The RagTime Traveler

The RagTime Traveler

Casey Karp and Larry Karp

Poisoned Pen Press

Poisoned Pen Press
4014 N. Goldwater Boulevard, #201
Scottsdale, Arizona 85251
www.poisonedpenpress.com
info@poisonedpenpress.com

Printed in the United States of America

Larry dedicates this story to Casey Karp,
his co-author and son, whose imagination, organization,
and energy have enabled an old inkslinger to explore some
wonderful new writing territories.

In turn, Casey dedicates the tale to Larry Karp, for believing
I had the ability to write, making it possible for me to
develop the skill, and offering me this chance to use it.

The Blackstones and Nowlins of Sedalia and Kansas City

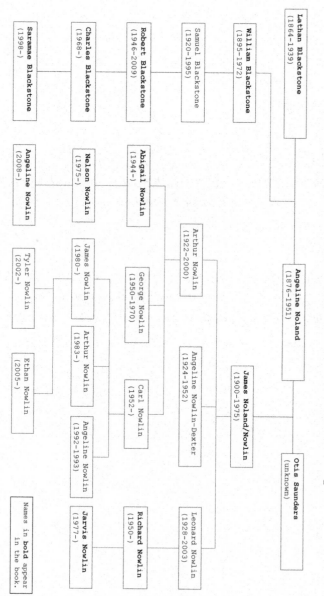

Names in **bold** appear in the book.

Chapter One

As long as Alan's fingers glided across piano keys, pain did not exist. He played the four-hand arrangement he'd written for his "Hybrid Slow Drag," testing the latest changes. A tiny smile waxed and waned at the left corner of his mouth. Occasionally, a "Yes" or "Right on" slipped unheard from his mouth. A corner of his mind gloated, *It went over big as a solo, but when Tom and I hit them with this arrangement at next summer's Joplin Festival, they'll really go wild.*

Doorbell. "Nuts!"

The old man twisted tension out of his shoulders. *Probably another solicitor. Ignore it.* He set himself to start again, but before he sounded the first note, the doorbell rang a second time, then a third.

"Am I the only person around here who answers the door?" he griped to the empty room. With his concentration blasted, Alan stood, a bit too energetically. He winced, groaned, and grabbed his lower back, shuffled down the hallway to the front door, and yanked it open as the bell rang again.

The mail carrier smiled. "Hi, Mr. Chandler. You've got an insured envelope that needs a signature."

Alan signed, mumbled "Thanks," and slammed the door shut.

• ● ● ● •

Cancer's a lousy traveling companion, never stops reminding you that your life's been hijacked and your arrival at your final destination has been changed. Alan rubbed his lower spine as he plopped into his recliner chair, leaned back, and tossed the supermarket flyers onto the little walnut table to his right. He scanned the envelopes. Mostly bills. Water, credit card, Tom's karate lessons, another credit card. Seattle Symphony…fall fund drive. All for Miriam. Not that he was about to complain. Without her money-managing over the past sixty-four years, he might be resting his cancer-ridden bones in a doorway somewhere. He'd known pianists who'd come to that.

The insured envelope, the only piece of mail addressed to Alan, was at the bottom of the pile. No return address, but it was postmarked Sedalia, Missouri. Could be any number of people, though Alan couldn't think of anyone there likely to send him anything requiring extra insurance. The shaky hand, probably of an old person, maybe writing in a hurry, didn't narrow the possibilities much. Except for the staff at the Scott Joplin Ragtime Festival, everyone he knew there was almost as old as he.

Alan tore open the end flap, and pulled out the contents. No letter, just a couple of pieces of cardboard sandwiching four pages of music paper filled with notes. The title at the top of page one: "Freddie." Freddie? Alan narrowed his eyes. His heart began to beat harder, faster. Even at a quick glance, there was something about the music.…

But no explanation? Alan spread the envelope, peered inside, spotted a small piece of white paper. He adjusted his glasses. The message, in the same shaky writing as the address, was short. "Call me. Mickey."

Not just age affecting the handwriting, then. Only one person it could be: Mickey Potash. They'd been friends forever, played together at countless ragtime festivals throughout the United States, Europe, and Asia. If not for an unfortunately low resistance to booze, Mickey could've been with Alan, right at the top of the ragtime pianist heap. Even potted to the gills, he could outplay almost any tickler on the premises. But why did he send this music? Only one possibility. Money and booze made Mickey's world go round, and Alan couldn't see any connection to the latter.

He looked more closely at the music. The paper was yellowed, creased and crumpled at the corners. Old-looking…A diminished seventh chord in the eleventh measure, resolving to the tonic…

"Holy shit!" A breathy whisper. "So typical, but how did Mickey ever get hold of something like this?"

Alan lowered the music, looked across the room at his Steinway grand, took a deep breath. Automatically, he reached into his shirt pocket, popped open a small metal container, extracted an oblong white pill, and gulped it down. Vicodin, his savior. Give it a little time and he'd be able to put his butt back on the piano bench without the goddamn back pain locking him down. Yes, he could read the music just fine, and utter improbability notwithstanding, he was certain of what he was holding. But he had to hear it on the piano. *Had to.*

• • ● ● •

Upstairs, out of range of the doorbell, Miriam dabbed a handkerchief at her eyes. "I just can't get him to stop doing concerts," she said. "But he's got to stop. Someone on chemo like he is simply can *not* keep up that pace."

Tom patted her hand. "He'll never give it up, Gramma…but suppose he did. What would he do then?"

"He could still compose."

"Without playing for audiences? He couldn't. If he could, he wouldn't be Alan Chandler."

"Thomas! He's going to run himself into the ground. Watch him walk, would you. It's like a slow-motion movie."

"Yeah, but when he's at a piano, you'd never know there was a thing wrong with him. It's the music and the applause that keep him going."

One edge of Miriam's thin lips curled upward. "You're a pair, you and your grandfather. I'll bet you and he have been plotting."

Tom grinned, shrugged. "'Course we have. You're formidable, Gramma. You'd run right over us if we didn't double-team you."

Miriam sighed, wiped at her eyes again. She pulled herself out of the chair, leaned forward, and kissed Tom's cheek.

"We've gotta do the best we can for him." Tom's voice cracked on the last word.

Miriam gazed at her grandson. Wide-eyed, cheeks glowing, dark hair tumbling over his forehead to nearly cover his eyes. Spitting image of his grandfather the day, sixty-odd years ago, when she'd trailed him into the high school music room, listened to him play "Maple Leaf Rag," and knew she'd found someone she'd never part from. "You're only sixteen years old," she murmured. "There's been too much death in your life."

Tom shook his head. "There's been a zillion times more life than death. Since you and Alan stepped in after Mom and Dad… you know. I've been awful lucky."

Miriam opened her mouth, but the sound of piano music from downstairs cut off whatever she was going to say.

Tom listened, then squinted in concentration. "Gorgeous! That heartbreaking thread sneaking behind the happy foreground…wow! What *is* it? Not one of *his* pieces—we woulda heard him working on it before now. But we haven't heard anybody else play it at a festival, either."

Miriam sighed. "Yes, it *is* beautiful. But beyond that, all I can say is it's a rag. That's it."

Tom laughed. "But you know plenty of stuff that leaves us tunesters in the dark, Gramma. The way you can turn a buck into a million? Alan and I would be SOL without you. Come on. Let's go down and see what gives."

They tiptoed downstairs as the piece ended and began again. They stood outside the living room, watching Alan at the keyboard.

"My God, look at his face," Miriam whispered. "He's not the same man who couldn't eat his lunch a few hours ago. Now he could light a room."

"He's talking to himself. Can you hear what he's saying?"

Miriam shook her head. "He's sitting so straight, his back must not be bothering him at all. Why couldn't he just play piano here at home and take proper care of himself?"

"He will play here. It's called practicing. But he's got to practice *for* something. I feel the same thing he does, Gramma. Prepping for a concert gets your blood flowing, but only because it's for the show. Stepping out on stage and nailing it? *That's* what it's really about."

"Like a drug."

At Miriam's sharp remark, Alan stopped playing, mid-tune, turned, then smiled at his audience. They applauded ostentatiously.

"What *is* that?" Tom asked. "Nothing I've ever heard before, I'm sure."

"No, you haven't. Neither have I. It's a Scott Joplin piece, a new one, can you believe!" He waved a hand, tried to control his excitement. "Of course I'll have to do the academic things to really nail it down, but any halfway decent ragtimer would know immediately only Joplin could've written this." He jabbed a finger at the music on the rack. "And the title, that's the clincher. 'Freddie'." He raised an eyebrow at Tom.

Tom got it. "Joplin's wife...his second wife. The one who died of pneumonia right after they got married. Holy shit! Where did you get it?"

Alan held up the little white scrap of paper. Miriam and Tom stared at it, then at each other.

"'Call me. Mickey'?" Tom read.

"From Sedalia—it must be Mickey Potash."

"So what're you gonna do?"

Alan smiled at his grandson, then rose from the piano bench like a young athlete. "Call him—what else?" He walked across the room to the phone, flipped through the pocket notebook Tom jokingly called Alan's backup brain, and dialed.

Miriam and Tom settled on the edge of a sofa. They leaned forward, as if that might allow them to hear through the receiver.

"Yes," Alan said. "Yep, good old caller ID, it's me. I just got your envelope." Brief pause, then, "Mickey, what the hell have you got going there?"

Another, longer pause. Alan looked ready to dive through the phone. "You're kid—no, you're *not* kidding, you're serious. Where did this duffel bag come from?"

"Hey, hold on, Mickey. You send me a manuscript that's clearly an unknown Scott Joplin piece, you tell me there's a whole bunch more in a duffel bag, and that's it? Where'd you get them? And what do you want from me?"

"Oh, for Christ's sake! Mickey...all right, listen. Give me a few more titles...Okay? Anything we know of as lost...? All right, good. What else?"

Alan flipped to a blank page in his notebook, and after a moment, began to scribble on it, now and again murmuring, "No. No." Finally, after a long silence, he said, "Well, Mickey, I guess you're calling the shots. Count on it." He hung up the receiver.

"So what's up?" Tom nearly danced on the edge of the sofa.

Alan shook his head. "I can't believe it. He says he's got a duffel bag full of music. Printed, handwritten. Drafts and fragments, too, not just completed tunes. He's sure they're Joplin, but he needs me to give an independent opinion and help him decide what to do with them."

Miriam raised a finger. "And just how did Mickey get his hands on these pieces? Mickey Potash is not exactly a model of honesty or propriety."

Alan shook his head. "He's keeping it close to his vest. You heard me ask, but he wouldn't say. Just said if I come to Sedalia and check out the music, he'll tell me the whole story."

She was on her feet instantly. "'Come to Sedalia'...Oh, no, Alan. That is not going to happen."

Alan raised his eyes. "For a duffel bag full of unknown Scott Joplin compositions? Oh yes, that *is* going to happen. Tomorrow, in fact. It can't not happen."

"Alan, you're a sick man. You can't—"

"Please, Miriam, don't tell me I'm sick. I know better than anyone that I'm sick, and just how sick. But I'd have to be dead to not follow this up. No, not even being dead would stop me."

Miriam's eyelids descended into a severe squint, a sure sign of impending battle. "He could send you the music. And you could sit here in your own house, at your own piano. Where your doctor—"

"Stop right there. I'm sorry, Miriam, but that's ridiculous. Mail a package of just-discovered Scott Joplin tunes? I can't believe he mailed *one!* That's like…like mailing the original Declaration of Independence!" He took a deep breath. "This is the greatest find of music in the history of the world, and frankly, I'm at least as qualified as anyone to verify it as Joplin's. Or to be fair, to verify it as not Joplin's. This is the most exciting thing that's ever happened in my life, and if I *were* on my deathbed, I'd figure a way to get up and go to Sedalia. Now, that's the end of it." He reached for the phone. "I'm going to make my plane and hotel reservations. For tomorrow."

Miriam's outflung arm stopped him like a tollgate. "Alan, when you get like this, I know better than to keep fighting. But you are *not* going halfway across the country alone. If you're going to Sedalia, I'm going with you. But I can't go tomorrow or the next day. There's a little matter of my annual meeting of investment advisers, where I'll be sorting out our strategy for months to come. The music can wait a few days or even a week. Make those reservations accordingly."

Tom thought the air in the room felt the way it had the year a tornado blew past the Sedalia ragtime festival one June. Didn't happen often between his grandparents, but when it did…He reached to rest a hand on Miriam's shoulder.

"I'll go with him," the boy said quietly.

The combatants stared at him.

"I'll look after him." A pleading note came into Tom's voice. "Won't let anything happen to him. And if he needs help with the music, I can do that, too."

Miriam's glare had built serious strength through decades of practice against Alan. The modern form, the Gramma Glare of family legend, worked on Tom, even at low levels of intensity. The full-strength version she focused on the boy could have scorched ivory. "Ganging up on me again? Aside from anything else, you're just happening to forget a little thing like missing how many school days? And right near the beginning of the term."

"Miriam!" Alan, red-faced, was clearly on the edge. "The boy's right. This is a one-time opportunity for him too. Look what's happened for us in our sixty-five years because *I* took off for Sedalia when I was just his age. How many school days did *I* miss? And how much has it mattered?"

The tornado spun in place for a long moment, then veered south, sparing the combatants, the way the Sedalia twister had veered off into Arkansas. Miriam sighed, raised her hands in surrender, and plopped back onto the sofa. Alan walked over to pat her hand.

"I'd be glad to have you along. As always. But yes, somebody's got to bring in a buck here and there. You keep the home fires burning, and I'll call every day and tell you what's going on. Having Tom come makes so much sense in so many ways. We've never passed up a good opportunity, never. And we've never regretted it."

"There's a first time for everything, my dear." She fixed him with a mocking glare, only ten percent. "'Most exciting thing,' is it? Do you want to reconsider that claim?"

Alan chuckled. "Maybe that was a slight exaggeration… maybe." He picked up the receiver and started to push buttons.

Chapter Two

Tom wiped sweat off his forehead. "You know, the car *is* air-conditioned."

The old man grinned. "Yes, Thomas, I'm aware of that. But I enjoy riding with the windows open...feeling the breeze. It takes me back to the time before air-conditioning in cars, driving from venue to venue through the goddamn hottest weather you've ever known. Usually your grandmother in the passenger seat there. Makes me feel—"

"Fifty years younger and up for anything. And just as glad there's no airport in Sedalia."

Alan nodded. "Yeah. And you can't tell me taking the back way—Kans' City to Lone Jack to Knob Noster to Sedalia—it's a hell of a lot nicer than chugging down I-70. Especially with the windows open."

Tom smiled when Alan slurred off Kansas City's final syllable, as he did when he was in a good mood. "Long as you're not in a hurry, I suppose," the boy admitted.

"Believe it or not, it's no slower than the freeway."

"*Sure* it isn't."

"I've timed it. Just a bit over an hour either route. We'll be there in plenty of time for dinner. Oh, the barbecue in 'Missoura'—worth the trip just for that alone."

Another smile, a little wistful, from the boy. The alternative pronunciation of the state tickled his grandfather's fancy. Tom decided to not ask whether the chemo might throw off Alan's taste for barbecue.

He pushed the control button to open his own window, took a few deep breaths. It did smell good, cut grass rather than burned gasoline. *Real glad Gramma couldn't make the trip. It'd've been dire if I'd hadda stay home. Miss out on maybe being the first person in a century to play a Joplin piece? This is gonna be epic!*

Alan began to hum "Maple Leaf Rag." As the diminished chord resolved into the tonic, the old man felt an odd sensation, a strange warmth filling his head, and he couldn't remember a moment in his life when he'd felt happier.

They pulled into Sedalia about four o'clock, turned off Route 50 onto Ohio Avenue, and drove the few blocks to the Bothwell Hotel. Before Tom could close the door to their room, Alan cranked up the heat.

"Chills?"

"'Fraid so. Chemo fatigue, too."

Tom set his grandfather's suitcase on the table and tossed his backpack underneath. "Sorry. That sucks bigtime."

Alan kicked off his shoes and stood in front of the heat vent for a long minute before he shucked out of his jacket and flopped onto one of the queen beds.

"Give me an hour horizontal, and I'll be fine. Ready for anything Mickey might throw at us."

Us. Tom couldn't hold back a smile at the word. "Sure, Alan." He kicked his shoes away, pulled the envelope with the music out of the suitcase, sank into the padded chair in the corner of the room, and began to study the work, humming softly. *It sure sounds like Joplin to me. But I've got a long way to go before my opinion means shit.*

Alan parked in front of Mickey's once-pretty house on East Third Street. Tom shook his head. "Jeez, it gets worse every year. One of these times, we're going to come out and find the place collapsed on the ground around him. He could at least paint it."

Alan chuckled. "I doubt that'd hold the thing together." He opened the door. "Music, booze, money—after those, Mickey just doesn't care. He could live in a tent or a palace, and he wouldn't notice any difference."

They walked up the sagging wooden steps to the porch, where an ancient glider, its cloth seat frayed to threads, hung limply from two hooks in the ceiling. Alan pushed the doorbell, heard nothing, and with a disgusted look, gave the front door a couple of sharp kicks. A moment later, it creaked open.

"Hello, Mickey," Alan said.

The little man took in his visitors and grinned. "I see you brought reinforcements. Didn't want to take me one-on-one, huh?"

Alan sighed. Genetics and circumstances had given Mickey Potash everything a man could hope for. Extraordinary musical talent, the constitution of a bull, a face that pulled in women like a magnet pulled steel. But he'd pissed away everything except the talent in a half-century of nonstop boozing. Alan felt simultaneous urges to put an arm around him and to smack him hard.

"Reinforcement's what I need, Mickey." He gestured with his head. "Okay if we come in?"

Mickey cackled, showing a row of crappy-looking dentures, and opened the door wide. "Please do enter my humble abode, gentlemen."

The living room was a mess. A pair of ancient couches with springs sticking through the seats. An oval hooked rug in the middle of the floor, so faded its colors were indecipherable. Mismatched, scarred wooden tables from the fifties, one holding a plate containing food remnants topped with a greenish-white fuzz. The only departure in the décor from disorder and deterioration was Mickey's prize possession: an inscribed, sepia tone photograph in a carefully dusted frame hung near the hallway. As he usually did, Alan smiled at the sight of Scott Joplin shaking hands with the pianist and conductor, Alfred Ernst. Mickey had at least a dozen different stories about how he came to own the picture, none of which corresponded to any of the others, or in all likelihood, to reality.

Tom plopped onto a sofa; dust filled his nostrils and he coughed. Alan carefully avoided the visible sag in the center and lowered himself slowly to the cushion at the other end. Before he could start talking, a lanky, black teenage boy sauntered into the room from the hallway. He wore patched jeans, and a red-and-black checkered work shirt over a faded, dark green T-shirt. The boy looked as surprised as Alan felt, and for a moment everyone in the room sat and stared at each other.

Finally, Mickey broke the silence. "Alan, Tom, this is my young friend, Jackson. Don't know what I'd do without him. He brings me my newspaper every morning, hot off the press. And if I need help around here, Jackson's my man. He's been patching a couple holes in the roof, getting that done before the fall rains hit. And I show him how to play a little ragtime piano."

Alan thought his friend was running off at the mouth. *More going on here than he's telling us.* All the while, Jackson stood in place, squirming as if he'd just realized he'd sat on a nest of fire ants.

"You've heard me talk about Alan Chandler, right, Jackson?" Mickey said.

The boy's eyes widened. "Yeah, sure, Mr. Mickey." He clomped across the room and pumped Alan's hand as if he expected to draw water from a well. "Mr. Mickey say you the Big Daddy of all the ragtime players."

"Well, I'm not sure—"

Mickey interrupted Alan's demurral. "Maybe he'll play some for you while he's in town. But I guess you'd better be heading on home now—don't want your Granny getting mad at me for making you late for dinner."

Jackson looked confused, then muttered, "Yeah, sure. See ya in the mornin', then. You know. With the paper."

"You bet, Jackson. Thanks."

As the front door slammed behind Jackson, Mickey said, "He's a good kid. Lives with his grandma in this little place up in Lincolnville."

Tom had been staring after Jackson, but pulled his attention back to the room when Mickey spoke. "The old black part of town? I didn't think anybody lived north of the tracks anymore."

Alan nodded. "It's pretty much deserted now that the city's integrated, but some of the old people still hang in there."

Mickey smiled. "Get to be my age with no kids or grandkids of your own, you do good to pick one up, even if he's a different color. Don't matter a bit that I'm white and he's black. He does whatever for me, and every now and again I give him a ten or a twenty to put on a horse. If it comes in, he gets a cut. And yeah, he's only seventeen, but he knows where to find a bottle of good stuff for me, cheap. I don't ask no questions about where, and he don't tell me no lies."

Alan chuckled. "I should've known. Is Jackson his first name or his last name?"

"Both."

"Come on."

"No, really. His father, mercy on his crooked, twisted soul, is Jack Jackson, so he named his son Jackson—Jackson Jackson."

"Poor kid." Alan shook his head, let silence spread for a few seconds. "Well, Mickey, I hardly know what to say. Your package was quite a surprise."

Mickey ignored the hint. "Rough trip, Alan? You don't mind me saying so, you're not looking so good. Getting old?"

Tom and Alan exchanged a quick glance, then Alan sighed. "Still getting older, but not sure for how much longer."

Tom raised a hand. "Alan—"

Alan's lips set into a tight line. "Prostate cancer, Stage 4. In my bones. I'm on chemo, lost twenty pounds since June." He gestured toward Tom. "My reinforcements."

Mickey ran fingers through the thin strands of gray behind his forehead. "Oh, jeez, Alan—I didn't have any idea. I'm sor—"

Alan waved him off. "No way you would've known. I've kept it quiet for as long as I could."

"But that stuff—the chemo—it's gonna fix you up, right...?"

Mickey ground to a stop as Alan shook his head slowly, side to side. "No. Once the cancer gets that far, it's just a matter of time. The drugs slow it down, but they can't wipe it out. I might have a year or three, or I might not. No matter. Once I saw that piece of music, nothing would've stopped me coming here. Which you knew."

A smile won out over Mickey's discomposure. "I kinda figured."

"Well, then, talk. I don't have forever."

Mickey looked at his wristwatch. "Jeez, Alan…listen, I'd like to give you dinner, but—"

Alan laughed. *That's Mickey.* "I didn't expect you would—and I'm not going to drop dead in the next hour. Let's go to Kehde's and have some barbeque. Then we can come back here, and you can trot out that duffel bag."

• • ● • •

Mickey burped into his hand as he pushed his front door open and motioned his guests inside.

Alan shook his head in wonder. "Don't you lock your door?"

"My deal with the burglars." Mickey laughed. "I don't make trouble for them, they give me a ten percent discount to buy back what they take."

Alan groaned and Tom stifled a laugh.

"Okay, have a seat, I'll be right back." Mickey gestured toward the dingy sofa. Then he disappeared through a doorway into the back.

When he returned, he was carrying a medium-sized black duffel bag in both hands as if he thought any jolt would set off an explosion. Alan and Tom leaned forward, stared. The old man suddenly realized he'd stopped breathing, and inhaled slowly, deeply. The bag had seen hard use, color faded irregularly, a few small rips in the fabric. Mickey set it down on a banged-up coffee table in front of the sofa, then pulled up a chair opposite Alan and Tom. He yanked the knot out of the drawstring, opened the duffel wide, then gestured toward the opening.

"Go ahead, Alan. Have a look."

Alan aborted his instinctive grab for the bag to pull a pair of white cotton archival gloves from his jacket pocket, and slipped them on. Only then did he reach into the duffel. He came out with several sheets, which he carefully spread onto the table. Then he blew out a deep breath, and began to scan the music, eyes following fingers across and down the pages. When he'd looked through the sheets he'd extracted, he went back to the duffel, pulled out another handful, repeated the scanning.

There were a number of published works, ranging from a first printing of "Maple Leaf Rag" to a few that Alan instantly dismissed as "modern crap." But most of the music was hand-written, primarily on yellowed music paper, 11 by 14 inches, crinkled and showing old fold marks. A few pieces were scrawled across 8-1/2 by 11 sheets, and there was a substantial sprinkling of smaller scraps that held short musical passages, almost all of which showed signs of multiple revisions. Alan examined every-thing until, halfway down the bag, he pulled out a hand-bound composition, thicker than any of the others.

Finally, he spoke. "My God, I can't believe this. It's a con-certo—a piano concerto."

"Better believe it," said Mickey. "You're the authority, but I'd put more than a little of the money I don't have on it being by Scott Joplin."

"You'd win," Alan murmured. "Mickey…where did you get this?"

Tom and Alan glanced at each other, sharing a thought, as Mickey opened his mouth: *He's going to spin a whopper.*

"Well, it came outa Kansas City. See, I got this call from an antique dealer, he cleaned out a house down in the District when the old lady went into some kind of a nursing home. He saw the duffel bag full a music, and said he figured well, it probably ain't worth much, but somebody might appreciate havin' it… and of course there might be a little something in it for him. So he talked to a couple other dealers, one a them was Rudolph Korotkin, I've sold him a few things over the years and Rudy told him to show 'em to me. He came up a few days ago, I scraped together five hundred bucks for him, and here we are. I guess it's a good thing Joplin didn't put his name on any of the manuscripts—but there's something else, bet you didn't notice."

"About the music? Like what?"

Mickey shook his head. "No, not the music." He picked up the empty duffel bag, turned one edge of the opening inside out. "Lookit here."

Alan and Tom came forward as a unit, and squinted into the bag. "Writing?" Tom muttered.

Alan craned his neck. "Pretty faint…well, look at that—a W and an S. Wilbur Sweatman."

"The guy who played three clarinets at the same time?" Tom asked, his eyes wide.

Mickey and Alan both laughed. "That's the guy," Mickey said. "He died, what, about 1960?"

Alan agreed. "He was Joplin's friend, and Lottie's, and when Lottie died, he got his hands on a load of Joplin's music. Then, when *he* died, the music went to his illegitimate daughter, and after her, it vanished. There's a story that one of the lawyers threw it all away, but that was more than fifty years ago, and nobody knows what really happened. Do you know whose house it was the antique dealer cleaned out?"

Shrug. "I didn't ask. He didn't say."

"Mickey, do you have this guy's card?"

A shake of the head, no. "I gave him the five Cs, he gave me the bag, why would I ask for a card? But if you want to know, Rudy could tell you."

Alan noticed Tom absently running gloved fingers across the music sheets. The kid was as taken up as he was. He looked back to Mickey. "So, what now?"

"Well, that's what I figured you were gonna help me decide. I mean, first thing is, is this really all Joplin stuff? And if it ain't, who wrote it?"

Alan nodded. "I did see a few things that Scott Joplin couldn't possibly have written, but on a first look—I admit, a quick one—I'm sure most of the handwritten pages *have* to be Joplin.

The published stuff—pretty much all of it looks more recent. I'll check all of it more closely, but I'm going to be surprised if Joplin didn't write at least three quarters of it." He groaned and massaged his lower back. "There's going to be a lot to think about, and authenticating it is only the first step."

He looked at the ceiling. *Give me strength.* "Proving provenance will be a mess. But after that…this looks like unpublished, uncopyrighted material. Who has the right to secure copyright on it? How about publishing it? How should you—we?—go about keeping it safe? Mickey, who else knows about this besides those antique dealers?"

For answer, a slow sidewise shake of the head and a shrug. "No one, far as I know. You guys, me, that's it…Alan, you okay? You're all of a sudden white as a ghost."

Alan waved off his friend's concern. "I get really tired, sometimes a little dizzy. It's the chemo…along with a long plane ride and some pretty exciting stuff happening. But mostly the chemo. I need to lie down for an hour every so often." He glanced at his watch and eyed the duffel bag. "Tom and I can go back to the hotel, I'll flop, and then I'll be good for a little more work. Okay if I take some of these sheets? I can check them out carefully, and we can get back together in the morning, look at the others, and go from there. We've got some big decisions ahead of us."

"Sure, Alan, sounds fine. You okay to drive?"

"Yeah. We're at the Bothwell. No sweat."

Alan dug into the bag for pieces he hadn't yet seen. A dozen sheets of manuscript paper, a few of plain paper, and a half-height piece of light card stock with a short musical passage, just a single theme.

"These'll do for tonight. About ten tomorrow, okay, Mickey?"

"I'll be waiting. Hey, take care, pal, okay?"

• • ● • •

Alan and Tom perched side by side on the edge of the bed, each holding a piece of music, running fingers across the lines of notes, every now and again humming a passage.

"Best I can tell, this is Joplin," Tom muttered. "I mean, this piece...'A Bouquet of Daisies'? Look here." The boy hummed a passage. "Isn't there something awfully like that in 'Heliotrope Bouquet'? Maybe he was writing them at the same time."

"Could be, but probably not. Remember, the first two themes in 'Heliotrope' came from Louis Chauvin, and they're not in 'Daisies' at all. I'd say it's more likely Joplin was experimenting with the themes he wrote. Look at this chord progression. That's something he never did as early as 'Heliotrope Bouquet'." Alan stretched, felt his shoulders pop. "If everything we've seen so far is typical, most of what's in that duffel is middle or late Joplin, things he wrote in St. Louis or New York. But look at this." He held up the piece of card stock. "Definitely early Joplin. He must have written it sitting at a table at the Maple Leaf Club, just a few blocks down the way from where we're sitting right now."

Tom looked puzzled. "How can you be so sure?"

Alan chuckled and flipped the card over and held it out. The card was printed with a few lines of text:

> *The Maple Leaf Club*
> *W.J. Williams, Prop.*
> *121 East Main Street*
> *Sedalia, Missouri*
>
> *The management of this club would be pleased to*
> *extend their hospitality to you and anyone you may*
> *wish to bring to an evening of music.*
>
> *Friday, September 1st, 1899.*
> *Scott Joplin, entertainer.*
> *Present at door. Admission 20c.*

Alan tapped the date. "I cheated." His eyes drifted to the wall and slid out of focus. "Can you imagine," he said slowly, "Joplin picking up a discarded invitation and writing out a theme that had been bouncing around in his head all evening?" He blinked a couple of times, dragging his attention out of 1899 and back to 2015.

Tom took the card from his grandfather, traced notes with his fingers. "It's for a cakewalk, isn't it? It's got that cakewalk rhythm, anyway." He started humming.

Alan watched him with a smile. *Knows more about the music than he thinks he does. Just needs a bit of self-confidence.*

After a few seconds, Alan tapped Tom's shoulder. "Hey, Thomas. Come back."

The boy blinked, looked sheepish.

"I'm glad you came along," Alan said. "I do feel better, not being alone all this way from home. And the chance for you to look into a music find like this one, at this point in your education?" He shook his head in amazement. "I think you'll be a big help to me—and you're going to learn a hell of a lot." He took the paper back from Tom. "I'd better call your grandmother, let her know we're all right, and then let's sack out. Get a good night's sleep and hit the ground running in the morning."

Tom gave his grandfather a quick hug. "Thanks, Alan."

• • ● • •

Sunlight poured around the edges of the window curtain as Tom rolled out bed and slapped Alan's annoying travel alarm. *Just past eight. That's what, six in Seattle? Ugh. Good thing Alan set a late meeting time with Mickey.*

The boy stretched and shoved his feet into slippers. "Hey, Alan—" he began, but cut himself short when he saw the empty bed beside his. He blinked once, twice, rubbed his eyes. The bed was still empty. Sheets and blankets thrown off toward the foot of the bed, a depression at the center of the pillow. Over on the night table, the invitation sat front and center, music side up, as though demanding to be studied.

"Alan!" Tom called. He checked: no Alan in the bathroom either. "Oh, shit!"

He reached for his iPhone, but stopped short of picking it up. *No, I can't call Gramma! We haven't even been here a whole day and I've lost track of Alan already. She'd kill me.*

Chapter Three

Alan woke a few minutes after four, his back screaming, and Joplin's newly discovered music playing over and over in his mind. He glanced at Tom, curled in a ball under the covers of the other bed, snoring softly.

The old man threw off the covers and eased himself up to sit on the side of the bed, then grabbed the Vicodin he'd left handy on the bedside table. Quick swallow, then he stretched and got to his feet. Sometimes it helped to move around while he waited for the painkiller to take effect. He straightened slowly and shuffled to the bathroom, took care of necessary business, then returned to the bedroom.

Alan knew he wouldn't be able to go back to sleep. With a sigh, he dressed in the dark, moving slowly so as not to aggravate his spine or disturb Tom's sleep. Then he walked to the bedside table, picked up the pile of music, extracted the invitational card, and dropped the rest back onto the table. The multiply-revised musical passage, short though it was, enticed him with its suggestion of a window into Joplin's creative process. He set the card down on the edge of the table, clicked the bedside light onto its lowest setting, and bent over the card, trying to define the evolution of the music. After a couple of minutes, he completely forgot the ache in his back.

A twinge brought him up short as he started to stand up and stretch. He glanced at the clock and shook his head at his own impulsiveness. Only 6:13. Much too soon to go back to

Mickey's. Too early even to wake Tom for breakfast. Alan finished his interrupted motion, and stretched cautiously. The Vicodin was working. Good. For the moment, standing was better than sitting; he leaned on the table and returned his attention to the music. In his head, he played his best guess at the earliest version of the passage on the invitation, then switched to the last. It was Joplin, he had no doubt about that. But a strain that had never found its way into any of Joplin's known pieces.

While he mentally played the final version again, he pictured the Maple Leaf Club as it would have been in Joplin's time. Gas chandeliers hanging from the ceiling. A massive walnut bar on one wall, a sign behind it touting the products of the Capital Brewing Company. On the opposite wall, a scattering of card and dice tables and a few pool tables. In between, heavy wooden chairs placed around large, square tables for drinkers. Against the wall between the bar and the gaming tables sat an upright piano, a very dark-skinned black man on the bench.

Alan grimaced. That wasn't right. Joplin wouldn't have been alone; the scene would have been more like a pianist's jam session at one of the ragtime festivals. He added a few more men to his mental picture. Joplin's students, Scott Hayden and Arthur Marshall, of course. His closest friend, Otis Saunders. Anyone else? Perhaps not. Joplin's face tightened as one of the standing men leaned over his shoulder and played a few notes; the composer shook his head and played a longer passage. Not quite the final version of the strain on the invitation, but close. He crossed out a few notes on a card resting on the piano's music rack, wrote a correction, and played it again. Closer, but still not quite there.

Alan stepped away from a table in the back of the bar and walked to the side of the piano bench. "I think you want an F-sharp minor run in the third bar, Mr. Joplin."

There was a moment of silence. Alan froze. *What in hell is going on? Am I dreaming? Or, my God, is this a dying experience? Am I dying in my sleep in that hotel room? Oh, please, no—that'd be something Tom and Miriam would never get over.*

Joplin broke the silence. "You were saying, Sir? An F-sharp minor run in the third bar?"

Alan glanced around the room. No question, he was in the Maple Leaf Club. The bar was as unmistakable as the man at the piano, who shot an accusing glare at Alan, even as his fingers played the phrase with the minor run. The glare modulated into a frown, apparently a habitual expression, as Joplin added another correction to the card and set down his pencil.

Hayden, Marshall, and Saunders studied Alan for a moment, then looked a question at each other. Saunders shrugged. No wonder, Alan thought. An old white guy in a blue-and-white-striped shirt and light-colored slacks who interrupts their late-late get-together is hardly going to get an open-armed welcome.

"You appear to know my music better than I do myself, Sir," said Joplin, a thick coat of ice covering every word. The "Sir" came across as an accusation.

Alan took a deep breath. Worry about the hows and whys later. "Hardly that, Mr. Joplin. Just a feeling. The result of listening to—and playing—ragtime for longer than you would believe." He stepped to the side and turned the closest chair to face the piano. "Please excuse me. I can't stand up for very long these days." He sat, cautious of his back in the unpadded chair, and leaned forward.

"Mr. Campbell told me you were often here at all hours, working on your music, but I never expected to meet you myself."

Joplin turned his eyes heavenward as his companions exchanged whispers. "*Brun* Campbell, that would be?"

Alan nodded.

Joplin's face tightened. "You're a friend of Brun's?"

"I don't know that I could go that far…well, maybe." Alan quickly thought better of saying that he'd gone out to the coast some sixty years before to take ragtime piano lessons from Brun Campbell. "I enjoyed talking with him and listening to him play. He's quite a…character."

Joplin's expression didn't change, but slim, light-skinned Saunders, dressed to the nines even in the early morning hours, grinned and stage-whispered to Joplin, "It look like maybe you gots yourself another white disciple on your doorstep, Scott. Way this be goin', you gonna have a full set of twelve by next Christmas."

Joplin turned his frown on his friend. "As I recall, Cracker-jack, you were the one responsible for unleashing Brun on us. Is this *gentleman* also one of your converts?"

Alan almost laughed out loud. *Right! That's what they called Saunders then. Crackerjack.*

"Never once saw him before."

Joplin looked toward Marshall and Hayden. Marshall shrugged; Hayden shook his head, no.

Joplin's cheek twitched. "Perhaps you'd like to explain a little, Mr…"

"Chandler. Alan Chandler."

"Mr. Chandler. How is it that all of a sudden, out of nowhere, you're here? Not to be rude, but the fact is, we don't see too many white folks in the Maple Leaf after hours. Just what is it that brings you to Sedalia? You say you've been listening to Brun Campbell play ragtime. *Are* you following in Mr. Campbell's footsteps? Seeking lessons in playing ragtime?"

"I didn't have any firm goal in coming here, but if I had, that wouldn't have been it. I'm content with my own style, particularly at my age, at least as much as any musician ever can be. I would be more interested in discussing composition with you." Alan nodded at the invitational card. "What, for example, do you intend for that little theme?"

Joplin ignored the question, and rose. "Let's not go quite so fast. You play, Sir? And compose? Then perhaps you could demonstrate."

Alan's thoughts churned. It wouldn't do to play something too modern, too distant from Joplin's first efforts with classical forms. As he sat, an idea struck him. "I'm sure you'll recognize the theme these variations are based on. Mr. Campbell told me you use it as a negative example—you gave him holy hell for playing "Maple Leaf Rag" like a funeral march. It seemed like an interesting challenge."

Alan had written his variations on Chopin's "Funeral March" for his own amusement, back when he was in his twenties. Now he omitted the initial statement of the theme, and jumped straight into the first melodic variation, heavy on passing tones and ragged enough to shake Chopin right out of his coffin.

As he worked his way through a series of harmonic variations, Marshall and Hayden nodded agreement, and Otis Saunders grinned and murmured a quiet "Yeah." Alan brought the piece to a close with a syncopated rendition of the theme, which set everyone but Joplin to chuckling.

"Perhaps not the most original notion, Mr. Chandler," Joplin said with a grudging nod, "but competently executed."

Alan's energy was beginning to run out, and his back began to escalate its complaints. "I'd be honored to share something more original, but another time might be better." He stood and tried to coax his spine to fully vertical. "It's still early morning, but I've already had a remarkably long day. I think an hour or two of rest is in order. Maybe I could come back another time and talk some."

Joplin nodded. "I'd be interested. For now, I think I'll do just what you have in mind." He pointed a thumb at his students. "And it wouldn't hurt these two young men to visit their pillows either. Crackerjack, well, he'll do what he wishes."

"Crackerjack gonna stay a little longer. Enough for one more drink, anyways."

Alan made his way down the stairs, then headed south on Ohio Avenue. He shivered. *If I'd known I was going outside, I would have worn my jacket.* He'd have to stop for a rest, but even so, he was sure he could make it to the hotel by 8:30. Then he'd worry about getting back to the twenty-first century. With luck, he might get there before Tom woke up.

• • ● • •

Alan dodged past a large man in front of the Blocher Feed Store, then walked the half-block to Ohio Avenue, and turned south. *I can't really believe I'm in 1899. But a dying vision—no, anything but that! It can't be that! Maybe…a hallucination? That would be far better. Would I see the dust in the street in a hallucination? So many places I've read about over the last fifty years of research. There's the St. Louis Clothing Store. Long gone, but it* was *a big-time operation in 1899.* The sight of a store advertising "Pianos, Organs, and Music" distracted him, and he smiled briefly. A few steps closer to Third, he nodded. *Right, the Ilgenfritz Block, all those small shops and offices. And Sicher's Hotel at the corner of Third.*

Shortly before nine, the old pianist stood on the corner of Ohio and East Fourth. The Bothwell Hotel, however, wasn't there. In its place was a row of small businesses anchored on the corner by the Bryant-Tewmey Dry Goods Company. A small sign in the window offered lodgings on the third floor.

Alan glared at the sign, but his concern wasn't the staircase the sign implied. Tom would almost certainly be awake, and that meant trouble. *God help us if he's called Miriam to tell her I've gone AWOL.*

After a few minutes, Alan shrugged. For want of a better idea, he opened the Bryant-Tewmey door, stepped inside, and blinked in surprise. He was standing in the dimly lit Oak Room Lounge, off the lobby of the Bothwell.

Chapter Four

Tom drew a deep breath. He tried to focus his mind by silently running through a few bars of "Maple Leaf Rag." *Alan wouldn't leave without me. He probably went for a walk or something.*

The boy grabbed his phone and called Alan's cell number. Across the room, Alan's phone, permanently set on "vibrate," buzzed. *He plugged it in last night and forgot it this morning. Figures.* Tom scribbled a quick note—"Out looking for you. Call me."—and set it on the table next to the invitation card. Then he threw his clothes on and started for the door, but quickly doubled back. *Can't leave the music just sitting out in plain view.* He emptied his backpack, slid the manuscript pages and card into Mickey's envelope, carefully zipped the bundle into his pack, and headed out, leaving the Do Not Disturb Sign in place.

Alan wasn't eating breakfast in the Palm Room. He wasn't in the Fitness Center either. Tom circled back to the reception desk, described his grandfather, and asked if the clerk had seen him. No luck.

A thought occurred to him. "Is there a piano in the hotel?"

"There's one on the balcony." The clerk pointed straight up. "But nobody's..." The clerk's voice trailed off when he realized he was talking to Tom's back.

If he was at the piano, I'd've heard it. Tom trotted toward the door. *Could he have gone over to Mickey's on his own? We weren't supposed to be there until ten, but could he not have been able to wait any longer? Don't really think so, but...*

The car was still in the lot, two spaces away from the street. "Damn it, Alan! Where *are* you?" It didn't seem likely that Alan would have walked to Mickey's. On the other hand, it was only four or five blocks, and Alan's doctors had been trying to get him to exercise more.

Tom checked his phone. 9:10. No messages. He called Mickey, but got no response. Nothing for it but to walk. He cut diagonally through the lot and set off along East Third.

• • ● • •

Alan glanced around the lounge and dropped into the nearest chair. *Does feeling this crappy mean I'm alive? If it does, I can't be dying. Chemo fatigue's bad enough by itself, but add an adrenaline crash and it's like staying up all night before doing matinee, evening, and midnight shows. I guess the real proof will be when I get back to the room. If I find myself in that bed*—He interrupted the thought, leaned left to look toward the elevator. *No, I can't handle it yet. Ten minutes to catch my breath and find some energy.*

Twenty minutes later, he pried his eyes open and reached for his phone to call Tom. It wasn't until his hand touched his belt that he realized the phone was still up in the room. With a groan, he dragged himself to his feet and into the hotel lobby.

As he passed the front desk, the clerk called him. "Mr. Chandler?"

Alan braced himself against the counter. "Yes?"

"Did you meet up with your grandson?"

"No. Where did he go?"

The clerk gestured toward the door. "He went out, oh, ten or fifteen minutes ago."

Alan sighed and suppressed a curse. *He must not have seen me sitting there.* He nodded thanks. "If he comes back, please tell him I'm up in the room."

"You got it, sir."

• • ● • •

Tom stopped short of the front steps. *Huh? Leaving the door unlocked is one thing. But leaving it* open? Tom listened, expecting to hear Alan and Mickey talking or, more likely, playing some of the music from Mickey's duffel bag. All he heard, though, was silence and the occasional passing car.

He climbed the creaking stairs and called "Hey, Mickey! Alan? Anyone home?"

No answer.

Tom pushed the door wide open and called again. He was about to go inside when he heard the opening passage of Alan's "Tomatillo Rag" behind him. He spun around, then realized the music was coming from his phone—his ringtone for a call from Alan.

He answered, shouting "Where are you? What did you think you were doing, going off without me? Gramma is going to kill me!"

Alan managed a chuckle. "I'm back at the hotel. Alive, thank God, and well enough, all things considered. You'll have trouble believing where I've been, but now that I'm back, I'm glad I went. No harm done, but I need a rest. And we will *not* tell Miriam about this."

Tom groaned. "She'll know. She always knows everything we do."

"She's good, Tom, but she's not quite clairvoyant. Listen, where's the music?"

"Don't worry, I brought it with me. Didn't want to tempt a maid by leaving it sitting around."

"Smart boy! I was worried for a second there. Okay, why don't you come on back here? Soon as I wake up, I'll tell you where I've been, and we can get our stories straight. Oh, and please call Mickey and let him know we'll be late."

"I'm at Mickey's house. Came here looking for you, but doesn't seem like he's home."

"That's odd. He knew we were coming over. Where would he have gone?"

Tom shrugged reflexively. "I don't know either, but he didn't even close the door. Look, I'm worried about the rest of the music. He hadda be joking about his deal with the thieves about stuff in his house, but there's those slimy-sounding antique dealers from K.C. I'm gonna go inside, look around a little, keep an eye on things. Take your nap and then come over."

"Fine. I'll make my nap short and come over as soon as I can. When Mickey shows up, tell him I'll be there about 10:30."

"Okay. Feel better."

Tom disconnected the call and walked inside. The living room was too crowded with battered furniture for easy pacing, but he made do, walking in circles around the dilapidated sofa. Partway through his fifth lap, he stopped and stared at a patch of considerably less-faded wallpaper, roughly eight by ten. A nail head protruded from the top of the rectangle.

"The picture of Joplin and Ernst," Tom murmured. "Mickey's prized possession…gone. I remember seeing it in June, but was it here yesterday?"

The missing photograph, open door, Mickey's absence when he knew Alan and Tom were coming over…it all made him nervous. Should he wait for Mickey to return? Or maybe snoop around a bit? Just to make sure the music was safe.

Who was going to stop him?

Once Tom stopped pacing, his bladder reminded him he hadn't used the bathroom in the hotel before he rushed out to find Alan. *The toilet's at the end of the hall. Mickey won't mind if I use it, and if I happen to peek into his practice room on the way and see the duffel bag, he'll never know the difference.*

The door to the practice room was closed. Tom gave a pro forma knock, and opened it almost before the hollow tap faded. Except for a carefully maintained path from the door to the piano, the floor was hidden under stacks of sheet music, overflow from the bank of filing cabinets along one wall. *He could hide an elephant in here.* Tom glanced around, figuring the bag couldn't be buried too deeply, since Mickey had brought it out quickly enough the previous night. He didn't see it, but there was a duffel-sized clear patch in the dust on top of the piano.

Tom circled around to the piano bench, careful not to brush against any of the stacks of music. No duffel bag on that side of the piano either, but on the bench lay a single sheet of music paper. His grandfather's name and the phrase "in case of trouble" leapt out at him from the space normally reserved for a title.

He scanned the page. First, four bars of music. It looked familiar, but Tom couldn't quite recognize it…"No, wait a sec," he muttered. "Swipesy Cakewalk!"

Below the music was written, in Mickey's shaky hand, "Hey Fats, you ain't exactly keepin' out of mischief now, is you? And you think I'se gonna b'lieve you ain't misbehavin'? Well, one just never knows…do one?"

Tom scratched his head. "What the hell? 'Swipesy' is Arthur Marshall with a bit of Scott Joplin, but then Mickey goes off quoting Fats Waller. Even for Mickey, that's pretty weird." The boy folded the note and shoved it into his pocket.

He edged out through the stacks of music, pulled the door shut behind himself, and continued toward the rear of the house. On his right was a door that had been held closed by a small padlock. The hasp had been torn from the wall and dangled from the lock, its screws on the floor, powdered with plaster dust. Tom's heart quickened. He turned the knob, opened the door, and flipped the light switch on.

Just a small closet. A few pairs of pants, a dark suit, and a topcoat hung on the wooden rail. The floor was empty.

A padlock on a coat closet? That's just so Mickey. Tom laughed out loud, then sobered. *Shit. If that's where the duffel was…nah, Mickey would've put it someplace he could get to it quickly.* He turned off the light, closed the door, and continued down the hall.

Mickey's bedroom was further down the passageway, on the other side; Tom could see that the door was open. But reaching the bathroom was becoming increasingly urgent, so he just glanced in as he hurried past. Nothing seemed obviously out of place.

Hydraulic pressure relieved, Tom returned to the bedroom door. *He'd want to keep the music close. Under the bed?*

Tom stepped inside, looked to his left around the door, and froze at the Halloween sight in the room.

Mickey Potash sat in the bed, his head lolling against the wall behind him. His swollen, purple tongue hung from the right corner of an open, gaping mouth; two hideously bulging eyes seemed to accuse Tom of all sorts of malfeasance. Thin streams of blood decorated Mickey's neck and stained the portion of his chest that was visible above the rumpled blanket. Round, purplish-black stigmata dotted his chest and face. A scream sent every hair on the boy's neck to attention; it was a moment before he realized that the sound came from his own throat.

Tom found himself on the front porch with no memory of how he got there. He still felt Mickey's accusing eyes on him. His stomach heaved, and he deposited some nasty-tasting mucus on the porch flooring. Quickly, clumsily, he wiped at his mouth, then leaped down the steps and sprinted for the hotel.

Alan'll know what to do!

Chapter Five

The hotel room door bounced off its stopper and slammed shut. The crash sent Alan into an awkward sitting position on the bed. Nasty electric shocks flew down the outer sides of his legs, crossed over below the knees, then continued downward to curl his big toes into painful upward spasms.

"Christ on a crutch, Tom," he barked. "Didn't I tell you I'm exhausted, I was going to take a nap? Couldn't you have been just a little considerate..." His voice faded as he looked at the intruder and he worked himself to the edge of the bed. "Tom? What...what's the matter? You're white as a ghost."

The boy jabbed a finger toward the door. "Alan...He's... Mickey...dead. *Murdered.*" Tom ran the few steps to the bed, then threw himself against his grandfather and began to sob.

Alan let him go on for a minute or two, then gently pulled free of the embrace, hobbled to the bathroom, and filled a glass with water. He used the first sip to swallow a Vicodin, then returned to the bedroom and pressed the glass into Tom's hand. "Here, drink," he said softly.

Tom drained the glass in a few swallows.

Alan nodded. "Good. Take some deep breaths."

Tom did as he was told. His body relaxed; he sank to the edge of the bed, then looked up, haggard, at Alan.

"Now tell me what happened. You said Mickey was—"

"Dead." The boy groaned. "Alan, someone killed him."

"How? Gun? Knife?"

Tom shook his head, then raised his shoulders in a shrug. "Not those…I'm not sure…but he looked awful."

Alan sighed out a chestful of air. "All right. Tom, you didn't see the duffel bag, did you?"

"No. I looked…at least until…"

The old man took the boy by the arm. "All right, don't worry about it. Come on."

"What? Back *there*?"

Alan started to suppress a smile, then let it spread across his face. "I think we ought to find out what's going on."

"Shouldn't we maybe call the cops?"

"Eventually, yes. But first we'll get a little more information ourselves, and decide how much of it to give them. Come *on*, Tom. We need to get cracking."

• • ● • •

Alan pulled the rental car to the side of the road in front of Mickey's house. "What if someone sees the car here?" Tom asked. "And then they trace it to us?"

"No problem." The boy's concern brought another smile to Alan's face. "We're keeping our appointment with Mickey from last night, correct? Once we see what's the story, of course we'll be calling the police."

Inside, in the living room, Alan turned to Tom. "Which way?"

The boy pointed toward the back. "Aren't you worried about leaving our fingerprints all over the place?"

The old man shook his head. "We already did that, yesterday." He set off toward the back, Tom following at a cautious distance.

In the bedroom, Alan moved quickly toward his friend's body, then bent slowly over the corpse. "Well, Mickey, you got somebody pretty upset, didn't you?" He shook his head, then looked back to Tom, who hung back halfway across the room. "We'll take a look around, but I don't think we're going to find the music, God *damn* it." He pointed toward Mickey. "This isn't just a robbery that got out of hand. Cigarette burns. Torture.

Unless somebody had a whole 'nother agenda to settle, I've got to think they were after that bag, and Mickey wasn't about to hand it over." He sighed. "Poor guy didn't just buy a bag of music, he bought a big bag of trouble."

Trouble! Tom's head jerked up. "Oh!"

He pulled the folded sheet of paper out of his pocket and passed it to Alan, who scanned it quickly, then half-whispered, "Yeah. I guess he was afraid something might be going to happen to him. But something as awful as this? Whew."

Alan handed the note back to his grandson before he bent over the body, taking care to not touch the bedding or the corpse with his fingers. "Hmm. Well, that's interesting—look, Tom."

The boy came up to the edge of the bed.

"Unless I really miss my guess, he was strangled with piano wire."

Tom whistled. "Jesus."

"Not only that—look close, Tom. That wire's corroded all to hell. It's got to be really old—either that or it was seriously mishandled, maybe left out in the rain. Or both."

Alan straightened, reached into his pocket, pulled out his Leatherman—a recent upgrade from the Swiss Army knife he had always carried for emergencies. Tom's eyes widened. "Alan, what are you doing?"

"There's a lot of wire hanging free there. I'm going to cut off a piece. It might come in handy."

"That's illegal isn't it? Tampering with evidence, or something."

"*Murder* is illegal. Not to mention grand larceny: stealing a duffel bag full of valuable music. Which, if it falls into the hands of the police—or if it's never found at all—*we'll* never see." He fixed a hard eye on his grandson. "Sixty-five years of playing and studying ragtime, and how much time do I have going forward? Somebody didn't exactly observe the niceties with Mickey, and I don't feel any obligation to follow the usual rules and procedures. How often do you think the Sedalia police get a case like this? *I'm* going to make sure whoever did this gets his wagon fixed good. *And* get back the duffel bag. But if you don't feel right about it, I'll understand, and go it myself."

Tom drew a shaky breath. "I've got your back, Alan. Whatever you do."

The old man fought back tears. "I hoped so. Good."

Tom managed a shaky smile. "Just be real glad Gramma couldn't come."

They both laughed. "Saints be praised," said Alan. He wrapped his handkerchief around the wire—it was already thoroughly corroded, but years of habit as a pianist prevented him from getting oils from his skin on it—and snipped off about four inches. He started to roll it up, then changed his mind and handed it to Tom.

"Tuck this into your deepest pocket, Thomas. Mickey's message too." He closed the Leatherman and dropped it back into his pants pocket. "Okay. Let's take a few minutes and see if by any chance the duffel bag *is* still here. And then we'd better call the cops."

● ● ● ● ●

Alan thought Detective David Parks seemed like a decent enough guy; given the circumstances, a certain amount of official grumpiness was understandable. Parks grimaced and shook his head when he saw Mickey's body, then turned to face Alan and Tom.

"Must have been a shock to find him like this, huh?"

The two conspirators nodded.

"Lemme see." The detective paused, then addressed Tom. "You found him first, and then you went and got your grandpa, right?

Tom nodded vigorously. "Right."

"Why didn't you call us then?"

Tom shook his head. "I guess I just panicked. I don't even remember going back to the hotel. All I could think was to get away and find Alan."

Parks turned to Alan. "And you didn't think of calling us then?"

"The boy was hysterical," Alan said softly. "I couldn't make out what he'd actually seen, so I drove us back here, we came in, found…" He gestured toward Mickey. "…and called you."

"You said you and Mr. Potash were going to talk about this duffel bag full of music. Did you find that?"

"We didn't really look," Alan said. "Yes, we checked around a little, didn't see it, and then we called you."

"Mind if I have a look out in your car?"

"Help yourself."

Alan dug into his left pants pocket, pulled out the car key, and gave it to Parks, who waved an officer over. "Duffel bag, music, anything like that," he said, jerking a thumb at the car. Then the detective turned back to Alan. "I'll need you both to come down to the station and make an official statement. You said you were staying at the Bothwell?"

Alan nodded. "Yes."

"Were you planning to leave town, now that this has happened? Because I have to ask you to stay, at least until—"

"We'll stay as long as you wish," Alan said.

Parks smiled with pursed lips. "Good. I appreciate that. But just for the record, let me get your home address. Can I see your driver's license, please?"

Alan took his wallet from his left pants pocket, extracted the driver's license, handed it to Parks. "I'm glad to do whatever I can to help. Mickey was a good friend for a lot of years. I want to see whoever did this to him brought to justice."

Parks' grin widened. "Not to mention you wouldn't mind locating that duffel bag, huh?" He finished copying Alan's license information and handed the card back.

"I won't deny it. This is the most important discovery in the history of music scholarship." Alan worked to pull himself to full height. "Scott Joplin was the king of ragtime composers. I've been studying his music for sixty-five years, I have Stage Four prostate cancer, and before I die, I want to have the chance to validate this music and be sure it enters the general repertoire."

"I can't stop you from looking for it," Parks said grudgingly.

"There's nothing wrong with my doing that, is there?"

"Not as long as you don't get in our way. Or do anything illegal yourself."

The men shook hands. "I'll get back to you very shortly," said Parks. "Today. About the statement."

"I'll be available."

• • ● • •

Back in their hotel room, Alan collapsed onto the bed. Tom dropped his backpack onto the desk. "When that detective searched my pack, I thought for sure he was going to keep the music you took last night."

"He'll probably make more of a fuss about it when he takes our statements. Time enough to worry about it later." Alan sighed, deeply and heartfelt. "I still need that rest, but I know you're worried about where I was this morning. It's not going to be easy to explain, but..."

He gestured toward the chair at the desk across the room. "Pull it over and have a seat."

Tom's eyes asked questions, but he dragged the chair to the bedside and sat.

Alan winced a couple of times as he kicked off his shoes and hauled his feet onto the bed. "All right. If this sounds funny—peculiar—in spots, bear with me. I was talking to Scott Joplin."

"Alan!"

The old pianist raised a hand in the classic stop signal. "I said, please bear with me. I'm not kidding around. Every word I'm going to tell you is true."

"Sorry. I'll do my best."

"Okay. Here's the way it was. I was studying the passage on that invitation, and I began to imagine I was listening to Joplin in the Maple Leaf Club...and the next thing I knew, I was *in* the Maple Leaf Club. I mean, really *in* the Maple Leaf Club. Joplin was at the piano, working on that piece. Arthur Marshall was standing to one side, Scott Hayden and Otis Saunders on the other side. They were as surprised to see me as I was to see them, and at first, things were a little tight. But after a bit, we got to talking about music, and then everything was copacetic. Funny thing, Joplin spoke very good Standard English, almost like formal speech. That's what all the sources say, and that it was supposedly because of the influence of the German music professor he studied with when he was a boy. I admit, I always took it with a grain of salt, but…

"I stayed until I started to run down and had to leave. I walked from the club back here. Not the hotel…there was a dry goods store on the corner of Ohio and Fourth. Tom, I swear, this is God's truth. I walked inside, and I was in the Bothwell lobby, exhausted and hurting all over. I flopped into a chair in the lobby for a little while, then came up to the room and hit the bed. Which is where I was when you came barreling in—no, not that I blame you. That's the story. I can't begin to understand how it happened."

"Time-traveling?" Tom's eyes widened. "That's an awfully big bite to swallow. Could you possibly have been hallucinating, you know…what with how tired and all you've been?" The boy's face brightened. "There must have been a name on the front of the shop—did you see it? We could go to the Carnegie Library and look in the 1899 City Directory. Then we might know what really happened."

Alan laughed out loud. "Nice try, but no cigar. It was Bryant-Tewmey—which I already knew. Remember, a few years ago, when I was researching those concerts they used to have on the courthouse lawn, right across the street from here? The name in the City Directory and the Sanborn maps stuck in my head because I wondered if that Bryant was related to the BBQ bigshot in K.C."

Tom returned the laughter, but then his expression went serious again. He rubbed his chin. "Any chance it could've been the chemo? That stuff does do all kinds of weird stuff to you."

Alan shook his head. "I don't think so. Fatigue, stomach cramps, and yes, it does affect the nervous system. You know how forgetful I've gotten. I have tingling in my feet and fingers, and I know I'm more irritable and have less patience than I once did. But Tom, I can't believe that was a hallucination. Would I have hallucinated all of my pain? I don't think so. And it was so quick; no disorientation, no confusion, just suddenly—ta da!—I was in Sedalia with Scott Joplin in 1899, and then ta da! again, I was back here in 2015."

The boy frowned. "Well, okay. The only other idea I've got is something called psychometry."

"What's that?"

"It comes out of psychic research—you know, mind reading, clairvoyance, seeing things at a distance, all that stuff. There are a lot of books about it, and I've talked to some people at science fiction conventions. There's this theory that a person with the right psychic abilities can sense the history of an object by handling it. Maybe you're just going one step further, visiting the object's past. You were studying that piece of music on the card, putting yourself into Joplin's head while he was writing it. And, hey! If Joplin wrote it at the Maple Leaf Club, he was only, what, a quarter-mile away from here?"

Alan made a go 'way motion with his hand. "Tom, that sounds like poppycock."

"Do you have a better explanation?"

"All right, Tom. Enough. Let's cool it for now. I'm really exhausted—too tired to try to think. Give me an hour or two horizontal; then we'll get some food and try to make sense out of all this."

Tom grinned. "While you're sleeping, I'm going to go over the music. I would anyway, but if I could go visit 1899…" His voice trailed off for a moment. "That would be *awesome*! And it would prove you're not hallucinating, right?" He didn't wait for Alan to answer. "If I'm not here when you wake up, you'll know where—or when—I am."

"Hmm." Alan lifted his knees, stretched a kink out of his lower back. "I said that piano string looked old. Wonder what might happen if I really study it…but not right now." He closed his eyes. "See you in a couple of hours."

The boy smiled. "Maybe."

Chapter Six

Tom waited until his grandfather started snoring before he pulled the envelope of music out of his pack. He set the invitational card on the desk in front of him, then stared at it in puzzlement. *Alan said he was imagining listening to Joplin working on this, but how the heck did he figure which scratch-outs and erasures went together?* He shrugged. *Maybe it'll be enough to go with the final version.*

He set his fingers on the edge of the table, fingering it like a keyboard, and played through the strain a few times. Once he was sure he had it down, he closed his eyes and pictured a slim, black man sitting at an upright piano, his fingers moving in synchronization with Tom's. At first it was tricky to keep the image in mind without losing the music, but after a couple of false starts, Tom thought he had it right. *1899, here I come!* He cracked one eye open and snuck a peek.

Still in the hotel room.

He tried again. Still nothing. *If I'm supposed to be feeling something from the card, I must be doing it wrong, 'cause I don't feel anything except silly.* He tipped his chair back onto two legs while he thought. *Maybe I don't have a good enough idea of what Joplin looked like. Or—didn't Alan say some of Joplin's students and Otis Saunders were there? Do I have to imagine them too?*

A few minutes with his iPhone turned up pictures of all four men. Tom studied them, closed his eyes again, and pictured the men gathered around a piano. He imagined Saunders saying something, and the others laughing. *Just another day, work's over, time for some fun.* Tom started to play the card music again, and realized it had slipped out of his head while he was looking at photos on his phone.

"Crap!" he said, then looked at Alan, who was still snoring. "He made it sound so easy," Tom muttered as he returned his attention to the card. He ran through the music a few more times, fixing it in his memory, and glanced back at the photos on his phone. Then he played the edge of the table again, letting his fingers remember the notes while he built up his mental image of the Maple Leaf Club. Slowly, his eyes closed, and the music in his head grew louder and louder.

• • ● • •

Tom jerked awake, the theme still running through his mind in dissonant counterpoint to Alan's snores. *Still right where I started. Either there's something I'm missing, or Alan's slipped a gear. I've got to be careful with him. If Gramma thinks he's losing it, she'll make us come right home. Leaving without finding out what happened to the music and who did in Mickey, that would kill Alan. I have to stay cheerful, take as much of the work as I can, and keep my mouth shut when we call home this evening.* Tom rubbed sleep out of his eyes. *And I'll keep trying to time-travel. 1899! That would be so epic!*

He tucked the card back into the envelope and pulled out one of the sheets of music paper. It began and ended mid-strain. Tom riffled the stack, hoping to find the preceding and following pages, but came up empty. It looked familiar, though. Tom played it through in his head, then laughed at himself. *Of course it looks familiar.*

"Still here, I see," Alan's voice interrupted the boy's train of thought.

Tom looked theatrically around the room and widened his eyes in a parody of shock. "I guess I am, at that." He shrugged, not ready to discuss the implications. "I didn't wake you, did I?"

"Nah. I had my couple of hours, plenty." Alan heaved himself up and leaned back against the headboard. "What's that you've got?"

Tom held up the sheet he'd been studying. "The middle of something. Unless I've forgotten half of what you've taught me, this is from a cakewalk—that rhythm is unmistakable—and we've got parts of two themes here. We don't have the rest of the piece, which is a crying shame, because the second theme looks a lot like the one on the invitational card."

Alan held his hand out, and studied the page for a moment. "Looks like it to me too—good job. Hope we can find the rest of the piece."

Tom grinned at the praise. "If we're lucky, it'll turn up in Mickey's duffel bag."

Alan grunted. "You sound confident we'll find it."

"Huh? *You* sure were when you were talking to the cops."

"If I hadn't, that Detective Parks would have walked all over me. I'm sure Parks is an okay guy as far as police go, but he still doesn't really want us underfoot." Alan shrugged and swung his legs out of bed. "Be polite, be respectful, but do what you need to. That's a good rule with police."

"If you say so." Tom stood up and stretched. "So what do we do next?"

"We find ourselves something to eat."

"Alan!"

"You've had nothing to eat since dinner last night and it's half-past lunchtime. That's not a natural state for a teenaged boy."

"I'm not sure I could eat anything. Not after seeing Mickey…" Tom's voice trailed off.

"Dinner tonight will be late if Detective Parks nabs us for statements. Bet you change your mind about eating when a burger looks you in the eye." He winked. "Besides, I ought to be eating too. At my last chemo treatment, my weight was down a few pounds, and the oncologist threatened me with Ensure if I didn't get it back up." Alan screwed his face into an expression of disgust. "Ugh! A fate worse than death, so to speak. Let's go over to that sports bar down at Fifth…Fitter's, right? Yeah. If we sit inside, nobody's going to hear us talking. And it's not likely the police would look for us there; if they can't find us, they can't tell us not to do whatever we decide to do next."

Tom gave him a dubious look, then slipped the music into his pack.

• • ● • •

By the time they settled into a booth at Fitter's, Tom's stomach growls were loud enough to convince him to risk a chicken wrap and onion rings. Alan looked the menu over and decided to stick with a plain burger and fries.

"Chemo tastebuds, Alan?"

"Nah. Just playing it safe. 'Sides, I like a good burger now and then. The more protein I can take in, the better, and the fat in the burger and the fries—calories!"

Alan looked around the room. Satisfied that no one was within earshot, he leaned forward. "The way I see it, that note from Mickey is our only real clue to where he stashed the duffel bag. Let me have another look at it."

He unfolded the paper and studied Mickey's scrawl. "Seems to me he was worried about someone coming after the duffel bag," Alan said, thinking out loud. "But why didn't he just say something last night?" Alan tapped the page against the table. "Look how sloppy his notation is. His handwriting's always been a mess, but his musical notation is usually clean. If he got this sloppy, he must have been in one big hurry, and maybe more than a little drunk. Something scared him last night after we left. Hmm."

"You think the music on this note is important? I figured it was already on the piece of paper Mickey happened to grab."

"Maybe you're right, but I doubt it." Alan flipped the page around and dropped it on the table. "Recognize the piece? I taught you this one a lot of years ago."

Tom grinned and nodded. "Took me a couple of seconds yesterday, but yeah. It's the intro to 'Swipesy Cakewalk'."

"You got it. Mickey's known that tune for decades. He wouldn't have bothered writing it down unless he was trying to send me a message. But what?"

"That someone was trying to swipe the music?"

Alan shook his head. "The note does that just fine. No, there's got to be more to it than that." He muttered "Swipesy, swipesy, swipesy…"

Tom spotted the waiter approaching with their food and stuffed Mickey's note back into his pocket.

Alan nodded thanks for the food, and picked up a fry, absently tapping it on the edge of his plate in time with his mutters.

Tom took a cautious bite of his sandwich. When his stomach didn't rebel, he followed the first bite with two more and an onion ring. "What we need," he said, mumbling through his meal, "is a native guide. Somebody who might know if there was some local significance to Swipesy."

Alan froze, then pointed his fry at Tom. "Of course!" he said, then looked at the fry and popped it into his mouth. "You remember the story about how Swipesy got its name?"

Tom had to wrack his brain over that one. His fingers always learned music much more easily than his brain learned the accompanying stories Alan told. "Uh…Joplin's publisher, John Stark, suggested it, right?" At his grandfather's nod, he went on. "Mr. Stark said the kid in the cover picture looked like he had just swiped something from the cookie jar. So?"

"So the 'kid' was a newsboy."

That clicked immediately. Tom's eyes widened. "Jackson? You think Mickey was worried Jackson was after the music? Maybe he was afraid Jackson was gonna kill him?"

Alan choked on a bite of burger and had to take a quick sip from his water glass. "I didn't even think of that! I figured that somehow, Jackson was protecting the music. That puts a whole 'nother slant on it."

The two were silent for a couple of minutes, eating and thinking, until Tom pushed his empty plate aside and snagged a handful of fries from Alan's.

Alan mock-glared at him and tugged his plate closer. "Stealing a hungry man's fries. For shame! See if I ever trust—" He held up an index finger. "Hang on. Mickey said he thought of the boy as almost a son, was teaching him ragtime piano. He *must* have trusted the kid. And probably every lesson included half a dozen stories about Joplin and his music. Jackson's probably heard the story about Swipesy a million times. Mickey never would have used it as a clue if he suspected the boy."

Tom shook his head. "That's a lot to hang on one little thing Mickey said."

"Getting cynical, are you? Well, how about this: Jackson had free passage to that house. He'd have known where to find the duffel bag, and could have just walked in and swiped it any time."

"Assuming Mickey showed it to him." Tom shook his head. "No, never mind. We both know Mickey wouldn't have been able to resist showing off his big score to his student. Okay, so Mickey wanted us to talk to Jackson. How about you let me take care of that?"

Alan half rose. "By yourself? I don't think so. I'm not going to sit around doing nothing while you go chasing after trouble!"

Tom made a couple of "sit down" patting motions. "Not 'nothing,' Alan. I'm suggesting a whatchamacallit…division of labor. Look, no matter what stories Mickey's told Jackson, he doesn't really know us. He's not going to trust some old guy he's just met. But someone more like his own age? Someone who can talk to him like just us guys? He might go for that."

"Humph." Alan settled back in his seat. "Maybe. But where's the division? So far all I'm hearing is what you're going to do."

"Somebody needs to distract the cops. Feed 'em a line of bull so they don't look too close at what I'm doing. And who could do that better than you?" Tom gave his grandfather his best deadpan look. "You said 'polite and respectful' earlier, but I didn't hear anything about truthful. Who could be better at spinning a tall tale than somebody who studied the art with Mr. S. Brunson Campbell, The Original Ragtime Kid hisself?"

That got a snicker out of Alan. "Sounds like you could spin a pretty good yarn yourself. Why's it so important for you to go chasing off after Jackson? Let's both go talk to the police. Feed them a line and then ignore them."

Tom shook his head and tapped his jeans pocket. "We lucked out this morning: the cops only searched my pack, when I was standing there with Mickey's note and the wire in my pocket. I don't think I should talk to the cops about a murder while I'm carrying around stolen evidence. If they find that stuff, we're going to wind up in the slammer."

Tom went on before Alan could do more than nod reluctantly. "I can't think of any place safe to hide the stuff. Can you?"

Alan shook his head slowly. "Damn it, no."

"Okay, then. So I'll hang on to it and stay out of sight. And that'll be a lot easier if you keep them distracted."

Alan sighed. "All right. You win this round. Go talk to Jackson, I'll talk to Detective Parks. But be careful! Even if we're right about Jackson, that just means the killer is out there somewhere. We've got to talk to your grandmother this evening, and I do not want to have to explain how you got hurt—or worse."

"I'll be real careful, Alan, I promise! I'll stay in public, won't get him mad or anything. If he gets weird, I'll run like hell. Okay?"

Alan sighed again and shook his head. "Better watch it, Thomas, or you're going to make me proud of you." He took a deep breath. "Give me your backpack. Most likely, the lieutenant will want to see the music, so I'd better have it to hand."

Tom stood and dropped his pack on the bench next to Alan. He gave his grandfather a quick peck on the cheek. "Baffle 'em with bullshit, okay? Meet you back at the hotel so we can figure out what we're gonna tell Gramma."

Alan looked around for the waiter, then changed his mind. *Too busy talking to eat. Still have half my burger, and I'm not going on Ensure. No way. It won't hurt the police to wait a little longer to hear from me.* He took a bite and stared off into space while he chewed. *Tom figures I've lost my mind over this time-travel business, but I don't think so. I may be forgetful, but I feel almost as sharp as ever. I don't know if I can get back to 1899, but if I can, I might find something or do something to prove it's real.*

He popped open the buckle on Tom's backpack and dug out the invitation, setting it on the table a safe distance away from the plates. He took another bite of burger as he recreated his image of the Maple Leaf Club with Joplin at the piano, surrounded by his students and friends, then hesitated.

If I could talk to him alone… That would be much better. Maybe a different time. Midafternoon, maybe, sneaking a few quiet moments before he heads off to work.

Alan erased everyone but Joplin from his mental picture and added the sun angling in through the windows, a few stray reflections off the unlit chandeliers. It didn't feel quite right. After a moment of thought, the old man imagined Joplin rising from the piano and stepping behind the bar, then bending over to look for something underneath it. That felt better. He let the strain on the card begin to play in his head, then added himself to the picture. *As easy as that.* He swallowed his food and said, "Mr. Joplin? My apologies for disturbing you—"

Joplin jerked upright, a pile of papers in one hand. "Oh! Mr. Chandler. You do have a way of appearing unexpectedly."

"It does seem that way, doesn't it? But it's just happenstance."

Joplin nodded and waved a hand at one of the tables. "If you say so, Sir. Please, have a seat." He bent behind the bar again.

Alan heard a "clunk-rattle-click" before Joplin straightened, tucking something into his pocket. He realized the sounds had been Joplin putting the papers into some sort of safe or locked box under the bar.

"I've been looking for you the past few days," Joplin said as he settled into the chair across from Alan. "Naturally, it wasn't until I stopped looking that you turned up."

"Days?" The word slipped out before Alan could stop it and he tried to cover for himself. "I hadn't thought it had been that long."

The musician gave him a dubious look, but let the statement pass. "Perhaps your arrival is fortunate. I've been vexing my free moments with a new composition for several weeks and have little to show for my efforts. A change of mental scenery—devoting some time to another problem—might help."

"Mozart's muse eludes you, I take it," Alan said with a grin.

"The one that allowed his music to flow from his mind to his pen as fast as he could write? Alas, it has. If there ever existed such a creature, and I have my doubts that it did, I fear it perished with Mozart."

Alan raised his hands and face heavenward. "Oh, Lord, give me patience with my muse. She knows not what frustration she brings upon me, yet I dare not tell her how I feel, for fear of reaping her eternal scorn."

The corner of Joplin's mouth twitched upward. "Amen. But tell me, Mr. Chandler, what brings you to this glorious venue at such an auspicious moment?" The sarcasm in Joplin's voice hinted that his opinion of the Maple Leaf Club was lower than that of future generations.

Auspicious? Good God, that's right! If this is September 1899, "Maple Leaf Rag" has either just been published, or will be any time now. Alan forced himself to look relaxed. "In a way, I suppose I could say it was your music. It's a long story, and I'm afraid if I stay long enough to tell it, my grandson will get himself into trouble. May I defer the tale for another time?"

"A cruel request, to leave me unsure whether I've been complimented or condemned, but family must take precedence. And I'll admit, my own time is limited this afternoon as well."

"Then a discussion we can set aside at any moment." Alan thought for a second. "The philosophy of music, perhaps? What do you consider to be the purpose, the reason for music?"

"Beyond the purely commercial? A subject best suited to a late night with friends, Mr. Chandler. But why not?"

Joplin returned to the bar, snagged a pair of bottles, poured, and brought the glasses to the table. "Capital Ginger Ale. Nearly as good as beer for philosophical disputation." Although his face was sober, a hint of humor lurked in the corners of his eyes. "And much cheaper than alcohol. Until recently, the bottler was housed in this very building. I believe our host receives a special price in exchange for displaying their sign."

Alan gave the brew a dubious look. He'd always considered ginger ale an insipid beverage, ill-suited for any purpose beyond soothing an upset stomach, but he took a polite sip—and coughed when the strong, spicy drink hit the back of his throat and tickled his sinuses.

He took another, more cautious sip. *That's…actually quite good.* A glance at his watch. *No more than an hour, then back to the hotel and Detective Parks,* Alan promised himself, shifting uncomfortably in the hard chair. *But next time I visit, I'll bring a cushion.*

Chapter Seven

Tom wiped his eyes as he walked away from Alan. He shot a glance backward at his grandfather, hunched over the table, studying God-knew-what as he chewed a mouthful of burger. Trying to keep up his energy and his weight, even though he knew it would ultimately be a losing battle.

Time was, and not that long ago, Alan Chandler was a living, breathing energy source in the world of ragtime. It was nothing for him to play a concert, instigate an after-hours jam till three or four in the morning, and be wide awake after a few hours' sleep, putting down on paper the tune that had entered his mind in embryonic form during the night. Now he needed an hour or two of—as he put it—going horizontal to get through a concert. He could still go directly from bed into composition, but not for anything like the uninterrupted day that used to be his standard. Half that at best, and only with a rest period in the middle. Tom felt a good deal of satisfaction at having given the old man a chance to go back to the hotel room and take it easy for a while.

We'd better get our hands on the music in that duffel bag quickly. The longer it takes, the harder it's gonna be to keep Alan from overdoing so much the effin' chemo knocks him on his ass.

But how was he going to find Jackson? Mickey had said he lived in Lincolnville with his granny. Not exactly specific information, but a start. Tom had come to Sedalia for the Scott Joplin Festival with Alan every year since he was eight, and he knew the layout of the central city as well as he knew Seattle—but that wouldn't help with Lincolnville, the neighborhood north of the railroad tracks. Until the late 1950s, when integration finally spread through Sedalia, it was the black section of town. Now most of Lincolnville was wide swatches of tall weeds where abandoned, century-old houses had collapsed and the rubble cleared. Even the old Hubbard High School had been bashed into nonexistence, replaced by a housing project for the elderly. Most remaining individual homes were small, but well-kept-up, statements of resistance by old folks.

But only an idiot would try to go door-to-door in Lincolnville. Lots of streets to cover, with strong odds that a white boy knocking at doors and asking about a black kid would be lucky to just get those doors slammed in his face.

Start with something simple, logical, and convenient.

Tom walked to the hostess at the little welcoming station inside the door, and asked for a phone book. The young woman smiled, reached behind the lectern, and handed the boy a regional telephone directory. He murmured thanks, then dropped into the nearest empty chair and flipped to "Ja".

Great. The list goes on for-freaking-ever. Tom checked the obvious possibility quickly. *No Jackson Jackson. Only one J. Jackson, and he's not even in Sedalia, let alone Lincolnville. Screw it. No point wading through all this.*

Tom drummed fingers on the page. He thought back to their meeting with Mickey the night before. Mickey had introduced him and Alan to Jackson, they shook hands...hang on! *His fingernails were stained black. Maybe he's not just a delivery boy; maybe he actually works on the paper.*

Tom jumped up, ready to run. What was the address of the *Sedalia Democrat?* If they'd moved out of Town Center, like so many businesses, he'd need a car, but at sixteen he was too young to drive the rental car.

He flipped to the Yellow Pages, Newspapers, *Sedalia Democrat*...700 South Massachusetts Avenue, corner of Massachusetts and Seventh, just two blocks down Ohio, then two blocks east on Seventh. *Score!* Tom slammed the phone book shut, returned it to the hostess with a "Thanks" and a quick salute, and tore out the door.

• • ● • •

Tom looked around the lobby of the *Democrat*. No printed directory on the wall. He shrugged and approached the security guard sitting at a small desk just inside the door. The guard looked old enough to have been on the job since the paper was founded; he blinked several times when Tom stopped in front of the desk, then said, "He'p you, Sonny?"

Tom flashed his best smile. "Can you please tell me where I could find Jackson Jackson?"

That drew a phlegmy laugh and a cough. The guard shot a glance at a brass spittoon beside his chair, but then swallowed and wiped his hand across his mouth. "That boy…He works the night shift, so I couldn't begin to tell you where he'd be right now. But I'd bet the farm he'd be into some sorta devilment."

"Could you tell me his address?" Tom asked. "Or at least his phone number?"

"No sirree, cain't do that. I'm a security guard. Givin' out personal information, that ain't so secure, now is it?"

"I've got to find him, though," Tom said. "It's very important—really."

"That's what they all say, Sonny. But I still cain't he'p you."

"I know he lives with his gramma, in Lincolnville. Can you tell me her name?"

The old man's face registered annoyance. "You're a persistent li'l cuss, ain't you? But you're wasting your time and mine. I cain't give you no personal information, none, nothing. Now git on your way, hear?"

Tom stifled an urge to brain the old fart with the phone on the desk. "Okay, can you call his house for me? Tell Jackson or his grandmother that Tom Chandler needs to talk to him, it's very important and it's got to do with Mickey Potash. That way, you won't be giving me any personal information."

The guard gave Tom a long stare. "I do that, you promise you'll go 'way? No more foolishness?"

"Yep. Promise."

The old man sighed extravagantly, opened a directory, ran his finger down the page, then began to punch keys on the phone. After a moment, he cleared his throat. "Hello, Elvira? Yeah, this here's Calvin, down at the *Democrat.* I got a kid here, a Tom Chandler. He say he's gotta talk to Jackson, it's real important… oh, okay, then. I'll tell him."

He replaced the receiver in the cradle and looked back to Tom. "She say Jackson's sleepin' now, and she don't know you and ain't got no truck with you. So…" He jerked a thumb toward the door. "On your way now. Scram."

"Well, thanks anyway." Tom turned, walked back through the lobby and outside. Once on the sidewalk, he flipped his middle finger at the wall between him and the security station, and immediately felt foolish. He looked around, didn't see anyone who might have noticed his gesture, and took a step into the street.

A hand fell on his shoulder. He jumped and spun around— *Who…?*—and found himself looking at a slim, light-skinned black girl, about his own age, a huge leather purse slung casually over her left shoulder. A single braid hung down to her lower back. She flashed Tom a smile featuring a luminous double row of shining teeth.

The girl grinned at Tom and flipped her own middle finger in the general direction of the security desk. "That Calvin, he one nasty ol' asshole. I don't like him a bit. You lookin' for JJ, right?"

It took a moment for Tom to catch on to the change of subject. "Yeah…Jackson Jackson…" The cartoon-balloon lightbulb went on over his head. "I saw you inside there, didn't I? Over by the elevator?"

"Yep. My daddy work up in the City Room, so I stops by 'most every day on my way home from school. I heard you two arguin'. Thought I'd offer you a friendly hand, but you done better'n I expected. Never thought anyone get the ol' bastard to do somethin' as hard as dialin' the phone." She changed the subject again. "What's it worth if I takes ya right to JJ's door?"

Tom squinted, shaded his eyes against the sun. "You mean money?"

The girl laughed. "'Less you got something better'n that."

Now Tom chuckled. "Sorry, but I don't think I need your help. I read the numbers while Old Mr. Get-Off-My-Lawn was dialing." He pulled out his iPhone. "Bet a quick search'll give me the address that goes with it. And I know my way around town—once I have the address, I can walk right over there, all by myself."

The girl put a hand on her hip, extended it to the side, and gave Tom an amused look. "Well, now, I thought you was cute, but I never woulda guessed you was clever, too. But maybe you ain't quite so clever as all that. Yeah, maybe you *could* walk over there by yourself, but walkin' back, that might be a bit tougher. See, Granny Elvira don't take too kindly to strangers—'specially white ones—and she pack some mean heat. But Granny know me. If I tell her you be all right, well, then you *be* all right. So how 'bout it? What's it worth to you?"

Tom sighed. "How about ten bucks?"

"You think I come pretty cheap, don't you? I was thinking more like fifty."

"Fifty? Forget it. Look at me. What do you think, I walk around with a wallet full of bills? No way. I'll give you ten…" He paused for a split second, thinking about "cute" and how close to him the girl was standing, and decided to risk it. "And if there's anything else you like…" He let his voice trail off.

The girl guffawed. "Why, Mr. Chandler, you offerin' your body 'steada cash? You got bigger balls than I give you credit for." She giggled, went on. "Well, what the heck. I ain't got no plans, and it might be kinda fun."

She leaned forward, planted her lips onto Tom's, and wiggled her body against his. After a long moment, she pulled back. "Not half bad; I've had a lot worse. Figure that's a down payment. Now, where's the tenner?"

Tom dug into his pocket, pulled out a worn black leather wallet, removed two fives, and passed them to the girl, who smirked, and started to slip them inside her blouse. When Tom's eyes widened, she giggled again and dropped them into her purse. "Okay, Tom, I'm Saramae. C'mon, let's go."

• • ● • •

Alan snuck another glance at his watch. He suspected that it was out of place in 1899, though probably no more so than any of his clothes. *At least it's a wind-up model, not one of those annoying digital monstrosities.* He and Joplin had been talking for a bit over an hour, moving from musical philosophy, through composition for the musical theater, to Joplin's intent to answer Dvořák's call for a truly American musical style.

"I know you compose at the keyboard," Alan said. "Do you also work away from it?"

"At times." Joplin tapped a pocket in his jacket. "I always carry some paper and a pencil in case the muse chooses to pay me a visit while I am out and about town. Nor am I likely to leave a warm bed on a cold night to search out a piano."

Alan grinned. "A sensible philosophy."

Joplin went on. "I find, however, that while I can imagine the music well enough, once I hear it through my ears instead of my mind, there is always something I wish to change. And you?"

"Much the same. I can put down an idea, even a draft, any- where, but music can't be complete until it's heard. Sometimes the necessary changes may be small, but there are always some." He smiled at his host and picked up his ginger ale. The glass was nearly empty, and a trace of guilt poked his conscience.

I promised myself no more than an hour, but here I am still, while Tom's chasing around town.

"Mr. Joplin, I'm afraid I do need to leave." Alan rose to his feet. "My ability to visit is not entirely under my control, but I'll return as soon as I can—perhaps even without catching you by surprise."

"Well then, until our next meeting. Which will be, I hope, long enough for you to tell the tale of how I'm responsible for your visit to Sedalia." Joplin glanced at Alan's wrist, then swung his eyes to the backpack the old man had dropped on the floor beside his chair. "And perhaps a few other tales as well?"

"Long and unbelievable tales. But I hope so as well." He worked hard not to grimace as an intense cramp worked its way through his gut. *Damn you, chemo!* He shook an Imodium out of his little pocket container and downed it with the last mouthful of soda. Then he shook Joplin's hand, and turned to the stairs.

• ● ● ● •

Alan stared in puzzlement around the Bryant-Tewmey store. The last time he had stepped through its door, he had found himself in the Hotel Bothwell, and had expected the same this time. Instead, he found himself before a display of brightly colored fabric. He blinked a couple of times, said "Sorry, wrong door," to the approaching clerk, and stepped outside again to think.

It took only a moment to recognize a significant difference between his visits to 1899: his departure point. When he had left from the Hotel Bothwell, returning there to end his trip made sense.

So this time I need to go to where Fitter's will be in another century.

He crossed East Fourth and started down Ohio. He couldn't resist studying the businesses he passed. Almost every storefront between Fourth and Fifth housed either a grocery, a druggist, or a dry goods store. Alan made a mental bet with himself that the future location of Fitter's would now be harboring a grocer. As he approached the corner, he found he was half right: the space was shared by a grocer and a millinery. Beyond them, a dry goods shop, a druggist, and a piano and organ specialist. The area in front of the grocer, where Alan was used to seeing Fitter's patio seating, was occupied by a number of sturdy tables holding baskets of produce.

As he crossed the street, a burst of swearing rose behind him. Startled, he stumbled over the curb and bumped into a teenaged girl, her nose buried in an iPhone. They mumbled apologies at each other, and Alan leaned against the wall to catch his breath.

He took two steps back toward the hotel, stopped, and slapped his forehead. *The card!*

He wheeled around and walked into Fitter's. "Excuse me," he said to the hostess. "I was here earlier, and I think I left some music on my table."

"Musician, are you?" She eyed him suspiciously. "Chicken wrap, onion rings, plain burger and fries, hold the mayo?"

Alan nodded. "That's right. You remember?"

"I remember everyone who leaves without paying."

"Did I really?" Alan gave her his best innocent look. "I'm very sorry. I've been forgetting things lately because of the chemo I'm getting for my cancer treatment." He pulled out his wallet. "Can we settle up now? And can I get my music back?"

"Chemo? Oh gee, sorry to hear it. My mother had breast cancer, and she had the same problem with her memory. Just a sec." She took Alan's credit card to the register at the end of the bar. Much to his disappointment, she didn't show any intention of looking for the invitation in a lost and found box.

The hostess returned to the front of the restaurant and handed Alan his card and the slip. While he calculated a larger than usual tip as an apology for skipping out, she pulled the invitational card from a box inside the lectern. Alan sighed with relief and upped the tip further.

"You musicians leave music behind during festival season. We're used to it. Still have some from this summer. Any of it yours?"

Alan made a show of thinking about it. "I doubt it. Best I can remember, I brought everything home with me this year."

He signed the slip and handed it back, then carefully tucked the invitation into the envelope in Tom's backpack before he put his credit card and the receipt into his wallet. "Of course, with my memory the way it is, who knows what I might have left? You don't have my grandson in that box, by any chance?"

The hostess laughed. "'Fraid not. But good luck with your chemo."

Alan nodded his thanks, and headed toward the hotel, hoping for a chance to rest a little before talking to the police.

• • ● • •

Saramae led the way up Ohio, past Main Street, across the railroad tracks, and into Lincolnville. They crossed Jefferson and Pettis, turned right on Cooper, then right again onto Lamine. A short way down the block, Saramae took Tom's arm and pointed at a small, well-kept house. "There ya go. You just make sure you let me do the talkin' at first, huh?"

Tom nodded.

The boy was surprised at the woman who answered Saramae's knock; she was well-proportioned, probably pushing eighty, an inch short of his own height, with an elegant beehive of black hair. Not even close to the clone of Aunt Jemima he'd pictured when he heard the name "Granny Elvira." *So much for prejudice.*

She gave Tom a quick up-and-down, then turned a questioning face onto his companion. "What's goin' on, Saramae?" she asked. "You got manners enough to introduce your friend?"

"This's Tom Chandler, Granny Elvira. I met him downtown, and he lookin' for JJ in a big way. Says it's real important."

"Oh, is it? Tom Chandler…this be the boy ol' Calvin call me about. You don't give up easy, do you, Boy?"

"No, Ma'am, I don't. And I don't mean to bother you, but it really is important for me to talk to JJ."

"You gonna tell me what it be about?"

Saramae elbowed Tom in the ribs and gave him a quick nod. "It's about Mickey Potash, Ma'am."

"Hmm. That old boozehound. What about him?"

Tom took a deep breath. He didn't see any suspicious bulges in the woman's dress. In for a penny, in for a pound. "He's dead, Ma'am. Murdered."

He could see that got Elvira's attention, but she caught herself quickly. "Well, I guess I'm sorry to hear it—he been good to my boy. But why's it so important you talk to Jackson about it?"

"Few things. One is that the cops are going to find him and want to talk about the murder. And…well, Mickey and my grandpa are friends from way back, they both play ragtime piano.

Mickey's got some music he wanted my grandpa to see. We were over there last night and met JJ. So we figured that with…what happened, we ought to talk to him about the music."

"Grandpa? And you a Chandler?" Elvira's hand flew to her mouth. "You tellin' me you be *Alan* Chandler's grandson?"

"Yes, Ma'am."

"Greatest ragtime piano player on Earth. Maybe the greatest ever. Don't think I've missed hearing him play at one single Joplin Festival since they begun, and when I go up and tell him how much I like his music, he just *so* nice, almost bashful." She squinted to get a better look at Tom. "An' you the boy been playin' with him these last years. His grandson! My! You know how lucky you are?"

"Yes, Ma'am. And I'm not as good yet as my grandpa, but I'm working on it."

The woman laughed, a silvery-bell sound. "However good you be, you got a way to go."

"Yes, Ma'am. I know that. But Alan also says I shouldn't ever aim low."

Elvira nodded, and motioned behind her. "Come on in. I'll wake Jackson up for you."

"Thank you, Mrs.…."

"Jackson. But you call me Granny, like all of his friends. He live here with me—he's all I got and the other way 'round too."

She led Tom and Saramae into a bright living room and motioned for them to sit on a sofa with a bright blue cover dotted with yellow flowers. "I'll be right back," she said, and walked off into a hallway to the right.

"You don't care if I stay, do you, Tom?" Saramae grinned. "Ain't nothing this much fun ever happened to me."

"No, it's fine." *What else can I say?* "You live around here?"

She shook her head. "No, way back in the sixties, my family move down on Moniteau Avenue, south of Broadway. Got white folks to each side." She flashed a sly smile.

"Cool. Want to give me your address and phone number?"

"Why? Am I important, too? Like JJ?"

"You just might be. One never knows…do one?"

The girl broke into a raucous laugh. "You could be Fats Waller, 'cept you white and you ain't fat."

"And I'm alive."

"Yeah, that too." She reached into her backpack, pulled out a notebook, and scribbled on a page. When she finished, she tore it out and passed it to Tom.

"Hmmm. Saramae Blackstone, 000 Moniteau Ave." He looked up. "Zero, zero, zero?"

"What kinda girl you think I am? Givin' out my address to some white boy I just meet? Hell, we ain't even been properly introduced!"

Tom snickered. "But you'll smooch me on the sidewalk?" He shook his head. "Phone number's just as good." He balanced the paper on his knee, fumbled his iPhone out of his pocket, and tapped the screen.

Elvira came in, carrying a little wooden tray with two glasses of lemonade and a plate of cookies, which she set down on the small coffee table in front of the couch. "Here you go," she said. "Can't talk about murder and music on an empty stomach. I'll go get the boy for you."

As she walked away again, Tom entered Saramae's name and phone number. He started to reach for a cookie, then remembered what he'd promised Alan. Here he was, sitting inside a house no one knew he had gone to, a house owned by a woman who allegedly packed some mean heat and didn't take well to white boys coming to her door. And now she was serving him food and drink. But she'd left the glasses for each of them to pick up, and there was only one plate of cookies.

Don't think she'd take a chance of poisoning Saramae. Better be polite and take a cookie.

• • ● • •

Alan groaned as he crossed the lobby toward the elevators. Detective Parks was leaning on the front desk, talking to the clerk. He considered trying to sneak past, but gave up when the clerk aimed a finger in his direction. As the detective walked toward him, Alan let his shoulders slump, stopped trying to ignore his tiredness and the ache in his back, and plastered on a cordial-through-the-pain smile.

"Mr. Parks. I was wondering when I'd hear from you."

"Wondered how long you could avoid me, I'm sure. Nobody ever wants to see me when it comes time to give a statement."

"Strange, isn't it?" Alan shrugged elaborately. "Is this something we can do up in my room? I need to sit for a bit."

"Sorry, Mr. Chandler. I need you to come down to the station. Procedure."

"Then you'll need to give me a couple of minutes to leave my grandson a note and take my pills."

"I can do that." The detective gestured toward the elevator. "After you, Sir." After a couple of steps, he went on with a carefully casual air, "Where is your grandson? Tom, right?"

"'Around' is the best I can tell you." Alan's reply was equally casual. "He's upset. Tom's known Mickey since he was a little boy; they were very fond of each other. He needed some time to himself. I told him to take a walk around town, burn some energy. Do something so he can…what do the shrinks call it? Process. So he can process what he saw. I was the same way at that age."

"Mmph." Parks didn't look like he was buying what Alan was selling, but he wasn't walking out of the store either.

Alan unlocked the door and tossed Tom's backpack on the bed, trying to make it look like the pack was unimportant. He stepped into the bathroom and selected a Compazine, a Vicodin, and another Imodium from an impressive lineup of small brown bottles on the counter next to the sink.

"Quite the pharmacy you've got there, Mr. Chandler."

Alan eyed the line of bottles with disgust. "And not a one of them does anything interesting. Cancer's no fun, and neither is the medication. If you need to copy the list…" He fished out his pocket notebook, started to flip through it.

"That shouldn't be necessary. It's not like Mr. Potash was poisoned."

Alan nodded and sat at the desk. He dashed off a note to Tom— "Gone to visit Detective Parks. Back soon. Wait for me."

"That's Tom's backpack, isn't it, Mr. Chandler?"

"It is."

"Mind if I have a look inside?"

"Go ahead. Nothing in it you didn't see earlier." Alan finished writing, then turned to Parks. "Like I said this morning, that's how Mickey got me out here," Alan said before the detective could speak. "Sent me the music with a note that didn't really say anything. Tom and I got on the first plane we could get, and here we are."

"And why is your grandson carrying it around town?"

"I'm not going to leave this music—a major discovery—sitting in a hotel room where a maid could mess with it or someone could break in and grab it. After what happened to poor Mickey, I'm keeping it where I can see it."

Parks flipped through the pages. "Looks like music, I suppose." He slid them back into the envelope. "I could impound these as evidence in Mr. Potash's murder. Probably should." He held up a hand, cutting off Alan's outburst. "I should, but I won't. *If.*"

"If?"

"Let me take pictures for the case file and I'll let you hold onto them."

"Absolutely."

"But if I find any evidence you're lying about how and when you got these, your name goes straight to the top of the list of suspects, and you go straight behind bars. Hear me?"

"Loud and clear. You can see the address and postmark on the envelope." Alan plucked the envelope out of Parks' hand and tapped the postage sticker in the corner. He tucked the envelope back into the pack and swung it over his shoulder. "Can you bring me back here when we're done, or should I drive myself to the station?"

As JJ came through the door with Elvira, Tom lowered his glass and held his breath. JJ hadn't bothered to change out of his blue-and-black-striped pajamas. His hands were empty, eyebrows at half-mast; he shuffled forward in bedroom slippers. *No concealed weapons there.*

"Sorry to bother you," Tom said. "But I figured this was real important."

JJ answered with a shrug, then plopped into a padded chair facing the sofa. "So, okay," he muttered. "I'm here. Talk."

"Well, it's about Mickey."

"Tha's what Granny Elvira say. What about Mickey, huh?"

Tom blew out a deep breath. "JJ, I don't have any good way to say it. Mickey's dead. Somebody murdered him last night."

The change in JJ's demeanor was astounding. He straightened to attention in the chair, eyes bulged. He leaned forward past the lemonade and cookies to grab Tom's shirtfront. "Man, you better not be trying to pull something on me."

Tom wriggled himself free. "No, it's God's truth, and I'm sorry to have to be the one to tell you. But…" He waved his hand, trying to summon the right words. "My grandfather and me found him this morning. Cops're all over it, so I figured I'd better find you and let you know. Good thing Saramae could get me here."

The girl flashed a quick grin at his recognition of her contribution.

JJ shot Tom a suspicious glare. "That ain't the only reason you come by, now, is it?"

"No." Tom's voice softened. "My grandfather and I flew out here yesterday because Mickey wanted his help figuring out who'd written some old music manuscripts. We went to see him last night, when we met you, and were supposed to go back this morning to do some work with him."

"Yeah, I get that. You still ain't tellin' me why you sittin' here today with *me*."

Tom made a quick decision to shade the truth a little. "After you left, Mickey told us that you were the best friend he had, and you knew where he stashed the music when he wasn't looking at it. That a good enough reason for you?"

JJ's face hardened. "It's gonna be good for *you*, sure. But how do I know it's good for *me*? And not maybe bad."

Tom wondered whether he should go ahead without Alan's agreement. *But I'm here and Alan's not...* "Try starting with this: we could play ball with the cops or we could play with you. And I'm here."

"But how do I *know* you ain't playin' on the cop team?" He leaned forward in the chair. "Pull up your shirt, Man. Let's see if you carryin' a wire."

Tom did as he was told. "We're not playing with the cops. My grandpa wants that music, and he also wants to nail the bastard who killed Mickey. You're our best hope."

JJ took a moment to think. "You never did tell me how they got Mickey. Gun? Knife?"

Tom shook his head. "He was strangled with a piano string."

"Piano string?! You ain't shittin' me, are you?" He took a moment to study Tom's face. "No, you ain't. Fuck."

Disgust covered Saramae's face. "Piano wire? That be all kindsa messed up shit!"

"JJ, do you have any idea who might have done it? *And* where that duffel bag with the music is."

"Well, it ain't here, if that's what you're thinkin'." JJ sat back. "Mickey wouldn't never let it out of his own hands, not for a minute, not for nothin'."

"I believe that."

"But yeah, I know where he keep it." The young black man considered, decided to go on. "He give me the key, jus' to be safe. That hall closet, were it still locked?"

Tom shook his head. "No, it was open."

"Well, hell. I tell Mickey that stupid padlock were a piece o' crap."

"The lock was still locked. Whoever it was ripped the thing out of the wall." Everyone was silent for a few seconds, then Tom added, "So the music's gone. Damn."

"Maybe, maybe not," JJ said slowly. He held up a hand, Stop, as Tom rose halfway out of his chair. "I ain't gonna tell you everythin' just like that. Here's what we gonna do: tonight, late, we gonna go by that house an' take us a look. You an' me. An' if we finds it, we gonna do some heavy talkin'. An' if we don't find it, we gonna talk maybe even heavier."

"But won't the cops have a watch on the house?"

JJ laughed. "Prob'ly not. What for? They doin' what they got to do there now, an' no reason for them to keep a man sittin' on his ass all night. An' it won't take but no time for us to know if the duffel's there or not."

"But if you work nights—"

"I gets an hour for dinner, three a.m. to four. Won't be no trouble a'tall to do what we gotta do in that hour. You'se probably a virgin, but I knows what we gonna have to do."

I'll bet you do. Tom nodded his head. "I'll have to talk to my grandpa—see if he wants to be there, too. But figure it's a go."

"Just one minute now, boys." For the first time, Elvira broke into the dialogue. "You don't think I'm just gonna sit back and let my boy go on by hisself with that monkey business. I be there with you; best you have a lookout while you'se pokin' around inside a hot house like that. An' I ain't no virgin either."

Saramae tried, but couldn't stifle a snicker. Elvira reached across to punch her arm.

"Yeah, Granny, okay." JJ smiled. "So let's figure we meet at, oh, ten minutes pas' three, on Third, halfway between Lafayette and Washington. Everybody wearin' black, right? An' not together. Tom, you be on the south side of the street, I be on the north, and Granny, you gonna be on the Lafayette corner. If a nice ol' lady, goin' first, see somethin' she don't like, she let us know: two hands up in the air, we all go back and tomorrow we gets together here, after my shift—say nine o'clock—and figure what's next. Got it?"

Nods all around.

JJ stood, stretched, yawned. "Good, then. Now if you all 'scuse me, I gonna go back an' finish up my beauty sleep. Gotta be at my best tonight."

Saramae snickered again. "Think you gots'nuff sleep time 'tween now an' then? Gonna take more'n a few hours to make *you* beautiful, I'm thinkin'."

JJ glared at her. "Knock off that crap, Girl. Straight-A student like you got no damn business talkin' like some country nigger ain't never seen the inside of a classroom. You oughta be 'shamed—your daddy be the editor of the paper, he talk beautiful English, an' I knows you did too, up 'til maybe a couple a years ago. I wish *I* could talk good as you, an' if I could, I sure as hell would."

Saramae shot a quick glance sideways at Tom, and blushed slightly. She held up both hands in an "I surrender" gesture and mumbled, "Sorry."

• • ● • •

Detective Parks dropped the typed copy of Alan's statement on the table. "Check it over, and if there are no mistakes, sign here and initial each page." He sighed. "I will need to take a statement from Tom too."

Alan looked up from the stack of paper. "You really think he could have done that to Mickey?"

"What I think is beside the point, Mr. Chandler. According to your statement, Tom was the first to see Mr. Potash's body, and he was alone at the time." He dragged the phone on his desk a little closer. "Is he likely to be back at the hotel by now?"

"Probably." Alan glanced at the clock. "Almost certainly, by now."

"Good. Ask him to come down here. We'll take his statement, then give you both a lift back." He dialed the hotel, identified himself and asked to be put through to Mr. Chandler's room. While the phone was ringing, he handed it to Alan.

"Alan!" Tom cried. "Is that you? Are you okay?"

"I'm good. Good enough, anyway. How're you doing, Thomas? Holding up?"

"I'm okay." Tom sounded wary, as though it was a trick question.

"Glad to hear it. Listen, I hate to make you do this, but Mr. Parks insists on taking your statement. Can you bring yourself down to the station?"

"I guess so…If you're sure I should."

"I do. Detective Parks is being careful and thorough."

"Gotcha, Alan. See you in a bit."

• • ● • •

On their way back from the police station, statements given, Tom's hangdog expression faded, replaced by a broad grin. Alan muttered, "You did good, but hold on now until we get to the room. Don't blow it."

As they got out of the Bothwell elevator, Tom turned down the hall, away from their room. "Hang on a second, Alan," he said. A short way along, the boy stopped before a vase in a decorative niche. He tipped the vase up on edge, pulled a small envelope out of the cavity on its underside, and set the vase back down before he rejoined Alan.

Inside the room, he opened the envelope to show Alan the snippet of piano wire and Mickey's note. "When you said Parks was being careful, I figured you meant he might search me. Seemed like putting these someplace outside the room would be safer than trying to hide 'em here."

Alan gave him a quick hug. "Smart kid. You read me just right." He stretched to release the tension in his back. "Ought to be safe to hang onto that, now he's done with us. Tuck it in the pack, and let's go find some dinner. You can tell me how you did with young Mr. Jackson, and then we have some figuring to do. I don't think Parks has the smarts to settle a case as weird as this, and I don't trust him to not impound the duffel bag if he finds it. I think it's up to you and me to get things straight, as soon as we can."

Chapter Eight

Comfortably settled in a padded booth in the railroad car at Kehde's Barbeque, Alan stretched his back. "Hope you don't mind barbeque two nights in a row."

Tom waved off his grandfather's concern. "You've brought me to Sedalia for the Joplin Festival every year for, like, half my life, and I don't think we've ever had anything *but* barbeque. Is there even anything else?"

Alan laughed. "It's strange—seems like my chemo taste aversions would have a field day with barbeque, but it's just the opposite. Most food tastes at least a little bit off, but it's mostly a loss of flavor, like I'm eating blotting paper. But barbeque sauce tastes right. Ketchup helps too. Fries without ketchup? Ugh."

Tom put a hand on his grandfather's. "Don't worry about it," he said quietly. "Whatever works for you works for me. Besides, this is good stuff."

"Thanks. I appreciate that. What would work for me now is to hear what went on with you this afternoon. What did you learn?"

As the boy wound up the account of his adventure, Alan nodded. "Good. *Really* good. I think you made every call right, and we're rolling…"

The waitress set two brisket sandwiches on the table, with a side of fries between them, then added a couple of Cokes to the array. "That do it for you for now, Guys?"

Alan inhaled extravagantly. "Very well, I think. Thank you."

He picked up his sandwich, took a big bite, chewed and swallowed slowly.

Tom suppressed his normal inclination to gobble his food, determined not to put any pressure on Alan to hurry.

It's part of his routine. If he puts it in too fast, he fills right up, and can't eat the whole thing—and then he imagines the server's gonna bring him a bottle of Ensure. Jesus, I hope it's not the same for me, sixty years down the road! But if it is, I hope I handle it as well as he does.

Alan snagged a napkin, mopped his lips, took another bite, set his sandwich down, swallowed. "Well, let's go along with what you've set up, just one small change. I'll go into the house with JJ, and you'll stay out with Elvira."

He held up a hand as he saw Tom about to object. "I'm not being pushy here; I think there are good reasons. If one of the lookouts needs to come inside to give a warning, there'll still be another one outside to keep monitoring. And if the lookouts need to do more than just look, you'll be of more help to a woman in her sixties than I would. Besides. Let's just suppose JJ knows more than he's told you, and he may not play altogether straight. Let him know he'd need to face you if he comes outside alone, and he might think twice before he'd try any funny business with me. And if he doesn't think, well, maybe you'll get some use out of those karate lessons you've been taking for the last couple of years. Fair enough?"

Tom's face said he didn't like it, but he nodded. "You're a tough man to argue with."

"I've got a few years on you." Alan gestured at the food. "Okay, let's eat, then go back to the room, call your grandmother, and get some sleep."

"You gonna be up for this, Alan? At three a.m.?"

Alan patted his shirt pocket; Tom heard the little pill container rattle. "Five, six hours in the sack and my little pocket pharmacy'll get me through almost anything." He picked up his sandwich, and took another bite.

• • ● •• •

As Alan reached for the hotel room phone, Tom asked, "Wanna use your cell? You've got unlimited long distance."

Alan shook his head. "Good point, but it's not going to be an easy conversation, and I don't want us cutting out on each other. Worth the extra few bucks."

"You sure you wanna tell her the whole story? She'll shit a brick if she hears Mickey got murdered."

"I'm sure. I've learned over a lot of years that it's best to be straight with people, especially your wife. Sooner or later, that little fact would have to come out, and if she knows I kept it from her, it'll be a lot worse than if I just tell her now." He picked up the receiver, began to push numbers. After a few rings, he said hello, how are you, and then launched into his report.

When he stopped talking, Tom, on the bed, could hear Miriam's voice past his grandfather's ear. "Alan—you're both all right?"

"Fine, Miriam. Really."

"So what now? I assume you'll be coming home soon."

"Not quite yet. For one thing—the main thing—Tom and I are under orders from the police to not leave town. It was us who found the…Mickey. They had us make a statement, then told us we needed to stay around while they continue their investigation. And…well, we don't have the music, and I am determined to get it."

Tom grimaced as "Alan!" cut through the air from the phone.

"Miriam, you know me better than to react like that. I've been fortunate enough to not just drop dead one day or go out in my sleep from a heart attack. I've been given an opportunity unlike any I've ever had in my life, and a wakeup call to not let it go by. I won't do anything foolish. I'll take good care of Tom and myself, and I will keep you posted, call every day. But I'm not leaving until the cops tell me I can—*and* until I'm carrying that duffel bag."

Tom could not make out the short reply from Seattle, and figured it was just as well.

"How's your conference coming along?" Alan asked. "I trust we are not going to go broke over the next year."

• • ● • •

At ten after three, two pairs of black-clad figures made their way up opposite sides of East Third Street toward Lafayette, where Granny Elvira had arrived a minute or less earlier. Tom and Alan walked up the south side, JJ and Saramae on the north. JJ had spent the past block—since Saramae had joined him—getting his temper under marginal control. Now his voice came out as a hoarse whisper.

"What the hell you doin' here, Girl? We didn't say nothin' about you bein' here. This ain't exactly a 'more the merrier' job."

"Well, just fuck me upside down, huh? This's the most excitin' thing I ever—"

JJ clapped a hand to her mouth. "God damn, Girl, keep quiet! You gotta talk, you keep it way down, got it? Don' make me *have* to shut you up."

She squirmed away, threw her arms in the air. "Okay, okay. I'm just about whisperin'. Happy? Jesus, JJ, ain't no way I'm gonna miss this show."

JJ threw his arms skyward. "Fine! Looks like Tom bring somebody 'long too. Who the hell's that?"

"Probably his grandpa, the ol' piano player. Mickey's friend. Tom said he might wanna come."

"Jesus! Hope he's got his Pampers on." JJ shook his head, disgusted. "I shoulda come by myself, not try an' do a job with a buncha am-a-choors."

As they approached Lafayette, Elvira set out half a block in advance, leading them past the wide weed-filled lot to the west of Mickey's house. All lights were off at the closest neighbor's, on the far side of the lot. Tom saw JJ crouch and scamper noiselessly closer toward the front porch, then give a hand signal to advance. They followed him and Elvira around to the back. Elvira crouched beside the tiny rear stoop on the side away from the street; Tom followed her. Her eyes shot him a question, he answered with raised palms: cool it. JJ, Alan, and Saramae ducked under the yellow crime scene tape, and continued up the three wooden stairs to the stoop.

JJ took a deep breath, put a finger to his lips, then slipped on a pair of thin black gloves and turned the doorknob. The door opened, creaking more loudly than Alan would have liked, but he said nothing, just followed JJ inside. Saramae brought up the rear.

At JJ's gesture, Alan took Saramae's hand, then held out his other hand to the young man. JJ grabbed the hand and murmured, "I knows this house like my own. We go slow. Jes' follow me, don' trip, an' don't nobody but me touch' nothin'."

He led the party through the kitchen, stopping periodically to listen for any noise that might be coming from a policeman stationed inside, then through the living room and down the hall to the closet, where he freed Alan's hand, turned Saramae back the way they had come and whispered directly in her ear, "Keep watch. Don' pay no attention to what I be doin'."

She glared, but didn't object when JJ pushed her a few steps toward the living room.

JJ opened the closet door wide, blocking the hall, and dropped to his knees just short of the threshold.

Alan watched, fascinated, as the young man hooked fingers into knotholes in the baseboard on both sides of the closet and pulled. The wood slid forward an inch, hitting the front wall of the closet with a pair of subdued thunks. JJ winced and froze, waiting to see if anyone came to investigate the sound. After ten or fifteen seconds, he put his hands flat on the closet floor and pushed to the right, then back. The entire floor shifted, exposing a gap at the front of the closet. JJ grabbed the edge of the floor, lifted slightly, then swung it up on concealed hinges to rest against the rear wall. He glanced up at Alan with a mischievous grin, and Alan mimed applause.

JJ took a tiny flashlight from his pocket, and played the light around the opening. Alan could see an empty shelf at the back of the space, but no more than that. JJ leaned forward, then sat back on his heels. "Shit, fuck, damn," he whispered. "Gone."

He waved Alan to squat, then whispered, "Lookit down there, see? Mickey, he usedta put the bag on that shelf. But sometime it fall down below, 'specially if he been drinkin'. I don' wanna go down there, leave footprints an' all that. So you hold my legs while I lean in an' look 'round."

Alan nodded and waited as JJ lay facedown, halfway into the closet. He knelt between the young man's feet and raised an ankle onto each of his calves. JJ bent forward at the waist, his head and arms dangling into the darkness. Alan caught glimpses of the flashlight reflecting off whatever was down below. After less than half a minute, JJ straightened, then rolled to one side. Alan shifted his weight to help, and extended a hand, which JJ ignored. He sat up, then stood. "Nothin'."

JJ gently lowered the closet floor into place and shoved the baseboards back to their original positions. He made a let's-go movement with his right hand, led the way outside, then motioned to Elvira and Tom, and the five housebreakers walked silently back to the corner of Lafayette and Third. JJ checked his wristwatch.

"Okay, then," he said in a quiet voice. "I got a quarter of an hour to get back to work. We gonna meet up at home, nine o'clock, right?" He looked at Alan. "That all right with you, Old Man?"

"I think we were introduced, and the name's Alan, Alan Chandler. And yes, nine o'clock will be fine."

That earned him a grin from JJ and an admiring glance from Elvira.

"Good. See you then."

As he turned toward the *Democrat*, JJ unbuttoned his shirt pocket and pulled out a notebook and pen.

"I'll have us breakfast," Elvira said.

JJ nodded without looking up from the page. "Huh. Didn't have no doubt about that." He started walking, still writing.

• ● ● ● •

By a few minutes past nine, the five conspirators were seated around Elvira's living room, balancing heaping plates of pancakes, eggs, and sausage on their laps, a huge pot of steaming coffee on a centrally placed card table. JJ was the first to speak. "Mmm-mmm. Granny, this so good, it almos' make me forget how pissed off I were 'bout surprises on the job."

"Now, Jackson. How 'bout you give the people half a chance to digest they food, huh?"

"Granny, I been havin' indigestion for five hours. Only fair t' share it." JJ stared at Saramae. "Like for example, Girl—what you doin' here now? You already late for school."

She flashed him a look, half-annoyed, half-teasing. "Ain't the first time, and so what? I told you last night—this's the funnest thing ever happened to me. I know I've got a big mouth, yeah, but I also know how to keep it shut. So I wanna be a part of this stuff."

"Okay," JJ said, a look of resignation making it clear how little he wanted to agree. "But I tell you, and I talk seriously: you open that mouth in the wrong place to the wrong person, and you find out jus' how much fun this ain't. Hear me?"

Saramae pouted. "You don' have to be that way."

In an instant, JJ set his plate on the floor, grabbed the throat of Saramae's blouse, and yanked her forward. "I be a dead man by now if I not be 'that way,'" he growled. "We gettin' involved here with some fuckhead who wrap wires around peoples' necks. That mean no carelessness. None, zero, zip. Okay?"

"Okay," the girl whispered.

JJ released her, and went back to his breakfast.

Alan was surprised at Elvira's calm reaction to the exchange. He wondered whether he should say something about the possible consequences of hothead actions. But it occurred to him that the older woman's behavior might have been due to her having confidence in her grandson, and perhaps also having sufficient acquaintanceship with Saramae to figure the boy's threats contained at least some degree of put-on, and might have been advisable, even necessary.

Alan swallowed a mouthful of pancakes, cleared his throat. "I think it's a good idea to keep each other fully informed. I apologize for not calling you to let you know I'd be there."

JJ nodded. "You, I shoulda jes' figured on. But thanks."

"And I trust you'll keep Tom and me up-to-date as well. We're at the Bothwell, Room 412."

If JJ was annoyed by what might have seemed a challenge to his leadership, he didn't show it. "It work both ways. But okay, enough bullshit. We gotta figure out what we gonna do now."

"That's what I think," said Alan. "And unless you've got a better idea, I also think that's going to depend on what you and I can tell each other." He pulled a quarter from his pocket. "Heads, I go first, tails, you do." He flipped the coin in the air, caught it, raised his upper hand, and extended the coin toward JJ. "Tails. Go."

The boy guffawed. "Let's see the other side."

Alan laughed, flipped him the quarter. JJ checked both sides, smiled, shoved it into his pocket. "Okay, then. We gonna be partners, so I be straight with you. Honest truth is I don' know a whole lot. One day, maybe a week ago…little less? Anyways, I come in with Mickey's paper, and right off I know something big's goin' on. Mickey looks like he got a stick up his butt, an' there was more empty bottles in the livin' room than usual. 'I'm on to something big,' Mickey tells me. 'An' I'll let you in on it if I know you can keep your mouth shut.'

"'Well, if you don't know that by now, you never will,' I tell him."

"'All right, then,' he says. 'I'm sittin' on a pile of music manuscripts that could not only be the greatest music find in history, they could bring enough money to make us both comfy. Crap, Boy, I'm over seventy, ain't got no wife, no kids, an' you're the closest I got to a son. It'd make me happy to set you and your granny up for life.'"

"Well, I gotta admit, I was so choked up in the throat, I couldn't say nothin', and he went right on talkin'. 'A man was here last night with a duffel bag fulla music I bet no one has ever seen before. I'm pretty sure it's by Scott Joplin, but it's gonna be easy to find out yes or no. I got a friend in Seattle, Alan Chandler, and if he says it's by Scott Joplin, there ain't no one in the world gonna argue with him. I'm gonna get him out here, have him look over the music, and we'll go from there. How you like them apples?'"

Tears coursed down JJ's cheeks.

Alan's eyes widened at the show of emotion. *He's not faking that. He loved that man.* "Did he say anything about who it was that brought him the music?"

JJ sniffed, shook his head. "He jus' say the five hundred bucks he give whoever it was, was nothin' near what that music'd bring in a resale with a copyright." He sniffed again. "He showed me his hidey-hole an' give me the key fo' the padlock. Had me come over every morning to open it up, 'cause he couldn't mess with that floor when he were drunk or hungover. But no way he was gonna leave that music sittin' out at night."

Tom looked back and forth between the two. "Hidey-hole?"

"It's quite something," Alan said with a laugh.

JJ nodded. "I ast Mickey about it. He tell me his father and grandfather made it back in the twenties. He put in a whole room down there to hide bottles of booze afore he sell 'em."

Elvira sniffed. "He brag about his granddaddy bein' a boot-legger. Even had it in his bi-o-graffy at the festival a couple a times. Like father, like son."

"We're wandering off the subject," Alan said. "You have no idea where he got the duffel bag?"

"Iff'n I had a clue, I'd tell you…Podnuh."

Alan grinned. "Fair enough. Okay, my turn. Everything you've said so far clicks with what I know from Mickey, and I can add a little. Mickey told us an antiques dealer was cleaning out a house in Kansas City, found the duffel bag full of unsigned music manuscripts, and thought he could turn a few bucks on it. He showed it around to some other dealers, one of whom was named Rudolph Korotkin, who had done business with Mickey before. Korotkin sent the dealer to Mickey, Mickey gave him five hundred bucks, and he gave Mickey the music. I don't know who the dealer was, but it shouldn't be hard to find Korotkin, and go from there."

He paused, quickly decided to go on. "Scott Joplin had a friend, Wilbur Sweatman, a clarinetist—he was the executor of Joplin's estate, and a bunch of Joplin's music went to him after Joplin died. But nobody knows what happened to it when Sweatman died, more than fifty years ago. *And* there were initials inked inside the duffel bag—WS. Wilbur Sweatman."

While Alan had been talking, JJ had been scribbling in his notebook. Now he looked up and leaned forward in his seat. "That it?"

"That's all I've got."

Tom raised a hand: Teacher, I got a question. "Just one thing. When Mickey was telling us where he got the music, I had a feeling he was cooking up a whopper. But you guys know him better than I do. What do you think?"

Alan shrugged. "He probably didn't tell us the uncontaminated truth. Mickey'd stretch a story on any excuse, but he'd never tell an outright lie when it mattered. He knew how much money was going to come in, he had the music in his hands, so I don't think he'd cook up much of a story."

"The man did drink way too much." JJ's voice was soft. "And he love t' tell a wild tale when he had a couple a drinks. But he were cold sober when you come to his house."

"And what he told you does fit with what he told me," Alan said. "I guess the next step is to talk to Korotkin, and if he *can* give us a lead to the dealer, we'll know for sure. We also might be able to find just whose house he was cleaning out."

JJ nodded, then loosed a raucous bark. "Guess you guys are on for that. Ain't no antique dealer gonna give a seventeen-year-old black kid the time a day, 'specially if he askin' 'bout some guy who got hisself murdered. Phone calls won't work real good, either. You up for a li'l drive?"

Alan and Tom looked at each other, then nodded in unison. "This afternoon," Alan said. "But there's another thing."

"Like what?"

"Like who else, here or in Kansas City, besides Rudy Korot-kin, knew Mickey had that duffel bag?"

"Good, Old Man…Alan. You take K.C. I'll take here."

Saramae cleared her throat. "If I can say somethin', there's one other thing."

"Go 'head," growled JJ. "You on the team, you can talk."

"What if the guy who sold Mickey the music finds out what it's really worth? Think he mighta come back for a second visit?"

Elvira burst into a full-throated laugh. "Girl, maybe you got more upstairs than I give you credit for."

Alan nodded. "It *is* a good thought. We'll be careful."

Chapter Nine

Mid-September in Missouri is still warm; the breeze through the open car windows felt soothing on Alan's face. How many times over how many years had he driven Route 50 between Sedalia and Kansas City with Miriam in the passenger seat? Then as now, the breeze served as a buffer, precluding any sort of conversation, and leaving Alan's mind free to run audio clips of ragtime. He smiled, a little sadly, as he recalled the skinny teenaged girl who would have killed him if he hadn't agreed to link their fortunes in life. She was crazy for him, didn't seem disturbed when he told her straight-out he could never return her passion, that for him, such a feeling was focused onto music and only music. Yes, he'd said, he was fond of her, and he appreciated all she did for him, but she cut him off, telling him we all have our different ways, and that was fine with her, so long as they were together.

"I think about 'September Song,'" she'd once said. "I'll play me a waiting game, and you'll come my way." In fact, she had and he did, though never with anything resembling the feeling she had for him. Did he love her? He thought so.

Alan glanced across the car at the kid staring out the window. God only knew what was turning over in that mind right then. From the moment of Tom's birth, Alan knew something special existed between them, kind of like they were one person who'd somehow been split into two bodies, but with a common mind. Was this what Miriam felt for him? Who could tell? If he didn't understand it, that was all right.

The days dwindle down…He shook the melancholy out of his mind, let the invitation card theme have full play for a moment. *Think, Alan. You're not taking a joy ride, and you're not speeding into K.C. to get to a concert on time. You're hunting down a bag full of what could be the most glorious music you've ever heard, something that's going to justify the eighty years you've been on Earth. And you're going to find the son of a bitch-bastard torturer-killer who had the audacity to put the end to a friendship of more than half a century. Get yourself ready.*

• • ● • •

Tom stared out the window without seeing anything; the landscape and the sounds of the breeze and tires on pavement were white noise, isolating him with his thoughts. Most of his attention was on his self-imposed vow to take on as much as he could of the work of tracking down the duffel bag. But how to get information from an antique seller? Did he even need to do anything? Talking was a lot less stressful than running around Sedalia looking for mysterious newsboys and breaking into crime scenes. Maybe just let Alan take charge on this trip, be ready to jump in and volunteer for any physical activity. But…

The rest of his brain was occupied with Saramae. She was really hot, and a great kisser. He shifted uncomfortably in his seat. Alan had an uncanny ability to tell what he was thinking. Tom really, really hoped his grandfather wouldn't notice what was on his mind. She had called that kiss a down payment. Tom looked forward to paying the next installment.

• • ● • •

Rudolph Korotkin's antique shop was at one end of the Forty-fifth and State Line Antique, Art, and Design Center, a two-block row of toney establishments on the border between Missouri and Kansas. Rudolph's Treasures occupied about twelve hundred square feet offering a wide selection of high and mid-level antiquities, tastefully displayed in glass-front cabinets and on shelves. Pottery, glass, medical, and scientific instruments; tasteful Victorian jewelry, some smaller furniture pieces. The real stuff.

From behind a graceful walnut desk, Korotkin looked past the computer to give Alan and Tom a simper of acknowledgement when they opened the door. He listened to Alan's story with clearly increasing discomfort: squirming in the chair gave way to mopping a handkerchief across his beefy forehead and cheeks. Alan silently warned himself not to scare the man off. When he got to the part about the murder, he left out the ugly details, and simply told the dealer Mickey had been killed and the music stolen.

"So you understand where I'm coming from," Alan said. "I want to find that music. I am *going to* find that music."

"Well, I'd say that's what the police are for," Korotkin said laconically and blew a cigarette-scented chest full of air across the desk. "I might be wrong, but you don't look like a detective to me."

Alan pushed his temper back under cover. "Looks can be deceiving," he said with a little smile. "I'm eighty years old, Mr. Korotkin, and my neighborhood is not one where many people hold long-term leases. Right now, I'm impatient."

"Mr...?"

"Chandler. Alan Chandler."

"Sorry. Mr. Chandler, I'm sorry, but I can't help thinking that if you get too impatient, somebody might want to cancel your lease altogether."

Don't push him. "Oh, I'm sure you're right, Mr. Korotkin. But I think you'll understand this: sometimes a person needs to seize an opportunity. Take a risk. I'll bet in your business you've had to go out on more than one pretty shaky limb. So I'm asking for your help—won't try to get you to do or say anything illegal that could get you into trouble. Please, would you give me the name of the dealer you referred to Mickey?"

Korotkin tapped a cigarette out of a package, thought better of the idea, slipped it back in.

"It's my funeral," said Alan.

"You may be eighty, but that kid's not even twenty. How're you gonna feel if...?"

"Like dirt. Garbage. How else would I feel? That's why I've got to be sure to not let it happen."

Two quick nods, more "I hear you" than "I agree." Cigarette out and back in again. "Okay, Mr. Chandler. I need to say, Mickey had his failings and faults, just like all of us. Never mind the drinking, he was the greediest sumbitch I've ever seen. But basically he was a decent little guy; he didn't deserve to end up like that."

"Most of the time, we don't get what we deserve," Alan said quietly. "And most of the time, that's a good thing. But not this time."

Korotkin allowed a chuckle to work loose. "Okay. Your man is Sylvester Maggione, right up the street here. He told quite a little story about that duffel bag. Maybe he'll tell it to you. But you didn't hear that from me. Get it?"

Alan smiled and nodded. "I appreciate that, Mr. Korotkin. Thank you."

• • ● • •

Old World Antiques and Collectibles was at the far end of the Center from Rudolph's Treasures, both geographically and economically. Some nice things, but mostly *dreck* from the fifties to the seventies—the nineteen fifties and seventies—and nothing displayed in any particular order. The place reeked of mold.

Alan coughed. "I can understand you don't want trouble, Mr. Maggione. But I'm not going to give you any or bring you any. And I'm willing to make it worth your while." He dug his wallet out of his pocket, pulled a hundred-dollar bill from the back compartment, and passed it to the cadaverous little man perched on the countertop.

Maggione made a show of inspecting the bill, then grinned, revealing a double row of browned teeth. "Nice piece," he said. "I like it. But y'know what? In my business, what's better than a single nice piece is a pair a nice pieces. I've always had trouble saying no when somebody offers me a real nice pair a something." He coughed consumptively.

Alan and Tom exchanged the quickest glance, then the old man pulled another hundred from his wallet and gave it to the dealer. "Long as I get honest value," Alan said. "Give me the real story, and you'll never have to hear from me again. But I swear, try to screw me over with a whopper, and you'll be missing another nice pair I'm sure you're fond of."

Tom took that as a cue, and looked as fierce as he could.

Maggione shoved the two bills into his pants pocket, then waved off any concern Alan might have been harboring. "Nope, you ain't got no worries. I ain't exactly on the top of the feeding chain, but I never in my life screwed a client over, and I ain't gonna start now. Okay, then. Where I got that duffel bag. Damndest thing I ever saw in my life. There was this estate sale over East a Troost, usual stuff, y'know, nothin' I could get a hardon over. Crap. Garbahge. All out on the front lawn, people pickin' it over, not much goin' away. But the family—the whole famn damily was there, musta been fifteen of 'em at least, and it sounded like they didn't know how to say a civil word to each other. Fightin' about everything. 'Who the hell put two bucks on this ol' camera—it's gotta be worth ten times that.' 'Why'd'ja let that blanket go for a lousy buck? Go try an' buy a blanket like that for a dollar at Goodwill, never mind Bed Bath and Beyond.' Fuckin' circus. I grabbed a lamp I can probably unload on some disco burnout case, and a coupla other cheesies and sleazies." He waved an arm at the far wall.

Tom followed the gesture and had to suppress a gag at the quintessential seventies-green pole lamp beside a pair of wooden music stands badly carved to resemble musical clefs, a battered Papasan chair without a cushion, and a box of sheet music.

Maggione was on a roll. "I had the crap in my truck and was just about to split when one of the freaks latches onto my arm and says do I see anything else I like? I told him I'm a dealer and I ain't seen nothin' at all there I like, so how could I find somethin' else? Went right past the moron.

"'Well, maybe I can turn that around,' he says, and makes with the finger, I should follow him. We go inside the house, he takes me kinda through to the back, and tells me to wait a minute. Then he goes inta the next room and less'n a minute later, comes back with this duffel bag. I give him a funny look, I guess, and he says, 'Just hold your horses,' then opens the duffel bag. And it's full of these music papers.

"'This's real old stuff, the McCoy,' the guy says. 'Ragtime, you know. No one's ever proved it, but it's supposed to be written by Scott Joplin. Been in the family here since, jeez, like forever. It's gotta be worth somethin', right? Gimme a thousand and go make your fortune on it.'

"Well, that got him a real good horse laugh. 'These papers ain't even signed,' I said. 'How the hell do I know Scott Joplin wrote them, not Joe Schmuck?' I ended up givin' him a hundred bucks, got in my car, and went right to Rudolph Korotkin's to try and find out where to dump it. Rudolph sent me to that guy Mickey in Sedalia…and the rest's history. Okay?"

Alan felt as if he'd been run over by a steamroller. "And you sold it to Mickey for…"

"Five Cs. Hey, I'm not greedy. I hope he ain't unhappy."

Alan shook his head. "No. He's not at all unhappy."

Maggione held out his hands, palms up. "So, good, then. Everybody's makin' out. Right?"

"Just about. Everybody but me. Mickey was your pigeon; I'm his. I'm supposed to be the expert on Scott Joplin, and it does look very much like the music really is his. Which would make me very happy. But if I'm going to authenticate it, I need to know where the music came from. If it's been in that family for a hundred years, how did they get their hands on it, and what have they been doing with it all this time?"

He smiled, and poked a finger into Maggione's ribs. "History. Provenance, you know the drill. I want to talk to some of the people in the family. Give me the address…"

Alan ground to a halt as he saw doubt smear itself across Maggione's face. He sighed, pulled out his wallet, extracted a fifty, and pushed it into the dealer's hand. "There. Now, I'm betting you haven't had a payday like this in your shop in the past year.

Give me the address and a name, and I'll be in your rearview mirror in nothing flat."

"I ain't got a name," said Maggione. "I didn't give a damn, just wanted to get the hell outa there and make my resale. Like I said, it ain't all that far from here, maybe a ten- or fifteen-minute drive." He peeled a blank page off a pile of paper. "Here, lemme write you directions. But if they come back at me, I'll be tellin' them I never heard of you or saw you in my life. Capiche?"

Alan nodded.

• • ● • •

Saramae fluttered her lashes at JJ from across the little table in Fitter's outdoor space. She sucked at her straw, drained the liquid with a slurp, and sat back in her chair.

"Thanks for the Co'cola," she said. "And for lettin' me help find out what's going on."

"Huh. You're welcome. I just figure, better I keep an eye on you, not let you go pokin' 'round on your own. 'Sides, I gotta admit, you gotta pretty good idea, sayin' maybe the guy who did Mickey were the same one as sold him the music, when he figured he sold out cheap. If he did, Mickey wouldn't'a given him a bigger cut. I been thinkin' about it, an' I remember now, Mickey did say it was a dealer from K.C., some Italian, maybe. I think let's go over to the library, get a K.C. phone book, and see if we can narrow it down some. Then we give Alan and Tom a call; see if they can find this guy and get sense outa him."

JJ smirked. "Done with that Coke? C'mon, le's get movin'." He pushed back his chair—and found himself looking up into the concrete face of Detective Parks.

Saramae looked around for the nearest exit.

"Mr. Jackson, I'd like you to come down to the station with me. I've got some questions I'd like to ask you."

"What, about Mickey? I—"

"Please just come along with me, would you, Mr. Jackson?"

JJ and Saramae exchanged a long look. "Go on, JJ," the girl said lightly. "Thanks for offerin' to help with my homework, but I guess I can jes' go over to the library."

JJ grinned and flipped her a quick salute. "Catch you later."

• • ● • •

East of Troost was clearly a long-established black enclave, small houses generally well-kept-up. Alan parked in front of 5708 Virginia Street, a beige bungalow with gray trim and a covered front porch, killed the motor, and raised a finger as Tom started to open the door. The old man coughed, cleared his throat.

"Just give me a few minutes, and we'll take in Act 2."

He rested his head against the seat and closed his eyes. Tom wondered whether his grandfather was going to fall asleep, but in less than five minutes, he opened his eyes and said, "All right. Let's go."

Peeling paint on the mailbox identified the resident as "A. Nowlin." More peeling paint under the eaves of the house suggested money had been too tight to deal with a leaky roof for more than just a couple of years. A yellowed Venetian blind over the front window sagged at the near end.

The woman who answered the bell put Tom in mind of a superannuated alley cat, hanging onto life for all she was worth, which was not a whole lot. Probably his grandfather's age, wisps of scraggly white hair going in all directions, a yellow and blue flower-print dress that showed no evidence of a human female form underneath. Eyes red and watery, cheeks and arms covered with brown splotches and scaly circles. She leaned heavily on a black wooden cane as she took in her visitors. Then she spoke one word: "Yeah?"

"Ms. Nowlin?"

"Yeaaaah? That's me. What the hell you want? Who are you? If you're sellin' something, you can get your white asses outa here."

"We're not salesmen. We're just looking for some information, if you can help us. Now, I understand that at your estate sale last week, you sold a duffel bag with some music manuscripts in it, and—"

The transformation in the woman's appearance chased Alan and Tom a step backward. Eyes sizzling, cheeks flaming, she shed a decade of decay and raised her cane threateningly. Sunlight reflecting off the heavy ring on her right hand caught Alan's attention. It was silver-colored metal, but didn't look like silver. The upper surface was etched with a monogram filled with something black.

"Is it *youse* that gots my music?" she screeched.

Alan extended a protective hand. "No, we didn't buy it. But we're looking to find it, and I'm hoping you can tell us—"

"I ain't tellin' you *nothin*," the woman howled. "Wasn't *me* sold that music! Wouldn't never have been me. I'd'a never, ever sold that music. And I tell you this—when I find out which one of my shit-ass nephews copped it, he better never get inside six inches of ground around me, 'cause that'll be where he dies."

She swung her cane like a broadsword, underlining the threat. "Now, get your fucking shoes offa my porch and keep 'em off. Bastards, alla youse!"

The glass in the little window in the door rattled as the door slammed.

"Jeez, Alan," Tom said. "You think she didn't like us?"

"What gave you that idea?" Alan snorted. "Charming lady. Interesting ring, though. 'A L'. If she's A. Nowlin, I wonder who 'L' is. Someone else we could talk to, maybe?"

Tom shrugged. "More likely her maiden name."

"I suppose. Grasping at straws, I guess. She sure didn't give us much to go on."

• • ● • •

Elvira sighed and shook her head as she pushed the basement door open. Her normally erect posture drooped. She snaked her way onto the stairs, balancing the tray carefully as she descended. The place smelled of mold and damp. Slowly, she moved along the dirt floor, bending to be sure to not knock her head on a beam.

She was getting too old for this stuff, but what was she going to do about it? What else could she have done, turned him away, right into the hands of that redneck honky son of a bitch sheriff, with his dogs and his guns and his way of handling troublemakers?

Wouldn't do that to nobody, 'specially not him. But how long this gonna go on?

She turned the corner, saw him sitting on the edge of the cot, staring at his feet. "Gotcher dinner," she called.

"Huh. What we got tonight, huh?"

She forced a smile. "Some nice po'k chops an' collards. An' I made my banana cream pie—cut you a nice big piece here. Think that'll do?"

The "Yeah" was sullen, but it was followed quickly by, "Sorry, Momma. That sound good…real good. I jes' don't…" He waved his arms, taking in the dark, damp space. "Alla this jus'…you know?"

"I know. I sure do." She set the tray on the little table next to the cot. "But that don't make no never-mind." She put hands to her hips. "You jes' can't be sneakin' outa here. You gotta promise me, you won't be doin' that no more."

He'd already shoveled in a mouthful of pork, chewed, swallowed. "Well, I be sorry. Damn, I really is. But sometimes I get to thinkin', well, maybe I can make things right, an' not have to live the rest of my life like some kinda animal, hidin' in the basement. An' it jes' take me right over."

"Oh, hush, now, Jack. Don't you be a damn idiot. You ain't never gonna be able to set it right, not with the temper you got. Keep sneakin' outa here and what you gonna find is trouble and death. Ol' sheriff, he gonna send you right back to that place, no trial or nothin'. Now, promise me, you ain't gonna let that happen. Promise."

Another mouthful of pork dispatched. "I promise."

• • ● • •

As Alan and Tom got back into the rental car, Tom's cell phone went off. Alan stifled a laugh at the outrageous melody. "Is that Saramae? Better not let her find out what you're using for her ringtone. 'Pussy Cat Rag'? She'll scratch your eyes out."

Tom rolled his eyes. "It's not like she'll recog—" He interrupted himself and answered the call. "Saramae? Whoa, slow down! What's the matter?...He did what?...that bastard. Well, we're headed back now—soon's we get there, I'll give you a call. But don't worry. Alan'll fix it. Huh? Oh yeah—we already found the Italian antique dealer...yeah. Tell you all about it when we get there." He hung up. "Saramae says the police arrested JJ. She doesn't know why."

"And you think I can fix it? Without even knowing what it's about?"

"You're gonna try, right?"

"Of course I am."

"Then it's in the bag."

Alan laughed. "High praise, Thomas." He thought for a second. "Did you give her your number?"

"No. I got hers, but I didn't give her mine. Wonder how she got it."

"Wonder what else she got, too. And if I were you, I wouldn't count on her not knowing that tune." Tom opened his mouth, but Alan added, "The odds are in your favor, but this *is* Sedalia, and if there's any place in the country where anybody you meet might be a ragtime fan, this is it. 'One never knows...do one?'"

Tom fumbled for a retort, then closed his mouth with a snap remembering how quickly Saramae had picked up on Fats Waller's famous tagline when he had used it on her. After a second, he made a show of changing Saramae's ringtone to one of the generic sounds.

Ten miles down the road, Tom broke the silence. "Alan?"

No response. The old man stared through the windshield as if he were hypnotized by the sight of Route 50 speeding end-lessly under their car.

"Alan!" Louder this time, accompanied by a gentle poke in the ribs. "Shut the damn window for a minute so you can hear me."

"Oh...sorry. Sure." He pushed the button; the window closed. "What's up?"

"You looked like you were a million miles away. You thinking about what to do to get JJ out of jail?"

Alan nodded, but it was a silent lie, at least in part. What he'd really been thinking about was that ragtime ringtone. Not that he was envious of his grandson's teenaged goatishness—kids are supposed to be that way, and besides, with the chemo, though you know your libido has gone straight down the toilet, the odd thing is, you don't care. It doesn't seem to matter. Next to the fatigue, the intestinal cramps, the numbness and tingling in your hands and feet, and that goddamn chemo brain, "a little chemical castration," as the doctor had called it, is inconsequential.

And what was bothering him most right then was the memory loss. He wasn't demented; he knew that, could still solve problems, could get himself where he had to go, could play the piano. But he had lost so much of his ability to bring up memories when he needed them. Over sixty-five years, he'd heard that particular version of "Pussy Cat Rag" so many times, but now he could not remember the name of the performing group. Like losing a basic piece of his past.

He cleared his throat. "Actually, Tom, I was trying to remember who it was playing "Pussy Cat Rag" on your cell phone."

Ready to come back with "Alan, you're kidding me, right?" Tom caught the expression on his grandfather's face and regrouped. "Polk Miller and his Old South Quartette," he said simply. "Imagine what it must've been like to hear them in person?"

Alan nodded, then the distress broke through. "Yes, I can. But Tom—I couldn't remember their name. I've been trying to think of it since your phone went off."

"Well, okay, Alan, it's the chemo. We know that—"

"It's not okay, and it doesn't really help to know it. Tom, my brain is like a chunk of Swiss cheese. How can I trust myself to remember what I need to do to get JJ out of the clink? *And* find the music and the guy who killed Mickey. If I can't keep all this stuff straight in my head, I could screw up the whole business and maybe even make matters worse. Could get one of us killed. I'm starting to think it might be better for me to back out and let the cops do what they need to do. Maybe see if they'll let us go back home."

"And just forget about a duffel bag full of Scott Joplin music."
Each word tinged with acid. "What's with you, Alan? All of a
sudden, you don't sound like my grandfather."

"Tom, watch your mouth—"

"I'll be your memory, Alan."

"What?" The car swerved over the center line; Alan quickly
corrected the path.

"I said I'll be your memory if your notebook isn't enough to
keep you straight on details. There's still nobody to match you
on figuring out what to do with problems. You tell me what
you're thinking, and I'll feed it back to you whenever you need it.
Hey, listen: have I ever forgotten anything you ever taught me?"

Silence.

"No, I haven't. So you teach me what I need to remember,
I'll keep every bit of it on file in my head, and we'll get that
music back."

Alan sighed. *That's the kind of teenaged balls I regret losing.*
"Okay." Another sigh. "Deal. Get back on your phone there and
call Harry Feffer, my lawyer, back in Seattle." He reached into
his pocket and passed his notebook to Tom. "His number's on
the inside back cover. We'll ask him a few questions."

• • ● • •

A little after five, Alan, Tom, and Saramae sat in the Sedalia Police
Station waiting room. The hardback chair was murder on Alan's
back; electric shocks flew down the outside of his thighs. With
some misgiving over the monitoring camera mounted in the far
corner, he took a Vicodin from his pocket stash, limped to the
water cooler, and swallowed it. Then he walked slowly around the
room until the pain began to melt into a more tolerable mild ache.

At 5:27, Detective Parks came through a door to the rear,
nodded to the small group, and made a come-in gesture. But
when everyone stood, he shook his head and pointed at Alan;
then, before the old man could say anything, added, "Just you."

"Go ahead," Tom whispered. "You've got your notebook—
take notes. That should make him a little nervous."

Alan followed Parks down a dreary hallway, walls painted a uniform gray. Neither man spoke. When they came to an office door on which a nameplate identified the space as Parks', the detective opened the door and stepped aside to let Alan go in ahead of him.

Two chairs—hardbacked, of course—had been placed opposite the gray metal desk, behind which was a huge corkboard decorated with photos of Mickey's house and body. As Alan moved toward the chairs, the door to the office opened again, and a sergeant led JJ inside. The young man's expression would have curdled milk. But when he saw Alan, the pianist saw hope light in his eyes. Moment of anxiety: *I can't let him down.*

Parks plopped into a swivel chair behind the desk, flipped the switch on a small recorder on the desk, then leaned back and folded his hands over his paunch.

"You wanted to talk to me, Mr. Chandler?"

Alan pulled out his notebook and a pen, flipped the notebook open. "I do. I want to know why you've arrested Mr. Jackson."

"I don't need to tell you that. I have my reason."

"I'm sure you do, but I want to know what that reason is."

"I'm sure you do."

Alan tapped fingers on the edge of the desk. "All right, then. Let me put it this way. What have you charged him with?"

"Any way you put it, I'm not obliged to tell you. I can't have you interfering with my investigation."

"All right. *Have* you charged him at all? And before you tell me you don't have to tell me, let me remind you that a person who is not being charged is free to leave at any time he chooses. I'm not so foolish, Detective, that I've come here on my own. I'm not a lawyer, but I've spoken to one. If you force me to do it, I will call him again. I have to think you'd rather deal with me, but I won't mind being wrong."

Neither Alan nor JJ missed the glance Parks shot toward the recording machine.

That's one record that's never going to see the light of day.

"Short and simple, Detective. Is Mr. Jackson in custody, or have you just requested him to stay?"

Short pause. "I have requested him to stay for further questioning. It would be in his best interest to do that."

"Good." Slowly, Alan got to his feet. "Then I can assume he's neither been declared a suspect nor a reluctant material witness. Is that right?"

Parks nodded.

Alan looked at the recorder. "I'm sorry. I didn't hear you."

"Yes. That's right." Words dripping with venom.

"Good. Thank you, then. Come on, JJ. Let's get on our way. We've got a lot to do."

The detective sat forward in his chair. "That what you want, Jackson? You want to go off with this guy against my wishes?"

"Yes, Sir. I believe I do. Sorry, but I think he be better company."

JJ got up, stretched, walked to the door. From near the desk, Alan motioned him through. "I'll catch up with you in a minute." Then he turned back to Parks. "If that boy turns out to have anything to do with the theft and murder, I will be shocked. *But* if I do see or hear anything that might in any way change my opinion, you will be the first to know it. That's a promise."

"You want a nice shiny little deputy badge? That's not the way this game is played, Mr. Chandler." A clipped monotone.

Alan bit back the impulse to snap back "Badges? We don't need no stinking badges!" and waited until his back was turned before he allowed himself a short-lived smile.

Where the hell did that line come from…oh, right! The Treasure of the Sierra Madre. *Take that, chemo brain!*

The smile returned, just a little broader.

The paperwork was slow—Alan was quite sure the police were taking far more time than they needed for every page of it—but he was firmly, even aggressively polite. When he and JJ strode into the waiting room, Tom broke into a huge grin, and Saramae jumped up and down, clapping her hands in a rapid rhythm.

"You done it," she squealed, then gave Alan a big hug, and over his shoulder, fist-bumped JJ.

Alan worked loose of the girl's embrace. "Let's get out of here before our luck changes," he said. "Almost eight o'clock—get some dinner and make some plans. We're in this for good now."

"Kehde's again?" Tom asked.

"Nah, let's go to Little Big Horn," Alan said. "Also good barbeque, but a little different menu for a change. More important, the tables are a lot farther apart. Still have to keep our voices down, but every advantage we can take, we will."

• ● ● ● •

Everyone was hungry, and the pork and brisket were dispatched in record time. Alan wiped a napkin across his mouth, then looked across the table at JJ, sitting next to Saramae, and sporting a subdued look Alan wouldn't have thought the young man had in him.

"In a way, you're the key right now," Alan said. "They did question you some, didn't they?"

"Huh! They sure did, fo' three hours. Same things over and over, like between what they heard and what they got on their damn recorder wasn't enough. Probably tryin'a get me to say something different about something, then hang me up."

"Did they?"

"Hell, no. Ain't the first time cops've tried to get me to spill."

A small headache blossomed between Alan's right eye and ear. "JJ...could you tell from their questions why it was you they decided to pull in? Whatever it was, it wasn't enough to charge you, but there must've been a reason why they were looking at you."

"Yeah, well, start with what color I am."

"Damn it, JJ. Fine, you're black. So are how many people in Sedalia? Of all those black men, why was it you they brought in? Tell me that."

Saramae had been looking at her cell phone, but suddenly, she slammed it into her cavernous purse, sat up straight, and delivered a solid punch to JJ's upper arm.

"Tell him what you can," she barked. "Wasn't for him, you'd be eatin' shit right now down at the station, and the same tomorrow and the next day. If you can't see he's your friend, you're about the dumbest thing on this planet. Hear?"

Alan held his breath. He'd have sworn JJ squirmed in his seat. The young man's lips contorted at the left corner. "I hear ya," he said, very softly. "Yeah, I gonna trust you, but you gotta trust me jes' a little bit more. 'Fore I can say why they grab me, I gotta talk to my Granny. I do that, an' then I'll tell you whatever you want to know. Deal?" He extended a hand.

Alan suppressed the urge to roll his eyes, and extended his hand to shake JJ's. "Deal. You can talk to your Granny when we're done talking here?"

"Yeah, man. I gotta get ready for work, but I'll talk to her. Don't matter what she say, I'll tell you what happen, but it be her problem just as much as mine, so she gotta know I tellin' you."

"Okay." Alan nodded, one sharp motion. "One thing—we'd better not have you be alone right now. That detective was pissed off beyond reason, and he's going to have every cop he can get to be watching for you. Wherever you go, wherever you are, even inside, you have to make good and goddamn sure you have somebody with you. You with me on that?"

"Be a fuckin' fool if I wasn't."

"Good. Now. Tom and Saramae, can we get you to start looking for facts and clues here? Stuff we can build on?"

"Yeah." Tom held up an index finger. "I've been thinking about that."

Alan knew he had been thinking about that. They'd rehearsed this scene in the car, on the way back from Kansas City.

"Saramae's father's the city editor on the newspaper, the *Democrat*. He had a short piece on the case in today's paper, and I'll betcha anything he's going to have a big article tomorrow. Maybe with all kinds of stuff in it like autopsy reports, the time of Mickey's death, any clues the cops have found. Maybe even clues we'd recognize and cops might not." The boy slid a sly look across to Saramae. "You think we could get him to tell us anything?"

Saramae snickered. "'We?' No way. 'Me!' You keep your big mouth shut and I'll get him talkin' about the case for hours."

"All right, then," Alan said. "So the two of you can go down to the paper and take it from there."

"No, Daddy works days." Saramae grinned. "We'll go over to my house. Be a piece a cake. My daddy, he's a real integration-ist. Won't care if I bring over a white boy or a black one. Long as he can put on his "*Sedalia Democrat* City Editor" show, he wouldn't care if I brung a Martian 'round."

Alan managed a tired chuckle. "Okay, get as much detail as you can. Anything could be a key here. Saramae, does your dad go to bed early?"

"Nah. Not before the late news, anyways."

"Good. Maybe the two of you could walk JJ home before you go on to your house. I'm sorry, but my age and my…condition are catching up with me, and if I don't hit a bed soon, I'm in real trouble. JJ, you figure to stay home till it's time for you to go to work. Then, Tom and Saramae could come back and walk you to the plant."

"Less'n my Granny do that…no, don't worry. Nobody, an' I means nobody, not even cops, gonna ever mess with my Granny. She can pick me up in the mornin', too, and if you want, we can all figure to get back together like we did today, nine o'clock, and see what be what."

Heads nodded all around the table.

Chapter Ten

As Tom, Saramae, and JJ crossed the tracks, entering Lincolnville on North Ohio Street, Saramae pursed her lips, and poked a finger into Tom's side. "Your grandpa's got some kind of *condition?*"

I knew she wouldn't let that rest. "Yeah. He gets really tired, and has to lie down."

"My grandpa had The Big C. That what yours has?"

"Yeah."

"I'm sorry." She rested a hand on his shoulder. "Can they cure it? You hear all about how people are living with cancer now, but it sure as hell must be tough."

"Thanks. It's as tough as it sounds. They can't cure it, but they give him medicines that make it grow slower. The medicines make him feel lousy, at least some of the time, but he still plays the piano and writes his music, so he says he's okay."

"Man, I don' know as I could ever say that," said JJ.

"He'd tell you that you just haven't had a life yet," Tom replied.

They walked in silence the rest of the way.

● ● ● ● ●

Alan set his alarm for thirty minutes, then changed his mind and made it an hour. Wouldn't be as good as a night's sleep, not even the partial nights he was getting more and more often, but it would be enough to see him through for another few hours. He thought that was the most he could afford.

When the alarm rang, he woke feeling surprisingly alert. After a moment he realized it was because he was in the zone. Not quite the same feeling of total control he had when he was performing, but closely related. His head was near-bursting with unfocused thoughts about Mickey and the missing music. He'd have bet the farm he was on the right track to finding Mickey's killer and the treasure-packed duffel bag.

He settled himself at the bedside table and looked at the card without really seeing it.

I'm pretty sure the scene I cook up controls where I arrive. I doubt Joplin was alone in the club very often, so trying to catch him when there's nobody else there might mean a very long time after my last visit. And I don't want to surprise him again.

Alan considered the possibilities, then built up a new scene in his mind. Late morning, maybe ten o'clock. A few napkins, bottles, and glasses scattered around the tables, legacy of the previous night's entertainment. A pile of papers on the end of the bar closest to the piano, as though someone had been interrupted while looking through them. Nobody in the room.

It felt wrong. Not wildly wrong, just slightly off. Alan added more mess to the tables and floor, a "not cleaned up" scene. Better, but still not quite right. On a sudden impulse, he changed his mental picture, setting the piano's lid beside it against the wall. That felt right. Odd, but right.

Alan let the card's strain pour through his head, and stepped forward. To his left, he heard footsteps descending the stairs. He looked in that direction just in time to see the backs of two heads disappear down the stairs.

Give them time to get clear of the door.

He peeked into the piano. Shards of glass littered the cavity, and liquid had been splashed across the mechanism. A strong odor—beer and urine!—filled the interior.

What kind of jackass does that to a piano?

He shook his head, and walked as quietly as he could toward the stairs. As he neared the top of the staircase, he heard someone coming up. Heavy footsteps that sounded too firm to be Joplin's.

A moment later, a burly black man carrying a broom stepped out of the staircase.

Alan spoke before the man noticed him. "Have you seen Mr. Joplin?"

The man jumped, nearly dropping his broom, but collected himself quickly. "Who you to be asking that?"

"A friend of Mr. Joplin. Have you seen him?"

The man crossed to the bar and leaned his broom against the end. "He not here."

Alan laughed. "I can see that. And you can't be slow enough to think you can fool me by acting stupid. You don't have the look of a janitor, and a bartender needs more brains than you're using. Or are you the club owner?"

"Could be both, Sir."

"Which would make you one of the Williams brothers. Alan Chandler."

"'Deed I be, Sir." The black man shook Alan's extended hand. "Walker Williams."

"I'm pleased to meet you—but I do need to speak to Mr. Joplin."

Williams gave a one-shouldered shrug as he picked up his broom. "You jus' miss 'im, Mr. Chandler. You kin have a seat and wait, but I don' know how long he be gone."

"Do you know where he went?"

"He turn down toward Ohio, him and Otis Saunders, but I didn't hear where they goin'." Williams started sweeping behind the bar. Alan heard the tinkle of broken glass over the scrape of the bristles.

"Thanks. I'll go take a look for him."

Alan took a step toward the stairs, then stopped and turned back, gave Williams a half-wave. "If I don't find Mr. Joplin, I'll come back and wait."

Outside, Alan turned right, glancing in windows as he walked. At the corner, he looked in all directions. The sheer number of people passing made it obvious he wasn't going to spot Joplin, so he turned back—and found himself a few steps behind his quarry. Joplin and Saunders had stepped out of a hardware store and headed toward the club. Alan was about to hurry his pace to catch them when he realized they were arguing.

Saunders was the more agitated of the pair. He threw his arms in the air and made punching motions several times as they walked—or in Saunders' case, stomped. Alan couldn't hear any of their discussion, but could tell Joplin was trying to calm his friend. At the door to the club, Saunders whirled to face Joplin.

Alan caught the last few words he shouted, "…if it takes the rest of my life!" before he stomped away.

Joplin sighed, watched Saunders disappear in the crowd, and then walked slowly inside.

Alan waited several minutes before he went up to the club so Joplin wouldn't think he had been eavesdropping. He found his man sitting at a table, staring not so much at the piano as through it. The papers Alan had seen on the bar earlier were on the table in front of the composer. Alan tossed a salute at Williams, who was clearing debris from the tables, and slid onto a chair next to Joplin.

After a few seconds, Joplin spoke without looking around. "It's a sad thing, Mr. Chandler, when a man lets his pride do his thinking."

"Sometimes all you can do is give that man some space and hope he lets go of his pride before it gives him too nasty a fall."

They sat in silence for a few minutes before Joplin shook himself free of his melancholy. "Well, Mr. Chandler, what brings you back to the Maple Leaf Club so soon? Was last night's excitement not enough?"

Alan blinked. *Last night? But…Oh!* "I must have left before the real excitement began," he said in an attempt to conceal his ignorance. "What did I miss?"

"The death of an old friend," Joplin said with a nod to the piano. "I didn't hear what started the fight—the first I knew was when a couple of out-of-town rowdies began to shout and punch each other in the back of the room. Then one of them grabbed a glass off the table and threw it. He missed his opponent, but hit the piano squarely. The glass went right over Arthur's head and smashed against the lid."

"And liquid and glass don't do good things for pianos. RIP, piano. My sympathies on your bereavement."

"Thank you." Joplin turned a weak smile on Alan. "I doubt the club will be open tonight. Without a piano, there's little reason for anyone to come here instead of the Black 400 across the street."

Alan stared absently at the instrument and considered what he had seen inside it.

There was far too much liquid in there to have come from a single glass. And even beer that tastes like horse piss doesn't smell like horse piss. Joplin is missing something.

"What happened to the lowlifes, Mr. Joplin?"

"The what? Oh, the fighters? They ran out while everyone was still looking at the piano and making sure Arthur hadn't been hurt."

Those thugs must have been working with someone else. Someone who wanted to make sure that piano was put out of commission. I'll have to find a way to come here last night. Watch from out of the way, see who might have used the commotion to cover dumping piss into the piano. Follow the thugs. Alan's back twinged. *Well, maybe. Change the subject.* "The reason I'm here is that I owe you a story—more likely, several stories—and last night wasn't the right time to tell them." He stared in thought at the table. "I guess the right place to start is with the music." He locked eyes with Joplin. "I've been playing ragtime almost my entire life. I heard "Maple Leaf Rag" when I was sixteen, and that was it. I've been listening to ragtime, playing it, and writing it ever since."

Joplin leaned back in his chair, disappointment written large on his features. "A shame you've aged so much in just a few months, then." He shook his head sadly, pushed his chair back, and started to rise. "I see no point in listening to such ravings."

"Wait! Please, Mr. Joplin, every word I've said is true. I hardly believe it myself, but I'm not lying and I'm not insane. Give me a few minutes to try to explain."

Joplin's expression didn't change, but he didn't leave the table.

"The simple truth is what I said. I first heard your music when I was sixteen—in 1951. It's been more than sixty years since that day, and I believe I've played ragtime—your own music often enough—on all but a handful of those days. Just two days ago, I was studying a scrap—a piece of a work in progress—I had never seen before. I was trying to put myself in your head, to figure out how the strain had evolved and imagine what you might do with it, and I suddenly found myself here, as you were writing that strain."

"Ridiculous!"

"Completely."

Joplin dropped back into his chair. "If I hadn't heard the way you play, I'd dismiss your tale out of hand, and you along with it."

"Then you're more generous to me than I am to myself. I've lived this tale, and I'm not convinced it's real. For all I know, I could be lying in a hospital bed, dreaming this conversation."

A moment of silence as Joplin stared at Alan. Then he said, "I'm not a drinking man, but somehow I believe this conversation requires something stronger than a soft drink." He called over his shoulder, "Walker, bring me a beer, please?" After a hesitation, he added "And one for Mr. Chandler."

"Comin' up, Scott."

Alan said quietly, "I can't pay for a drink. I can't pay for anything." At Joplin's raised eyebrow, he pulled a few coins out of his pocket. "Mr. Williams wouldn't be happy with my money." He held up a battered penny. "1970." He dropped it on the table and sorted through the rest of the change. "2008 quarter." He flipped it over. "Alaska. It's a state now—or, no, make that *then*. Hmm. 1986 dime. Another quarter. Florida Everglades on the back." He shoved the pile over to Joplin. "None of 'em legal tender today. Hell, they're not even worth their face value as metal, now *or* then."

Joplin studied the coins. "I don't believe the cost of a beer will break me," he said absently. He dropped the coins back into Alan's hand as Williams brought a pair of glasses to the table.

"Thank you," Alan said to both men. He pushed his glass aside.

Williams caught the motion. "You don' want no beer after all?"

"Oh, I want it plenty. But alcohol doesn't mix well with the medicines I have to take."

"That be a true shame."

Williams reached for the glass, but Joplin snagged it. "No harm done, Walker. I'll drink them both. And perhaps you could bring Mr. Chandler a Co'cola?" Joplin turned to Alan. "Would that suit you?"

"Yes, it would, and thank you. My apologies for the inconvenience, Mr. Williams."

"Ain't much trouble. The bar's just a few steps away. Funny thing, though, now's I think about it, you might jus' be the first piano player to pass through here without tryin' to sweet talk me inta givin' him a beer to keep his fingers loose."

Joplin cleared his throat meaningfully.

"Oh, not you, Scott. You not passin' through; you damn near lives here—an' you allus pay for your drinks." Williams stepped to the bar and returned a moment later with Alan's soda. "But, Mr. Chandler, I prides myself on 'membering every face I meets. When you taked me for a janitor this morning, after callin' me by name las' night, I was afraid my memory was playin' tricks on me, 'membering a body I ain't never met."

"More like *my* memory playing tricks on you, I'm afraid," Alan lied smoothly. "No way did I intend to deceive you. But when a man gets to be my age…" He shrugged.

Williams nodded. "I understands. Right sorry to hear it, Mr. Chandler. But I let you gentlemen get on with your business."

Joplin gave Alan a suspicious look. "I doubt your mind suffers the failings of age any more than mine."

"It does, actually, though my forgetfulness is due more to medication than to age. But it was a convenient explanation. I could hardly tell him today was the first time I'd ever met him, when he remembers speaking to me yesterday."

Alan took in the blank look on Joplin's face. "Traveling in time has some unique confusions. I wasn't here yesterday. Not yet, anyhow. But it seems that at some point in my future, I'll be visiting your past. Don't try to make sense of it; I certainly can't."

"Maybe I had best not think about it at all." Joplin took a large swallow of beer. "So when you told me it was my music that brought you to the Maple Leaf Club, you were speaking the literal truth."

"In several ways."

"And when you said you had spoken to Brun Campbell?"

"That was misleading, I admit. He was my first teacher. Taught me to play ragtime just the way you taught him."

Joplin pounced on the implication. "In 1951?"

Alan sat mute.

"If you were playing my music, but didn't come to me—"

Alan interrupted. "I'm not going to answer that question, Mr. Joplin. There's no way your knowing the answer would be a good thing."

"But if I knew, I could plan! There's so much I need to do!"

"The muse moves at her own speed, and no one has found a way to hurry her. You have time, but it's best that you don't know how much, just like the rest of us. It's not enough time, but none of us ever has enough. The man who says he's done everything he set out to do and is content to die is a liar, a coward, or a fool, Mr. Joplin."

Joplin thought for several minutes. Alan didn't interrupt. "I believe I understand," Joplin said at last. "And just by your presence, you assure me that I will achieve some of my goals."

"You will, Sir. Your popularity will rise and fall, but you won't be forgotten. Millions of people will enjoy your music. You'll be remembered as one of the great American composers, and ragtime will be considered a true American musical style."

Alan considered, and then smiled a little. "In your future, you'll tell other musicians that you won't be properly recognized until a quarter century after your death. They may laugh at you, but it's true—and generations of scholars will be amused at how accurate your prediction will be."

Joplin thought that idea through and back. "I'll say that because you told me I will. But you told me I will because I did say it." His face took on the puzzled expression of a dog whose chew toy has been stolen between bites. "What if I don't say it?"

Alan assumed a similar look. "I think you will because you did. If you don't, I won't have had any reason to tell you to say it."

"I think this is another one of those things I had best not think about." Joplin drained his first glass and reached for the second. "All right, Mr. Chandler. Let us put my life aside, at least for now. You've played your introduction—and quite impressive those four bars are. Now let's have the rest of the piece."

Alan squirmed in his seat, momentarily feeling as if he were seventeen again. "Call me Alan, please. Being your student's student, I don't feel right hearing you say Mr. Chandler."

A considering look. "Very well. Your tale, then, Alan."

"Your music's tale as much as mine. It's well known that some of your music was lost. Never published, in some cases never seen by anyone but you and your wife." He stopped and shook his head, forestalling Joplin's automatic question. "You wouldn't thank me for spoiling any of life's pleasant surprises. Anyway, imagine opening your mail and learning a friend had sent you a previously unknown piece by Chopin or Mozart. That was how I felt a few days ago when I received a letter…"

Alan left out many of the details of his story. He worried that he might already have told Joplin too much about the future, so he didn't say anything about Wilbur Sweatman, Freddie Alexander, or Lottie Stokes. He snipped everything he could have said about Joplin's time in St. Louis and New York, nor did he mention the titles of any of Joplin's compositions. And he carefully avoided any mention of his suspicion that the attack on the piano had been aimed at Joplin.

When Alan finished talking, Joplin shook his head. "You have my sympathy for the loss of your friend, Alan." He looked pensive. "All those years, and men still torture and kill for profit. That's hard to hear. Harder still to know that I'm responsible for your friend's death."

"Don't ever think that! You had nothing to do with Mickey's death, not one little bit. I don't hold you responsible for anything anyone did over your music, and Mickey wouldn't have either."

Joplin closed his eyes and didn't respond for several moments. Alan was beginning to worry if he had said too much, when Joplin stood. "Forgive me, Alan. I believe I need some time to think about what you've told me before I can comprehend anything more. If you'll excuse me?"

"Of course." Alan watched Joplin collect his music from the table and return it to the lockbox under the bar. "I'll see you soon, I hope," he added as Joplin passed his table on the way out of the club.

Alan waited until Joplin had disappeared down the stairs, then crossed the room to the pool tables, where Williams was collecting the previous night's garbage. "Mr. Williams, will you take some advice from a worried man?" He didn't wait for a response. "Be careful, and keep an eye on Mr. Joplin. I don't think last night's fuss is going to be the end of this business."

"You think Mr. Joplin be in trouble?"

"I think it's possible. Maybe whatever is going on is aimed at the club, but I have a feeling…Mr. Joplin would never notice a threat until it came right out in the open."

"You gots that right, Mr. Chandler. Long as he can compose his music, he don't see nothing." He fixed Alan with a considering look. "You the same way."

"When I was his age. For a lot of years after, too. Hopefully I've outgrown it, at least some of the time."

"Hmmm. Okay, I keeps alert. Would anyways."

The walk to the future location of the Hotel Bothwell was uneventful, allowing Alan to think. By the time he opened the door into Bryant-Tewmey, and stepped into the hotel lobby, he was sure he needed to visit the previous night as soon as possible. Back in the room, he glanced at the clock.

Ten forty-five. Miriam first.

Alan kept the nightly call as short as he could, little more than "I'm fine. Tom's fine. We've got a lead on the music. No, we still don't know when the police will let us go. Don't worry any more than you have to." He could tell Miriam wasn't buying it any more than she had the previous night, but she also didn't threaten to hop on a plane and drag him back to Seattle, so he counted it a victory.

Another glance at the clock. Alan downed the handful of pills he'd normally have taken at bedtime, reloaded his pocket container, and sat at the table again.

• • ● ● •

JJ reached across the couch to take Elvira's hand. "Granny, I know what you're gonna say, but we gots to tell Alan...the old man..." He held up a hand, palm out, to halt the steamroller he saw coming, but it didn't even slow down.

"Boy, you hear me now, an' hear me good. We takes care of our own, and that be all there be to that."

"No, it ain't, Granny. It *ain't* all there be, by a long shot. You listen at *me* 'fore you say anything else. All my life I been takin' more'n anyone oughta have to carry from that man, but now—this gotta be the end of it, I don't care if he *be* my father. He weren't *ever* supposed to go outside, *not ever*, not for nothing. But did he go? Did he? An' did you call me, and did I go out lookin' for him 'steada eatin' dinner, and bring him back? An' did a cop see me out there, a nigger-boy goin' around lookin' a little crazy on East Third, a block away from where a white man got killed? An' did that cop tell his boss, and did his boss lock me up for 'questioning'?"

JJ punched the sofa cushion. "We gives that man shelter an' food, an' what he do for a thank-you? Jus' plain luck the cop see *me*, 'steada him, else we got a SWAT team outside the door there, the house is fulla tear gas, an' you and me are both downtown, maybe forever. But this Alan—he one smart guy, I'm tellin' you, an' a smart white guy is what we needs to get us outa this mess. 'Cause I sees on'y two things for us right now.

We tell Alan about Pop an' see what he figure we oughta do. *Or* we gives Pop a ticket for the next train to K.C., so long and don't let the door hit ya in the ass. An' if anybody with a badge asks us, we never saw hide nor hair of him. 'Cause takin' care of our own only go so far iff'n he ain't gonna help hisself. We kin trust Alan, Granny. Not Pop."

Elvira sighed from the deepest part of her soul. "I hear you, Boy. But sometimes trust ain't enough."

"Sometimes it's the best you got, Granny. An' don' forget, it were Alan got me outa the clink—and you shoulda heard how he talked to that cop. I had all I could do to keep from bustin' out laughin' a couple times. White cop don' like him none, but he listen to Alan 'cause he talk their language. Hell, he even call a lawyer, had him all ready to spring me if he had to. I owes him big."

JJ paused, took a deep breath. "Come hell or high water, that man gonna find the duffel bag fulla music, an' who it was killed Mickey. That what he want, so I owes him my help. An' that mean I gotta give him everythin', so he know what the cops be thinkin', and why they pick me up. An' I gotta tell him quick. He say if the cops get to that music first, he never see it again. It be locked up fo' evidence till he dead and gone. Or worse, if whoever snatch it get spooked and throw it in a fireplace—"

"Sweet Jesus. And he think it all be by Scott Joplin?"

"Yeah. His grandson say nobody in the world know more about Joplin than Alan do. He's got cancer, and he need to take care a that music afore it too late for him." Another deep breath. "Now, you say no, you gonna keep hidin' that bum in your basement, I does two things. One, I finds me a new place to live, startin' tonight. Two, I tells Alan everything he wants to know, and I figure I'm helpin' us all." Now, what do you say?"

Elvira's eyes shimmered. "I guess I say you now for real the man in this house, so we do what *you* say." She hugged JJ's hand. "When you gonna go bring Mr. Alan 'round?"

"Not now. He back at the hotel, layin' down for a while. We all gonna get together tomorrow, nine o'clock. Think you can do one mo' breakfast?"

She patted his hand. "Got a feelin' it gonna be more'n one."

• • ● • •

Once they'd delivered JJ to his house, Tom and Saramae started down Lamine toward downtown. After a few steps, Tom broke the silence. "Your folks aren't going to have a problem with this, are they?"

"Not folks," said Saramae. Just 'folk'—Daddy. Momma died when I was four, don't know exactly why, I think her kidneys. Daddy never talks about her, and I hardly even remember her. As for missing dinner without checking in, hangin' with a couple of strange white dudes, and investigatin' a murder…well, Daddy, he's pretty used to the first two. We might have to roll with a punch or three on the last."

"If he's pissed at me for getting you in trouble, we're not gonna learn much, right?"

Saramae giggled. "Nah, it's cool. Can't get a girl in trouble by kissing. If you don't know that…" Tom mimed a punch at her shoulder as she went on. "No, seriously, we're cool. Daddy says his job is reporting the news, so somebody else needs to go out there and make it. He ain't gonna lock me in my room for the rest of my life. And I'm havin' too much fun to be ashamed."

Tom held his hands up in surrender. "Okay, yeah, I get it. So how we gonna play this?"

They walked half a block or so in silence while Saramae considered the question. "I think better we be straight with Daddy. Like I said, he loves to talk about his stories, but he also says 'nothing's free in the newspaper game.' You're probably gonna have to trade him info for info."

It was Tom's turn to think for a block. "I guess there's some stuff I can maybe tell your father if I have to. More, if he promises not to put it in the story. At least make sure the cops don't know where he got it. Would he do that?"

"Oh, yeah. He does that all the time. Police keep stuff quiet while they investigate, and Daddy has to work with them or they won't tell him squat no more. So he doesn't always put everything he knows into the paper. 'Price of doing business,' he says."

A couple of blocks later, Tom said, "Hey, meant to ask you before, but I forgot. How'd you get my phone number, anyway?"

"Off your phone."

Tom made a grab for his pocket.

A giggle. "Not like that. I saw it at the top of your address book when you put my number in."

"The hell you did. No way is it there."

"Wanna bet?"

Tom didn't answer, just pulled out his phone and opened the Address Book app.

"See? 'My Number.' Might be a good idea to turn that off before someone nasty gets it the same way I did."

"How the hell did you read it that fast? And remember it?"

"I've got a good memory, and you were juggling that paper and your phone for ages. Gotta admit I didn't get the whole thing. Wound up callin' a bunch of folks in Seattle trying to work out the last number. Too bad it's a seven, instead of a one or two."

Tom grunted sourly and shoved the phone back in his pocket, thinking it was a damn good thing he hadn't downloaded "Pussy Cat Rag" while Saramae was around.

●　●　●　●　●

Saramae's house was an unpretentious two-story building, as was almost every other within several blocks. The green paint had once been cheerful, but now its faded color nearly matched the pale grass in the front yard. On the other hand, the couch and chairs on the front porch were a bit worn, but still bright and comfortable-looking.

Her father was sitting in one of the chairs, writing on a clipboard, as they approached. He looked up when Saramae's shoe scuffed on the front steps. "Is that you, 'Mae? Finally remember the way home?" He stood up, setting his writing on the arm of the chair.

Saramae sighed and shook her head. "Pretendin' you an old-fashioned reporter again?" She waved to Tom. "Come on up here and meet the old fraud. Daddy, this is Tom. Tom, this's my father. Don't let him kid ya. When he really workin', he use a laptop like anybody else."

She showed Tom the clipboard—the lined, legal-sized paper in it was as free of marks as the day it came from the store. "Didn't even notice he didn't have a pen, didja? He pull this stunt every time I bring a boy home."

Tom blinked.

What the heck's going on with her? All of a sudden, she's talking like JJ's country n—

He chopped off his thought, refocused. *No, I didn't notice he didn't have a pen; I was too busy staring at him....*

Mr. Blackstone was at least six-five, and massive enough to look almost square. His grin looked faintly piratical, an image the fuzzy, alligator-shaped slippers he wore somehow failed to dispel.

The boy ignored the family byplay. "Pleased to meet you, Sir." He held out his hand.

"Likewise, Mr. Chandler." He smiled at Tom's surprised start. "My daughter, for all her failings, knows better than to bring someone by to pump me for information without making sure I have something to share. Text messages are one of the few good reasons to tie yourself to a phone around the clock." He didn't wait for Tom to respond. "C'mon inside, and let's talk."

As they walked into the house and through the living room, Tom noticed a piano, a well-kept but obviously much-used baby grand, against the front wall. He leaned sidewise to read the music on the rack: a softbound set of Chopin's polonaises, then turned a silent question onto Saramae, who responded with an embarrassed little shrug.

Tom was impressed.

If she's good enough to handle those, asking her to play 'em for me might be a way to get on her good side.

Mr. Blackstone opened a door on the right wall of the room. "Welcome to my lair," he said with a theatrically evil laugh.

Saramae sighed again—it was obviously an old family joke—but she held her tongue as she detoured into the dining room for a couple of chairs.

As he sat, Tom looked around curiously. Despite its title, the room didn't look much different from any other home office he'd ever seen—a desk with the promised laptop, a cheap office chair, a wall full of filing cabinets, and a couple of crammed bookcases.

"You want to know about Mr. Potash's unfortunate demise, Tom? Seems to me that you might know more than I do, being the person who found him."

Tom paled as an image of Mickey's face popped up from his memory, but he pushed it aside and said, "Which didn't exactly make me Detective Parks' best buddy. He's not about to share anything his investigation turns up with me. I know what I saw, but that's about all. You've got the newspaper behind you; he has to have told you something."

"Good, so we've got the basis for an exchange." Mr. Blackstone leaned back in his chair.

"Told ya!" Saramae chimed in.

"Shush, 'Mae. Tom, much as I hate to admit it, I don't know a lot that wasn't in yesterday's story. The cops are being unusually tight with details. If they're holding back this much, it probably means they don't have a lot to go on in the first place."

Tom sighed. "I sorta figured Parks was stingy like that, but haven't you heard anything? Autopsy results, maybe?"

"That I can do." Mr. Blackstone unlocked his laptop and pulled up a file. "Time of death, four-thirty—"

Saramae jumped in her seat and interrupted her father. "So the cops can't think it was JJ! He were back at work by four!"

Mr. Blackstone shook his head. "Was he? According to this, he's listed as a person of interest because an officer saw him looking agitated near your friend's house at ten 'til. Would have been tough for him to get back to the paper by four from there. But even if he did clock in by four, it wouldn't help his case. Time of death is an estimate. Four-thirty means it could have been any time between three and six. Sorry, 'Mae."

"Damn!"

"Preliminary cause of death, strangulation with wire."

Tom nodded. "A piano string. But why 'preliminary'?"

"Piano? Interesting. That's something Parks didn't say." At Tom's stricken look, he added "Relax, Kid. The police don't give me their informants, I don't give them mine. Preliminary because it'll take a while for all the drug tests to come back. Okay?"

Tom nodded.

"Smaller bruises, cuts, and scrapes consistent with his having been repeatedly hit or punched by someone wearing rings. Cigarette burns, suggestive of torture, but no indication of restraint. That would be something like rope burns or more extensive bruises."

"Huh? Who sits there and lets someone burn him with a cigarette?"

"Someone drunk or stoned, maybe? That would be one reason for the toxicology tests. Or it could have been that the killer was strong enough to restrain him without ropes."

"Oh. Anything else?"

"Not from the autopsy. One thing Parks asked me not to publish. During the initial investigation, the police found signs that the house had been searched multiple times."

Tom repressed a flinch. "What kinds of signs? And how many times?"

"Unfortunately, he didn't share that information. I take it you could shed some light on the subject?"

"Well...Maybe. I—I mean, Alan and I—looked around a little for the music before we called the police, but it wasn't really a search. I mean, we didn't open any cabinets or anything."

Mr. Blackstone gave Tom a dubious look, but let the question drop. "About the music: your grandfather believes it to be by Scott Joplin?"

Tom nodded. "There's a lot of work to do to prove it, once we get the bag back, but he's sure."

"The bag?"

Saramae jumped in. "The music's in a whadyacallit—a bag like sailors use. A duffel! Right, Tom?"

"Yeah. A lot of music, and as far as Alan could see, most of it is nothing anyone knew about before. That's why it's so important."

"That much? I had the impression from the police that it was only a few pieces…" Mr. Blackstone leaned his chair back and thought for a minute, then spoke to the ceiling. "You know, not everyone was a big fan of Mr. Joplin in those days. By what my great-grandfather used to say, there were plenty of people, even blacks, who thought he was arrogant, or what we'd call a sellout." He sat up and looked at Tom. "You know the black clubs like the Maple Leaf weren't popular with the gentry?"

Tom nodded. "Alan told me. Even the black preachers were against them. 'Dens of depravity' and like that, right? Didn't the city shut them down pretty quickly?"

"Exactly. And it wasn't just preachers complaining. There were legitimate concerns about public drunkenness and violence. My great-grandad's father saw some of it first-hand. I don't know if the authorities would have taken action against white clubs, but…" Mr. Blackstone shrugged. "Great-granddad was a boy when Mr. Joplin lived in Sedalia. He always said he was 'powerful proud' to have shaken 'a great man's hand.' But he also said some of the trouble that got the clubs shut down was aimed at Mr. Joplin." He shook his head. "But I'm getting off the subject. Is there anything else you can share with me, Mr. Chandler?"

"Uh…I don't think so. Not right now, anyways."

"All right. Saramae, I have an uneasy suspicion that you intend to continue to assist this gentleman with his investigations?"

"Heck, yes! I be havin' a great time. Most fun I'se had since I broke up with El'Ray."

"It's not a game, 'Mae! You could be in serious danger—and how many times do I have to tell you to speak Standard English? This is important business!"

Saramae glared at him. "What do Standard English gots to do with importance? 'Sides, this investigation be mos' important to black folks." She started counting on her fingers. "JJ an' his granny, the ol' lady who useta have the music, me, even Mr. Joplin…Hell, Daddy, after Mickey, Tom an' his granddaddy be the only white folks mixed up in this at all." She flipped a hand in dismissal. "I got me a well-developed sense a preservation, Daddy—why you think I'se not seein' 'Ray no more? I be real careful. I don' want you writing no stories 'bout me. But some things is worth takin' a few risks for." She winked at Tom. "Leastwise, if you gonna write 'bout me, it gonna be my story, not some kinda sidebar to someone else's story. Okay?"

"I could chain you to your bed, but you'd probably just pick the lock." He shook his head. "Much as I'd like to stop you, you're eighteen, old enough to make your own decisions, so I can't force you to stay out of this. Tom, you be careful too. Don't drag my daughter into any trouble you can avoid." He leaned forward. "Hear me?"

"Loud and clear, Sir."

A chuckle as he settled back in his chair. "Good."

Saramae stood. "Now, if you be done 'timidatin' Tom, how's 'bout I walk him back to the Bothwell?"

Mr. Blackstone glanced at his watch. "How about you walk him to the door? Tomorrow's a school day—and even if you don't care about your senior year, I do."

On the front porch, Saramae touched her lips to Tom's cheek and whispered, "Wait for me at the corner."

Tom leaned against the street sign for a quarter of an hour before Saramae showed up, brushing leaves out of her hair and rubbing a scratch on her left arm.

"Guess I'm gettin' too big to climb out the window and down that tree," she complained as she approached.

Tom eyed the mini-skirt that did little to hide her tights-covered legs. "Must have been quite a scene. Ow!" He rubbed his shoulder.

"Wimp. I didn't hit you that hard." She frowned at him. "I was gonna collect another payment on what you owe me for hookin' you up with JJ. Now I don' know…"

"Oh, come on! Put yourself in my position. 'Course I'm going to want to have seen that. Any guy woulda!'"

"Yeah, but some guys would have had the class not to say anything about it." She sighed theatrically. "I suppose I gotta work with what I've got." She pressed herself against Tom and pinned him against the sign pole.

Tom put his arms around her, somewhat awkwardly, and bent his head to kiss her.

A long minute later, Saramae pulled away. "You're getting better. Might not be sorry about settling for something besides cash."

"Does that mean I can have my ten bucks back?"

"Don't be stupid. Now shut up. That's not the only reason I came out here. I wanted to tell you, Daddy cleaned up what he said about his great-great."

"What do you mean?"

"I mean, Triple-Great-Granddaddy didn't just *see* the violence, okay? Daddy's not proud of that, so it's somethin' he doesn't share outside the family. But your granddaddy being who he is, I know he's gonna want to hear Daddy's stories. When this's over and we have the music back, if he asks nicely, maybe we can talk about it. Not now, no way."

"Hey, credit me with some sense! Alan, too. You don't want to talk about it, that's your call."

Saramae looked embarrassed. "Sorry. Just, y'know?"

"Yeah. We're cool."

● ● ● ● ●

I can't just pop into the club the way I have been. Not when it's full of people. What about outside? Can I do that?

Alan built a mental picture of the ground-level storefront at 121 East Main Street as he had seen it when he went looking for Joplin. *But the night before.* He darkened the scene, then added patches of light from the windows of the Maple Leaf Club and the other late-night businesses. After a moment's thought, he added more illumination from the gas streetlight at the corner.

The scene didn't feel alive the way it had on his previous visits to 1899. The sense of rightness or wrongness that helped him build the image was missing. He let it go.

Up until now, I've started with the music on the invitation. That makes a kind of sense.

Alan pictured the card tucked into the lockbox under the end of the Maple Leaf Club's bar. Slowly, he broadened his mental picture to include the entire club. Joplin at the piano in his role as the club's entertainer, the tables filled with customers, gamblers at the gaming tables, money changing hands at the pool tables, Walker Williams filling orders behind the bar. The feeling of rightness was back.

He stretched the picture further, bringing in the staircase, a man leaning against the wall near the top, sipping from a glass. Straining further, he added the street outside, with the club and the staircase more felt than seen. It didn't diverge much from his original picture, but the shadows were a little different, and there were a few people in the street, though none close by. Still right.

Alan let the card music play in his mind. A gust of wind from down the street and a burst of laughter from the window over his head hit him simultaneously. A moment later, he heard applause as Joplin brought "Maple Leaf Rag" to its conclusion. Alan grinned and stepped inside, out of the wind, and started up the stairs. He nodded to the man drinking at the top and approached the bar. Williams spotted him and frowned.

"'Scuse me, Sir. We not open to the public tonight. Club members only."

"Walker—" Alan started. *He doesn't know me from Adam yet.* He corrected himself. "Mr. Williams. It's all right. I'm here as a musician. Mr. Joplin will vouch for me."

"Wait here, please."

Joplin was playing something that was almost "Swipesy Cakewalk," stopping every so often, backing up, and playing it again a little differently. Arthur Marshall leaned over his shoulder, reaching in to interject a few notes. Williams hurried over and spoke in Joplin's ear. The composer looked up, saw Alan, and nodded.

Williams returned to the bar, nodding sideways to indicate Alan could go to the piano. As he did, Joplin stood, allowing Marshall to take over. He shook Alan's hand.

"Mr. Chandler. Good to see you. Come to grace us with a tune or two, have you?"

The temptation was irresistible. "I'd be delighted, if it wouldn't be an inconvenience."

"Not at all. I'm pleased to have the opportunity."

As Marshall brought the almost-Swipesy to a close, Joplin tapped him on the shoulder, then waved toward Alan. Marshall yielded his seat, and Alan took over. He began with Joplin's "Original Rags," then went on to his own "Emerald City Rag," a classic ragtime tribute to his hometown. As he finished, he found himself wondering whether any of the pianists present would be tempted to snag his themes for their own compositions.

I suppose if anyone does, it won't go over well enough to survive. But if it does or did, or however you put it, I could have wound up defending myself against accusations of plagiarizing myself!

Alan appreciated the applause, but cheerfully returned the hot seat to Marshall and Joplin. As long as he was playing, the unknown thugs who attacked the piano couldn't make their move. He slowly worked his way to the back of the room and took a seat where he could watch everyone.

Forgot to bring a cushion again.

He found it difficult to concentrate on the audience. Not only was Joplin's performance a significant distraction, but Alan's attention was repeatedly caught by a woman in a bizarre hat seated near the front of the room. The hat was decorated with lace and what appeared to be real flowers, but its most striking feature was a pair of gauze butterfly wings. Every time the woman moved her head, the wings flapped, catching Alan's gaze.

It wasn't until Joplin and Marshall had been playing for more than half an hour that Alan finally noticed a pair of men at a nearby table who looked out of place. They didn't seem to share the general air of good cheer, and the younger one was tapping his foot in an irregular rhythm that bore no relationship to the piano.

Suddenly, the younger man reached across the table and deliberately pushed the other man's glass into his lap.

The beer-soaked man leaped to his feet, shouting, "What the hell you do that for?"

"You keep your dirty mouth offa my Mabel!" the first retorted as he stood and threw a punch.

As the two men traded blows, most of the room turned to watch them, including the musicians. Abruptly, the older man rushed at the younger, forcing him a few steps toward the front of the room. In a single motion, the younger man grabbed the remaining glass from their table, hurled it past his opponent's head, and dashed for the stairs.

The contents of the glass sprayed across the room as it flew, leaving it empty when it smashed against the underside of the piano's raised lid. At the sound of the crash, the second fighter followed the first out of the club.

Alan's attention was locked on the space around the piano; almost absently, he noted that the glass had actually come closer to Joplin's head than Marshall's. The audience rushed to the front of the room, crowding around the piano so quickly Alan couldn't tell who reached it first, or see whether anyone was dumping pee-infused beer inside. He swore under his breath, before his attention was caught by the butterfly hat again.

Why is she moving away from the piano?

Something else about the woman's appearance nagged at Alan, but he couldn't take the time to figure it out. As she moved toward the tables in the middle of the room, Alan tried to get Joplin's attention.

Wait a second. I can't talk to him now, or he'll know tomorrow I didn't leave before the commotion started.

He froze in indecision as the woman and a male companion walked past him. Alan watched them move toward the stairs and suddenly realized what had caught his attention were the puffed shoulders of the woman's dress: one was distinctly less puffed than the other, giving it the appearance of a deflated balloon.

On impulse, he followed the couple outside. By the time he reached the sidewalk, they were several doors down the street. He tried to catch up, but his spine wouldn't permit him to move that quickly. He followed at his best pace, and gained a few steps on the couple when they stopped to exchange a few words with a man walking past. As they resumed their walk, Alan realized with a start that the man they had been speaking to was Otis Saunders. Alan stopped and waited for Saunders to reach him.

"Mr. Saunders!"

"Beggin' your pardon, Sir. You looks familiar…"

"Alan Chandler. We met in the Maple Leaf Club not too long ago. But that's not important. That couple who just passed. Do you know them?"

Saunders flinched, then quickly turned and looked back, as though he was trying to determine which of several couples Alan might have meant. After a second, he returned his attention to Alan. "Not real well. I'se seen him—Mr. Noland, I think he is—'round the Maple Leaf Club a few times. Ain't never been introduced to his wife, though."

Another Nowlin? Here?

Before Alan could ask Saunders where he could find Mr. Nowlin during the daytime, Saunders spoke rapidly. "'Scuse me, Sir, they needs me upstairs." He pushed his way through the crowd beginning to leave the club and vanished inside.

Alan sighed, dropped the question, and set off for the hotel.

I'm getting a little tired of this walk. No, very tired. As he went along, his brain filled with speculations about the aerodynamics of filled and empty glasses, the feasibility of concealing bags of liquid inside dress sleeves, and violent words and actions.

There's plenty of evidence Otis Saunders' claim to have written part of the "Maple Leaf Rag" destroyed Joplin's friendship with him, but I've never heard it went beyond words. And two Nowlins involved with Joplin, one here in 1899, and the old bitch in K.C. Coincidence?

• ● ● ● •

Some time later, Saramae backed away again, buttoning her blouse. "What time is it?"

Tom pulled out his phone and checked. "Bit after eleven."

"Huh. Hadn't thought it was that late. I'd best go home, and you should check on your granddaddy."

"You sure?"

"Hell, yeah. Maybe I'll collect another payment later, but that's enough for now."

"I suppose." A thought struck Tom. "How're you going to get back inside?" Wistfully. "Climb up the tree?"

"In your dreams. I'll use the front door; Daddy's not gonna want to keep me *out*, y'know."

• ● ● ● •

Alan wasn't in the room. Tom looked around, as though Alan might be hiding in the tiny excuse for a closet.

Did he duck out to the ice machine or something? Or is he time-traveling again?

After five minutes, when Alan still hadn't appeared, Tom called his phone. The call bounced to voice mail. "Hey, Alan, it's me. I'm back here at the Bothwell, and you're not. I mean, heck, you know what I mean. Give me a call, huh?"

Tom dropped onto his bed and pulled one of the sheets of Joplin's music out of his pack, determined to wait for Alan. Ten minutes later, he was sound asleep.

• ● ● ● •

As he shut the room door behind himself, Alan grinned at the sight of Tom sitting on the bed, slumped forward with his head on his backpack.

Good instincts. Too tired to lie down, but he put the music aside before he conked out.

Alan carefully packed away the card he had left on the table and the page Tom had been trying to study, and stretched out on his own bed to give his back a chance to unkink.

I wonder if there's any way to hide the card nearer the Maple Leaf Club. I don't dare risk losing it, but it's such a pain coming back here each time.

Chapter Eleven

Alan glanced at his watch as Saramae and JJ burst into Elvira's living room. "Yeah, we're late," JJ groused. "Took my little nursemaid here forever t' show up."

"Jeez, not *my* fault," Saramae shot back. "The asshole principal called my father because I've been cuttin' so much lately." Her face brightened. "But Daddy was really cool. He wrote me a note for school tellin' them I'm working on a special newspaper project for him and it's great experience. He even said they should excuse me, maybe even give me extra credit. Epic, right? But the school's way the hell out on Sixteenth, and, like usual, I hadda wait for Daddy to get ready for work and drive me out there. Then he waited while I dropped off the note, so I didn't have to walk all the way up to the paper to meet up with JJ."

Tom raised his eyebrows. "Boy, that *is* cool of your old man."

JJ looked as if he were eyeballing the floor for a spittoon. "Yeah, Mr. Blackstone is okay. But it still pisses me off, I gotta have somebody with me alla time. On account of I'm black."

Elvira, walking into the room with a tray of food and coffee, gave her grandson a hard look, obviously preparing a reprimand. Before she could say anything, Alan cleared his throat.

"You've got it backward, JJ—you don't need to be covered because you're black; it's because Detective Parks is an asshole." He held up a hand to shut off the retort he saw coming. "It's a shame on us that there are people like that around, and they have the authority to do what they do, but that's what's what, at least for right now. But I believe you can look forward to a time when all Parkses *will* get their asses handed to them for stuff like they're pulling now. In the meantime, you need to stay alive to see that day. And you'd be smart to take the opportunity to learn from your experiences."

"Huh! Learn *what*? What the hell have *you* learned from the experiences you havin' now, 'sides you gonna die?"

JJ winced as Saramae landed a serious punch to his upper arm. "*Jesus*, JJ!" she hissed. "Talk about bein' an asshole."

"That's something I knew already." Alan spoke softly, slowly. "I've never known when, I still don't, and neither do you know when *you're* going to die. Probably after me, but no guarantee, is there? You know what? I've learned I have to go slow chewing my food, swallow it a little at a time, else I start to feel sick. And funny thing—that's also true about how I need to swallow my days. I go a day at a time, enjoy every minute of every experience just as much as I can, and I don't think more than I have to about what I'm going to do tomorrow."

Suddenly, his mind's eye filled with an image of Scott Joplin's face. "Mr. Chandler," he heard, as if spoken from a great distance. "Good to see you. Come to grace us with a tune or two?"

"And you know what else? Everything considered, my life is still pretty good."

Alan smiled, then shook his attention back to the moment. "JJ, do you really think that because you're black, every white man is your enemy? I thought by now you'd learned that some white guys are even *on* your side." A wicked smile spread across Alan's face. "At least one of them."

Another "Huh," but all the steam had leaked out of the syllable, and JJ couldn't stop the grin that spread across *his* face.

Elvira had set the tray on the coffee table; now she straightened, nodded at Alan, jammed hands to hips, and favored her grandson and guests with a wry smile.

"If you people can quit squabblin' for a few minutes, maybe you'd like to put away some pancakes and sausages before you get down to your business."

Once Elvira had collected the plates and coffee pot onto the tray, the group refocused. "All right," Alan said, and gestured toward JJ. "Let's start with you. Did you pick up anything at the paper last night? Hear anything? Anything at all?"

The young man took a moment to think, then shook his head slowly. "No…no. Guys talked some 'bout Mickey—a lot of them knew him—but nobody said nothin' we di'n't know. Nobody had any ideas 'bout who did it and why. They didn't even talk about the duffel bag or the music."

Alan nodded. "Okay. Tom, Saramae…what did you come up with…" Sly smile. "…from the city editor?"

"Well, he—" Both spoke at the same time, then stopped and laughed. "Go ahead," said Tom. "He's your father."

Saramae laughed again. "Well, he said the detectives were a whole bunch tighter on details than usual, which makes Daddy think the cops don't have a lotta ideas."

"Which is probably why they picked up JJ," said Tom. "He had a solid connection with Mickey, and on the night of the murder—"

"He couldn't prove he had an alibi," Saramae broke in. "The time of death was set at four-thirty, but that just means it coulda been any time between three and six."

JJ bit his lower lip and looked away.

Saramae talked on, a mile a minute. "And the cops didn't seem to know the wire was a piano string. It seems like the cigarette burns musta been done by somebody real strong, because there weren't any rope burns—no signs of restraints. Or maybe Mickey was stoned or drunk and didn't feel anything. So they're doin' toxicology studies."

Alan shook his head. "Drunk is a good possibility for Mickey."

"And the cops think the house was searched more than once. *And* that there were only a few pieces of music."

Alan shrugged. "Anything else?"

Saramae squinched her eyes in thought, then looked at Tom. "Did I forget anything?"

The boy hesitated. "What about what your dad said about… how everyone back in Joplin's time was not a fan of his. Can I…or would you…?"

"Sure. Go ahead. He told us, so it's okay."

Alan realized he'd stopped breathing. He worked at keeping his face straight.

"Well…set me straight if I get it wrong, Saramae. Sounds like Mr. Blackstone's family goes all the way back in Sedalia, and his great-grandfather—Saramae's great-great—knew Joplin. He was 'powerful proud' that he'd gotten to shake Joplin's hand. But there were some people, even blacks, who didn't like Joplin—thought he was arrogant, even a sell-out. Right, Saramae?"

She nodded. "Right on."

Tom smiled. "He also said he thought some of the fighting and stuff that got the Maple Leaf Club and the Black 400 shut down was somehow set off because of Joplin."

Alan tried to speak, but felt as if his vocal cords had been inactivated. Tom picked up on his distress, and signaled to Elvira. "Could my grandpa have a glass of water, please?"

She was out of the room, then back within thirty seconds. Alan nodded thanks as he took the glass, swallowed slowly, once, twice, a third time. Then he blew out a long sigh. "It's that chemo med…sorry to concern you. I'm fine now."

The tension in the room declined noticeably.

Alan flashed Tom and Saramae his best smile. "That's really interesting—and maybe important. Very important. What else did Mr. Blackstone say about that?"

"That's pretty much it," Tom said, very quickly. "He said he was getting off the subject, and went back to trying to see what *I* could tell *him*." He shot Saramae a quick glance.

Which Alan did not miss. "Saramae," he said. "Can *you* tell us anything more?"

The girl's body tensed.

"I don't mean to push you too hard," Alan said. "But there could be an important connection here. For example, your great-great-grandfather? Was that on your grandfather's side?"

She chewed on her upper lip.

"Listen, Saramae. You've put a lot of energy into becoming part of the team. Your father's even given you a note to miss school and work on this project. We're glad to have you, always have been. But every one of us needs to put whatever we possibly can into the case. Can we all agree that whatever is said among the five of us will stay there, and will never, not for any reason, be told to anyone else?"

He looked around the room. Tom's hand shot toward the ceiling; slowly, Elvira's followed it. JJ nodded, then raised his hand. Staring at Saramae, Alan did likewise. Tears coursed down the girl's cheeks, but her hand went up.

Alan stood as rapidly as his back would accommodate the changed position, then pulled his handkerchief from his pocket and handed it to Saramae. She wiped at her face, then managed a weak smile. "You're tougher than you look," she said.

"Believe it," said Tom. "Be on his team and never cross him."

She blew a deep puff of air into the room. "Okay, then. "Yeah, we're talkin' about Blackstones all the way back. Triple-great-granddaddy Lathan and his son. From what I hear from my daddy and *his* daddy, Lathan and Will were both big men, and big storytellers too. Like Tom said, Will was high on Scott Joplin all his life, had nothin' good to say about the people who tried to drive Mr. Joplin down. Daddy, he told me Will used to say 'When a black man try t' make somethin' of himself, there *always* someone right there ready t' unmake him, and some of those somebodies are gonna be black. That just be the way of things, and it mean we need t' watch out for each other, not just ourselves.' So Lathan—Triple-great—was up to his neck in the fuss that got the black clubs closed down. It was just something he figured he had to do, or else Scott Joplin could've been hurt real bad."

"But who was it that wanted to hurt Mr. Joplin?" Alan asked.

"Oh, jeez." Saramae made a go'way motion with her hand. "That's where I don't know much. There were people who had it in for Joplin, but I really don't know why, exactly. I know it had *somethin'* to do with who composed some piece of music, and I'm pretty sure a man named Saunders was the big troublemaker. But I don't know how Triple-Great Lathan got mixed up in it. I suspect there's more—probably *lots* more—Daddy never told me, because I'm a girl and all."

Alan's legs wobbled. "That could be really helpful, Saramae, thank you." He walked back to his chair and plopped into it. Then he looked around the little circle. "Well, now, let's figure where do we go from here."

"Nowhere yet." JJ dropped his notebook into his shirt pocket. "I've got something else to tell about."

Alan waved his hand, palm up, a "go ahead" motion. "The floor's yours."

"Okay, Granny?"

"I already say it be your call, Jackson. Don't need to ask me no more."

Before Elvira finished speaking, Alan's cell phone rang.

He fumbled it out of its holster. "Hello? Alan Chandler here."

"Mr. Chandler. This is Rudolph Korotkin. In Kansas City."

Alan put a finger to his lips, then hit the "speakerphone" button. "Yes, Mr. Korotkin. What can I do for you?"

"Well, I just heard something *terrible*. Sylvester Maggione is dead—murdered. Gruesome. He was bludgeoned to death with an antique music stand. Blood all over his shop. I'm hoping you can tell me I don't have anything to be concerned about."

Alan looked at his phone as if the device might be in need of psychiatric counseling. "Mr. Korotkin, I'm sorry to hear that. It *is* terrible. But I don't really see how I can tell you whether or not you're also in danger. I had nothing to do with what happened to Mr. Maggione."

"You're certain of that, are you?"

Alan almost said, 'Well, one never know…' but caught himself. "I don't see how I could have."

"Did he tell you anything that made you wonder whether he was swimming in shark-infested water?"

"No...no, I can't think of anything like that. We talked for just a short while, he said he'd picked up the duffel bag and music at a sale in Brookside, I asked him to let me know if he got hold of any more information, and that was about it. I did get the impression that Mr. Maggione—and the person who sold him the music—were both totally focused on money. Perhaps one of them, I wouldn't know which, got a little greedy. So unless there's something I'm not aware of, I don't imagine you're in any danger."

"Well, if you hear anything or think of anything else, I hope you'll call me."

"I will. And you, me. I'm sorry, Mr. Korotkin."

Alan turned off his phone and returned it to the holster. Four pairs of eyes studied him, then JJ loosed a low whistle. "Man, that were smooth as snot. 'Less I ain't remembering straight, you 'bout the best liar I ever did hear. Didn't say Word One 'bout goin' to that ol' lady's house."

Alan grinned. "I also gave him the wrong neighborhood. We wouldn't want him to go snooping where he shouldn't, do we? I doubt Ms. A. Nowlin's ever even dreamed of moving up to Brookside, so that ought to throw Rudy off the scent nicely."

"Like I said, you good. Now, *I* suppose to just believe what you tell *me*?"

Alan nodded. "We're all in this together. It wouldn't do any of us any good, me included, to not be straight with you and everyone else in this room."

JJ guffawed. "You really good...Hey, there, Tom." JJ winked. "*Am* I supposed to believe him? He ever lie to you?"

"Not so I could ever tell. And not so I ever got hurt. Yeah, you'll do better believing him than not."

"Mmmmm. Guess I'm in, fo' good or bad." JJ paused, collecting his thoughts. "Like I was sayin' 'fore your phone went off, I got somethin' to tell alla you. 'Bout why I were out when Mickey got it." He paused, pursed his lips, then fixed a hard stare on Alan. "Granny and me, we got us a secret. See, there be a man, he live downstairs in the basement, been there for what, Granny? Six month now?"

Elvira nodded. "Just 'bout that. A good halfa year."

"He come to us lookin' for help, we should hide him away 'cause he runned off from the County Nuthouse, and if they catched him, they'd lock him up where he wouldn't never get out no more. So, what could we do, huh? We put him away downstairs, and when the cops come by, we tell 'em no, we ain't seen him. An' when they come back with a search warrant, we had him tucked away nice and snug in the chimney. Elvira take him his food, an' he got a li'l music player an' a cot, so he be happy as a clam."

JJ stopped talking, and tapped his index finger on the coffee table. Alan sensed this was a test of some sort. "Well, all right," he said. "But why would a person…two people…take in some runaway mental case, and hide him for half a year? Especially when the police are doing a search? The trouble you could've gotten into…You're leaving something out. Something big."

JJ pointed to Alan, then looked at Elvira. "See, I tell you this one sharp white guy! Okay, Alan, yeah. Guy we got down our basement just happen to be my ol' man. Granny's son. An' like she allus say, you takes care of your own. But you don't have to be no kinda genius to see that sooner or later, this ain't gonna work out so good. 'Cause he cain't never be goin' outside, not for nothin'. But the other night, he did just that, went outside, lookin' for a man prob'ly been dead an' gone for years. Granny, she call me, so I went out to find him, which I did, and hauled his sorry ass back home. But a cop seed me out there, he tol' Detective Park-it-in-'is-asshole, and I get picked up. Now, we cain't have that hap'nin', no way, so I tol' Granny we be smart to tell you. Maybe it helps you find what you're lookin' for, and also maybe you can just help us figure out what we can do with Pop. Fair deal?"

Alan smiled. "One for all, all for one. Sure, I'll do whatever I can to help with that. But you're still not giving me full disclosure, and you need to. Who was this man your Pop was chasing, and why was he chasing him?"

JJ nodded, looked at Saramae, who nodded back. "Don't sweat it, JJ. I won't say nothin' to my daddy about yours."

"Okay, then," JJ said. "Here it be. My Pop was never the brightest bulb in the 'lectric store—sorry, but that be truth. When he have a job, it something like pushin' a broom, or loadin' stuff onto trucks in a warehouse, kinda thing that take muscle, but don' need no brains. My mama got sick and tired of not havin' no money, and one day when I was maybe five or six, she was gone, out the door, no note, no nothin'."

JJ took a deep breath, then another. "People allus took advantage of him. Way back 'fore I was born, some guy take him to a bar, a crummy place outsidea town, offa Fifty. The guy makes like he Pop's best friend, tell Pop he had the chance to make a nice li'l bit a money, real easy. All Pop hadda do was swipe a duffel bag offa someone."

The room filled with soft murmurs.

"Oh, nothin' real valuable in it, you know. Just that it b'longed to Pop's new buddy there, and a scumbag had nicked it off him, an' he wanted it back. Easy, you know—wait'll real late at night, go in this guy's house, get the bag, bring it on over. But when Pop come by with the bag, his pal don' give him no money, just give him a good one upside the head with a baseball bat. Knocks him colder'n a walk-in freezer, an' then dump him in an open field. If Pop wasn't so sharp before, he even worse after that."

Elvira nodded, and dabbed a handkerchief at her eyes. "That all happen in '73, and for the rest of the seventies an' into the eighties, he had these bad times when he think he know where he could find the guy who did him wrong and fix him for it. Jes' keep walkin' 'round town, lookin' for the bar and the guy he say call himself Mr. Raney. It happen less an' less, but he never quite stop lookin', an' finally, one day 'bout ten years ago, he did something he shouldn't'a, and ended up where Jackson said. An' then, 'bout a half a year ago, he show up on our doorstep, pleadin' with Jackson and me to hide him away, said they treated him so bad, take away the food I brung him, make funna him for bein' dumb, sometimes hit him with a switch. What else I gonna do? We been keepin' him downstairs all this time, but Jackson be right, it ain't gonna come out good in the end. I can't take him back to that place, though, no how. Not my own son. Mr. Alan, I sure hope you can help us figger out what to do."

"I will do my best to help you," Alan said. "Do you know who Mr. Raney was? It sounds like you don't think that was really his name."

Elvira's face hardened. "Jack allus called him Mr. Raney, but you be right, I'm sure's I can be that weren't actually his name. Nobody know who he be—but I can tell you this: the person Jack stole the bag from was Sam Blackstone…" Elvira gestured with her head toward Saramae. "Her grandpa, Charley's father."

Saramae jerked erect, but couldn't find any words. Alan cleared his throat. "JJ, Elvira…how sure can we be that the duffel bag Jack stole is the same one we're trying to hunt down now? And do you think he could give us a description of what 'Mr. Raney' looked like?"

Elvira laughed dismissively. "Oh, he could tell you, I be sure of that. On'y problem is, he still be lookin' for the man what hit him, an' he not real clear how long it been, how much the man musta change, 'sumin' he ain't dead already. And as for the bag—" She shrugged.

"That's fine, I understand." Alan worked his jaw side to side. "Do you think it'd be okay to bring him up here and let me talk to him a little? Could he handle that?"

Elvira and JJ studied each other. "I'll go down, talk to him," JJ said. "Tell him you're our friend and you're gonna help us figure out how t' get him outa the nuthouse for good. I think it'd be okay, but if not, I'm stronger'n he is now."

JJ rose from the sofa, then disappeared out the doorway behind the living room. Five minutes later, he returned with an older man at his side. Alan wondered whether his idea had been a good one. The man was, he guessed, about sixty. He walked hunched over, making him appear to be shorter than his full height, which would have been something over six feet. His head was shaved, eyes bloodshot, and his expression was one of combined fear, hope, and barely suppressed anger that pulled at Alan's heart.

The pianist forced a smile and extended a hand. "Glad to meet you, Mr. Jackson."

"People, they calls me Big Jack," the man rumbled.

"Big Jack, then. I'm Alan."

"You my friend—my boy, JJ, he tell me you gonna get me 'way from them bad peoples at the hospital."

"I'm going to try my best. You've been there a long time, huh?"

"Longer'n I got numbers in my head. Mr. Alan, I don't want to die there. Know what they do with me when I do die?"

"Bury you, I guess."

Jackson loosed a raucous, bitter laugh. "Sure, they does. They buries me, but it be in a hole with ten other peoples, an' it got quicklime and vitriol in it, so nobody could ever know who's me and who's somebody else." The man's face went to grief. "Please he'p me, Mr. Alan. I wants to get buried right when I die."

My God, where does this end? Find Mickey's killer, find the music, now get this poor man out of his mess. What's next?

"Well, I'm going to do my best for you. Can you tell me why you're in that hospital, how you got to be put in there? Everything you can remember."

"Oh, I remembers it all. Back when I were Jackson's age, mo' o' less, this Mr. Raney, he tol' me if I would sneak into Mr. Sam Blackstone's house an' come away with a duffel bag an' give it to him, he'd have a hundred dollars for me, cash on delivery. Well, maybe that was something I shouldn't'a did, I knew it then and I knows it now. But a hundred dollars, shoot. Two months' pay pushin' a broom. Wasn't no trouble at all. So back I goes with the duffel, gonna meet Mr. Raney at the bar. He be happy as a pig in mud, say he get me the hundred right then. But he come back with a baseball bat, an' I turn around jus' in time to see him start his swing.

Nex' I know, I's in the Colored Ward over by Bothwell Hospital, and they tell me it's July, an' it was May when I took the duffel bag. I figger Mr. Raney go back to that bar now 'n' again, so *I* go there now 'n' again, lookin' for him. But the guy owned the bar, he didn't like for me to be comin' 'round there, and sometimes he call the cops an' they 'rest me. I don' make no trouble, though, so in a few days, they allus let me go. But one time, I *did* see Mr. Raney, sittin' right at the bar there, an' I went and hit him one in the jaw that stretched him out cold. Didn' need me no baseball bat, neither. So when they 'valuate me, they say I be dangerous, that it weren't Mr. Raney no how, but some other guy—"

"Did you get his name?" Alan asked.

Big Jack shook his head slowly. "They say it, but not so's I could 'member. But it don't matter. He was for sure Mr. Raney. Looked jus' like I 'member him, sure's you' born."

Alan thought the man was getting upset, so he assured him that was fine, not to worry. "What was in that duffel bag? Did Mr. Raney tell you?"

Jackson's face went crafty. "No, he never did say…but he didn't hafta. I done looked. It was a whole buncha music-type papers. I had to watch I didn't laugh out loud and waken up Mr. Blackstone, why anybody'd want to give me a hundred dollars for some old music papers."

Alan clapped his hands. "Good, Big Jack. I think that'll do it for now." He shifted his gaze to JJ, who took his father by the arm, and led him back downstairs.

Elvira moved to clear away the remains of breakfast, but Alan motioned for her to wait. "Do you remember just when Jack found the man he thought was Mr. Raney, Elvira? Close as you can come?"

"Somethin' I'll never forget. My on'y child, taked 'way from me an' sent off to the county. It was ten years ago, just like he say, in August. Jack, he get in one of his moods, and off he go, no one could stop him, no way. An' they had the hearing just a couple weeks later and send him right off. I go an' see him every Sunday, no fail, every Sunday till he snuck off and came here."

"Ten years in that place…" Alan sighed. "Nobody should have to deal with that," he added, more to himself than anyone else.

JJ came back into the room, dropped back on the sofa. "Okay, Boss," he said to Alan, "What now?"

"Whew." Alan mopped a handkerchief across his forehead, then looked at his wristwatch. "Just past ten-thirty. I had some ideas about what to do next, but now I think the first thing's got to be that we find out the real name of your dad's 'Mr. Raney,' and any other information, like where he lived, what his work was…anything that might help us track him down quietly. Tom, Saramae, and Elvira—you go down to the *Democrat*, get Mr. Blackstone into his office for a few minutes, and find out what he's willing to tell you from what he knows about that incident. Elvira, maybe if you're there, you can give a little support to those 'two kids' who'll be trying to pump him for information. The duffel bag stolen from his father's house—why was it there, how did it get there? Does he know who Mr. Raney was? Whatever you can find out might help. I'll go over to the courthouse and see whether I can have a look at the records from the case. Then, let's figure to meet back here, say one o'clock, tell each other what we found out, and go from there."

Tom had a puzzled frown. "What good is finding the man he knocked out going to do? It couldn't possibly be the same guy."

Saramae snorted, fisted him in the ribs. "Didn't you hear what Big Jack said? 'Looked jus' like I 'member him,' right? Maybe it ain't the same guy, but if he looked that much the same, maybe it was his kid, or something like that."

Alan nodded. "Exactly right. Or if there's another connection we haven't thought of that we could use to get him out of that hospital."

Tom blushed. "Okay."

JJ looked at Alan. "I didn't hear my name called. What you got for me to do?"

"Hadn't come to it yet. You stay here, JJ, get yourself some shuteye so you'll be sharp for whatever we do this afternoon. And I can't be sure we didn't shake up your dad to where he might decide to go looking for Mr. Raney again, and we don't want that for anything. You're the only one of us who could stop him. And since you can't go outside, either of you, that makes it your job."

"Hmmmm."

"Don't worry. There's going to be plenty for all of us to do, once we've found out who Mr. Raney is."

As JJ picked up cushions to spread before the front door, Tom sidled up to his grandfather. "*Did* you ever lie to me?" he whispered.

"Have you ever thought I did?" Alan's face was as droll as his voice.

"No, 'course not."

Alan shrugged. "Then, there's your answer. Come on, Thomas. Get moving before your team leaves without you."

copper. But the amount of corrosion set it apart from any other piano string Alan had ever seen.

He studied the pattern of rust and verdigris with the same intensity he normally brought to a new composition. Reaching the end where he had snipped it free of the longer string, he pictured it continuing, reconnecting into a single whole. The peculiar sense of rightness that accompanied his visits to the Maple Leaf Club guided his image. It took several minutes, backtracking whenever the sense of rightness faded, but at last he had it. The steel core was exposed at one end where the wire had been cleanly cut free of the tuning pin. The other end, a little more than four feet away, was cut raggedly, as though the cutter had needed several attempts with a dull tool to snip through the winding and central core.

How would the murderer have carried it to Mickey's? His pants pocket, maybe?

Alan mentally coiled the string and pictured it surrounded by cloth. The image felt right, but he couldn't keep it stable. The size of the coil grew and shrank, the light brightened and dimmed, and the texture of the fabric shifted, rough, velvety, soft. Alan tried to expand his mental image away from the wire, the same way he had earlier expanded his picture of the invitational card away from Joplin's lockbox. The harder he tried to picture Mickey's house, the harder it became to hold on to the image of the string. He began playing the card strain in his head, hoping it would improve his focus. Instead, he lost hold of the picture entirely.

"Hell!" Alan admitted temporary defeat. "It felt right, but…" He leaned back in his chair and stared at the ceiling. "If the problem is that I'm nuts, there's nothing I can do about it." He let his mind go blank for a moment, then slapped his forehead.

I'm not trying to go to the Maple Leaf Club and I'm not using the card. That's too many changes all at once—and the card was in Mickey's house right up until the killer left.

He pushed the wire aside and set the card in its place on the table, then easily built a mental image of the card in the duffel

Chapter Twelve

Alan forced himself to not slam the hotel room door. Nearly two hours of being sent from one department to another before anyone told him flat out to just give up. Alan mimicked the whiny voice of the last bureaucrat he'd spoken with. "'For any case involving a committal, our policy is to restrict release of information to situations where there exist sufficient legal or medical considerations. Mental illness carries carries such a *stigma*, it's necessary to preserve the privacy of the unfortunate sufferers.' *Stigma*, my ass! What a jerk! I sure hope Tom got something useful out of Saramae's father."

The old man ducked into the bathroom to catch up on his medication, then dropped back into the desk chair. Tom's backpack was leaning against the wall next to the TV table.

Not much point in keeping the music in that thing if we don't remember to take it with us. Still, long as it's here...Maybe I'm approaching the problem backward.

Alan opened the pack and was reaching for the envelope of music when he spotted the snippet of piano string. He dropped the wire onto the table and pushed the backpack out of the way.

If this works, we'll...well, we won't wrap everything up, but we will be miles ahead. If I can prevent Mickey's death in the first place, that'd sure also solve a lot of problems right there. Including proving I haven't flipped out.

Alan looked at the length of wire on the table, a typical piece of bass piano string—steel wire tightly wrapped in a spiral of bag. Alan smiled to himself and began spreading his picture outside the bag. His grin vanished when he imagined the duffel in the hidden space under Mickey's closet. The pile of paper in the bag began shuffling itself in his head, the light strobed from noon-bright to midnight-dark, and the surface under the bag flashed from dirt floor to chipped Formica, blotter-covered wood, bare concrete, and the worst 1970s shag carpet. Playing the strain in his head sped up the changes until they all blurred together.

"Fuck!"

Felt like trying to change the channel on a TV with the vertical hold on the fritz and the channels overlapping. Mickey's murder is too, hmm, call it loud. So if I step back… Worth a shot.

Alan put the card back into Tom's backpack and returned his attention to the wire. Rebuilding his mental image of the longer wire was simple. Instead of trying to force an image of its surroundings, he let his fancy fill in the details.

Sunlight slanting down, but shadows around the wire, dangling from someone's hand. Outdoors? Yeah.

Alan started his mental play-through of the card strain, but stopped after the first bar.

Not right. Maybe that music doesn't have anything to do with this scene? What would…? Of course!

Alan could, and often did, play "Maple Leaf Rag" in his sleep, so playing it in his head should have been easy.

No. Right music, wrong style.

He sped up. *Getting there.* The music turned showy, highlighting the pianist's skill at the expense of the composer's design—not just fast, but with sudden tempo changes and improvised variations. Alan could play it that way—any ragtime pianist worth his salt could—but it set his teeth on edge.

As the piece went on, the sound got clearer and increasingly unpleasant in Alan's head, with mistuned notes, missing notes, and a peculiar rattling buzz around the middle octaves. The imaginary pianist slammed the final chord with a particularly awful combination of buzzing and unintentional dissonance.

Alan took an involuntary step back, banging his shoulder on a door frame. He found himself standing just inside the door, looking out at a partially covered yard which held pianos in various stages of disassembly. The instrument furthest from the door had been stripped of much of its cabinet; the top, front board, desk, and shelf had all been left leaning against the side of the cabinet.

The young, dark-skinned black woman Alan had last seen wearing a ridiculous hat reached inside the dismantled piano, doing something he couldn't see. After a few seconds, she straightened and glanced around warily. Her gaze passed over Alan, standing in the comparative darkness of the shop. She reached beneath the keyboard and removed the lower panel. She touched the strings, then straightened and moved her fingers over the keys without touching them, apparently counting from the left. She pulled a tuning lever out of her purse, and reached into the cabinet.

She yanked the lever, repositioned it, yanked again, and dropped it back into her purse. She rummaged and came out with a pair of wire cutters. Another furtive glance around the yard, and she reached into the piano with the tool.

Alan winced. Even with the tension reduced, piano strings whip violently when cut, and the woman hadn't reduced the tension very much.

She obviously understood the danger, but was unwilling or unable to take proper precautions. Once she had the clippers positioned, she buried her face in her free arm. A couple of seconds passed—Alan figured she was steeling her nerve—before she quickly pulled her hand out of the cabinet. Even across the width of the yard, Alan heard the string snap against the keyboard as the cut end whipped forward and down.

The woman took a deep breath, and extended the wire cutters into the piano again. Another cut, another snap, and the clippers went back into her purse. She bent, grabbed the cut wires, and yanked them down and out of the piano. She coiled the wires quickly but carefully, avoiding the cut ends whipping through the air. Alan caught a glimpse of the ring she wore on her left hand—heavy, silver metal, a design worked in black in place of a stone. The woman tucked the wires into her purse as she turned toward the door.

An interesting hobby you have, Mrs. Nowlin. Which means that piano—

Alan interrupted himself.

Later. Don't let her see you.

An organ console stood at an angle to the back door. Alan sat on the bench and bent over, pretending to study the stops. He heard rapid steps, and then a male voice from further inside the store.

"Find what you needed, Miss Angeline?"

Alan started.

"'Fraid not, Mr. Taylor. Nothin' looks to fit m' Concord. Guess I'll jes' have t' play 'round the gap a while longer."

"Too bad, too bad. I shouldn't say it, as I could certainly use your business, but might Lathan carve a whippen for you? Your husband's gift for the mechanic arts should certainly be up to that."

Alan missed the next several exchanges.

Angeline—A.—Nowlin? And a Lathan? Even if he's a Nowlin instead of a Blackstone, the idea is ridiculous. And that ring could have been the same as the one I saw on the old bag in K.C. Maybe I have slipped a gear or two. He shook his head. *But if I don't trust my own mind, I'm not going to find the music, or the killer.*

A deep breath.

And Tom's right: I can't give up, not on Mickey and not on Mr. Joplin. Not even on JJ's father, God help me. I've got to treat these visits as real unless I see something that proves *they're hallucinations.*

Alan returned his attention to the conversation on the other side of the console.

"…pleased to inform you, should I find one."

"I'd be powerful 'bliged, Mr. Taylor. The club'll prob'ly hold a letter for me." Alan heard Angeline's footsteps crossing the floor and a burst of noise from the street as she opened the door.

"Oh! I beg your pardon, Sir! I didn't hear you come into my shop." The speaker, a well-dressed man in his early forties, looked like a prosperous businessman, despite the dusting of sawdust on his legs and chest.

"Quite all right, Mr. Taylor. You appeared to be occupied, and I needed the chance to sit for a moment." Alan decided to take a chance. "I was at the Maple Leaf Club when the disgraceful incident with their piano took place."

Taylor nodded. "Disgraceful, indeed, Sir. A real shame to treat a fine instrument that way." He hesitated, then went on. "I know some would say such ill behavior is natural to the black race, but accidents will happen, Sir. Even in the best homes and churches. If my pianos could speak, they could tell you stories! Fortunately, I don't believe the damage was mortal. I shall, I am quite certain, be able to restore it, if not to its full capacity, good enough for common entertainment."

"Really? I would have thought it was beyond help."

"You are interested? Come, come." Taylor led Alan out the back door and across the covered yard, talking non-stop as he went. "Luckily, very little of the…liquid reached the soundboard. I shall have to refinish the cabinet to eliminate the…odor, and of course I shall have to detune it while the action dries. Some strings will no doubt need to be replaced, and of course more than a few of the hammers will need to be refelted…" He stopped in front of the piano Angeline had pillaged.

Alan caught up. "But the broken glass?"

"Primarily large pieces. Most fortunate. It will take several cleanings to remove all of the shards, of course, but it can be done. It will be done."

"Lucky for Mr. Williams."

"Indeed, indeed." Taylor's gaze sharpened for a moment. "His wallet may not agree. But even with the cost of renting an instrument while I work on this one, he'll still be better off than if he had to replace it." He turned back to the piano.

Alan leaned into the cabinet, holding his breath—one whiff made it fully clear that this was the piano he had seen at the

Maple Leaf Club. To cover his interest, he asked "You're still disassembling it, then?"

Which strings…Ah, both of the A-flat 1 strings. There are easier ones to reach, so she must have wanted that note in particular…

"Indeed, Sir. It arrived just today, and I've been working on it between customers. I shall leave the cabinet here to air while I clean and repair the action indoors. Then I shall refinish the wood, and be done." He frowned. "Though I confess, I don't recall removing the lower panel. A haunted piano? I daresay Mr. Williams would not appreciate that."

Alan straightened and laughed. "Haunted? An amusing idea, but unlikely. Perhaps the young woman who just left…?"

"Mrs. Blackstone? Perhaps, perhaps. Though why? She was looking for a whippen. Not something she would have needed to remove the panel to see."

Alan forced a smile. "Maybe she was doing you a favor to thank you for allowing her to look for used parts."

Taylor looked dubious, but shrugged. "It could be. But…" He collected himself and peered closely at Alan. "No matter. But you, Sir—are you all right? You seem disturbed."

"Just a passing thought." Alan waved a hand dismissively, and started walking toward the shop, drawing Taylor with him. "I am curious. Mrs., ah, Blackstone, you said? She's a pianist? At a church, perhaps?"

"Nothing so elevated, I fear. She is, I am given to understand, a quite good performer of the lower sort, though I haven't heard her myself, of course. She plays at the Black 400 Club—you know of it? Of course you do, you said you were at the Maple Leaf Club two nights ago."

Alan nodded. "An unusual profession for a woman."

Taylor's expression combined sympathy and disdain. "I quite agree, Sir. How her husband can permit it—even let her appear in such places unaccompanied and using her maiden name—I shall never understand. But such is the modern age, I fear. Even my own wife wishes to claim the vote."

Alan hid a smile as he entertained a mental image of Miriam's likely reaction to Taylor's statement. "I'm glad the Maple Leaf Club's piano is in such good hands and I look forward to hearing it once you're finished with your work."

He shook hands and exited through the front door of the shop before Mr. Taylor could think to ask why he was there. He glanced around. *Just a couple of blocks from the hotel. Up Ohio, past the grocery where Fitter's will be. Convenient.*

• ● ● ● •

Alan closed the hotel room door behind himself, not at all tempted to slam it. "Food for thought," he informed the empty space. He glanced at his watch. "But that can wait." He set the alarm for forty-five minutes and stretched out on the bed.

• ● ● ● •

Tom thought Blackstone was making no effort to conceal his contempt for the two kids and the old woman who'd come to his office to weasel information from him. The city editor leaned forward in his desk chair to focus on his daughter.

"'Mae, I already told you this isn't a game. You're getting into dangerous waters." He waved an arm to include all his visitors in his comments. "The three of you—you need to stay out of the way of the police. Don't screw up their work and don't get yourselves into trouble. Let the cops do what they've got to do." He turned to Elvira. "I'd hoped you might have a little more sense than these kids, for Christ's sake."

Elvira sat upright. "Mr. Blackstone, this's 'bout my child. You don' want *your* child gettin' hurt, I knows. But *my* child already get hurt, hurt real bad, a lotta years ago. Man hit him with a baseball bat. My Jack, he think he fin' the man what hurt him, that 'Mr. Raney'. An' now he gotta live in the house for dangerous peoples. A day don't pass, I don't cry for him at least one time. Mr. Alan, he think if he know who 'Mr. Raney' really be, he might could get Jack outa there and back home with me. You say you wants me to go home and let the p'leece, who never did nothin' for my boy, 'do what they gotta do?' No, sir, I'm sorry. I thinks you oughta be 'shamed a yourself, talkin' to me like that."

Tom clenched his teeth, then his fists. "I'm sorry, Sir," he said, speaking slowly, in a level tone.

He may be able to ignore Granny and his own daughter, but Alan needs that name, and I'm not going to let Blackstone ignore me.

He stared hard into the editor's eyes. "We know we aren't playing some kind of silly little game. And if it was just the murder, I might agree with you about letting the cops do their thing. But the music changes everything. The police don't care about the music at all. Even if they find it, you know it's just gonna disappear into some evidence room and never be seen again."

He took a deep breath, then went on, a little faster. "I can't believe you don't realize how awful it'd be if a bunch of compositions by Scott Joplin got destroyed or lost, so no one ever gets to play them or hear them. And my grandfather's been studying Joplin and his music for more than sixty years. He's eighty years old, he's got cancer, he's in pain, he knows he's not going to be around a whole lot longer…"

Tom's hand flew to his mouth as he tried to stifle a whooping cry. Saramae set a hand on his shoulder; Elvira shot a look of pure malice at Blackstone. The boy swallowed hard, forced himself to go on. "We're not asking you for anything unreasonable, or that could get you in trouble. We think there was a story in your newspaper some years back that could give us a real lead in finding that music. All we want is for you to find that story for us."

Blackstone looked as if he didn't know whether to be angry or sympathetic. "But, how does—?" He interrupted himself, shook his head, started over. "You just want a story from the paper? That's all?"

"If that doesn't have what we need, maybe we'll need you to dig deeper. Reporter's notes or something. But we hope the story will be enough."

"All right, all right. Give me the information. Soon as I have a chance I'll look into it and get back to you."

"Mr. Blackstone, I'm sorry. We need the information now. It really shouldn't take long. We can give you dates and some names that'd be in the story."

Saramae leaned across the desk. "Daddy, what you doin' stonewallin' us? Ain't no big deal, an' it ain't like you gotta find anything yo'self. Petey, down in the morgue, he a sweetheart. Iff'n I ast him nice, he find that story right quick. An' I bet you went more'n a li'l outside the lines one time or another, gettin' a story. This ain't even outside the lines, none."

Weird, Tom thought. *Every time she starts talking to her father, she starts sounding more like JJ than JJ does.*

While his daughter was talking, Blackstone stiffened, his eyes bulged, and he half rose, only to settle back with a sigh when she finished. "We're going to have words about your attitude, young lady. But if it'll get you out of my office…" He turned to Tom with an exaggerated shark-like grin. "Make with the details."

Tom counted them off on his fingers. "Big Jack Jackson, ten years ago in August, slugged somebody in a bar, sent to the county house." He turned to Elvira. "Is there anything else?"

"My boy tho't the man's name were Raney, but that prob'ly not right. That be enough?"

Blackstone picked up the phone, dialed a number. "Yeah, Petey. Blackstone here. I need a story from ten years ago last month, about a bar fight involving Big Jack Jackson—and I need it on the double."

An uncomfortably silent eight minutes later, Blackstone's secretary walked in, handed her boss a sheet of paper, and walked back out. The city editor scanned the paper, then without a word, passed it to Tom. The boy read the report aloud: "Last night saw some unfortunate activity at Rudy's Roadhouse on Route Fifty. A man from Kansas City was beaten senseless by 'Big Jack' Jackson of Sedalia. The victim of the unprovoked attack was identified as Jarvis Nowlin, a well-known trad-jazz enthusiast and sometime critic. According to witnesses, Jackson shouted 'You son of a bitch' and began punching Nowlin. Nowlin was treated at Bothwell Hospital and released the next morning.

Jackson is being held without bail pending evaluation of his mental stability."

Elvira began to cry, and Saramae leapt up to hug her.

Tom stood, extended a hand to Blackstone. "Thank you, Sir," he said. "I really appreciate your help. I think this is going to help a lot."

The walk back to Elvira's house passed in silence, but Tom's mind was bubbling with activity.

Alan set me up for that to see if I really can help him. And okay—I did it. Got what we needed. But he's gotta open up some. He made everyone tell their secrets and all, he has to do the same. Tell them all about his time-traveling. If he doesn't volunteer, I'm gonna have to push him.

Tom barely let the group seat themselves in Elvira's living room before he passed the newspaper story to Alan. JJ leaned over the old man's shoulder to read the account. As Alan finished, he held up the paper like an athletic trophy.

"Jarvis Nowlin! From Kansas City, a jazz enthusiast! Way to go, the three of you. This is a real breakthrough."

"It was Tom," said Saramae. "Daddy shot down Miz Elvira and me, but Tom told him just exactly right. You shoulda heard the way he talked to Daddy. We had this in our hands practically before Tom was done."

Tom blushed, but said, "You helped a lot, threatening to go to Petey yourself."

Saramae shook her head. "That wasn't much. He wasn't even listenin' to me or Granny. You got him started, I just pushed him a little."

"Teamwork," said Alan with a nod. "And a good thing, 'cause I struck out at the courthouse. By the time I'd filed the request they said I needed, and had it reviewed by the proper authorities, that music would be *two* hundred years old. But Jarvis Nowlin, K.C.? I think we're ready for another trip down Route Fifty. JJ, I think you better come along on this job. We don't know whose particular skills we might need."

JJ chortled. "Tha's more like it! We gonna be back 'fore I gotta go t' work? If not, best I call in sick."

Alan glanced at his watch. "I can't imagine we wouldn't be back by midnight."

"Okay, then. Lemme get some stuff we might be needin'." He disappeared down the hall, then returned less than five minutes later. "All set. Let's roll!"

Tom couldn't miss the look of regard Alan turned on him. *But he's still got to tell them about the time-traveling.*

• • ● • •

"Shotgun!" Tom called as he grabbed the door handle.

Alan shook his head, tapped Tom's shoulder and jerked a thumb toward the rear of the car. "I want you behind me this time. Saramae! Front seat, please. I don't want you distracting the boys."

"You not worried 'bout me distracting you?"

"Distracting the driver? You're brighter than that."

Saramae snickered and got into the front seat while JJ settled into the seat behind her.

Tom hadn't moved. When Alan started around the car, Tom put a hand on his arm. "Alan, can we talk?"

"Now?"

"It won't take long, and this is the best time to do it."

Alan took in the expression on Tom's face. Worried, almost fearful, but determined. "Okay, Thomas. Go ahead."

"I've been thinking…we need to tell them about your memory and the time-traveling. Not knowing what's going on, that's not fair, especially after everything they've told us. And there's another thing. You were thinking I was biting off too much to chew when I said I'd be your memory, right? Maybe they can help with that, too. Help me remember everything you learn in 1899, help us both put it all together. Okay?"

For a moment, Alan couldn't answer; then he gave Tom a hug. "Thank you, Thomas. I wanted to tell them, but I was afraid you were going to think I didn't trust *you* to help me. Couldn't figure out how to bring it up, make sure you understood. But you were one step ahead of me the whole time." He gave the boy another squeeze. "There's something else, too."

"What's that?"

"Saramae's family stories. That's really why I want her up front, so I can quiz her, get her to remember more. Maybe she knows something that'll prove whether or not I'm really going back in time. That's a question I've got to answer."

"Even if the answer is that you're hallucinating?"

"Even if. Knowing would mean I could get help. Probably more drugs, but that's inevitable at this point anyway." Alan gave Tom one more hug, then looked theatrically at his watch. "Guess we better stop holding up the show here. Like JJ said, let's roll!"

When Tom and Alan opened their doors, JJ was leaning forward between the front seats, talking to Saramae. The conversation cut off abruptly. Tom glared at JJ and considered asking him to slide over, but changed his mind. It felt too awkward, too much like a junior high school kid trying to sit behind the prettiest girl in class so he could look at her while pretending to pay attention to the teacher.

Everyone was silent until they reached the freeway, then Saramae said "Can we have some travelin' music?"

JJ laughed. "Somethin' we kin all go for? Not likely!"

Alan headed off the developing argument. "I'd rather we talk. We've got some planning to do, but there's something else I need to tell you first…" More musing out loud than talking. "Looking at the three of you takes me back, way back. My wife and I were not any older than you when we set out from New Jersey in a beater, and drove all the way across the country to Los Angeles—Venice, specifically—and visited Brun Campbell."

"Brun Who?" JJ and Saramae pulled off a spontaneous baritone-soprano duet.

"Brun *Campbell.* Well, fair enough—I guess you wouldn't know who he was if you're not deep into ragtime. He was an old man then, only sixty-seven, but a half-century of hard living had pretty well used him up. In 1899, he rode a freight car to

Sedalia to get Scott Joplin to give him ragtime piano lessons. Then he played ragtime for seven, eight years in low joints all around the Midwest. When ragtime faded out, he got married and worked as a barber.

"In the 1920s, he moved his family and his shop to California. But when ragtime started coming back in the forties, Brun was right up front and center. I met him in Sedalia in 1951 when they had a ceremony to honor Scott Joplin. Before I left, he gave *me* a piano lesson, imagine that. After the ceremony, I went back home, but I ran right away again, this time to California, to get more lessons from Brun. Your grandmother came with me on that trip, Tom. We practically starved all the way out, figured when we got there, Brun would feed us like royalty.

"But that poor old guy had less money than we did—and even worse, since ragtime was the devil's music, no hell-spawned ragtime pianist was ever gonna set foot in Mrs. Campbell's home. We played in Brun's garage or his barber shop."

"Gettin' married's bad business. Serious bad business." JJ nudged Saramae's arm.

She snickered. "Especially for the woman."

Despite himself, Alan chuckled. "Depends on the woman. And the man, for that matter. But don't distract me. That trip formed me for life. Brun made sure I knew he was 'learning me how to play ragtime,' especially 'Maple Leaf Rag.' Oh, he was a character. He had no trouble telling people straight-out he was the best ragtime player in existence, both in 1900 and 1945."

"Well, maybe he was," said Saramae. "He did 'learn' you, right? And aren't *you* the best player of *your* time?"

"Damn right he is," Tom chirped.

Alan tried to wave away the complimentary flood. "We're in dangerous territory," he said. "Am I really the best? Maybe on some days, yes, but only on some days. Listening to John Arpin used to make me feel very modest. Same for Trebor Tichenor. All that's important is to be out there at a piano, playing your best for the people who pay good money to sit and listen."

As if for punctuation, Alan pushed the open buttons for his window and Tom's. As the early fall wind whistled through the car, Tom stiffened.

I can't let him get away without telling them.

He cupped a hand to his mouth, and shouted, "Shut those effin' windows, Alan!"

Alan shot the boy a curious look in the rearview mirror. He'd never heard anything out of Tom remotely resembling that remark, either in content or manner.

"Shut the windows," Tom repeated. "Can't hear anything over the wind. And if you keep going on like this, we'll be in Kansas City before you ever get to the point. Like you said, they gotta know. Rip the Band-Aid off and just say it."

Alan sighed and shut the windows, but still couldn't find the right words.

Tom marshaled his courage. "What my grandfather's trying to tell you is he's got trouble with his memory because of the chemo. It's not like he's got Alzheimer's or anything; he's still sharp as a tack. But he can't always remember stuff. So I told him I'd be his memory—but I think this is a time where four heads are better'n two."

The boy took a deep breath.

Fill your lungs before you jump into the deep end of the pool.

"And there's something else, something I know just a little about, and I think maybe all of us need to know a lot more about. Since we've been in Sedalia, Alan's been time-traveling. Going back to 1899, talking to Scott Joplin…"

He ground to a halt at the expressions on JJ's and Saramae's faces. The girl snickered, but cut it off when Tom glared at her. He turned back to his grandfather. "Start at the beginning, Alan. How you do the time-travel, who you've been talking to, all of it."

Alan nodded. "I wish I knew how I did it. Tom can tell you later how he thinks it might work, but since he's never time-traveled—"

"I've been trying, every chance I get."

Alan ignored Tom's interruption. "There's no way to know if he's right. The first time I did it, it just happened. Late on the first day we were here—actually, early in the morning—I was concentrating on a little musical theme Joplin had written on a card from the Maple Leaf Club, and all of a sudden, I found myself *there*...in 1899. Talking to Joplin. It lasted a couple of hours, and then suddenly I was back in the present. It was a couple of hours later here too—Tom had woken up and gone looking for me—but I had no idea how I got back.

"When I tried to do it again, I couldn't, but it worked when I stopped trying to go to the exact same time. I think I failed because I had already been there. I guess you can't be in the same place twice. But the thing is, if I fix on a particular time and place while I study the musical theme, that's where and when in the past I find myself."

As Alan paused to consider his next comment, a low whistle came from the backseat. "Jeez, man," JJ half-whispered. "Now, we're supposed to be takin' that serious, right? That's what you're sayin'?"

"Yes, JJ, that *is* what I'm sayin'. So far I've engineered five trips to 1899, and I've met some very interesting people. But I'm not asking you to believe I've really, actually, been traveling in time and space. Maybe I have been—it sure does feel like I have. But like it or not, I know I'm sick, got a very serious disease, and I can't be sure that either the illness or the awful treatment isn't doing weird things to my mind. Chemo does have mental effects—Tom said it: my memory's in the toilet. And I'm a lot more irritable than I've ever been. I've got tingling and numbness in my hands and feet—it's called neuropathy. The way the doctors explained it, those are all effects of damage to my nerve cells by the chemo. So put all that together with the fact that I've been studying ragtime and Joplin for more than sixty years, and maybe my mind and my imagination are playing tricks with me. Maybe Tom couldn't find me that first trip because I was wandering around Sedalia with my brain just plain shut down. Maybe easier to swallow than time-travel. But I don't

think that's what happened. The trips are just too detailed and consistent for me to believe I'm making it up…but of course I *would* think that, wouldn't I?"

Silence hung in the car like a heavy woolen blanket.

"And here's the kicker," Alan continued. "I've made five trips back so far, and on every one, I've seen people and found out stuff that seem to be connected to Mickey and the music in the duffel bag. Saramae, the stories about your triple-great-grandfather Lathan could be very important. I think I saw him on one of my trips. What you know could prove whether I'm really going to 1899."

"Huh. But I told you about him first, before he showed up in your dream, or whatever. Don't mean nothing."

"Right. But I think I saw his wife, too. You've never said anything about her. What can you tell me about her? Her name, whether she grew up in Sedalia, when they married. Anything like that?"

"I get it. Lemme see. Daddy never told me anything about when Triple-great came to Sedalia, but I kinda got the idea it was after he was grown up. I wanna say his wife and son, Great-great Will, were with him then, but I don't remember why I think so. And I don't know the wife's name. Pretty sure Daddy never said."

"Damn," Alan muttered, then quickly added, "sorry. That would have been really useful. Anything else you can remember about Lathan?"

"Well, I know Triple-great Lathan worked for one of the black newspapers, *The Sedalia Times*. Daddy's real proud about that, even though he wasn't a reporter or an editor. He did something mechanical with the press, I know that. But accordin' to Daddy, he was the first Blackstone to work in the news business, and all the sons and grandsons are following him." She looked up at the car's ceiling and closed her eyes. "Only one other thing I can think of. Daddy said Great-great Will used to tell him Lathan was the least musical man he ever knew. He liked to listen to music just fine, but couldn't sing or play a note. Great-great Will

say, 'It prove white folks who say all blacks got nat'ral rhythm is jus' as wrong as the ones who say all blacks be lazy and stupid.'"

Alan and the boys laughed, then Tom said "Sounds like your great-great grandfather was a pretty sharp guy. Way ahead of his time, y'know?"

"Oh, yeah! I wish I knew more about him. Daddy was maybe seven or eight when he died. Wonder what he thought about the Panthers, and the civil rights movement, and all."

"Prob'ly thought they was a buncha pussies," JJ said.

"He does sound like a smart man," Alan added, "Maybe we can come back to him later?"

Saramae looked embarrassed. "Sorry. Was any of that useful?"

"I don't know. Maybe." Alan was silent for a few seconds, but went on before anyone could jump in. "It doesn't contradict anything I think I learned in 1899, but it also doesn't seem to support anything I couldn't have already known." He glanced to his right and into the rearview mirror. "Saramae, JJ, before I catch you up on the details, tell me what you're thinking about all this."

"Not me, no way," JJ said. "Granny give me what-for, if I say what I think 'bout time-travel."

Tom punched him in the shoulder. "Since she's not here, I'll do it for her."

"Hey!"

"Knock it off, you two. Tom, it's probably a good thing he's skeptical. It won't hurt to have somebody taking my story with a big grain of salt. What about you, Saramae? You agree with JJ?"

Before Saramae could answer, Alan's phone rang. He fumbled it out of his pocket without taking his eyes off the road and passed it over his shoulder to Tom. "Don't answer. Just tell me who it is."

Tom flipped it open. "Caller ID says 'Sedalia PD.' Probably our pal, Detective Parks."

"Yeah. Thought it might be." Alan waved his hand— 'gimme'—and put the phone back in his pocket. "He can leave a message. I'll call him back later. Saramae, what do you think? Am I crazy?"

"Not gonna make up my mind yet. Sure, you're probably nuts, but maybe not. And if it's real, well, that'd be epic."

"Thank you. I think. As I said, I don't believe I'm nuts. The trips are just too detailed and consistent for me to see how I'd be making it up. But whatever it really is, time-travel or mind tricks, I'm going to keep doing it, and see what I can come up with that might click into place and help us find the killer and thief. I'd like you to get yourself thinking about your long-ago family. If anything I say rings a bell, tell me. And when we get back to Sedalia, we're going to have to talk some turkey to your Daddy. I hope you're not sorry you've signed on with us."

"Hell, no! I might be a little scared here and there, but not sorry, not even a teensy bit. Wasn't for you guys, I'd be half-asleep in Social Studies class right now."

Alan laughed. "We're better than Social Studies? High praise!" He thought for a few seconds. "Thomas, you've heard the first part of this already, but these two should hear the whole thing. Like I said, the first time I went to the Maple Leaf Club in 1899, Joplin was just finishing the piece of music I had been studying. I talked to him and a few of his friends, including Otis Saunders, before I came back to the present. Saunders, Saramae—the man you mentioned before who was the 'big troublemaker.' He did have a long dispute with Joplin over who wrote which parts of 'Maple Leaf Rag', but until I started to time-travel, I'd never heard that anything went past angry words. But now I have to wonder if there was more going on in 1899 than historians ever got hold of."

"Otis...Saunders?" Saramae sounded puzzled. "That does sound kinda familiar, maybe. So he was at the club hanging out, even though he was fightin' with Scott Joplin about 'Maple Leaf Rag'? Huh!"

"Nobody can argue all the time." Alan changed lanes to pass a slow truck and glanced at the dash clock. "I want to finish this before we get to K.C., so I'll stick with the important stuff."

"You'll tell us more later?" Saramae asked. "I wanna hear everything, especially if it's about my family."

"Fair enough. But yes, later." Alan gathered his thoughts again. "When I got to the club on my third trip, I found out there'd been a fight the night before, and during the fight, the piano had been damaged, maybe destroyed. That's also when I heard Mr. Joplin and Otis Saunders arguing. Well, actually, I didn't *hear* the argument, but I saw it, and from something Mr. Joplin said later, it could have been about 'Maple Leaf.' But it might also have been about the fight in the club. The story about what happened to the piano sounded suspicious, so I made another trip back, to see the fight happen."

"Hang on," JJ interrupted. "I'm confused. You go back to the night before the one you went back to in the first place?"

Alan had to think about that for a few seconds. "I went back to an afternoon in 1899, returned to the present, and then made another trip, to the night before the afternoon."

"My head hurt."

"Yours isn't the only one. Mr. Joplin's did too. Never mind, later for that. I think the fight was planned, and I'm not sure the piano was supposed to be the intended victim. The fight may have been an attempt to hurt Mr. Joplin. That's a lot of speculation, I know. But I saw a couple, a man and a woman, acting suspiciously. I tried to follow them, but couldn't keep up; I did get their name, though. According to Otis Saunders, it's Nowlin."

"Nowlin! Like the guy who bashed m' old man!"

"And like the old bitch in Kansas City that had the duffel bag!"

"Thomas! Better not let your grandmother hear you use language like that. But the most interesting thing is what I learned on my last trip. Nowlin is, or rather was, her maiden name. Her husband was Lathan Blackstone."

"What?!" three voices chorused.

"According to my source, Mrs. Blackstone used her maiden name while working as a pianist at a number of establishments polite gentlemen don't speak of."

"He mean ho' houses, Girl."

"Well, duh! Shut up, JJ. She played ragtime, Mr. Chandler?"

"At that time and place, most likely."

"So she knew Saunders. Why'd he tell you her husband was a Nowlin?"

"An excellent question. Even more interesting, what Otis said was that her husband was Mr. Nowlin, but that he had never met *her*. Interesting, isn't it?"

"Whoa, yeah!"

"Assumin'," JJ added, "that you're not crazy."

"Thank you, Captain Obvious," Tom said with a sneer. "Can we pretend my grandfather is at least as sane as you are?" Without waiting for an answer, he went on, "Did you pick up anything else?"

"Two more things. The 1899 Nowlin's first name is Angeline. And she stole both of the A-flat 1 strings from the Maple Leaf Club piano. She seemed to be after those strings in particular. Assuming, as Mr. Jackson would say, that I'm not crazy."

There was a moment of silence, then Tom carefully asked "Are you suggesting that Mickey was strangled with *Scott Joplin's piano string?*"

"Sounds pretty crazy, Thomas, and the piano didn't actually belong to him, but you could look at it that way. Remember how corroded the wire is? Being splashed with beer and piss, then sitting around for a century or so, could have done that." Alan held up a hand to prevent Tom from interrupting. "I know, it wouldn't necessarily take that long or need anything more than being touched by bare hands to corrode that much. But it's certainly not impossible. Maybe JJ's right, and this is all just my subconscious telling me there's more of a connection between Mickey and the not-so-charming Ms. A. Nowlin in K.C. than just the duffel bag. But if we're going to consider the possibility that I really have visited 1899, then there are two things we should do."

"Only two?" Saramae asked.

"Two that we weren't already doing."

"Like what?"

"First, while we're looking for anything on Jarvis Nowlin, let's keep an eye open for stuff about Angeline too."

"An' what else?"

"Remember that the killer might have more piano strings. I'd hate for any of us to wind up with one wrapped around his or her throat—even if it is a historical artifact."

As Alan half-turned to give Saramae what he hoped was a reassuring smile, he saw JJ writing in his notebook again. He came close to asking what the boy had been writing, but caught himself up, and locked his jaw.

"None of my business, really," he silently admonished himself.

Chapter Thirteen

At Lee's Summit, Alan turned off Route 50 onto 476, then headed west on I-70. Coming up on three-thirty, traffic was building toward rush hour.

"You know how late the museum's open?" JJ called from the backseat. "We gonna have long enough to do our thing?"

"No trouble," said Alan. "It's open till six, and with four of us splitting up the research, it should be a piece of cake. But we need to get organized. Much as I hate to say it, it's not the greatest museum in the world. You could see the whole thing in an hour and a half, two hours at the most. There're a lot of neon signs, some of the exhibits aren't working, and they don't have much in the way of historical information. But that can work to our advantage; it won't take long to go through what they *have* got. Either we'll find something or we won't. JJ, you and I can look for anything about Jarvis Nowlin. Tom, you get your hands on a phone book; check for our Mr. Nowlin and nasty Ms. Nowlin. And Saramae—"

"I want to see if I can find anything about your Angeline Nowlin in 1899. Or is it Angeline Blackstone? I oughta be the one to find out if she's my triple-great granny."

"Good. A personal motivation won't hurt at all. Try both names. Can't hurt."

They got off the highway at the Paseo exit, headed east, and lucked into a space at 18th and Vine, right in front of the museum's gift shop. "Good parking space, good omen," Alan said. "Okay. We ready?"

JJ snapped off a slick salute. "Yes suh, Mr. General Alan, suh! Let's go."

• ● ● ● •

Tom was back in the neon-studded lobby in less than ten minutes. He killed three-quarters of an hour wandering around the perimeter of the room, trying to guess what had become of the businesses where the signs had originally hung. When Alan and JJ appeared, Tom could tell by their expressions they'd been successful.

"So?" he asked as they approached.

"Let's wait for Saramae," Alan said. "Go through everything once, then head out.

"While we're waiting," said Tom. "That call from Detective Parks—you want to return it?"

Alan grinned. "In a word, no. Let's catch up with him after we get back to Sedalia. Let him stew a little."

"You like livin' dangerously." There was respect in JJ's tone.

"Know what?" Alan punched the boy's arm lightly. "I think you're right."

Ten minutes later, Saramae danced into the room. "Well, lookie her." JJ snickered. "Betcha she thinks she found somethin' sweet."

Alan shepherded the little group to a spot beneath colorful signs for the Top Hat Grill and The Pink Door. "Okay," he said. "JJ and I found a little something, probably not of much practical use. Jarvis Nowlin, our 'sometime critic' wrote an article for the museum on Ella Fitzgerald, about six years ago, and another one on Louis Armstrong a year later. He seems to know what he's talking about. Not that that'll help us a whole lot. Tom, what did you find?"

The boy waved a small slip of paper. "Something more useful. Jarvis Nowlin's phone number and address. And a phone number for 'A. Nowlin'. Same address we met the old you-know-what at. But no first name."

"Too bad," Alan murmured. "But finding Jarvis' information—excellent." He turned to Saramae. "Okay now, let's hear from you."

"'Fore you piss your pants," said JJ.

"Piss on *you*, wiseass." The girl waved a sheet of paper at Alan. "I went on back and found a guy I could talk my way around pretty good. He took me back to somethin' he called a 'resource room'—I call it a junk room, because all it's got is two lousy boxes of stuff, mostly letters and things like that. And lookie what I found."

She pushed the sheet of paper into Alan's hand. The old man's eyes bugged. "If you hadn't told us about that Brun guy, I mighta just turned it over and never noticed it's about my triple-great gran. Miz Angeline, I mean."

Alan scanned the paper, read aloud. "'A Woman Pianist in the Sporting Houses. By Brun Campbell. I only ever knew of one woman who played piano in the sporting houses in Kansas City, St. Louis, and other places in the Midwest. Her name was Angeline, and she used her maiden name, Noland. She came from a very well-off family in St. Louis, and got piano lessons starting when she was four years old. But she liked a good time and had a real liking for the bottle, and she didn't much care for playing in opera houses and tent shows.

"'Angeline was married to a guy named Blackstone, and if you ever wanted to meet a man who did not have a musical note in his body, that was him. Yes! He was very mechanical, though. There was trouble because Angeline liked the men as much as she liked playing ragtime and having a few drinks, and while she was in Sedalia one time, she took up with Otis Saunders, who was Scott Joplin's best pal who helped him with the third theme in 'Maple Leaf Rag.' Well, Angeline left her husband and their kids, and took off from Sedalia and went to Wichita. Saunders followed her there, and after that they went to Arkansas City, Kansas (my old home town), Oklahoma City, and El Reno, Oklahoma. Then they went back to Sedalia, but it got to be all over between them, and they went their own ways on the ragtime circuit…' Saramae, you just might've hit the jackpot."

The girl clapped her hands. "Maybe you ain't crazy after all." She shot JJ a withering look.

"Maybe, maybe not," said Alan. "To be honest, I can't swear I've never seen this article before, in all my years of research. Or maybe Brun told me about it when I was out in California in 1951. Also, it looks like Angeline's maiden name was N-o-l-a-n-d, not N-o-w-l-i-n, so maybe Ms. Nowlin really doesn't have anything to do with all this. I might've misheard what Otis Saunders said, back in 1899."

"But the names are awfully similar," said Tom. "And that duffel bag came to light in her house."

Alan shrugged and gestured toward the door. "We'll just have to keep our eyes open. Let's get on our way. We've got a lot of places to go to. How about we start with Maggione's shop? Korotkin said he was killed with a music stand, and I want to know if it was one of the ones he got along with the duffel bag."

● ● ● ● ●

The group stared through the front window of Maggione's shop. Three strips of yellow police tape covered the entrance.

"I thought it would look different," Tom said, half to himself. "The way Korotkin was talking, it should look like a Halloween haunted house."

Alan laughed. "A really tacky one. Fake blood dripping down the inside of the windows and flowing under the door, right? He's a bit excitable, our Mr. Korotkin."

Tom nodded, and put his nose against the window. "Wonder what a ghost-hunter might find in there," he mused. After a moment, he brought his hands up beside his head to block the reflection from the evening sun. "Not that pile of junk he got with the duffel bag, anyway."

"You sure?"

The boy moved a couple of steps closer to the door. "No, there it is. Dresser was in the way. I see the pole lamp, anyway. JJ, you're taller 'n I am. Take a look, okay?"

JJ plastered himself to the window. "What'm I lookin' fer?"

"Halfway back on the right. See that ugly lamp with the green shades?"

"Huh. Yeah, got it. Piece o' crap."

"You see any music stands near it?"

"Jus' one. Wood thing carved into a whozits. Treble clef."

"There oughta be another one, a bass clef."

"If it be there, it gotta be lyin' down. Or maybe the cops took it away if that's what whoever it were use to bash his head in. Too bad he di'n' use the lamp."

"Goon," Saramae said. "What difference does it make what he used? The guy's dead."

"Esthetics," Alan answered. "The lamp is crap from the seventies. Destroying it would make the world a measurably more beautiful place." He looked at JJ. "You've got good taste, Mr. Jackson." He clapped his hands. "Let's go pay Ms. Nowlin a visit."

"Huh?" Saramae interrupted. "I thought we were going to check out Jarvis."

"There's so much garbage in there the killer could have picked from. Why would he go out of his way to use something from her house unless he was trying to send some kind of message? So let's go take a look and see what we can see. Besides, her house isn't that far out of the way from here to Jarvis' place."

• • ● • •

Alan parked and slid down in his seat. At Saramae's questioning look, he said, "I don't want her to spot us hanging around."

From his seat behind Saramae, JJ called, "So what're we lookin' for?"

"Anything that looks out of place."

"Outa place where? Saramae 'n' me ain't been here before, y'know."

"Oh, right." Alan pointed across the street and up a couple of doors. "The little brown one with the gray trim."

A derisive chuckle. "How you esspec' me to see anythin' from back here?" A sigh. "Now, look, Alan—she don' know me from nobody."

JJ got out of the car, quietly eased the door shut, and crossed the street. He ambled up the block as though he knew where he was going, and wasn't in any hurry to get there. Just past the Nowlin house, he stopped and leaned against a tree. He pulled a pencil out of his breast pocket, mimed lighting it as though it was a cigarette, and pretended to smoke it, gazing vaguely back the way he had come. After several minutes, he continued up the street and around the corner.

Saramae had snickered when JJ lit his "cigarette." "He pulled that trick in math class one time before he dropped out," she explained. "Got it backward and poked himself in the tongue. Said he tasted lead for a week."

A few minutes later, JJ strolled up the street from behind the car, and tapped on Tom's window. "Slide over," he said when Tom rolled it down, then settled behind Alan and shut the door. "Place look quiet. On'y one person home, I think. Least there on'y one light. Room in back, maybe a bedroom."

"If we come back, say, in the middle of the night, can you get us in there to look around?"

"Like at Mickey's? The whole herd of you elephants? Real bad idea. Jus' me? Sure, no problem. 'Less she gotta 'larm, be a snap."

"Hmm." Alan thought for a minute. "You'll know what to look for?"

"'Sides Mickey's bag? Old piano strings. Old music. Anythin' show she in Sedalia when Mickey was kilt, or her nephew were. Like that, right?"

"You got it."

Alan was about to start the car when the front door of the Nowlin house opened. "Whoops! Hang on."

Ms. Nowlin locked her front door and, despite heavy use of her cane, managed to march to a dilapidated Ford parked in front of the house. Her hair was pulled back, and she had traded her shapeless dress for an old, but well-kept suit.

Tom leaned forward between the seats to see what was happening, and whistled. "Cleans up impressively, doesn't she? Alan, she's not dressed up like that to go down to the corner store. She's going all out to impress someone."

"Right. Let's hope she's not just meeting her boyfriend. JJ, you stay here while we follow her. When we're out of sight, get inside, look around, and get out. Should be safe enough: she's got a partly enclosed porch, and the houses aren't one right on top of the next. We'll come back for you as soon as we can."

JJ reached for the door handle, but stopped when Tom put a hand on his arm.

"Just a sec." Tom pulled out his phone and quickly set it to vibrate. "Not gonna unlock it, but at least we can call you if something comes up. If it vibrates, slide the green phone icon to answer it, okay?"

"Coulda figgered that out myself."

"Now you don't have to." Tom bit back the urge to tell JJ to be careful with the phone. "Go, man. Move it, before we lose her."

Alan kept a careful half-block behind Ms. Nowlin. After the first turn, Saramae looked over her shoulder. "Hey, Tom, gimme your granddaddy's number, in case we gotta split up."

"Two oh six," Tom and Alan said in stereo before Alan laughed and let Tom finish.

● ● ● ● ●

A man in his mid-forties, closer to three hundred pounds than to two, wearing a garish red shirt, was guarding the parking space closest to the front door of Niecie's Restaurant when Ms. Nowlin pulled up in front. He waved her into the space and offered an arm to help her out of her car as Alan cruised past on the far side of the street.

Saramae and Tom twisted in their seats and saw the old woman give her parking guardian a peck on the cheek before the mismatched couple moved to join a group of thirteen, seven men, five women, and a young girl, standing by the door to the restaurant. They clearly were waiting for her arrival.

"Pull over so I can get out!" Saramae said. "Looks like a family dinner with every damn Nowlin in creation."

Alan pulled a quick left onto Sixty-fifth, and stopped in a no-parking zone. "What are you thinking?"

"I'm gonna go in there and tip an ear at 'em. If Jarvis is part of that mob, I can give you the heads-up and you can go hit his place like JJ is doin' to hers. And maybe I'll hear somethin' else we can use. 'One never knows,' right?"

"Are you crazy?" Tom exclaimed.

"Heck, no. It's a great idea, even if I gotta say it myself. None of them knows me any more than they do JJ. I go in, have a bite, and nobody'll pay me no nevermind."

Alan stared at her, then nodded. "Don't do anything foolish."

"Who, me? I'm the carefullest girl on Earth."

Alan sighed and stared at Saramae's outthrust hand. "What?"

"If I'm gonna buy some food, I need some money."

Another sigh and a twenty crossed the front of the car before Saramae got out and Tom moved into her seat.

Saramae leaned through the window. "Hang loose a couple of minutes. I'll let you know what I hear." She walked slowly to the door of the restaurant, and made a little show of waiting impatiently at the door.

Two hefty middle-aged women came up behind her and smiled. "You gonna like the food here, Honey," one of them said. "Best food in K.C."

The girl nodded politely, then gave the women a couple of minutes to get inside and seated before she followed. The Nowlin party had pulled several tables together in the center of the room and were seated seven to a side. The little girl was sitting cross-legged at one end of the table, pouting. Saramae glanced around quickly, then slid into a booth near the other end of the table, behind the old woman. After a moment, she flipped open the menu and pulled out her phone.

• • ● • •

Alan's phone signaled a text, which he read aloud. "not happy family. 14 & 1 little kid. jarvis b 1 4sure, & he mixing it up with abigail about a legacy. she ur old lady & a real bitch. they could b hours, and they loud. Food smells good, c u"

Alan and Tom exchanged shrugs, before Alan turned around and headed back north on Troost toward Jarvis Nowlin's house on Forest.

• • ● • •

Saramae decided that even though the Nowlins looked thoroughly wrapped up in their discussions, she'd better make sure she didn't blow her cover. When the waitress came by, she ordered chicken and waffles. *Should last me long enough if I eat slow.* Then she sat back at her table, took out her phone again, and began to type. Anyone looking at her would think she was just another teenager who couldn't stop texting even to eat a meal.

"they fighting over what 2 do with the music," she wrote. "Jarvis & half of them wants to sell it and make a bundle. old bitch abigail & some others mean 2 put angeline's name on it. Couple wants 2 burn it up & be done. whoops, gotta stop. more later."

• • ● • •

"Jesus," Tom whispered. "You think she's in trouble?"

"Probably not," said Alan. "If she were, I think she'd have ended with some kind of 'Help' message. Let's go on with what we were planning; then if we haven't heard anything else from her, we can go back and check after we pick up JJ."

Jarvis Nowlin's street was a carbon copy of Abigail Nowlin's. Small houses, generally well-kept, with semi-enclosed porches, separated by wide, scruffy side lawns. The house itself was a small step above his aunt's. The white paint had been applied recently enough not to be peeling noticeably; beyond that, the only significant difference was a small sign warning the curious that the house was protected by an alarm.

"Now what?" Tom asked, pointing at the sign. "It's not even worth bringing JJ over if there's an alarm."

"Maybe not, but we can take a look around." Alan reached for his seatbelt release and winced.

Tom caught the expression and quickly opened his own belt. "Peeking in the windows? That doesn't need both of us. Take a break; I got this." He jumped out, leaving the door slightly ajar, as JJ had done at Abigail's.

Alan swallowed a Vicodin while Tom walked to the front door, tucked his hand into his sleeve, and rang the doorbell.

The door stayed closed. After a minute, Tom turned, glanced casually around, and strolled across the lawn. He peeked quickly between the bars over the living room window, shrugged and walked around the corner of the house.

Alan crossed his fingers and held his breath when Tom disappeared and let it out in a long sigh when he reappeared almost immediately.

"See anything?"

"Nada. The only light on was behind frosted glass. Bathroom, I guess. Everything else was dark. Maybe we should bring JJ over."

"Maybe." Alan sounded dubious. "Let's go pick him up and see if he learned anything." He tossed his phone to Tom. "Give him a call and let him know we'll be there in a few minutes."

•　•　●　•　•

Saramae quickly tucked her phone away, and turned a big smile onto the little girl, maybe seven years old, at the long Nowlin table. The girl was glaring at the plate the waitress had just set in front of her, then pushed the plate away and turned sideways in her chair toward Saramae, her expression all but screaming "I'm *bored* and *starving* and *pissed off*." All the adult Nowlins were engaged in their dispute; no one else was paying Saramae any attention. She made a "come'ere" motion with her finger at the little girl, who responded with a "You really mean it?" expression.

Saramae nodded and turned her smile up another notch.

The little girl slid off her chair and walked across to Saramae's booth. "Hey, how you doin'?" Saramae patted the child's shoulder.

"Not so good. I had to come with my mom 'cause the baby-sitter punked out." She inclined her head toward the Nowlins. They's gonna be there forever, just fightin' and fightin'. An' I'm starvin' for something good. My mom made me order the liver an' onions, but I hate that stuff."

"Boy, that's tough. Hey, my name's Saramae. What's yours?"

"Angeline."

Saramae thought she'd managed to keep a straight face. "Nice name."

"Aw, there's Angelines all over my family. The first one was like a zillion years ago. She wrote some music, an' so a buncha us is named after her. Dunno what's so great 'bout writin' music. When I does it, only Grammy ever listen to it. Ev'rybody else, they just tells me to shut up." She pouted. "They all fights over Great-great-great—" she stopped, counted on her fingers, and nodded her head decisively, "Grammy's music, but they don't care nothin' 'bout mine."

"That sure ain't fair. I'd love to hear one of your songs some-time," Saramae said, mentally crossing her fingers. "Not right now, of course," she added quickly when the little girl's face lit up. "It's not polite to go singin' in a restaurant, right?"

"Angie, what you doin' over here, botherin' this lady, huh?"

Angeline's mother—*probably also an Angeline*—looked about thirty, and thoroughly irritated. *Talk fast, Saramae.* "Oh, Ma'am, she ain't botherin' me at all. Fact is, I'd be glad to have her for company. I was supposed to meet my mama here for dinner, but she called at the last minute and told me she was sick. But I was here already, so I came inside to eat. If you don't mind, I'd be happy to have little Angie sit with me and be my guest." She slid a sly grin at the little girl. "They've got awesome peach cobbler here—we could have it for dessert, if you eat all your dinner first."

"Oh, Mama, could I do that? I likes this lady."

The mother squinted. Saramae held her breath.

"You're sure you don't mind?"

"I don't mind a bit, Ma'am."

"Well, okay, then. Guess maybe we'll all be happier."

Little Angeline clapped her hands. Her mother walked off, back to the Nowlin table, returned a moment later with Angeline's liver and onions.

Saramae realized she was covered with perspiration. "Well now," she said, pushing Angeline's plate aside and sliding her own into the middle of the table. "If you don't tell your momma you didn't eat the liver, I sure ain't gonna. You help me with my chicken, and then we'll get us some of that cobbler. Sound good?"

Angeline nodded enthusiastically, and grabbed her fork.

"And while we eat, you can tell me all about that music they're fightin' over. Your Auntie Abigail has it at her house, right?"

"Nah—she's my gramma, not my auntie. She useta have the music, 'long with all the other stuff she keep from that Old Angeline, and she wants to get it back. But now my Uncle Jarvis got it, and he says he ain't gonna give it to her, no way. He say it be worth a bunch a money, a lot more money than it be worth to put Old Angeline's name on it, like Gramma want to do."

• • ● • •

JJ all but danced out of his hiding place beside the tree in front of Abigail Nowlin's house. He plopped into the seat behind Tom and grinned.

Tom glared at him. "You didn't find anything either, huh?"

"You kiddin'? JJ done brang the bacon!"

Alan sat up straight. "You found the duffel bag!"

"Well…" JJ visibly deflated a few PSI. "Okay, I di'n't get the bacon, but I found the pig. Sorry."

"Found the pig? What the—?" Tom censored himself. "What are you talking about?"

"Lissen. The ol' lady don't got an alarm, so I was inside five minutes after you left. I 'member what you say the dead guy, Maggione, tol' you 'bout the bag bein' in a room at the back of the house, so's I start there. An' when I open that door, I hit the jackpot." He paused and looked smug.

"What kind of jackpot?" Alan was on the edge of his seat.

"Somebody turn a big closet into a kinda shrine. Old photo, really old, on the wall, couple a shelves full of junk, little table in front. Stack a music paper on one side o' the table, an' a buncha pieces a wire on the other."

"Wire?!" Alan and Tom chorused.

"Piano wire. One 'bout yay long." He held his hands up about a foot apart. "Look like somebody cut it offa bigger piece. The rest is smaller, mebbe half. Check it out." JJ pulled out Tom's phone, unlocked it, tapped a couple of times, and handed it to Alan.

"Hey! That's private!"

JJ shot Tom a withering look. "Cool down, okay? I didn' look at anythin' 'cept the camera."

Alan ignored the squabble in favor of swiping through JJ's photos. A long shot of the closet shrine. A close-up of the portrait on the wall, showing a pinch-faced woman in her sixties glaring directly at the camera. The wires, the long piece raggedly clipped at one end, mottled with corrosion along its length, the shorter pieces cleanly cut. And the top of the stack of music, a hand-written page titled "Lowdown Rag" and signed "A. Noland." Alan held the phone near his face.

"Tom, how do I zoom in with this thing again?"

"Touch with two fingers and spread them apart."

Alan turned the phone sideways and zoomed in on the music. Zoomed back out and scrolled back to the portrait, studied it. Scrolled again to the shot of the whole closet and zoomed in on the shelves. "Huh. Bunch of junk. Who keeps old lipsticks?" His mumbles trailed off into silence.

"Alan."

No response.

"Alan!" Tom tapped him on the shoulder. "Can I see?"

"Sorry, Thomas. What does that piece of music look like to you?"

Tom took time to study it. "Sounds familiar." He hummed a couple of bars under his breath. "It's almost the same as the trio from 'Maple Leaf.' Not quite, but darn close."

"Not as polished, I'd say," Alan said. "Good ear."

Tom dug the snippet of wire out of his backpack and compared it to the piece JJ had photographed. "Looks about the same, but I can't tell if they really go together. Maybe an expert could. Wait a sec!" He swiped back to the music. "'A. Noland'?" He swiped over to the picture of the photo, held it up to Alan. "Does she look like the woman you saw in 1899?"

Alan shrugged. "Maybe, maybe not. This one's easily forty years older than the one from 1899. There *is* a resemblance, but…" He shrugged again. "Well, in any case, good work, JJ. You're right. It's not the duffel, but I think your pig's ready for the smokehouse."

JJ's stomach growled, cutting off any reply. A moment later, Tom's stomach growled in sympathy.

Alan laughed. "Teenaged boys' stomachs. I could do with a bite or three myself. How about we go find Saramae and make her watch us eat?"

Tom gave JJ a final glare as he switched apps to send Saramae a text. "r u ok? meet outside 10 min"

• • ● • •

Alan slowed to a crawl as he drove past Niecie's. No sign of Saramae. "No reply, Tom?"

"Nothing. Pull around the corner where we dropped her off. If she's not there, I'll go in and look for her."

"You mean, I go look," JJ said. "Still don't want ol' Ms. Abigail t' rec'nize you."

JJ popped out of the car as soon as Alan stopped, saying "Keep the engine runnin' but don' go nowheres till I gets back, 'kay?" He strolled into the restaurant and looked around casually. The Nowlins were easy to spot at their long table, but at first, his eyes slid past Saramae. He expected her to be alone and ignored the young woman sitting with a little girl. It wasn't until he had scanned the room twice that he recognized what he was seeing.

"What the hell?"

He didn't want to attract the Nowlins' attention, so he stayed a few steps inside the door, trying to catch Saramae's eyes, but she was focused on the kid. Finally, he gave up on subtlety and took a step toward Saramae's booth; naturally that was when she glanced up and spotted him. He looked at the kid, looked back at Saramae, and then jerked his head toward the door.

Saramae nodded and held up an index finger to JJ, who nodded and left.

Between mouthfuls of cobbler, Angeline was telling Saramae a rambling story about some kind of a battle. Saramae couldn't quite figure who all the characters were and which ones were fighting with whom. She let the story flow past, since it seemed really important to Angeline, and tried to pick out something she could use to direct the conversation back to Old Angeline's music.

"…stole that music, an' that's why everybody hate Misser Saun."

Saramae jerked upright. "Stole it?"

An enthusiastic nod. "He stoled Ol' Grammy's music and gived it to Misser Doplins."

"Well that was sure a mean thing to do." Saramae realized JJ had come back into the restaurant and was standing by the door, doing everything but jumping up and down. She waved him off; he turned and stomped outside. Saramae turned back to Angeline. "And Mr. Doplins did what with Ol' Grammy's music?"

Angeline pouted. "I tol' you."

"I'm sorry, Honey. It's a long story, and I forgot that part. You're a very smart girl to remember all that."

"Well…" Angeline decided the compliment made up for the insult. "He play the music fo' the white people and he get famous and maked lots and lots of money, and Ol' Grammy didn't get nothin'."

"Mr. Saun didn't get anything either. Bet that taught him not to steal."

"Sho did. He get nothin' and nobody like him, even Misser Doplins. They had a big fight an—"

"It's time to go home, Angie. Go say your good nights."

"Aw, Mama, I was jus'—"

"Now!" Angeline's mother turned to Saramae as her daughter flounced back to the Nowlins' table. "Thank you much for keeping company with Angie. She weren't too bad, were she?"

"Oh, no. She was real good, Ma'am. Uh…I wondered. Are you an Angeline too? Seems like almost every woman Angie knows is one."

She laughed. "It do seem that way, don' it? Nah, I'se a Mary, not a Angeline. But I weren't born a Nowlin, I done married one. Tha's my husband over there, the big lug in the awful red shirt. Nelson Nowlin, an' ain't that a hoot of a name?"

Saramae laughed along with her. "It sure is, Ms. Nowlin. I appreciate you lettin' Angie sit with me. The company sure made my dinner go down nice."

Angeline returned, towing her father. "Bye, Miss Saramae."

"Good night, Angeline. Hope I see you again."

"Me too!"

Saramae waited several minutes to let Angeline and her parents get clear of the restaurant. While she sat, another couple left the table. She cocked an ear toward the remaining members of the group. Jarvis and Abigail were still going after each other full blast while the others just threw in an occasional word. Saramae shook her head as she stood.

Some people don't know when to shut up.

On the way out, she checked her phone and found Tom's text. *Whoops!*

"Sorry," she said as she settled herself in the car behind Alan. "Those Nowlins were so loud I didn't hear my phone. Let's get over to Jarvis' place! He's got the music!"

Alan caught himself before pulling away from the curb. "You sure? How'd you find out?"

"I made a little friend named Angeline. She told me lots about that family. But let's get going. I don't know how much longer Jarvis and Abigail will keep snipin' at each other, so we gotta hurry."

Tom said, "His house has an alarm. JJ, you think you can get past an alarm?"

"Maybe. Depend on the 'larm. Some's easy, some ain't. Can take me a look."

Tom rested a hand on Alan's shoulder. "I don't want to go back to Sedalia without trying to get that music, and I bet you don't either."

"No argument, Thomas. JJ, if we all stand lookout, are you willing to try to get into that house and look for the music?"

"'Course!"

"All right." Alan put the car in gear and headed back to Forest Avenue. "Saramae, what else did your friend tell you?"

"She said Ol' Angeline, the same one who's my triple-great gran, is her triple-great too. Jarvis has the music now, and he ain't gonna give it back to Abigail. You shoulda heard her yellin' at Jarvis. Not that he's any better. Anyway, Abigail worships the ground Ol' Angeline walked on. She's got some of her music and everythin'. She wants to use the duffel music to prove Ol' Angeline was a great composer. Jarvis wants to sell it and cash in on Joplin's name. And a couple of Nowlins nobody paid any attention to want to burn it and be done with the whole mess."

She stopped and thought. "There was somethin' else…Oh, yeah. They think Ol' Angeline is the one who really wrote "Maple Leaf Rag," and that Otis Saunders stole it and gave it to Scott Joplin. How about that?"

Alan's mouth was hanging open. The two boys gawked at Saramae.

"What? I got syrup on my face or somethin'?"

"You get all that from the kid I seed you talkin' too? Damn!"

"She's one smart girl. Probably knows a lot more, too!"

"That's not going to help us much," Alan pointed out. "We don't know where she lives—or how reliable her information is."

"I got Angeline's Daddy's and Momma's names, so I bet we can find 'em if we want to. Can't be too many Nelson Nowlins around, even in a city this big. Reliable?" She shrugged. "Sure, we gotta take what she says about Ol' Angeline with a big grain of salt, but it sure sounded like the Nowlins believe it. Heck, she's probably as reliable about that as I am about Triple-great Granddaddy Lathan."

"Fair enough. Nice work, Saramae. You and JJ both hit it big today."

Chapter Fourteen

On the way to Jarvis Nowlin's house, JJ laid out the possibilities. "If he just got a li'l alarm sign on his front lawn and there really ain't no alarm on the house, I be inside in two minutes. But if there be an alarm, mebbe I can deal with it, mebbe I can't. If it gots magnetic sensors, that ain't bad. I brung magnets fo' that. But to crack a fancy wireless set-up, that take radio equipment. Back in Sedalia, I knows someone who'd lend me one. But he ain't here. So here's what we do: I go up and open the front door slow and careful, checkin' for magnetic sensors. If nothin' happen, I'm cool. But if the alarm goes off, or somebody see me and start shoutin', I'm back in nothin' flat, we're outa here in less time than that, an' we come back another time. Got it?"

Soft yeahs filled the car as Alan eased up to the curb across the street from Jarvis' house and cut the engine. JJ threw the rear door open. "Be ready to move in one big hurry," he snapped, then jumped to the ground, leaving the car door ajar. He trotted up to the house and worked at the front door for not more than a minute and a half before he gave it a push. No alarm sounded and he vanished inside, closing the door behind himself. Three people in a car exhaled noisily.

Less than fifteen minutes later, another car came down the street and parked in front of Jarvis' house. A large black man got out and walked around the front of the car.

"Oh, fuck!" Saramae breathed. "That's him."

Alan passed his cell phone to Tom. "Give JJ a call," he barked. "Quick! Tell him to go out the back way. I'll start the motor when I see him."

"I can't! He didn't take my phone."

Jarvis Nowlin put his key into the front door, stopped, and stared at the lock.

"Oh, shit," Alan muttered. "JJ left it unlocked. Jarvis knows something's up."

The big man disappeared into his house, leaving the door ajar. Immediately, Tom opened the car door and charged up the concrete walkway.

"Tom!" Alan called after him. "Hold up."

But the boy kept going, through the doorway, into the house, out of sight of Alan and Saramae. The girl started to open her car door, but Alan reached back to stop her.

"Wait," he said. "It's two against one there, and they're our two best bets. Better we should hope they come out, and be ready to bail when they do."

Inside the front hall, Tom paused, blinked his eyes several times. There was a faint light ahead, toward the back of the house. Suddenly, the light brightened, and a voice snarled, "Okay, you scrawny nigger. You dead if you move."

Tom flinched. Then, realizing the words couldn't have been addressed to him, he moved out of the hall into a dimly lit living room. There he saw Jarvis Nowlin's massive back; the man was facing JJ at a distance of three or four feet, and his right hand pointed a mean-looking pistol at his young opponent.

"Who you be, boy?" Jarvis roared. "What trash dump did Abigail pull you offa, huh?"

Well, that's something. He thinks Abigail hired JJ to get the music for her. Hope JJ goes along with him and doesn't give me away. Tom put a finger to his lips. *Play along, JJ!*

"I ast you a question, but I don't hear no answer. That's bad manners, and I don't like no bad manners. You don't make them manners better, you ain't never gonna talk to nobody no more."

Tom looked frantically around the living room. Fireplace. Set of tools hanging on a round holder. Without thinking, he moved silently, grabbed the fire iron, and walked as quickly and quietly as he could toward Jarvis' back.

"Hey, put the gun away, okay?" said JJ. "I ain't carryin', don't even got a knife. Miss Abigail, she tell me you got somethin' a hers, and she gimme a hundred bucks to get it for her. How I gonna say no to that, huh?"

"Easy." Nowlin sneered. "You just say it, 'no'. That's what you shoulda done, but it be a li'l late now."

Tom saw the man's right arm tense, his body bending slightly forward, his legs shifting to firing stance.

JJ recognized the movement. "You ain't gonna kill me for somethin' like this, is you?" For the first time, Tom heard a quaver in JJ's voice.

"Sure thing," taunted Nowlin. "Then I gonna cut off your balls an' dick, and give 'em to Abigail. Bitch oughta know better'n to bring an outsider inta fam'ly bidness."

Now or never. Tom told himself to keep breathing, raised the fire iron, paused an instant to draw back his weapon, then swung.

Jarvis Nowlin loosed a howl worthy of a wounded coyote, and dropped to his knees. The gun clattered to the floor. JJ leaped forward to grab it. Tom swung the fire iron a second time, bringing it down onto the top of Nowlin's head with every ounce of force at his command. Nowlin collapsed into a silent heap.

JJ and Tom faced each other for a moment, neither able to speak. JJ recovered first. "Thanks, man. I owes you big time. But let's move, huh?"

Tom dropped the fire iron and turned around.

"Hey, wake up. Don't be leavin' that thing with your prints all over it."

Tom blinked, shook his head, bent to pick up the weapon, and followed JJ outside.

Alan gave the fire iron an odd look, but he had the car moving before the two boys had their doors shut. "Looks like we're coming back for another visit, another time."

"I don't think so, Man," said JJ. "We're gonna have to talk, change our plans a li'l."

"You can fill us in on the way back to Sedalia," said Alan.

"No way," said JJ. "Saramae done had herself a good dinner, but not the rest of us. An' I wasn't sure there for a minute that I was ever gonna eat nothin' again, 'ceptin' dirt in my grave. How 'bout we stops somewhere, gets us a li'l somethin', an' Tom and me, we'll fill you in while we eats."

• • ● • •

After a quick dinner at Gates BBQ on Emanuel Cleaver, the gang piled back into the car, and Alan steered his way back to Route 50. According to some reviewers, Gates rivals Arthur Bryant's for the best BBQ in Kansas City, but the way Alan's stomach was churning, he doubted that claim. On the other hand, he admitted, he'd eaten fast and heavy, a full order of ribs downed in less than twenty minutes. *Should have known better.* He'd long ago learned there's no compromising with chemo, and if you don't eat slowly and carefully, you're going to pay. He loosed a belch that set Saramae into a loud giggle, then passed his little pillholder to Tom.

"Get me a Compazine, would you, please, Thomas?" he said. "The little round orange one."

That ginger ale just made it worse—and didn't taste nearly as good as what I had in 1899. Chemo poisoning my tastebuds? Or was soda really different then? Maybe I am hallucinating, after all. But it doesn't make sense for that to be the only thing that seems off.

The dinner conversation was more than a little manic, peppered with random bursts of laughter. Once in the car, though, the conversation stopped. *Adrenaline crash,* Alan told himself, trying to pull his thoughts away from possible hallucinations. He mused on a comment JJ had made.

"On'y seven-thirty. I be at work with plenty a time t' spare. Tha's good. I gots a perfec' record an' don' wanna ruin it. Saramae's daddy, I sees him every day when my shift be over and his getting' started, an' every day he give me some advice. He call me Mr. Ireland, 'cause old Mr. Tom Ireland never was late on his shift at the *Democrat* neither. He came to work every night at midnight, same as me, ridin' his bicycle, and he used to give the younger guys hell when they was late. 'I'm up in my eighties,' he say, 'and if I can still pedal to the paper before most of you kids get in, you's got no excuse.'"

Saramae's face had turned quizzical. "My daddy gives you advice? Pretty strange."

JJ saw he'd embarrassed himself, but had no way to go but forward. "Oh, yeah. He a smart man, your daddy an' a good guy. He know I likes the newspaper work. Always somethin' happening. You can't never move fast enough for the foreman, but it still way more interestin' than school." JJ hesitated. "Workin' the press is okay, but not so's I wants to do it for the next fifty years. I wants to be a reporter, and Mr. Blackstone tell me what I gotta do to make that happen. He say Mr. Ireland were a great man, but in his time, no black guy could be a reporter or an editor on no white paper. But today, things is different."

Alan swung past Elvira's to drop off JJ. As the young man was getting out of the car, Alan lowered his window. "JJ—I saw something in your hand when you came out of Jarvis' house."

"Yeah? So?"

"Yeah so, give it here."

"Hey—"

"I'm not kidding, JJ. Get caught packing heat, and none of us will ever see you again. Now, give me that cannon…I'll tell you what, I'll make you a trade. Tom, give him the fire iron. Get rid of it for us, JJ. Bury it somewhere, deep. And give… me…that…gun."

JJ tucked his notebook into his pocket, and then, a big smile on his face, slowly withdrew the pistol, and passed it to Alan. "You *do* like livin' dangerously. But you be careful with this baby. It be loaded." He took the fire iron from Tom, waved at the car, and went up to the door.

After they dropped Saramae at her house, Alan headed for the Bothwell Hotel. JJ's anecdote had triggered a notion he thought Tom should hear. "The first time I came to Sedalia, I was your age. And I had something happen I'll never forget. There was a KKK man after me because I had a journal of Scott Joplin's that he thought was worth a lot of money. He probably would've killed me, but a couple of black guys saved my life. One of them was called Sassafras Sam, because he dug sassafras roots and made tea to sell from them…and the other one was Tom Ireland. The KKK guy trailed Sam and me to Sam's house, and when we picked up on him, Sam hid me in the woodshed. When I saw that Sam's family was going to end up shot dead, I grabbed an ax, snuck into the house behind the bastard, and brained him. Sound familiar?"

Tom's eyes bulged. "Except for the fire iron…jeez, Alan. Same age, same town…what'd you do about the KKK man afterwards?"

Alan paused, then said slowly, "Sam sent me off to Tom Ireland's house, while he got rid of the body. I never did find out how."

"Rid of the body…Alan. You killed him?…oh my God, I never thought…could I maybe have killed *Jarvis?* I figured I knocked him cold." The boy started to cry.

Alan reached across the seat and gave his grandson's arm a quick squeeze. "Yes, Tom. That KKK man was deader than dirt. I was really upset for a little while afterward, but once the feeling passed, it never has bothered me since. That man would've killed me if it wasn't for Sam, and then he'd have killed Sam and his whole family. It was either-or. Tom, sometimes life deals us a hand we don't like, but we have to play it. I don't know if you killed Jarvis—we'll have to find out; you need to be sure one way or the other. But remember this—if you hadn't acted, we'd be only three of us back here in Sedalia now."

He paused to let the idea take root, then went on so Tom wouldn't brood on it. "What I can't get out of my head is how close your experience was to mine. We're not the same person, but we've got a close genetic relationship, we're on the same page with music—"

Tom wiped his eyes. "Kind of a time-travel, you're thinking."

"Well, maybe more like history repeating itself."

"Jesus…Does Gramma know you killed someone?"

"She knows the whole story. I think that's one of the reasons she's never wanted me to go anywhere without her." Alan shifted in the driver's seat, trying to ease the ache in his spine. "I'm about done for the night. As soon as we get back, I'm going to give her a call and then we should take a good rest. We've been running non-stop too long, and I think something close to a full night's sleep would do us both good."

As Alan and Tom came through the lobby of the Bothwell Hotel, the desk clerk reached behind him, then waved a piece of paper in their direction.

"Mr. Chandler—Detective Parks wants you to call him as soon as you come in. He seemed quite upset that he hadn't been able to reach you."

Alan's stomach did a flip. He read the paper, grinned, and thanked the clerk. In the elevator, he passed the paper to Tom and deleted his phone's call log. He pursed his lips and nodded.

"Good." A sigh. "So much for getting straight to bed."

In the room, Tom flopped on his bed as Alan dialed the detective's number. "Yes," he said. "This is Alan Chandler…well, no, Sir, I never…wait, now, hold on just a minute. The first I knew you wanted to see me was when the desk clerk gave me your written message…no, I'll be glad to talk to you…I—look, I'm an old man, I'm ill, and it would be a lot easier for me if you'd come here. You can have all the time you want…good. Thank you, Sir. I'll be waiting for you."

As the receiver settled into the cradle, Tom laughed. "For an old, ill man, sounds like you had the detective down on his knees."

"That's what I hoped." Alan looked at his watch. "Just a bit after ten—only eight in Seattle. It'll take him a little while to get here. I'll call your grandmother while I wait."

"Get the hard one over with first, huh?"

"Probably."

• ● ● ● •

"Miriam, hello. Did your meeting go well?"

"Just fine," crackled through the speakerphone. "We're set up perfectly for the next year. And you? I don't suppose you called to tell me you're coming home."

"No. I didn't. We're making some progress. We think we know where the Joplin music is, and we may be able to get it back soon. And in any case, the police haven't released us to travel away from Sedalia."

"Where is the music, Alan?"

"We think it's at the house of…" *Short version.* "…one of the descendants of a woman who felt Joplin had stolen music from her. The family is divided over whether they should present it to the world as their ancestor's, or cash in on Joplin's name."

"And they told you all that? How do you suppose you're going to convince either of those factions to give *you* the music?"

Alan thought of Saramae, pumping information out of Little Angeline at the restaurant. "Miriam, you know I've got my ways and means, and it would take more time for me to give you all the details now than either of us has to talk on the phone. Just take me at my word—"

"Oh, I do. But only up to a point. Fine. You don't want to tell me over the phone, you can tell me to my face."

"I told you, Miriam. If I try to come home now, the police will have the Seattle cops on me instantly, and—"

"I understand, Alan. Though I'll admit, I'm not sure how much faith goes in with that understanding. But if Mohammed won't come to the mountain, the mountain will get on the first plane to Kansas City in the morning. I trust you could meet me at the airport."

Loud sigh. "I could do that, Miriam, yes. I'm not going to try to talk you out of coming; that would be as futile as your trying to talk me into coming home. But I really am a bit concerned about what the police detective is going to insist I do and not do.

"Now, there are four of us involved in this business: myself, Tom, and two wonderful ki—young people—who live here. None of those three has access to a car, and I'm the only one of us old enough to drive a rental car. It would help if you'd come in, rent a second car at the airport, and drive to Sedalia, the Bothwell Hotel, you know where that is. Then we'll have a second car at our disposal, and a second driver. Would you do that?"

"Jesus, Alan…yes, yes for Christ's sake, I'll do that. After sixty-four years, I should be used to this stuff."

"Good. Wonderful. Send me a message so I'll know when your plane arrives, and I'll be sure I'm in the room by the time you get here."

"All right, Alan. Sleep well."

"You too." He hung up the phone and waved the conversation away. "Well, at least one of us will be here when you arrive."

Tom shook his too and snickered. "You want me to go out somewhere so you can be alone with our cop friend?"

"No. He'd only ask where you are and wonder why, at this hour, and it would be one more thing for me to explain. Sit tight. Or lie tight. Hang tight."

• • • • •

Detective Parks' knock was loud and long. Alan opened the door and motioned him in. "You won't mind if I sit," Alan said, and dropped into the desk chair. "My back is killing me."

"Nah. Go ahead." Parks shot Tom a quick glance, then sat on the edge of Alan's bed and gave him a long glare. "So you're saying you never got my call on your cell."

"I am saying that," said Alan. He reached for his phone, but Parks waved off the motion. "What number did you call?"

Parks pulled a slip of paper from his shirt pocket, dropped it on the table.

"That's it." Alan shrugged. "I don't know."

"Where have you been the past three hours, Mr. Chandler?"

"With all due respect, Sir, I don't think I'm required to tell you my whereabouts, but I will say we had some dinner. You had my phone number, the phone was on, but the call apparently didn't come through. Cell phones." An elaborate shrug. "Not my fault. I'm willing to stay in the Sedalia area as long as you need me to, but if you need to know exactly where I am every minute, you can have an officer google my cell phone location."

Parks chewed on his lower lip.

Alan leaned forward in his chair. "So here I am. What is it you'd like to talk to me about?"

A sarcastic smile distorted the policeman's face. "I think you might be able to help me with the case, Mr. Chandler. You're a piano professional, isn't that right?"

"Yes, that's right. I've played piano since I was eight years old, and it's been the only job I've ever had as an adult."

"Good." Parks reached into his pocket, pulled out a coil of wire in a clear plastic bag, and passed it to Alan. "What would you say this is?"

Careful. He made a show of studying it. "I've seen this before," he said. "If I'm not wrong, this is the string my friend Mickey Potash was strangled with…or one exactly like it."

"Yes, that's right. But I don't need help identifying it as a murder weapon. That was obvious. Can you tell me what it was before it became a murder weapon?"

"It looks like a piano string, one of the low bass notes…it's wrapped, you see. But, odd, it looks badly corroded, and I've never seen a piano string in that state. Never seen anything like these black stains here and there, either—"

"Those are bloodstains, Mr. Chandler. Your friend's blood, to be exact. But can you tell me how a piano wire would have gotten so corroded? You've never seen one like it, you say?"

Alan shook his head. "Piano wire's pretty sensitive—you don't want to go touching it because the oils in your fingers will ruin the tonal quality. After that, you'll see visible decay and the pitch goes off. But anybody who cares about their piano would replace the strings long before they get this bad. I'd have to think either someone spilled liquid into a piano, or the piano has been sitting outside, getting soaked in the rain."

"Do you have any idea why someone would have used this wire, of all things, to kill Mr. Potash?"

"Mickey was a pianist. Maybe someone with a warped sense of humor thought the string was appropriate in a sick way. Maybe Mickey didn't just hand the music over; he could be pretty caustic, especially if he happened to have a little of the sauce on board. But why an old, corroded string?" Alan shrugged. "What can I say? I guess I might look for a piano that had been left out in the rain, maybe in a dump, and try to trace things back from there."

The detective's face went crafty. "You're a pianist, Mr. Chandler. You want that music. You're a top scholar on Scott Joplin and other ragtime composers from a long time ago. This couldn't have been Scott Joplin's wire, could it? Maybe I need to go to Seattle and take a look through your research materials."

Alan shook his head slowly. "You're welcome to do that. But you'll be wasting your time. I assure you, if I had a piano string that could be authenticated back to a piano Scott Joplin played, it would be displayed in a beautiful glass case in my music room. *And* I never, ever, would have used it to commit a murder."

Parks tapped a finger on the bed. "Okay...for now. Guess I'll be turning Sedalia upside down looking for a piano left outside, with some of the bass wires—"

"Strings, Detective."

"What?"

"Once piano wire is cut to size and installed in a piano, it's called a string. See the loop on the end? Making that loop at just the right distance from the end of the wrapping is something you do when you size the raw wire and make it into a string."

"Thank you, Mr. Chandler. I'm sure that'll be a big help." Parks rolled his eyes. "I'll go looking for a soggy piano with bass *strings* missing. I'm not going to push the matter of where you were this evening, but I expect that you will remain in Sedalia for a while longer."

"Yes, I'll be here."

"And perhaps you'd like to take your phone to the Verizon store, let them look it over and make sure it's receiving calls.

One missed call, I'll overlook. More than that, no. Kapeesh, Mr. Chandler?"

"Loud and clear, Detective."

• ● ● ● •

By the time Alan finished his ablutions, Tom was curled up in bed, half asleep.

"Good night, Thomas."

"'Night, Alan." A pause. "Hey, what's that railroad thing Gramma calls you? About how you always know what's going on in the ragtime community."

"Ticket Taker on the Gossip Express?"

"Yeah, that. Too bad there isn't anyone in 1899 who knows everyone and what they're up to. Someone who could tell you what Angeline and Lathan are up to."

Alan chuckled. "That would simplify that particular mess, wouldn't it?" He dropped into bed, expecting to fall asleep immediately, but found himself staring at the insides of his eyelids. Tom's comment nagged him. He was sure he *did* know someone who knew all the players, but his damned porous memory refused to cooperate.

Shortly after six, Alan bolted upright, vaguely aware that he had been asleep. "Ireland!" he shouted, then clapped a hand over his mouth and looked guiltily at Tom.

Tom was flat on his back, arms flung wide. He mumbled something that sounded suspiciously like "Erin go bragh," and resumed snoring loudly enough to rattle the lampshade on the bedside table.

Tom Ireland! A newspaperman and a musician. In 1899, he was in his prime, and he knew everyone in town, black and white. And everyone, black and white, respected him. If I want to meet Lathan and Angeline…"

Alan eased himself out of bed. Six hours of sleep wasn't really enough, but he knew it was all he would get. Between his cancer, chemo-inspired insomnia, and a hot lead, no way he could get back to sleep.

Alan considered his options while he used the bathroom and got dressed.

I could look for him at his house on Osage, but that's way the hell north in Lincolnville. Not someplace a white man should be wandering without an escort, then or now. I could try to catch him at one of the clubs, but God only knows what his schedule is like. Best to go to the newspaper. It's downtown, at least.

He settled himself at the table, and set out the piece of wire. Picturing the wire in the piano was easy, and so was zooming his mental image out to include the yard behind Mr. Taylor's shop. He pulled back further, putting his viewpoint in front of the store.

The Democrat *was a morning paper, and Mr. Ireland worked nights. To catch him coming off shift…hmm…early morning, just before sunrise, I think.* He filled in shadows, a hint of gray in the sky to the east.

Alan started the music in his head. Not the theme on the invitation. "Maple Leaf," as Mr. Joplin would play it. He rigidly suppressed all memory of Angeline's cutting competition version. The music felt almost right, but not quite…*Of course!* He restarted the music, this time including the beer-induced tonal discrepancies and the buzzing of glass shards among the strings. As the piece continued, his recollection of the sour sounds improved, and by the end he was certain he had it down. He began again, and blinked as the light changed. He leaned against the front door of the piano and organ shop for a moment to collect his wits, then started north on Ohio, toward Third Street and the offices of the *Sedalia Democrat.*

Alan's original intention had been to wait outside the office until Mr. Ireland left. As he walked, he reconsidered. How good was his memory of his quarry nearly sixty years after the last time he had seen him? Even if his memory held up, Mr. Ireland would be a good fifty years younger.

Fortune smiled. Alan stepped into the building, intending to ask the first person he saw, receptionist, reporter, or delivery boy, for directions to Mr. Ireland. The only person in the lobby was a janitor pushing a broom. Alan didn't recognize his face, but his posture, especially the way he held his head, was unforgettable. Only Tom Ireland could turn sweeping the floor into a claim that he'd not only fix whatever problems the universe handed him, but he'd enjoy the doing. Assuming, of course, that he thought they were problems worth fixing.

"Excuse me, Mr. Ireland? May I have a few moments of your time?"

"Yes?"

"My name is Alan Chandler. I have a problem I hope you can help me solve."

Ireland folded his hands over the end of the broomstick and gave Alan a long, considering look. "I trust you can provide a few details of this problem you want me to solve."

"I can and will. But it's complicated and you have little reason to trust me. I believe Mr. Scott Joplin would vouch for me—but he's at the center of the problem, and until I know more, I'd rather he didn't know I was making inquiries."

That earned him a deep sigh. "I'm thinking this ain't the kind of problem that can be solved standing here. I've got more floors to sweep. Suppose you have a seat in the office there. Mr. Stratton won't mind. I'll finish up, and then you can tell me about your problem."

• ● ● ● •

"So, Mr. Chandler, I'd like you to start at the beginning. Who are you, where are you from, and what sort of a problem do you have with Scott?"

Alan had considered the best way to present the problem.

The truth, the whole truth, and nothing but the truth is all well and good for the courtroom, but explaining about time-travel isn't going to fly. Getting him to listen long enough to convince him I'm not crazy would be tough, and even if I pulled it off, it'd take too long. And it's a good way to make myself too memorable. Mr. Ireland didn't—won't—remember an old fart named Alan Chandler when he met—is going to meet—a kid with the same name in 1951. I'd just as soon keep it that way. Keep it simple, focus on Angeline.

"I'm sorry, Mr. Ireland. I didn't mean to suggest that I had a problem with Mr. Joplin. It'd be more accurate to say that I'm trying to solve a problem he doesn't know he has. But yes, let me start at the beginning. I'm a musician myself, from Seattle. I had an opportunity to visit Sedalia on business, and used the chance to meet Mr. Joplin." He paused. "Did you hear about the trouble at the Maple Leaf Club? The fight that damaged the piano?"

"I did. Night before last, wasn't it?"

Alan blinked.

Two nights ago? Three, isn't it? No, wait! If I followed the piano string to Mr. Taylor's store, Angeline hasn't stolen it yet. If it was still there now, that means she won't be there until this afternoon! Time-travel really does make my head hurt.

"I'm convinced that the fight—and the damage—wasn't random. Someone staged the whole affair as part of a plot against Mr. Joplin."

Ireland raised an eyebrow. "Plenty of folks who don't like Scott, sure enough. But that seems very…indirect. Most people would be happy just to give someone they don't like a punch in the nose. And most white folks who want to put an 'uppity nigger' in his place ain't going to mess around; they're gonna figure that's what a rope is for."

"This isn't that kind of mess, thank God. As far as I can tell, I'm the only white man involved. But it *is* more than a simple grudge that could be settled with a fist fight." He took a deep breath. "I'm sure you know that Otis Saunders is saying he wrote the trio of Mr. Joplin's 'Maple Leaf Rag.'"

At Ireland's nod, he went on, "Did you know he's not the only one?"

"Oh. Her."

Alan was crestfallen. "You knew about Ms.—uh—Mrs. Blackstone, or Noland or whatever she's calling herself? Why haven't you done anything about her threats?"

Ireland shrugged. "What threats, Mr. Chandler? What I hear is she talks a bunch about 'Maple Leaf Rag,' but I haven't heard about any threats—'cept for what you just said. And I don't know you. Now, if Scott came to me and said he had a problem with Miz Angeline, that'd be different."

"Oh."

"I don't know the truth of her story either. Maybe she did write that music. So? Credit goes to the man who writes the music down. Always been that way."

"True. But people get excited when there's a lot of money at stake. And I think Angeline's gotten entirely too excited."

That drew a laugh. "And you want to tell her to settle down?"

"If it were only that easy!" Alan said with a laugh of his own. "I doubt she'd be happy to hear anything of the sort, especially not from some old, interfering white man. No, I was hoping you could introduce me to her husband."

"Hmm. He is a sensible man. Not the smartest, no, but levelheaded. Loyal."

Alan waited while Ireland thought.

"All right, Mr. Chandler. I don't know if I believe there's a problem between Scott and Miz Angeline, but I can see *you* believe it. I wouldn't want to get between a man and his wife, like you're planning, but hell, you're a grown man. And even if I think you're wrong, I'd hate to have anything bad happen to Scott. So I'll introduce you to Lathan Blackstone. After that, you're on your own."

"Fair enough, Mr. Ireland. I hope you're right that I'm making more of the situation than it deserves. But I can't sit by and do nothing on the chance that I'm wrong." Alan stood and stretched. "I know it's an awkward time of day, but would it be possible to get that introduction now? Unfortunately, my time is limited."

"Now?" Ireland considered. "Possibly. He might still be at the paper. You have the time to visit the *Times?*" He chuckled.

"If it's not too far, and you don't mind walking slowly."

"Slow, I can do, Mr. Chandler. As to how far..." He eyed Alan's posture. "Can you make it to Washington and St. Louis?"

"If I have to, I will. At my own speed."

"'Fair enough,'" Ireland quoted. "The way I see it, that's how fast any man should go."

● ● **●** ● ●

Lathan was at the *Times*. Ireland and Alan found him bent over the press, tapping something with a hammer. As they approached, a thunderous curse floated out of the depths of the machinery. Lathan straightened, kicked the frame—much more gently than the volume of his profanity seemed to warrant—and then noticed the visitors.

"Mr. Ireland! Beg your pardon. Betsy here be stubborn as the mule Mr. Carter named her for. Sometime you jes' gotta use a hammer to gets her 'tention."

Ireland nodded. "Never knowed a press wasn't stubborn. Anythin' serious?"

"Nah. I has her right as rain pret' darn quick." He glanced at Alan with a puzzled expression as he set his hammer on the frame of the press.

"Tha's good. Mr. Carter be happy 'bout that. Listen, Lathan, this is Mr. Alan Chandler. He's a musician, an' he got a problem maybe you can help him fix."

"Sho' thing, Mr. Ireland. Be glad to. Mr. Chandler." He wiped grease off his hands onto his pants before he took the hand Alan held out. His heavy ring pinched Alan's finger as they shook.

He's as light-skinned as Otis Saunders. But he could tear Otis into confetti without even working up a sweat. The thought flickered through Alan's mind as he checked to be sure his fingers were all intact.

Lathan rolled down his sleeves and dug a pair of cufflinks out of a pocket. "What kin I do fer ya, Sir?" he asked while he fumbled the left link closed.

Before Alan could answer, Ireland added, "Lathan, I got to get to a band rehearsal. You come to the concert at the park Wednesday an' tell me how you fix Mr. Chandler's problem, okay?"

"I do that, Mr. Ireland. I were gonna come to the park anyhow."

Alan nodded to show he understood the message, and wouldn't give Ireland cause to regret introducing him to Lathan. "Well, Mr. Blackstone," he said, "I know you need to get back to work, so I'll come straight to the point. What your wife is doing is dangerous. Arranging that fight, wrecking the piano—someone could have gotten hurt, even killed."

Lathan started, but shook his head. "I don' know what youse talkin' bout, Mr. Chandler, Sir. What fight an' what piano?"

"Don't lie, Lathan. I saw you at the Maple Leaf Club two nights ago, and I saw Angeline pour that mess into the piano. All this trouble over a few bars of music." He shook his head sadly.

Lathan clamped his lips shut, folded his arms, and glared at Alan.

"Keep going the way you are, and the police are going to get involved."

"Ain't no need for the po-lice, iff'n—" The big man stopped and glanced at his hammer.

"They won't have a choice, Lathan." Alan stepped to the side, forcing Lathan to turn his back on the press. "Lotta powerful people already want to close down the black clubs. If the trouble doesn't stop, they'll make sure the police step in. Probably crack down on black musicians all over, not just the clubs. You don't want that. I don't want it either. You have to talk to me. Let me help you end this trouble before they do shut everyone down."

Lathan stood mute for several seconds, then visibly deflated. "Don't got no choice," he muttered, staring at the floor. He looked up at Alan. "It be a real mess, Mr. Chandler, an' it be my fault, too."

"Your fault?"

"I the one who tell Angie it weren't fair what Mr. Joplin done." He waved at the press behind him with his left hand. "If I invents somethin', like the guy who invent the printin' press, I gets a patent and anyone what wants to build one hasta pay me. Oughta be the same with music, is what I tells Angie. It ain't right that Mr. Joplin, he use the music she write 'thout payin' for it."

Alan nodded. "I agree with you about that. That's what copyright is for. But you can't copyright something until you write it down. Without a copyright, the most you can do is ask Mr. Joplin to pay—like Otis Saunders did."

"Otis Saunders! That lyin' weasel! Lissen, Mr. Chandler. Angie go to Mr. Joplin, jus' like you say. Went t' the Maple Leaf Club, sit down 'cross the table. Tol' him he owe her for the music what she writ. She say she didn' want no money, just fo' him t' put her name on the music and innerduce her to Mr. Stark, the publisher. You know what he say? He say he don' owe Angie nothin' on account of he get the music from Otis Lyin' Saunders, an' he don' owe him nothin' neither, 'cause Mr. Joplin, he the one what write the music down! An' then he go too far."

Lathan sighed. "We not rich, Mr. Chandler. Never had much money." He tapped his ring. "I wanteda buy Angie a ring when I ast her to marry me, but I couldn' 'ford that. So I done make us both rings. Carved steel and paint with the first letters of our names. 'Tain't fancy, but it get the job done. Things is better now, but still woulda been hard to pay a lawyer to go after Mr. Joplin. I woulda done it for Angie anyhow, but when that man go an' say Angie couldn'ta writ the music nohow, he make it too much fo' any lawyer. He say there ain't no way no woman coulda writ that music."

Lathan had been swinging his fists through his whole speech, apparently punching imaginary Saunderses and Joplins. On the last word, he'd flung both hands into the air before slouching back against the press.

Alan blinked and held up a hand. "Whoa, Lathan. That doesn't sound like something Mr. Joplin would say. Hell, he knows that isn't true. You know 'Eli Green's Cake Walk,' don't you? Think Sadie Kominsky wasn't a woman?"

That caught Lathan's attention. "I 'members that song, yeah." He hummed a couple of bars. Alan thought they sounded more like Schoenberg than Kominsky. "Didn' know was a woman wrote it."

"And there are plenty of others. Mr. Joplin would know, and a man who loves music like he does would never say that."

Lathan's face clouded. "She tell me that what he say. You sayin' she lyin' t' me?"

Of course I am! Alan kept the anger out of his voice. "I'm saying maybe she exaggerated. Or misremembered. I'm sure Mr. Joplin said he didn't owe her anything. Legally, that's true." He shrugged. "But the other? No way. Maybe he said he didn't believe she had written it. It's not so far from 'didn't' to 'couldn't' for someone who's too upset to listen."

The distinction went right past Lathan. "I don' think so, Mr. Chandler. That ain't Angie. She love me, she love our little boy, William, but she love the music more'n both of us put together. I knowed that when I marry her."

He smiled, eyes focused on the past. "We had us some real fights 'bout her givin' up playin' in the houses, but I knowed all along she wouldn' stop playin' *or* writin' her music, no matter what." The smile vanished when he refocused on Alan. "She wouldn'—couldn'—lie 'bout her music. She say Mr. Joplin tol' her she couldn'ta writ that music, that what happen."

Alan took that claim with an entire salt mine. *Okay, the horse isn't going to drink here. Keep leading it.* "All right. So what did Angeline do after that?"

Lathan grinned. "She look at Mr. Joplin and say all polite-like, 'If that what you think, I guess there ain't no real composers here at all, jus' a half-trained monkey what think he a piano player,' and she walk out."

"Oh, nasty." Alan winced. *That sounds like the kind of thing she might have wished she said. Assuming any of this story's true.* "And now she wants to prove she's the better composer?"

"No, Sir, Mr. Chandler. Now she want *revenge.* Mebbe later, after she hurt Mr. Joplin the way he hurt her, then she come back t' her music." Lathan folded his arms, hands cupping his elbows. "I don' like it none, Mr. Chandler. I help her, sure, 'cause she my wife. I puts that bladder in her dress so's she can mess up Mr. Joplin's piano, an' I pays them thugs she find—but I tells 'em iff'n someone get hurt, they don' get paid. I don' want nobody to get hurt, Mr. Chandler. I jus' want my Angie back."

"You know, it's not Mr. Joplin's piano. Losing it didn't hurt him much at all. The person it hurt is Mr. Williams. Getting that piano fixed up is going to cost him a lot of money."

"I'se sorry 'bout troublin' Mr. Williams, but Angie need t' get the piano outa the Maple Leaf Club so's she kin get somethin' from it."

"The strings."

Lathan's face was a study in confusion. "How you know that? She only tell me 'bout them strings."

"I have ways of finding things out that you wouldn't believe. I know she wants the strings. I even know which strings she wants. But I don't know why." Alan drew himself up, feeling faintly foolish—even on tip-toes, he'd still be a good eight inches shorter than Lathan—and was surprised to see the big man take a step back and cringe. "Why, Lathan? Tell me!"

"Don' hex me, Mr. Chandler! Mr. Ireland, he not like that."

Oh, that's why he's about to shit his pants. "I'm not going to hex you, Lathan. I don't need a hex. You're just going to tell me what I need to know, right?"

Lathan shook his head vigorously. "I done said too much already."

Closer. I'll make this horse drink yet. "Lathan, I know you're a sensible man. Matter of fact, that's the first thing Mr. Ireland told me about you. So if you think this mess is your fault, why are you making it worse? A sensible man would be trying to fix what he broke."

"But, Angie…"

"Revenge isn't what Angeline needs. Revenge breeds revenge. Nobody needs that. If you want to help her, then help her get past looking for revenge and back to her music."

"But…" Lathan spun around and looked heavenward for a long moment before turning back to Alan. "If I don' help Angie, someone else will. An'…." He fell silent again.

Ah. "Otis Saunders."

Lathan's face twisted. "He take her music an' play it fo' Mr. Joplin, sayin' it be his. Ain't the first time he play her music and say it be his, neither. But she still trus' him to help, and he happy t' do it. Happy t' do more'n that, once or twicet, but she swear that be over."

Another long silence, then Lathan nodded decisively. "Mr. Chandler, it just ain't in me t' work 'gainst Angie. She my wife, an' I think she got the right on her side. But you be right 'bout revenge bein' no good to nobody. I tell you what I knows, an' I hope you kin make somethin' good from it. I don' know what Angie gone do with the piano wires, but I knows it be soon. She want those two partic'lar strings, right enough. She tell me they's the lowest note of the 'Maple Leaf Rag,' an' she gone use 'em t' show Mr. Joplin he be the lowest of the low. I don' see how a piano string can show nothin', but she got it all figgered out, an' she prob'ly get that bastard Saunders t' help her do it."

Alan let that hang in the air while he thought.

History doesn't say anything about Mr. Joplin and a piano string, but there are an awful lot of things history doesn't talk about.

"Thank you, Mr. Blackstone. I can see how hard it was to tell me that. I'll do what I can—for your sake." He held out his hand again, and after several seconds, Lathan took it.

● ● ● ● ●

Tom woke just before ten. No sign of Alan other than the wire on the table.

He woulda woke me up if he had to go see Parks again. Time-traveling, I guess.

Tom bundled the wire back into his pack and went about his morning routine. Showered and dressed, he dropped into the chair to call Alan. But before he could reach for his phone, the door lock snapped open and Alan came in.

"Oh, good, you're up. How about some breakfast?"

"You're sure cheerful this morning. Good visit with Mr. Joplin?"

Alan laughed. "I didn't see Mr. Joplin, and I shouldn't be so happy, but I learned a lot. Can't prove any of it, of course, but it all hangs together." He glanced at his watch. "Think there's any place around here where we can get some pancakes at this hour?…Oh, wait. Hold on a minute."

He walked across the room, picked up his cell phone. "Yep. Your grandmother has reported in. Her plane lands at 2:33, so what with renting a car and driving out here, she should arrive by five."

Tom chuckled. "We'll keep that strictly in mind."

"Yes, we will."

• • ● • •

"As long as you allow for Old Angeline being a complete loon, that does kinda make sense," Tom said after he absorbed Alan's story and a stack of pancakes. "I don't see how it helps us, though."

"If nothing else, it gives us insight into that fight Saramae heard at the restaurant. Those people are still trying to tear down Scott Joplin, and promote Angeline." Alan paused in thought. "Too bad JJ didn't take a few more pictures of that music in Aunt Abigail's shrine. Be interesting to know how talented she was."

Tom shrugged. "I guess. Still wouldn't help us any, though. So what do we do while we wait for Gramma?"

"Two things we can do immediately, maybe more later. First, you find Saramae and bring her up-to-date. She's going to want to hear about her many-greats grandmother, no matter how unreliable the source. Second, while you're doing that, I'm going to find out everything about the Noland/Nowlin/Blackstone connection."

Tom choked on the last swig of orange juice. "Everything?" he said when he got his breath back. "How are you going to do that?"

"I've got a source. Betty Singer…Betty *Wasson* Singer. The Wassons have lived in this area practically since General Smith founded Sedalia, and Betty has spent endless hours, days, and years tramping through cemeteries to compose genealogies that could knock your eye out. If she can't find the answers, nobody can."

He dug out a credit card and looked around for the waitress. "When I'm done with that, you, Saramae, and I are going to have another talk with Mr. Blackstone, so wait at Saramae's for me to call you. I'm sure you can find some way to keep yourselves occupied."

• • ● • •

Alan turned left from Mt. Herman Road onto a narrow, hilly, dirt driveway and parked in front of a modest house. Before he could get out, a small woman with a smile like the sun dashed out of the house to stand at the side of the car. Alan slowly pried himself out of the driver's seat, then the two exchanged a brief hug.

"Well, Alan Chandler," the woman said. "Can you imagine how surprised I was to hear your voice on the phone? Whatever are you doing in Sedalia in September? I've never known for you to be here any time besides for the Joplin Festival in June."

"I'll explain, Betty."

"Well, of course. But not standing outside like this. Come on in. I've got coffee and some of my own sticky buns."

• • ● • •

Betty led Alan to the kitchen table, poured him a cup of coffee, then listened, wide-eyed, to his story. "Oh, my goodness!" she breathed. "I've been reading about that in the papers. You say you think I can help you somehow? I've never been involved in a murder investigation, but you know if there is anything I can do, I will."

"Well, you've certainly helped me with a lot of research for my books and articles for a lot of years. And I think maybe you can do some very important research for me now. I…don't exactly know how to say this, but as weird as it sounds, I think I might actually have traveled in time—gone back to 1899, talked to Scott Joplin…"

For the first time, Betty's smile faded. "Alan, I've known you for a long, long time. And I have to say, you're as sensible

a man as I've ever known. But I've got to admit, that *is* just a
little hard to swallow."

"I'm sure. And—Betty, I've got cancer. Prostate. They're
giving me chemotherapy for it, and it could be that either the
disease or the treatment is doing funny things to my mind.
But whether this is real traveling in time or my imagination, I
am learning things about people in ragtime from more than a
hundred years ago that seem to be related to those stories you're
reading in the newspaper. And right now, I need some help,
tying ends together."

While Alan was speaking, Betty had begun to cry quietly. She
dabbed at her eyes with a handkerchief, then reached across the
table to pat Alan's hand. "Oh, Alan, I am *so* sorry."

Alan shrugged. "I'm eighty years old, and when you get to
our age, you have to know that stuff is going to happen, and
you deal with it. Now, if I can find that music—and find out
who killed my friend—that will be the biggest thing that ever
will have happened in my life."

Betty sat up straight. "Well, I can understand—I'm eighty-
four. Okay, what is it I can do for you?"

"With all the books you've put together on genealogies in the
Sedalia area, you're the perfect person for what I need. I'm betting
you can get me information that might tie together a couple of
families in Sedalia—the Blackstones and the Nowlins—"

"The Blackstones? You mean Charles Blackstone, the *Democrat* editor?"

"The same. And also, there's some confusion about the other
family's name. Look for N-O-L-A-N-D and N-O-W-L-I-N. I'm
hoping you can tie them together. Let me explain."

● ● ● ● ●

Betty walked out to the car with Alan. "Okay," she said. "You're
at the Bothwell, right? I'll call you as soon as I have something
to tell you. I don't think it'll take very long."

"Thanks so much, Betty." The two old people hugged again,
then Alan slid into the car, waved, and drove off.

Chapter Fifteen

Alan thought Blackstone wasn't sure how to deal with the three people facing him across his desk. The editor began with a light touch. "You people might not have anything else to do," he said quietly. "But I have a job that takes a bunch of my time every day. It's not easy to have you constantly barging in, looking for information."

Tom, Saramae, and Alan glanced at each other, then Alan spoke. "I'm sorry, Mr. Blackstone. We'll try to take as little as possible of your time, but I think what you can tell us may be very important in finding a thief and a murderer, and retrieving some music that people will still think is important a hundred years or more in the future."

Blackstone leaned back in his chair and guffawed. "You're still all about that music, aren't you? Okay, go on. What is it today?"

"Two things. One, can you please check with the *K.C. Star*, and see what they can tell you about a man named Jarvis Nowlin, who suffered a head injury yesterday. Is he alive? Conscious? In the hospital?"

The editor lost his smile. "'Nowlin'? God in heaven! Those lousy Nowlins again. All right. Can you give me a little more information? Some background?"

"Whatever you need. We all went to Kansas City yesterday and found out the stolen music was being hidden at Mr. Nowlin's house. So we made an attempt—unfortunately, unsuccessfully—to find it. Even more unfortunate, Mr. Nowlin came home while JJ was…uh, inside, looking around, and Mr. Nowlin was carrying a gun. He was about to shoot JJ when Tom snuck up behind him and hit him with a fire iron."

"Jesus Christ on purple roller blades," Blackstone murmured. He shot a glance at Saramae. "And where was my daughter during this break-and-entry and possibly lethal assault?"

Alan motioned Saramae silent. "She was in the car with me. I told you we wouldn't expose her to danger."

"Oh, good. Just great. Chandler, if your grandson there killed Nowlin, my daughter'll get thirty years as an accessory.

"Only if the law knows she was there. And no one who knows would tell them."

The editor snatched up his phone. "Leah, please get *K.C.* on the horn. Find out if they have anything from last night about a Jarvis Nowlin—N-O-W-L-I-N—who was attacked in his house and had a head injury…right. There may be a local interest angle we can use…Yes, thanks."

He set the receiver back into the cradle, then turned heavy eyes onto Alan. "I'm sure I'll regret asking, but you said you had two things to talk to me about?"

"Yes." Alan took a deep breath. "Mr. Blackstone, I've found out some history that has a connection with this robbery and murder, and right now I have a very capable historian tying up the loose ends. But you may be able to give me information that will really put things together. Let's start in the 1970s. If I'm right, there was a duffel bag with a good number of Scott Joplin's compositions, and it was in your father's possession. But Big Jack Jackson stole it from him for a man whose name he thought was Raney. Mr. Raney paid him with a clout from a baseball bat and years in an asylum. But the man's name really was—"

"Nowlin. Richard Nowlin. Jarvis' father. You're right on, Mr. Chandler."

"Thanks, Mr. Blackstone. Can I ask you this: how did your father get hold of that duffel bag?"

Blackstone held up a finger in a "hang on" gesture. After a minute, he blew out a mouthful of air. "I can't give you much detail—remember, I was only four or five years old then. What I've put together over the years is that there's been bad blood between the Blackstones and the Nowlins going all the way back to Joplin's time. I don't know how it got started, but I do know it had something to do with a little hanky-panky in a marriage, and the Blackstones ended up being pro-Joplin and the Nowlins anti-Joplin."

Alan felt a little dizzy. *Either I really have been traveling in time, or I've got one hell of an imagination.*

"My father got a call from a lawyer in K.C. who had a duffel bag of music. He said he had gotten it from the Steadman estate and it might have been written by Joplin. Since he knew about the Blackstones and the Nowlins, he set up a little auction between them. My father and grandfather won. No idea what they paid."

"Amazing," Alan breathed. "But why didn't your father do anything with the music?"

"He and my grandpa were working on it, but they weren't in a hurry; they wanted to do things right. Keep in mind— they happened to buy that music in 1970, right before Joshua Rifkin's recording brought Joplin back into the public eye. All of a sudden, a bag with original, unknown Scott Joplin manuscripts was very hot stuff. The Nowlins were beside themselves, tried everything, no matter how far-fetched, to persuade Pop and Grandpa to sell them the manuscripts, or at least let them in on a deal. Relations between the families went from bad to completely impossible. While all the feuding was going on, Pop and Grandpa were looking into having Rifkin verify the music as Joplin's, and then they were going to copyright it—and that was in 1973, when *The Sting* came out. At that point, the Nowlins gave up any pretense of legality. Richard got Big Jack to steal the duffel bag out of our house."

Blackstone smiled, not pleasantly. "So they were forty-some years ahead of you, Mr. Chandler."

"And you're saying the duffel bag has sat in a Nowlin house for all this time?"

A knock at the door interrupted the conversation. Blackstone called, "Come in." His secretary entered and passed the editor a sheet of paper. He gave her a perfunctory thanks and started scanning the page before she was out of the room.

By the time he finished reading, Blackstone was chortling. "You're gonna love this," he said, and passed the paper to Alan. "World War Three starts in Kansas City, Missoura."

Saramae's and Tom's heads clonked together as they both tried to read over Alan's shoulder at the same time. He held up a finger at them and read silently. After a minute, he looked up. "Well, Tom, guess you didn't kill him. Listen to this: 'At eleven o'clock last night, police were called to the home of Abigail Nowlin on Virginia Ave. to break up a domestic dispute. Ms. Nowlin's cousin, Jarvis Nowlin, reportedly broke into her house and accused her of hiring a thug to rob and beat him. He then allegedly assaulted Ms. Nowlin, inflicting major bruises to her face and knocking out three of her teeth. Ms. Nowlin denied any knowledge or involvement in the incident at Mr. Nowlin's house several hours before. The two combatants were taken to St. Luke's Hospital, where their injuries were attended to; then Mr. Nowlin was removed to the police station and booked on charges of first-degree assault.'"

Saramae giggled. "That take Mr. Jarvis outa the picture for a while. An' ain't no cops gone be watchin' his place, neither."

"We'll have to think about that," said Alan. "Mr. Blackstone, you've been really helpful, thank you. I might want to come back after I've talked to my historian friend, and I hope you'll accommodate me."

Blackstone chuckled. "Your historian friend wouldn't happen to be Betty Singer, would it?"

"How'd you—?"

"A historian in Sedalia who can trace family relationships back to General Smith's days? There are only two possibilities, Betty and Rhonda Chalfont. I guessed and got lucky." He sighed. "I think I'm in with both feet now. Yes, I'll accommodate you, Lord help my sorry soul."

He looked at Saramae. "If I'd known this was going to get you mixed up in committing felony assault and worse, I'd never have written that note for your school."

Then the editor turned a baleful gaze onto Alan. "If you let anything happen to my daughter, it'll take more than God to help *your* sorry soul."

● ● ● ● ●

At the solid triple knock on the door, Alan and Tom looked at each other and grinned. Tom checked his watch. "Four-fifty-eight. You called it."

Alan pulled himself out of the desk chair, walked slowly to the door, and opened it. Miriam, a small suitcase in her hand, her face a mask of uncompromising disapprobation, gave her husband a quick up-and-down.

Alan leaned forward to peck her cheek, took the suitcase from her hand. "Don't just stand there. Come on in."

As Miriam walked into the room, Tom gave her a hug and a kiss. "Glad to see you, Gramma."

She tried, not altogether successfully, to suppress a smile, then flopped into the padded chair. "Jesus, getting older isn't easy. I'm whipped. Used to be, a trip from Seattle to Sedalia was a piece of cake."

Tom walked into the bathroom, came out with a glass of water, which he pressed into Miriam's hand. She swallowed half of it in one gulp, then blew out a long sigh. "All right, thank you, Thomas. Now the two of you can bring me up-to-date on what's going on here. What's new since you talked to me last night?"

Tom made a point of avoiding Alan's eyes.

Alan suppressed a snicker.

Oh, nothing much. A good meeting with Tom Ireland and Lathan Blackstone. Eventually, Lord help me, I'm going to have to tell her about my time-traveling…but not now, not right off the bat. Think, man. Tell her something to keep her satisfied for the time being.

Alan took close to three-quarters of an hour telling Miriam about Mickey's death, the hunt for the music, and his research into the tangled histories of a couple of families, when the room phone rang. He waved Tom off, then walked across the room and picked up the receiver.

"Hello?...Betty—I hadn't expected to hear from you so soon."

• • ● • •

Betty Singer smiled as she hung up the phone. She had never thought of herself as a proud woman, but right now, she found herself thinking she'd better be careful she didn't take a fall. How many people, for how many years, had poked fun at all the time she spent with her nose in hundred-year-old newspapers and books, and prowling through cemeteries with gravestones so ancient that some of them were unreadable? But here was Alan Chandler, the most prominent ragtime historian and musician on Earth, needing her help finding both a bag of lost music written by Scott Joplin and a murderer—and in just a few hours, she had the information he wanted.

She checked her wristwatch: just a bit before five. She had two hours to get dinner together and onto the table—tight squeeze, but far from the tightest she'd dealt with in her eighty-four years. Not enough time to make the pork roast she'd prefer to serve, but no one had ever turned up their nose at her ham and cheese casserole. And how lucky she'd baked a bunch of apple pies that morning for the meeting of the Scott Joplin Foundation. Three would have to be enough for that.

• • ● • •

As Alan pushed his chair back from the table, he loosed a monster belch, then covered his mouth with his napkin. "Sorry," he muttered. "The chemotherapy does that. I can't stop them."

Tom winced. Betty and Miriam nodded sympathetically. "I hear that in China, that's supposed to be a compliment to the cook," Betty said. "I'll take it that way."

"If you do, that would be perfectly appropriate," said Miriam. "The meal was delicious, thank you so much."

Betty smiled. "My pleasure. In all the years you, Alan, and Tom there have been coming for the festival, there's never been time for a dinner here, what with his performance and practice schedule." Quickly, she piled the dishes and carried them to the sink, then returned to the table with a couple of books and several pages of note paper and copies of newspaper articles. "Let me show you what I found," she said. "If I've missed anything, I'll go back and find it."

She set a notepad page in front of Alan. "Here's a pedigree—a family history—of the Blackstones, the Nowlins, and the No-lands." She pronounced the final name as two words. "See, it goes back to the turn of the last century. The central figure is Angeline No-land Blackstone, here. She lived from 1876 to 1951. She was married to a man named Lathan Blackstone, but, well…let's say she didn't take the marriage vows terribly seriously."

Betty laid a newspaper article next to the pedigree. "She played piano in less-than-reputable places in Sedalia, and took up with some of the men she met there. Her husband found out about one of them. There was a nasty scene which led to the end of the marriage."

Tom's eyes widened. "The whole mess made the newspaper. And, wow! Pretty blunt!"

Betty chuckled. "Yes, newspapers then didn't hesitate to publish local scandals—the readers couldn't get enough of them. And the reporters and editors did not mince words. They must have loved Angeline. Did you see this line? 'Scandalizing local society since her arrival this summer.' Doesn't say where she came from, though. If it did, I might be able to trace her family back further."

Alan waved a hand dismissively. "Doesn't matter. It's what happened after she got here that's important right now."

"Saramae might like to know," Tom pointed out.

"Fair enough. Betty, if you stumble on anything, pass it along, but don't put in too much time. I don't want you to feel obligated."

"Oh, it could be fun to try. But let me show you the rest of what I did find. For a few years, Angeline seems to have traveled around the Midwest playing piano, but then she came back to Sedalia."

Betty laid another couple of newspaper articles in front of Alan. "Angeline was at least a little unbalanced. Sometimes in her later years, she created scenes, shouting about Scott Joplin, how he'd stolen her music to write "Maple Leaf Rag," and claiming that the reason he'd moved to St. Louis was to avoid the lawsuit she was planning to slap on him.

"Now," Betty pointed toward the pedigree, "Angeline started two family lines. She and Lathan had a son, William, who stayed with his father when his mother left town. And three generations after William, here you see Charles Blackstone, city editor at the *Democrat*. The Blackstones have all been highly respected people here in Sedalia, at least since William's day.

"On the other hand, here are the Nowlins. The first of them is James. There's no way, I'm afraid, to find out with any certainty who his father was, or where he was born. James was just a baby when Angeline returned with him to Sedalia, so I'd guess whoever the father was, he'd abandoned Angeline not long after James was born."

Betty set another newspaper article in front of Alan. "From the time she came back to Sedalia with her baby, she lived here for the rest of her life, and as James got older, Angeline became more and more of a problem for him. In 1933, he petitioned to have his name and the names of all his family changed from No-land to Nowlin, to try to spare them the embarrassment his mother was causing them. Now that ragtime was over and the…places she played at were closed, she'd taken to begging on street corners and asking for money. But in a way, Sedalia's a small town, and the name change didn't do much by way of distancing the Nowlins from Angeline. So a couple of years later, James and his wife and children moved to Kansas City. But wherever they set down, the Nowlins seem to have been a wild bunch: one of James' grandsons was killed in a bar brawl and a daughter died under suspicious circumstances—according to one article I found, the police suspected her husband might have been involved in her death."

During Betty's report, Alan had been studying the pedigree. "Yes!" he shouted. "Look at this. There are a few lines of Nowlins. Here, we've got Jarvis in the…let's see…the fourth generation. And over there, look, there's Abigail Nowlin and her granddaughter, another Angeline. She'd be that little girl in Niecie's. Abigail's son is Nelson, and…Tom—didn't Saramae say there was a Nelson at the restaurant? I think it all checks out. Old Angeline died in 1951, plenty of time for her to have gotten Abigail Nowlin under her spell. So that's the branch of the family that wants to get their hands on the music to publish it as Old Angeline's. And the Jarvis branch, they're the ones who just want to make a pile of money on it. And the ones Saramae heard in the restaurant saying they want to burn it all and wash their hands of the whole mess are probably scattered around in the other lines."

"Yes!" Tom was bouncing in his seat. "And Saramae said nobody paid any attention to the burners."

"Right. So the only ones that matter, the only likely possibilities for the thief-and-killer, are the ones greedy for money or fame. Jarvis or Abigail. We just need to find out which."

Betty beamed. "So, I've been some help to you."

"A lot. A whole lot."

• • ● • •

The drive back from Betty's had been silent. Alan's back was aching again, Miriam was obviously thinking hard, and Tom was staring blankly out of the window.

"Thomas."

Tom winced. It was never a good sign when his grandmother used his full name.

"Weren't you the one who promised to keep your grandfather out of trouble? 'Won't let anything happen to him'—weren't those your words?"

Tom knew a rhetorical question when he heard one. He kept his mouth shut, but he couldn't stop himself from rolling his eyes.

"Don't you roll your eyes, young man," Miriam shot over

her shoulder. "I could hear it all the way up here." She twisted around in her seat to give him a half-strength Gramma Glare. "I know nobody can keep this old reprobate out of trouble. You're obviously just as bad, but you're young enough that you might still be teachable. Next time you go off on one of these little jaunts...You. Will. Keep. Me. Informed!" She turned the glare up to full-strength. "Hear me, Thomas?"

"Yes, Gramma."

"Good." Miriam rolled her own eyes. "Two of you, alike as two wooden nickels. Girl doesn't stand a chance with the pair of you ganging up on her."

Alan interrupted, "Wooden nickels?"

That got him a glare of his own. "Too weird to toss out, too worthless to keep. That's you. Both of you."

Alan grinned. "Weird and worthless? Sounds about right." He eased the car to a stop in front of the Blackstone house and hit the button to unlock Tom's door. "Give Saramae an update on what we learned from Betty," he said and glanced at his wristwatch. "By the time you've done that, JJ should be at the *Democrat*, and you can swing past there and update him—better than having to walk all the way up to his house and back."

"And then you get yourself back to the hotel," said Miriam. "Your homework will be waiting for you."

"Homework? Gramma!"

"Yes, Thomas, homework. A couple of pages of Math, some Social Studies and English reading, and the instructions for next week's Biology lab." She frowned. "A week to dissect a daffodil? I'm going to have a talk with your counselor when we get home."

• • ● • •

The hotel room door had barely closed behind Alan and Miriam before she demanded, "Out with it, Alan. You've been talking around something all evening, you and your junior delinquent."

Alan sighed. "Hard as it might be for you to believe, that's what I was planning to do." He eased himself into the desk chair with a sigh. "Car seat's too damn soft."

Miriam kicked off her shoes and settled herself on the bed. "Which has nothing to do with whatever you couldn't tell me in front of Betty. Something with your cancer?"

"No! Well...I don't think so, anyway. It's complicated."

"Isn't it always?" She thought for a moment. "It's got something to do with Saramae, doesn't it?"

Alan choked.

"Oh, I know it's not like that—though don't think I haven't noticed how Tom keeps bringing her up! But you've been talking about her however-many-greats-grandfather like he's a personal friend. I've heard you talk about Scott Joplin that way. Some of the other old ragtimers. But never a non-musician."

"I have been talking like I know him, haven't I? Brace yourself, Miriam. That's because I do. In a very strange way." Alan took a deep breath and dived back into the explanation again. "Since we got our hands on those few pieces of music, I've been traveling in time. I've visited 1899 five—no, six—times..."

• • ● • •

Miriam leaned against the headboard. "Okay. I think I get it. Either you're time-traveling—which I doubt—or you're hallucinating. But why is there any question? If you're imagining it, then your body ought to be sitting right here in the present. Correct? What does Tom say?"

Alan suppressed an urge to wince. He had been hoping Miriam would miss that point. "I've never done it when anyone was around," he said. For a moment he thought he was going to get away with it.

"Wait a sec. Wasn't there something...right. Your first morning here, when Tom couldn't find you. That was while you were on your first trip, wasn't it?"

"Well, yes..." Alan resigned himself to his fate.

"So you're wandering around Sedalia with your head in 1899. Alan! You could get killed just crossing the street."

Deep sigh. "I know. The most I can say is that I haven't been killed or even injured. That would be unlikely if I was hallucinating. It's part of the reason why I think I really am going to 1899."

Miriam's scowl spoke volumes. "You do, do you? It's ridiculous, and you know it! If you're hallucinating, walking around in some kind of daze, I want your doctors to see you right now." She folded her arms. "We're going to settle this once and for all. Go. Take another trip. If you vanish, well and good. But if not, and you try to walk out of this room, we're getting on the next flight back to Seattle, and your Detective Parks will just have to lump it. Take as much time as you need. Tom won't be in any hurry to leave Saramae, so we won't be interrupted."

Alan surrendered. "All right. Let's see…" He pulled the piece of piano string and the card out of Tom's backpack, set them on the table, and considered where and when to go. The obvious answer was Angeline's meeting with Scott Joplin. Alan tried to picture the scene, Angeline and Joplin facing off across a table. He had the mental picture of the card in the lockbox under the bar and the piano string in the piano, the sound of the card music, and "Maple Leaf Rag," but no matter how he put them together, that sense of rightness and wrongness eluded him.

Nor was the concentration he needed quite the same as he used in playing piano. The best performances depend on a feedback between performer and audience. He might not be disturbed by the audience, but he always knew they were there and how they were responding to his music. Time-travel needed a more self-contained level of concentration, shutting out the present to allow the past to take over. He couldn't summon it, not with Miriam's eyes digging into his forehead. After a few minutes, he shifted the chair around to the other side of the table, putting her behind his back. That was slightly better, but the necessary state still eluded him.

• • ● • •

Miriam shifted uneasily. Dinner had been delicious, but it was making its way through her digestive system and dealing with it was starting to become an urgent issue. Finally, she stood. "Don't do anything until I get back."

Alan absently waved a hand. He had given up on joining the meeting between Joplin and Angeline, and was ready to settle for catching Joplin alone and getting his version of the discussion. Without the pressure of Miriam's presence, the scene snapped into focus. Joplin at the club's rented piano, darkness outside the windows. The piano string, he felt, was under the bar. He started playing the card strain in his head. Yes, the string *was* under the bar. In an envelope, he was almost sure. The card was in the lockbox. He started the strain again. Once again, a night's accumulation of debris scattered around the room. Walker Williams descending the stairs with a box full of empty bottles. That was right.

Alan took a step forward. "Mr. Joplin! May I have a few minutes of your time?"

• • ● • •

Miriam flushed the toilet and washed her hands. As she dried them, she realized she hadn't heard any noise from the room in several minutes. "Alan?" No response. "Oh, that man!" No Alan in the room. No Alan in the hall. She wasted about a second and a half dithering between checking the stairs or taking the elevator straight to the lobby before deciding on the latter.

The elevator arrived quickly; the ride down was only slightly longer than the wait. No Alan in the lobby. Miriam shot a glance at the desk clerk. His attention was riveted on something behind the counter.

Must be watching a movie on his phone. Wouldn't notice a flock of loons flying through here, let alone one loony old man.

She loosed a sharp "Damn!" before looking around guiltily to be sure nobody had noticed.

• • ● • •

Joplin looked up and smiled. "Alan!" He stood, closing the fallboard over the keys, and crossed the floor, holding out his hand, then withdrawing it to cover a yawn. "I beg your pardon. A long night. It's always a pleasure to have an enthusiastic audience, but you know how draining that can be."

Alan shook the re-extended hand. "I do, and I'm sorry to burst in on you at a time like this. Unfortunately, I have little say in when I can pay you a visit." He shrugged and glanced around the room, making sure they were alone. "Tell me, please, how long has it been since I was last here, the day after the piano was damaged?"

After a moment's startled pause, Joplin thought aloud. "The fight was Wednesday night, and it's now Saturday—Sunday morning, to be precise." He frowned at Alan's muttered curse.

"My apologies. I had hoped it would have been sooner." Alan pulled a chair away from the closest table and sat. "I need to pry into matters that shouldn't be any of my business. Will you allow me?"

"If your questions are so important that you violate the laws of Nature to ask them, it would be foolish of me to deny you." A second later, Joplin smiled. "Still, the laws of Man allow me to decline to answer any question that offends me excessively."

Alan nodded to acknowledge the point. "Thank you. I'll be blunt. More so than I'd like to be. Mr. Joplin, I understand you recently met with Angeline Blackstone—or rather, Angeline Noland."

It hadn't been a question, but Joplin nodded. "She gave the latter name. An uncomfortable meeting. You wish me to describe it?"

"Please."

"It was, let me see, two or three weeks ago. She sent a note asking me to come to the Black 400 Club to discuss a matter of some importance. She was polite at first. Told me that the trio of 'Maple Leaf Rag' was hers."

Joplin's sigh, Alan thought, was more theatrical than the situation really warranted. "I explained that six other people had already laid claim to ownership of that piece, the only one of whom I had so much as met being Otis Saunders." He looked at

Alan. "Otis did, on occasion, play a theme I thought had some potential. Over several months, I developed it, brought out that potential, and used it."

Alan raised an eyebrow.

Interesting. A contribution to "Maple Leaf"? I don't think any ragtime scholar has found a hint that Mr. Joplin would give Saunders any credit whatsoever!

Oblivious to Alan's surprise, Joplin went on. "I told Mrs. Noland as much. That displeased her. 'Otis,' she said, 'took that theme from me. Listen!' She played a rag built on the theme. It was certainly similar to Otis' version, and despite being the first strain of the piece, far from fully developed."

He shrugged. "I pointed out that the question of who played what for whom was a matter she should discuss with Otis—but regardless of who the Muses first bless with an idea, music belongs to the man who develops the idea, writes it down, and publishes it. That being the case, neither she nor Otis was due any portion of the proceeds from 'Maple Leaf Rag.'

"She gave me a look then, Alan, that put me unpleasantly in mind of a lion in a circus menagerie: grim and with far too many teeth. 'Oh, I don't want any money, Mr. Joplin,' she said—you understand I'm paraphrasing, sparing your ears and my tongue her vulgarities—'You must admit that without my involuntary contribution, 'Maple Leaf Rag' would be a far poorer composition. I simply want my contribution recognized. An introduction and recommendation to your publisher and my name on the sheet music as co-composer.'"

Even though Lathan had told him what Angeline had demanded, Alan was still surprised. He had assumed she had shown Joplin several pieces. "A recommendation? On the basis of a single piece of music? Ridiculous!"

"My exact words, Alan. An introduction to Mr. Stark? Certainly. I've introduced many musicians to him. But a recommendation was quite out of question. Nor would he be likely to publish her music if she couldn't deliver it on paper. When I said as much to Mrs. Blackstone, she puffed up and raised a hand as though preparing to scream and strike me. I stood, getting ready to depart before she could carry out any assault, but she mastered herself. Between clenched teeth, she said 'I am quite capable of writing music, and "The Queen of Calico Rag" is hardly my sole composition.'

"I might have apologized for my assumption of her ignorance, however much her speech had justified it, but she then swore at me, accusing me of the commission of a variety of unnatural acts. I wouldn't allow a man to say such things about me, and I was not going to listen to a woman do it. I informed her that the interview was over, and left."

I doubt his exit was that easy or graceful. For that matter, I doubt he was really as polite as he claimed when she demanded credit for "Maple Leaf." But I suspect his version is closer to the truth than Lathan's.

"And since then?" Alan asked.

"I haven't spoken to her since, though she has dogged my footsteps, appearing at performances to glare at me throughout. She was here Wednesday night, in fact, wearing a ridiculous hat, I assume to ensure that I couldn't fail to see her."

Alan nodded. "I saw the hat." He wasn't ready to mention what else he had seen Angeline do.

Walker Williams had been moving around the room, cleaning up the previous night's garbage, but keeping enough distance to allow Alan and Joplin some privacy. Now, however, he approached the table, an envelope in his hand. He nodded at Alan. "Mr. Chandler."

"Mister Williams. Good morning."

"Good enough. 'Pologies for interrupting, Scott, but I found this behind the bar 'long about midnight. Wanted to give it to you afore I went home."

Joplin took the envelope with a smile. "And it was a good excuse to tell me to get on home so you can lock up."

"Now, I never said that!"

"Doesn't mean you weren't thinking it. All right, Walker. A few more minutes to finish our discussion, and I'll pick up my music and we'll clear out. Alan, let's move to another table so Walker can clean this one—or have you learned what you came for?"

Alan was looking at the envelope, blank except for the word "Joplin" in slightly uneven block letters. His impression that the piano wire had been in an envelope under the bar remained with him, and the question of what else might be with it was an uncomfortable one.

When Joplin spoke to him, he shook himself free of thinking, and stood. "I thought I had my answer, but I have a feeling that envelope will ask some new questions." He crossed to the piano with Joplin following. "It's silly of me, but I feel safer in front of a keyboard."

"Safety in Euterpe's arms? Not so silly, I'd say. The Muse should take care of her own, after all." Joplin sliced the envelope open with a clasp knife and shook the contents onto the fallboard.

Much to Alan's relief, the envelope held nothing more than a single sheet of paper and a foot-long piece of piano wire, cleanly snipped at one end and crudely hacked at the other. Alan waited impatiently while Joplin scanned the unsigned letter. It wasn't more than a minute before the composer frowned and handed it to Alan.

You lousy son of a bitch,

The Bible say if you be proud, God will destroy you. Preacher say the higher you look, the easier it be to stumble and the farther you fall.

You steal my music and you proud of the tiny fame your theft has brought you. You the lowest of the low, no matter what you think, and soon you be reminded where you belong.

This wire and another helped you up where you think you is, and soon they show you how low you truly be.

And remember, you fucking bastard, the tool that cut the wire can cut other things too!"

"She has quite an impressive command of the vernacular, doesn't she?"

Joplin sighed. "If she had worked half as hard on her music as she has on pursuing her grievance against me, she could have found a publisher on her own and never had a reason to plague me."

"Only half?"

"Three-quarters, then. But it sounds as if you don't think she's harmless."

It wasn't quite a question, but Alan answered. "Someone with a screw loose can be just as dangerous as anyone else. And it sure looks like she's got more than a couple of loose screws."

"Loose screws? Is the piano falling apart?"

Alan looked up in surprise. "Otis."

"Mr. Chandler. Scott."

Joplin glared. "The piano's fine, Crackerjack. What do you want?"

Saunders was wearing a black suit that had seen a few better days and a faded blue shirt. He winced slightly, but said evenly, "I was hopin' to catch Arthur Marshall 'fore he went home."

"Arthur left hours ago. Something about a young woman, I gather."

"No doubt." Saunders shook his head. "Iff'n you sees him 'fore I do, tell him Ernest Edwards ain't happy 'bout the attention Arthur be paying to his girl."

Alan laughed. "Pot, kettle, Otis? Your girlfriend's husband isn't at all happy about the attention you're paying to her."

"I guess you means Angeline Noland—"

"Oh, so you do know her!"

Saunders ignored Alan's interruption. "Don't you believe everything you hears from her—or her husband, neither."

"Including her claim that you stole her music?"

"She botherin' you with that blather, Scott?"

"It's no bother, Otis. No more than your ridiculous claims against 'Maple Leaf Rag.'" He looked Saunders up and down. "Wearing the contents of your rag bag won't make me any more sympathetic to your claims of poverty. Mrs. Noland's threats against my life, however, are more than just a bother."

"Threats?"

Alan thought Saunders' look of surprise lacked sincerity, but he waved the letter. "These."

Saunders took the sheet and read it quickly.

"Should we believe this?"

"'Course not, Scott." Saunders tossed the letter onto the piano. "Angeline be all talk. 'Thout a man, she helpless." He tugged at one of his cuffs.

"Hardly a gentlemanly thing to say about your girlfriend," Alan said. "But then, if you were a gentleman, you'd hardly have taken up with a married woman, would you?"

Saunders' face darkened. "Mr. Chandler, you an ol' man, so I let that go. But if you be a wise ol' man, you gonna watch where you walk. Sedalia ain't safe for nobody who let his mouth run."

Alan and Joplin watched Saunders storm out of the club before Joplin asked "Was that necessary, Alan? Otis has been a good friend, outside of his insistence on claiming credit for 'Maple Leaf Rag.'" His eyes narrowed. "Or is he involved in something you can't tell me about, something you know from history?"

Alan shook his head. "I don't *know* anything more than that he's been quarreling with you over that claim. But I suspect he knows a lot more about what Angeline is up to than he's letting on." He held up a hand to stop Joplin from interrupting. "I'm not going to accuse him of anything without proof. I hope you'll be careful, though. Maybe Angeline does need a man to do anything—though frankly, I doubt that—but if she does, she's got at least one."

He picked up the letter, slipped it back in the envelope, and looked for the piece of wire. It wasn't on the piano's fallboard, nor, when Alan bent to look, was it on the floor. "Do you have that piece of wire?"

Joplin shook his head. "Wouldn't want it, to be honest."

"I can't argue with that. But someone wanted it, and if it's not you or me, there's only one other candidate." Alan tapped the envelope against his hand. "If you don't mind, I'll take this and dispose of it."

"Dispose...?"

"In more normal circumstances, I'd tell you to take it to the police. But consider who the police report to, and who is currently demanding that the black clubs be closed. Something like this would only add fuel to that fire."

Joplin nodded slowly. "I take your point. But then, what should I do?"

Alan tucked the envelope into his jacket pocket. "Let me see what I can do. For now, don't talk about this mess to anyone. And be careful when you're alone. Walking home, for instance."

Another nod. "I will. It's just up Washington, not that far, and the sun will be up soon."

"Not that soon. But regardless, keep people around you. People you know and trust." Alan noticed Walker Williams leaning against the bar. "I'd best get out of here before Mr. Williams throws me out. I'll be back when I can." They shook hands, and Alan left with a nod to Williams, as Joplin began straightening up around the piano.

"Scott!" As he started down the stairs, Alan heard Williams call, "Give me some he'p with these bottles 'fore you go. Hey, Scott, come on, get your head outa your music!" The closing door cut off any reply Joplin might have made.

● ● ● ● ●

"Mr. Chandler!"

Alan looked across the street toward the voice calling his name. Lathan Blackstone trotted over. "Lathan! What are you doing here?"

"I was...I gotta..." A look of confusion crossed Lathan's face before he shook his head violently and restarted his speech. "I were gonna talk t' Mr. Joplin. Mr. Chandler, I been thinkin' 'bout what you say fo' the last coupla days. I talk t' Mr. Ireland, and he say the same 'bout Mr. Joplin you do. I don' wanna think Angie been lyin' to me, no way, but if she is, I gotta do somethin'. Like

I say, I gotta talk t' Mr. Joplin. Gonna ast him what he done say t' Angie. He tell me true, an' then I knows fo' sure."

Alan suppressed a groan. "Why are you so sure he'll tell you the truth?"

"Because I gonna tell him 'Mr. Chandler an' Mr. Ireland, they say you be an hones' man, so you gotta tell me true or they not respec' you no mo'." He gave Alan a wide-eyed look of innocence that expressed total confidence in the logic of his argument.

That stopped Alan cold. He ran the idea back and forth in his mind a couple of times before giving up. "Mr. Blackstone, your faith in your fellow man puts me to shame." He held out his hand and Lathan, the confused expression back on his face, shook it. "Unfortunately, this is a very bad time to talk to Mr. Joplin about your wife." Alan hesitated, then pulled the envelope out of his pocket and extended it to Lathan. "I don't know if you can read it in this light—"

"The light don' matter none. I gots my numbers an' enough letters t' sign my name, but tha's all."

"Oh. Then you should ask Mr. Ireland, or someone else you trust to read it to you. It's a letter from your wife to Mr. Joplin. You should hear what she said in her own words. I don't want to say more than that."

"It be bad, then."

"I'm sorry, Lathan."

Lathan shook his head. "I ask Mr. Ireland to read the letter, Mr. Chandler. If it be bad, I do what I has t' do." He sighed. "Iff'n I can't see Mr. Joplin now, I best be gettin' back t' work. Mr. Carter give me an hour fo' my dinner, but I come here steada eatin'." He started to walk toward Washington Avenue.

Alan hesitated, then fell into step beside Lathan. After a few steps, he said "Did you see Otis Saunders leave the club a few minutes ago? Which way did he go?"

"I seed him, sure. He go this way, and turn onta Washin'ton." Lathan hesitated. "If he go the other way, up Ohio, I woulda follered him, in case he were goin' to see Angie."

"I need to go after him." They turned the corner onto Washington while Alan was talking.

"Inta Lincolnville? That a bad idea, Mr. Chandler."

"I know it is, but I don't have a choice. Mr. Joplin's house is that way." He gestured in the direction they were walking. "I'm afraid Otis is going there to set some kind of a trap for Mr. Joplin."

They walked up the block in silence. Lathan stopped at the corner of Washington and St. Louis and put a hand on Alan's shoulder. "You know where Mr. Joplin live?"

Alan paused. *Chemo brain again, shit!* "I can't remember the number, but it's somewhere up Washington."

Lathan stared at him. "You jus' gonna go wanderin' around Lincolnville in the middle uh the night lookin' for Otis Saunders? By yo'self? Is you crazy, Mr. Chandler?"

"Probably. But I can't just let him do whatever he's going to do."

A deep sigh. "Then I come with you. You tryin' t' do the right thing. I cain't let you get yo'self hurt or kilt."

● ● ● ● ●

They crossed St. Louis and continued north. Their pace was slow, sparing Alan's back and letting them peer behind the trees and shrubbery separating the houses. Streetlights were non-existent north of Main Street, and Alan was grateful for the light given by the moon, just past its third quarter.

Beyond Johnson, Alan was ready to throw in the towel, when Lathan whispered, "Somethin' movin' ahind the trees across the street."

Alan leaned forward, trying to see, and immediately felt foolish. "Is it Otis?"

"I'se not sure it even be a person. We has t' get closer."

The trees stood close together beside a two-story white house. A gravel path ran straight from the curb to the bottom of three stairs leading up to the front porch; the trees were just a few steps from the porch.

As they reached the curb, Alan caught a flash of movement between the trees. He nudged Lathan in the ribs and pointed, just as Lathan was doing the same to him. Lathan whispered harshly, "Preten' you don' see nothin'. We walk pas' an' look back, see what goin' on."

Alan nodded, and kept walking, resolutely keeping his eyes on the sidewalk until they were well past the trees. That view was even worse: a third tree stood directly between them and their target.

Lathan blocked Alan's move toward the trees. "Lemme go firs'. White man shouldn' go sneakin' aroun' in Lincolnville. If that be Otis Damned Saunders, I call you. Else, I comes back an' we keep lookin'."

Splitting up sounds like a bad idea—but he's right that I'd be a risk if that's not Otis. Alan nodded and waved a hand treeward.

Lathan turned and moved surprisingly quietly across the grass in the moonlight. Alan lost sight of him as he stepped into the trees' shadow. A few seconds later, he heard Lathan shout, "What the hell you doin' wit' my wife, you son of a bitch?!"

Damn it to Hell! Alan started forward at his best speed, only to reflexively dodge aside, allowing Angeline to fly past and avoiding the slap she aimed at his head with one gloved hand. His automatic grab for her was late, and her tight-fitting men's shirt and pants wouldn't have given him much purchase anyway. She was down the street and turning the corner onto Johnson before Alan could take more than a few steps after her. He shook his head and went on toward Lathan.

The big man had Saunders trapped against the trunk of one of the trees, his right hand on his opponent's sternum, anchoring him as securely as if he had been nailed in place. Saunders' unbuttoned fly and dangling penis made the answer to Lathan's question obvious. As Alan approached, Lathan buried his left hand in Saunders' stomach, then released the smaller man, who gagged and doubled over. Lathan kicked him onto his back and stepped on his stomach, causing another gag.

"Wait, Lathan! Let me talk to him a minute."

Lathan ground his foot into Otis' gut, then swore as Otis vomited explosively onto Lathan's leg and his own chest. "Talk quick, Mr. Chandler. I got somethin' to tell this bastard, an' I don' wanna wait."

Alan leaned over Saunders. "What did you do, Otis? What were you planning for Mr. Joplin?"

"Wire...on..." A cough. "Stairs. *Her* idea." Another cough and a deep breath. "Trip him an' tell him how much worse it gonna be if...if he don't pay what...he owe."

"I'm thinking there was more to it than that. Somebody threatened Mr. Joplin with a pair of wire cutters. You telling me that wasn't you two?"

Saunders managed a faint laugh as Lathan frowned. "That jus' be a bluff. She done put the other wire in her pocket, but she di'n't even look at the cutters."

As if a piano string is harmless. He looked up. "I'm really sorry you had to hear this, Lathan. Don't assume he's telling the truth about who was planning to do what."

Lathan nodded. "I knows, Mr. Chandler. Man like that, he say anythin' if he think it get him outa trouble. Me 'n' Angie is gonna have a long talk when I gets home."

Alan squeezed his shoulder before he turned back to Saunders. "And what were you planning to do if someone else came along first? There are other people living in that house. Come down the stairs quickly, hit that wire, someone innocent could have been killed."

"We was watchin'—"

Alan laughed. "Doing a lousy job of it, I'd say." He stepped back. "Don't kill him, Lathan. You don't need that on your conscience."

"Wasn' gonna kill 'im." Lathan dug his foot into Saunders' stomach until he gagged again. "Just gonna learn him 'bout messin' where he shouldn' oughta."

"Fair enough. More than fair." Alan looked back at the man on the ground. "Consider what's about to happen to you as a lesson in not mixing business and pleasure, Mr. Saunders." He headed for the front of the house, trying to tune out the sounds of Lathan's teaching method.

The piano wire had been stretched between the lowest pair of newel posts. It was anchored with two shiny screw eyes, a few inches above the top of the lowest step, the perfect height to catch a careless foot. Alan pulled out his Leatherman and snipped the wire off the screws at both ends. He started to put the tool back in his pocket, then changed his mind. *Don't want Otis taking this wire back to Angeline so they can try again.* He quickly snipped the wire into six-inch lengths and carried the pieces back under the trees.

Saunders was sprawled on his back, gasping for breath. His nose was obviously broken, bent to the right and bleeding. The rest of his face bore a large collection of scratches and rapidly developing bruises.

Alan dropped his handful of wire snippets on Saunders' chest. "Don't try it again, Otis." He turned to Lathan, who was wiping his hands on a grease-stained cloth. "Are you done?"

Lathan grunted something that sounded vaguely affirmative, then stuffed the cloth into his back pocket. "S'pose I is. He still alive, but he not gonna be happy fo' a long time." He looked around absently, his ring catching a stray bit of moonlight as he turned. "Le's get you back south o' Main, then I guess I gotta have it out with Angie." He sighed. "I ain't gonna thank you for tellin' me what Angie doin', Mr. Chandler, but I ain' gonna blame you none, either. 'Magine I woulda found out sooner or later."

He took a couple of steps toward the street, then ducked back under the trees. "Some un's comin'."

Saunders groaned as Alan looked down Washington. "It's Mr. Joplin! Lathan, keep the bastard quiet."

Lathan whipped his rag out of his pocket again and shoved it in Saunders' mouth. When Saunders groaned around the gag, Lathan added a knee on his chest, pressing down on his ribs. Otis' breath rushed out, and he gasped, but quietly.

Alan watched Joplin shuffle along the gravel path and up the stairs with a lack of energy that spoke eloquently of a long day after not enough sleep. He stumbled slightly on the top step, and Alan had to force himself not to smack his forehead in dismay. Joplin closed the door behind himself, and Alan turned back to Otis.

"If Mr. Joplin ever hears about what happened tonight, I'm going to assume it came from you. You won't like what happens after that. Get it?"

A nod.

Alan pulled the cloth out of Otis' mouth and handed it back to Lathan. "Better wash that well. No telling what kind of slime he's carrying around."

● ● ● ● ●

Alan glared at Bryant-Tewmey Dry Goods' locked door. *Hell! All I want to do is take my meds and collapse for a couple of hours, and I'm stuck here until they open for business. Are they even going to open on a Sunday? Shit. How am I going to explain this to Miriam?*

Chapter Sixteen

Saramae's face brightened when she opened the door for Tom. "I'm sittin' in the living room with Daddy," she half-whispered. "We're talkin' about what's been going on. You got something new?"

"Heck, yeah!"

"Sweet. You kin tell the both of us."

● ● ● ● ●

Charles Blackstone rose to shake hands with Tom. "I'll say this for you and your grandfather—I've never seen my daughter so serious about anything. I think she just might be finding her niche in life. I was afraid she wasn't ever going to take an interest in anything besides her latest boyfriend. I'd be happier if it was a less...well, *adventurous* news story she was chasing, but at least she's getting into the family business, and I can't object to that." He waved Tom toward a group of chairs. "Since you're here, I suppose that means Betty Singer turned up something."

Tom settled into the left side of a loveseat; Saramae plopped down next to him. Blackstone sat in a large wingback chair opposite. "Well, Betty found a lot of information about both the families who've been chasing Joplin's music."

Blackstone's eyes opened wider. "Really? Like what?"

"She started with Angeline No-land—that's how she pronounced it—and her husband and son, Lathan and William, and how the Blackstones have been respectable people. Right down to you."

Blackstone chuckled. "Meaning my daughter isn't?"

Saramae kept silent, unwilling to interrupt Tom's recitation, but couldn't resist sticking her tongue out at her father.

"Betty said Angeline left her husband and went around the Midwest playing piano, and then came back to Sedalia with a baby, James No-land. It sounds like Angeline was a real nut case. That was why James changed his name to N-O-W-L-I-N and moved his family to Kansas City—just to get away from her."

Tom paused. Anything further, about the way the Nowlins had separated into the Greed Clan and the Fame Clan, had not come from Betty's work, but from Saramae's eavesdropping in the restaurant. He was sure Blackstone wouldn't be happy to hear about that episode, so he went on talking as if the material had in fact come from Betty.

"It looks like over the years, James' descendants have separated into two groups, both of them chasing this batch of Scott Joplin's music. Don't know why they haven't worked together, but they absolutely won't cooperate. So now we've got at least three factions, two bunches of Nowlins and the Blackstones. That's about it, I think."

Blackstone shook his head sadly. "What a shame. Two bashed heads—maybe more—and a murder…and over what? A torn-up old, black duffel bag with a bunch of yellowing sheets of paper in it. I'll give you that they're special sheets of paper, but are they worth a man's life?"

"Oh, horseshit, Daddy. It ain't like Joplin wanted anyone to git killed. He ain't 'sponsible fo' what people try an' do with his music papers."

Blackstone grunted, and they shared a rare moment of familial silence.

Eventually, Tom looked at his watch. "I've got to update JJ too, and then get back to the hotel." He didn't mention homework. "I can catch him at the *Democrat*—Saramae, you wanna come?"

"Sho'. Of course."

Blackstone frowned. "It's getting pretty late...aw, nuts. I know when I'm fighting a losing battle. You will see her back here before you go to the hotel, I trust."

"Promise."

As soon as the couple reached the sidewalk, Tom said, "I wanted you to come so I could say something I couldn't say in front of your father."

"That the only reason you wanted me along?"

"'Course not."

She grinned and linked her hand into the crook of his arm.

"That business about the two lines of Nowlins...how they separated into the Greed Clan and the Hooray-for-Angeline Clan? You're the one who found that out, but I figured we didn't want your father to know how you learned it. But I wanted *you* to know that *I* know who really gets the credit."

"Good thinkin'. That wasn't so bad as breaking and entering, but try tellin' him that." She chewed at her upper lip. "But something's not quite right..."

"Something like what?"

"Dunno. Can't put my finger on it."

"Maybe it'll come out when we talk to JJ. You think it'll bother him or his boss if we come in looking to talk to him?"

"Nah. Won't take long; we'll probably be gone before his shift even starts."

● ● ● ● ●

Updating JJ didn't shake loose whatever it was that bothered Saramae. Tom kept sneaking glances at her on the way from the *Democrat* back to her house.

She's usually chattering like crazy. Why so quiet all of a sudden?

As they turned the corner onto Moniteau and walked toward the Blackstone house, Saramae suddenly let out a whoop and grabbed Tom's arm. "I got it! Son of a bitch, I *got* it!"

"Ow! Hey, don't tear off my arm. Got what?"

She didn't answer directly, just towed him up the front walk, through the hall, and down the basement stairs. At the speed

Saramae yanked him down the rickety wooden stairs, Tom was afraid they'd miss a step and wind up in a heap at the bottom. Saramae flipped a light switch at the foot of the stairs and pulled him across the room to an ancient furnace. She yanked the door open and pulled out a duffel bag.

For a moment, neither of them spoke. Then Saramae erupted into a barrage of the foulest language. "Oh, that fucker!" she screeched. "Jesus H. Fucking Immaculate Conception Christ on a crutch. That son of a bitch, bastard! With his goddamn pure-white-fancy-ass Harvard talk. Cocksucker talks whiter'n *you*, for Chrissake."

Tom slapped a hand over her mouth. "Shh! He's gonna hear you and wake up."

Saramae pulled the hand away. "No fuckin' way. When he goes to sleep, he might's well be dead. I could be yellin' 'fuck you' in his ear, and he wouldn't do more than turn over."

She gave a savage tug to the strings at the top of the duffel bag, peered inside, then held it out for Tom to see. "That's it, all right. If that ain't all the music, I'll eat it.

"See, now, here's what was botherin' me before. Remember what he said: 'A torn-up, old black duffel bag with a bunch of yellowing sheets of paper'? But the Nowlins grabbed it way the fuck back in the seventies! He was what? Five? Four? And we're supposed to believe he ain't seen it since? Horseshit! Bullshit! *Pigshit!* If his old man even showed it to him at all—a little kid like that—he ain't gonna remember it that well all these years later. I *knew* he had to have seen it pretty damn recently."

Tom pointed at the furnace. "But how did you know…?"

"He thinks he's so fuckin' smart. He stashes all kinds of stuff in there. This old coal furnace hasn't been used since Granddaddy put in forced-air heating before I was born. When Daddy's workin' on a juicy story at home, he doesn't want to leave stuff that could be embarrassin' out in the open where li'l ol' me might see it and get my tender li'l titties all in an uproar. But I saw him sneakin' my Christmas presents down here when I was five or six. Found 'em hidden in the furnace along with a bunch of papers and even a little money—some kind of emergency fund, I guess. Wasn't interested in the papers back then, but now I sneak down sometimes to see what's really goin' on—the stuff he doesn't put in the paper."

The girl began to cry. "My father's a crook. A thief and a murderer. Well, fuck that shit! He's not gonna get away with it." She yanked the duffel bag strings closed. "Come on."

"What? Come on where? What the hell've you got in mind?"

She planted a hand on one hip, and regarded the boy as if he were an idiot. "Where do you think? I ain't gonna go to the fuckin' cops! We're goin' to the hotel and find your granddaddy. He'll know what to do."

• • ● • •

Tom turned his key in the room door lock, pushed the door open, and motioned Saramae inside. From the bed nearer the window, Miriam stared at the youngsters. No one spoke.

Tom glanced at the bathroom; the door was wide open, no Alan there. No Alan anywhere in the room. Only one possibility. "He's…t-time-traveling again?" the boy stammered.

He thought his grandmother might fly from the bed and do a couple of loops around the room, but she settled to turn a disapproving face on her grandson. "Either that or he's wandering around the city somewhere, hallucinating," she grumbled. "And I don't know which to hope for. But don't you think you might introduce me to your friend there? The one carrying a duffel bag."

"Sure, sorry, Gramma. This is Saramae Blackstone, and she's working with us…" He jabbed a finger at the duffel bag. "*And* she just found the missing music. Saramae, this is my gramma, Miriam Chandler."

"I'm pleased to meet you, Saramae," Miriam said as she swung her legs off the bed. "Tom's mentioned you once or twice since I got here." She winked at the girl. "Maybe a few times more—certainly no more than a dozen, anyway."

"I'm glad to meet you, Mrs. Chandler…" Saramae extended the duffel bag toward Miriam, then lost her precariously held composure and started to bawl. "My goddamn…father's a crook and a…murderer." She dropped the duffel bag onto the floor and covered her eyes with her hands.

Miriam hustled over to the girl's side, steered her toward the desk chair. "Come sit down and let's talk about it." She turned to Tom. "Sit down, young man. Let's see whether we can all get to the bottom of this business."

Tom dithered, then scooped up the duffel and set it on the table, covering his homework, not entirely by accident. He sat on the bed, close to Saramae.

Miriam bent and put an arm around the girl. "I can't believe it. A respected man, raising a daughter, wouldn't do something like that." Saramae sniffled for a moment, then buried her face in Miriam's shoulder and started crying again. Miriam looked at Tom and mouthed, "Help me out here!"

Stalling for time, Tom said "Saramae." He touched her shoulder. "Saramae, look at me, please. Your father didn't do it."

Slowly, she turned toward him. "The hell he didn't!" she said between sobs. "The bag was in his hiding place!"

Tom waved a hand dismissively. "But he didn't kill Mickey. I'm sure of that. Gramma's right. Your father might get all pissed off and take it out on somebody. But torture and kill someone? No way!"

Saramae's expression said she wanted to believe Tom, but couldn't quite bring herself to it. "But…"

"But, nothing. No way he'd do anything like that!"

Miriam nodded. "I don't know your father, but from everything Alan's told me, I'm sure Tom is right. Take a deep breath, wipe your eyes, and let's figure out how to prove it."

• ● ● ● ●

Alan kicked Bryant-Tewmey's front door.

Damn it! No, of course they're not going to open today. Nobody in Sedalia is open on Sundays, even in 2015. They're sure not going to be any more liberal now. He kicked the door again. It rattled, but didn't open. He glanced around. *I could break the display window, but the sun's up. Somebody might see me, and then I'd be well and truly fucked. Maybe there's a back door.*

He walked the few steps to the corner and looked down Fourth. There was a gap between the back of the dry goods store and the next building along the street. *Or a window that isn't so obvious.* Alan walked slowly down the sidewalk, staying close to the building in an attempt to stay hidden in the shadows. A dozen steps, and the light changed, early morning sunlight replaced by late night darkness broken by electric streetlights.

What the hell? Alan leaned against the wall next to the Both-well's front door and took a deep breath. A moment's thought gave him an answer.

Like when I time-traveled from Fitter's. I came back when I got close to the music. This time, I bet it was the wire. Nothing to do with going inside. The wall of the building must be close enough to our hotel room to do the trick. Good to know.

He swallowed a Vicodin and stretched his back, trying to work out the pain before facing Miriam.

• • ● •• •

Saramae wiped an arm across her eyes, stared at Miriam and Tom for a second. "Can…can I have a tissue?"

"Here you go," Alan said, handing her several.

"Alan!" A duet by Miriam and Tom, followed a second later by Saramae's solo "Mr. Chandler!"

"Sorry. I didn't mean to startle anyone. I must have been right behind you kids—somebody was going up when I got to the elevator. Saramae, they're right. Your father might've stolen the bag from Mickey, but he didn't kill him. Remember the autopsy report?" Before she could answer, he held up a hand. "Hang on a second. I'm really behind on my meds." He stepped into the bathroom and started gathering pills from the bottles on the counter.

Miriam asked the room, "Will somebody please tell me what the autopsy said?"

"The cause of death was strangulation with piano wire," Tom replied.

Saramae nodded. "And—" A vigorous sniff. "'Scuse me. And he was burned with cigarettes and beaten up." Her face lit up. "And my daddy doesn't smoke."

Alan came back into the room and claimed the chair. He rested a hand on the duffel bag, but forced himself not to open it. "It also said the pattern of bruises and scratches suggested that the torturer was right-handed and wore rings. I don't recall your father wearing a ring."

"He doesn't. He took off his wedding ring a couple of years ago when he tried online datin'. It didn't go anywhere, but he never put the ring on again. *And* he's left-handed, like me." She took a deep breath and looked relieved for an instant, then frowned. "But none of that proves anything. Easy enough to buy cigarettes. And the other stuff, he coulda done to fake out the cops."

Alan nodded slowly. "True. It's all what a lawyer would call circumstantial evidence—like JJ being out looking for his father around the time Mickey died. None of it is proof, but pile up enough, and it does a good job."

Miriam harrumphed. "Maybe in a court, Alan, but not in the heart. There's only one way to prove her father's innocence where it matters." She tapped her breastbone. "You—we—have to find the real killer!"

Alan held both hands up at head level, palms forward. "You're right, you're right. But a lot easier said than done."

"Heck, it's gotta be Abigail or Jarvis," Tom put in. "That's what you said at Betty's. They didn't steal the duffel bag, but that doesn't let 'em off the hook for Mickey. Makes one of 'em even more likely—trying to make him tell where the bag was, but he couldn't because he didn't know."

A long moment of silence passed while everyone processed the idea before Alan slapped his forehead. "That's what Mickey was trying to tell me! Tom, where's that note?"

Alan snatched up the page from Tom, and tapped the music at the top. "*Swipesy Cake Walk.* That's what pointed us to JJ in the first place."

Miriam and Saramae exchanged baffled looks, which Alan missed completely.

"I'll explain later," Tom whispered.

"We thought Mickey wanted to say he was afraid the thief might come back." Alan was caught up in his brainstorm. "And he was, but it's also a clue. He mentions two of Fats Waller's songs—mischief and misbehaving—and even wrote Fats' name to tell us the thief was a big black guy. Like your father, Saramae. Right? And we know the thief didn't come back. Why should he? He had the music."

"Still just more circumstantial evidence."

"But it also backs up Tom's idea. The thief left and Mickey didn't know if he got away with the duffel bag or not, because he was too drunk to open the hidey-hole. So when the killer started torturing him, Mickey couldn't tell him anything."

Saramae nodded, a little reluctantly. "Okay, I see that. But Daddy coulda come back and—no, wait, I get it. Even if Daddy thought Mickey recognized him, and came back to shut him up, there wasn't any reason to torture him."

"Right." Alan didn't point out there was no evidence proving the torturer was also the murderer. "So now what?"

Miriam spoke up. "Now we get some sleep. It's the middle of the night, and Saramae's father isn't going anywhere. Neither is the killer. So let's pick this up in the morning. You'll plan your next move better with clear heads."

Saramae glanced at the bag. "I gotta talk to Daddy about this."

"Not now, though," Alan said. "Wake him up in the middle of the night, accuse him of being a thief…That's not going to be a good conversation. And it'll cause a big fuss. Let's find the killer, settle the whole mess. *Then* you can talk to your father."

"But how am I gonna sit there at breakfast and not say anything?"

"That, we can fix." Miriam reached for the desk phone. "We'll get you a room here. You don't want to be going home this late anyhow. Tomorrow, you can tell him you're following a hot lead. That's nothing more than the truth." She turned a mild Gramma Glare on Tom. "Put your tongue back in your mouth, Puppy. You're sleeping right here, in the same bed you've had all week."

• • ● • •

A little after eight, Alan gave up trying to get back to sleep. He sat up slowly and quietly so he wouldn't wake Miriam.

These days, five hours is doing well. Might as well get up and dig into that bag while I wait for everyone else.

"All right, Buster, just what did you think you were doing last night?" Miriam sat up and leaned back against the headboard.

Alan groaned and leaned back as well. "Well—"

"Skip the three lies you have queued up. It's too early in the morning for your nonsense."

"Lies? Moi?"

"You." Miriam elbowed him in the ribs. "I asked you to wait until I got back. Why did you take off?"

"It wasn't entirely my idea. Time-travel is more like composing than performing. You know how I get wrapped up in the music when I'm writing. You've complained about it often enough—dinner cold because I needed five more minutes that turned into a couple of hours. If you asked me to wait on the time-travel, I didn't really hear you."

"You had me scared to death, Alan! You could have been in trouble—dead, even—and I never would have known!"

"Shh, let's not wake Thomas. I'm sorry, I really am. Once I went, one thing led to another. And then I had trouble getting back. If you thought nothing happened on Sundays in Sedalia now, you should see it in 1899. I had to—well, that can wait."

"The only reason I agreed to let you do it—"

"Agreed?"

Miriam ignored the interruption. "—was to settle the question of where you were once and for all. You disappeared for hours and came dancing in here like nothing had happened, and we still don't know what's going on with you. No more!"

"Miriam—"

"No. More. I mean it. Alan, I go where you go. That's always been our agreement. Whether you're going to 1899 or someplace inside your own head, I can't follow you. And I can't protect you if I'm not there."

Alan shook his head. "Sorry, I won't accept a fiat decree. I have too much unfinished business in 1899 to just stop time-traveling—but I won't go off again without talking to you first."

• • ● • •

Tom woke to an unseasonably cool atmosphere. It wasn't the first time his grandparents had been at odds, but it wasn't common, either. Even half-awake, he knew better than to step into the middle of the disagreement before he knew what the issue was. *Keep my mouth shut, go about my business, and they'll sort it out.* Aside from morning greetings, he didn't say a word until he was showered and dressed. At that point, he figured he should make sure one important issue was resolved. "What are we doing about breakfast?"

Alan started. Breakfast hadn't been anywhere on his mental to-do list, but he rallied quickly. "Depends. We should bring JJ and Elvira up-to-date. Why don't you give them a call? Make sure JJ doesn't go to bed as soon as he gets home from work, and see if they want us to bring something over."

"Or if Elvira volunteers to make another of her pancake spreads. Got it."

Tom was still on the phone when Saramae knocked on the door. Miriam let her in, then interrupted Tom. "Whatever you're agreeing to, make it a half-hour later. We need to get this girl some fresh clothes." He nodded, and Miriam turned back to Saramae. "I should have thought of that last night. Sorry, Honey."

"S'okay, Ms. Chandler. I'm fine for now, and I can run out and pick up somethin' later."

"Don't be silly. Nobody can do their best work if they don't feel their best—and nobody feels their best wearing the same clothes day after day." She fixed Alan with a quarter-strength glare. "Something you gentlemen might want to keep in mind. How many days' clothes did you pack?"

"Enough."

Saramae was jittering in place. "I appreciate the thought, Ms. Chandler, but I can't take—"

"Nothing to worry about," Alan broke in. "We'll swing past your house on the way over to JJ's. Your father'll be at work by then, so you can run in, change, pack up enough clothes for a few days, and leave him a note saying you're chasing a lead. You won't even need to talk to him until this is settled."

"Elvira says to come over in about an hour and a half." Tom tried to duplicate the old woman's soprano, "'So's I kin show Miz Chandler some proper Sedalia hospitality.'" Halfway through, he choked and finished in his usual tenor.

"Perfect. Okay, Saramae?"

"I suppose. But what if Daddy's workin' from home?"

"We'll cross that bridge when we come to it. I can come in and talk to him. Or, better yet, Miriam can—he'll believe her, where he'd doubt anything I told him."

Miriam shook her head sadly. "Anyone would doubt you." She looked at Saramae. "He'd have starved to death decades ago if I hadn't been booking gigs and looking after him."

Tom nodded to himself.

That's what they're fighting about, all right. Gramma wants to get Alan home, close to his doctors, and he's not ready to leave Sedalia. He'll out-stubborn her, but it's going to be frosty for a while.

"This is more of the same thing he always does," Miriam went on. "Loves to make everything up on the fly. Half the time, he doesn't even have a set list when he goes on stage." She crossed her arms. "Is there any more of a plan than the next step? You brief JJ and his grandmother, then what?"

"Well…" Alan paused to think, but went on quickly when he saw Miriam opening her mouth again. "We can't plan without JJ. He's as much a part of this as anyone else."

Tom decided it was time to step in. "Alan…JJ is going to bed when we leave. Whatever we do today will be without him. And we gotta do *something*, so let's figure out what."

Come on, Alan. Don't argue.

Alan gave in. "Sorry, guys, you're right. I suppose I'm just being ornery." He looked around the room. "What are we going to do today? Anyone?"

"We're gonna prove my daddy didn't kill anyone."

"Yeah, but how?"

Saramae shot Tom a poisonous look. "Duh! Like we agreed last night: we find out who the real killer is. Abigail or Jarvis, right? I figure it's gotta be Jarvis. He's a big man, almost as big as Daddy, and he was runnin' a bluff, tellin' Abigail he had the music. No way he'd try a game like that unless he knew the bag wasn't at Mickey's." She turned to Alan for support.

Alan frowned. "I…think you're right. I have a feeling we're missing something, but…" He shrugged. "Sooner or later, I'll think of it. For now, we focus on Jarvis."

"Like Saramae said yesterday, we know he's locked up," Tom said. "We never got to look around his house, so let's do it. See if we can find something to tie him to Mickey. Or Maggione. That'd be almost as good."

"Thomas! Are you planning to break into someone's house?"

"I guess so, Gramma, since he wasn't nice enough to give us a key last time we dropped by."

Miriam rolled her eyes. "Was picking locks part of that homework I brought you? Social Studies, maybe?"

"Uh…I bet JJ can teach me. How hard can it be?"

"If it was easy, everyone would be doing it," Alan said.

"We can ask him!"

"We can. But if he's going to teach anyone, it's not going to be you."

"Who? You? And why?"

"No, not me. In case you've forgotten, Detective Parks is getting downright mad about us leaving Sedalia. Right now, there are only two people who can go check out Jarvis' house."

"What?!" Miriam sat up straight. "Alan! You can't be serious!"

"I'm very serious. You said 'we' had to find the killer, and right now you and Saramae are the only ones who can go to Kans' City." He smiled. "Think of it as an adventure."

"But—"

"Don't forget— if you go, I don't have to. Wouldn't you rather have me stay here, close to emergency services?"

Miriam slapped both hands onto her thighs. "You're being stubborn, as usual. I could stand on my head and spit nickels, and you wouldn't budge an inch, would you?"

Alan shook his head.

"Fine. First you drag your grandson into a life of crime, and now your wife. Saramae, how do you feel about learning to pick locks? At my age, I'd make a poor housebreaker—but I promise I'll be the best getaway driver you've ever had!"

That drew a giggle from Saramae. "Never had one of those before. If JJ can teach it, I can learn it, and it sure sounds like more fun than anything they teach in school." She bounced to her feet. "Daddy'll be at work now. Let's hit the road."

As the rest of the group stood, Alan said, "Don't get too excited, Saramae. You can learn how to pick locks if you want, but Miriam has to be the one to go into Jarvis' house."

Miriam's jaw dropped and Saramae stopped mid-step. "What? Why not, Mr. Chandler?"

"Yes, 'Mr. Chandler,' why not?"

"Because Saramae went into Niecie's during the Nowlin clan gathering. If Jarvis comes home while you're there—unlikely as that is, seeing how he's currently a guest of the K.C. police, he might recognize her. But Miriam's never been anywhere near him. She could convince him she's got nothing to do with the duffel bag and the music. Saramae, though…if he remembers he saw her at the restaurant, right before he caught JJ in the house, he'll know it's about the bag, and it's got nothing to do with Abigail."

Miriam dropped back onto the bed. "No."

Alan didn't say anything, just widened his eyes and gave her an innocent look. *How can you resist those puppy-dog eyes?*

"No, Alan."

"Miriam, *please*. For Mickey's sake."

"That old bum."

Alan lowered himself onto the bed beside her. "All us old bums have to stick together," he said quietly. He dropped his voice to a whisper. "And do you really think Saramae is the right person for the job? Smart girl, yes, but impetuous. Undisciplined. What if she misses a clue because she skips a room or doesn't recognize it? Leaves a clue to her identity behind?"

"Well…"

"You'd err on the side of safety. Take precautions, miss nothing."

Miriam sighed and buried her face in her hands. "You're the consummate bullshitter. You know that, right?"

"So you've told me, many times." Alan stood and held out a hand. "Come on. Elvira makes a mean pancake."

• ● ● ● •

Alan couldn't help smiling as he looked around the room. Elvira wasn't taking half-measures in showing Miriam real Missoura hospitality. The white tablecloth on the dining room table was spotless. Polished silverware gleamed. Six settings, dishes neatly placed, sparkling water glass and small juice glass at each location. At the center, a pitcher of orange juice, a steaming coffee pot, and a platter heaped with enough pancakes for a small army. Which, Alan thought, was probably the way his hostess conceived of Tom and JJ. He couldn't argue.

As the younger members of the party demolished the feast, the old man ate slowly. On one hand, he needed to keep up his nutrition: as hard as he was working, traveling between centuries and getting little sleep, he was putting his octogenarian, cancer-and-chemo-ridden body under a nasty stress. *Eat slowly, get more down.*

Bringing the group up to snuff on his latest trip and how Saramae had found the duffel bag, now carefully tucked under his chair, helped him stretch out his dietary intake.

JJ shot Alan a curious glance as the story ended. "Hey, Man, you be something different from anything I ever know 'bout. You probably crazy, but you know what—I almos' *believe* you. Maybe you really *is* runnin' around in Sedalia more'n a hundred years ago. Guess that mean I a li'l bit nuts too."

A sympathetic chuckle circled the table. Tom speared the next-to-last pancake and set it onto his plate.

JJ nailed the last cake. "So, where we goin' from here?"

Alan took a moment to lean back in his chair. "Well, we've taken care of the matter of the missing music—found it, got it, won't lose it. Eventually, we'll have to deal with Saramae's dad, but there's no hurry. I'll take care of it—"

"Hey! Don't I get a say in dealin' with my own daddy?"

"What? Oh, yes, of course. *We'll* deal with it later. Sorry, Saramae. But what's topside now is to find the bastard who killed Mickey, and give him to the cops. We both said our man almost has to be Jarvis. It's either him or Abigail, and all in all, he's certainly more of a logical suspect."

JJ drummed his fork on the tabletop. "So? How you figurin' we supposed to nail him?"

"Unless you can think of any better way, I'd say we need to get into his house again, and look for something, anything, to tie him to the murder."

"Oh, man." JJ sagged. "Two things. One is, I'm wasted. Last night was a bitch at the paper, didn't stop for a minute the whole night through. An' besides. If that big mother…" He picked up Elvira's expression. "…sees me in his house again, I'm a dead man, for sure. I think you gotta do better'n that."

"I can and I will. For one thing, it's not likely Jarvis'll come in again. Remember, the K.C. cops are still showing him their hospitality because of what he did to Abigail. But you're right,

JJ, you can't go back in, that's for sure. Neither can Saramae. Jarvis might've seen her in the restaurant. As for Tom and me, we'd be best off not leaving Sedalia again and getting our friend Parks exercised. And Elvira's confined to her quarters to keep watch on your dad.

JJ looked around the table. "So that leaves…" His eyes settled on Miriam, and he threw a hand over his mouth. "You're serious?"

Alan judged Miriam's Gramma Glare to be three-quarters strength. "Very serious, JJ. And Saramae will be her getaway driver. The two of them will get this job done. *Your* job is to show Miriam how to get into the house."

"Like I've gotta tell her how to pitch a rock through a window? Listen, Man. I ain't sayin' nothin' against her, but you just don't show a person how to pick a lock in ten minutes. It's complicated, and it takes a ton of practice…but hold on, hold on, wait a minute. That lock on Jarvis' door ain't a worldbeater… I know what. Miz Chandler, I can show you how to bump a lock. If you can't do that, I'll be very disappointed in you."

Bump a lock? That was a new term to Alan.

"S'cuze me a sec." JJ pushed back from the table and trotted down the hall. He came back less than a minute later and dropped a door key onto the table. Alan picked it up. "Funny looking—the teeth are set so low, but they're really steep and jagged."

"Right on, Alan. You're one sharp ol' guy. That's what's called a universal bump key. Ain't really universal, but it'll work on a whole buncha locks, includin' that Jarvis dude's. Made it myself, back when I were learnin' 'bout locks. Got a whole set that'll open near any lock."

Tom asked "How come you didn't use 'em at Jarvis' place?"

"'Cause it be a damn fool move for a black guy to carry a buncha bump keys around. Cops stop him, he go straight to jail." He jerked a thumb at Alan. "Iff'n I had 'em with me when that Detective P. picked me up at Fitter's, ain't no way he woulda let me walk outa the joint, no matter what your grandad tell him.

My picks be a whole bunch easier to hide or get ridda quickly, but I don't carry them around alla time neither. That's why I take my notes in code, too. Always a risk somebody might get into my business otherwise." He plucked the key out of Alan's hand and handed it to Miriam with a flourish. "But one key on a white granny-lady's key ring? No cop even gonna notice it. Come on. Take you out by the back door and show you the ropes."

Everyone scrambled from the table and followed JJ. Alan trailed the group, having stopped to grab the duffel bag.

Once they were all in the backyard, JJ closed the door, locked it with a house key, then pulled a big jackknife from his pocket. "Here's all you need, Miz Chandler: the universal key and a decent-size jackknife. Some people use a hammer, but I don't like that, it can damage the lock, and besides, it's a hell of a lot easier to carry around a knife than a hammer. Now, watch. I puts the key in the hole, just like any key, see? All the way in. Then I pulls it out, slow. And right when I feels two clicks—remember, it's gotta be two—I gives the key a pretty decent hit with the knife. And right at that same time, I turns the key to the opening side…like so. Gotta be real together on it, y'know?"

As the door glided open, the little group applauded. JJ made an exaggerated bow, then reached to pull the door shut and re-lock it. He passed the key and knife to Miriam. "Your turn."

Miriam smiled without showing teeth, then slid the key into the lock, started pulling it out, then suddenly slapped the knife against the key and twisted clockwise. The door slowly swung open.

JJ whistled. "Holy shit, first try! Miz Chandler, seriously, my hat is off to you. You's right, Alan. She really be goooood."

Miriam humphed and pulled the door shut. "Lock it again, Teacher. I don't want Alan thinking that was beginner's luck."

"He wouldn't dare, Miz Chandler. That were slick!" JJ locked the door and gave Miriam a wink and a grin, then stood back.

Miriam's second attempt went as smoothly as the first. "Nothing to it." She scowled momentarily at the key. "I'm surprised there's any house in the country that hasn't been burgled." She turned her disapproving look on the knife, then smiled and tossed it nonchalantly in the air, caught it, and held it out to JJ.

He pushed her hand away. "You jes' hold onto that key and knife. Take good care of them, an' good luck to you—I'm goin' off to grab me some shuteye."

"Tom and I'll go back to the room and get into the music," said Alan. "See if we can start making some headway into cataloguing it."

Miriam turned an undiluted glare on Alan. "And God help us housebreakers, we'd better head out too."

Chapter Seventeen

Miriam slid out of the car, leaving the driver's door open.

Saramae scowled. "You get to go inside and do all the fun stuff," the girl said. "I don't get to do anything."

Miriam turned a hot eye on her. "And if I get caught, I'll be dead, and you'll still be alive."

The girl walked around the car to the driver's side. "Hell, it's not even legal for me to drive this car."

"Young woman, it's no more legal for me to break into that house. Now, calm down. I don't like this any better than you do, but we all agreed on the plan, and here we are. I'll get back as soon as I can."

Saramae slammed the driver's door just a bit harder than strictly necessary.

Miriam clutched her purse and the clipboard JJ had forced on her "just in case you gotta look like some kinda social worker, or somethin'." She strode up the block, stopped in front of Jarvis Nowlin's house, drew herself up, and put on her busy executive face. She couldn't repress the urge to look right, left, and behind her before she rang the bell. No answer, of course. *Good.*

She opened her purse, pulled out the key and knife, bumped the lock. The door swung open. *Smooth as silk.* She walked inside, gently pulling the door closed behind herself. An odd thought occurred to her: this *is* kind of fun…oh, *damn* you, Alan.

She sighed, blew out a long breath.

All right, woman, get to work. What am I looking for?

Something to tie a man I've never met to a murder I've only heard about.

Easy.

She made a sour face, then got to work.

• ● ● ● •

"Can we really afford to spend time washing clothes?" Tom asked as they entered the Elite Laundromat. "We're, like, a zillion miles from the hotel, and this is going to take forever."

"Relax, Thomas. The ladies'll be gone for at least three hours. We'll have plenty of time to start organizing the music."

Tom let the discussion rest until they had a washing machine running. "Okay, but why did you bring my textbooks? There's gotta be something more useful I could be doing, isn't there?"

"More useful than keeping your grandmother happy?"

"Uh…When you put it that way…" He settled down with his Social Studies textbook.

"Thomas?"

"Yeah, Alan?"

"Not a word about this detour to Miriam. Got it?"

"Got it."

• ● ● ● •

In the Bothwell parking lot, Tom hoisted the laundry, the duffel bag, and their newly acquired office supplies, then headed for the hotel door.

Alan slammed the trunk closed, revealing Detective Parks, standing on the passenger side of the car.

"Good morning, Mr. Chandler."

Alan jumped, but composed himself quickly. "Mr. Parks. I doubt any morning that includes washing clothes is a good one." He put his hands on his hips. "Thanks for making the morning perfect. What can I do for you?"

"Oh, nothing. Just came by to make sure you hadn't accidentally snuck out of town again. If that happened too often, I might start thinking you lacked respect for the law."

Alan frowned. "Believe me, Sir, if I go anywhere, it won't be by accident. But as you can see, I'm here. Being a good boy."

"Glad to hear it, Mr. Chandler." The detective started to lean against the side of the car, hastily straightening when Alan thumbed the alarm button. "Since you're being such a good boy, perhaps you can help me out a bit. I heard something interesting while I was looking for that soggy piano. Care to guess what that might have been?"

"I wouldn't dare."

"No? Oh, well. Seems you spent some time at the store of one Sylvester Maggione, a man who is now violently dead. Unpleasant deaths are following you around, Mr. Chandler."

Alan raised an eyebrow. "All deaths are unpleasant. And I'm sure many people have visited Mr. Maggione's shop."

Parks snorted. "You saw the place and you say that?"

Alan shrugged, conceding the point.

"And what was your business with Mr. Maggione?"

"Looking for the music, of course. He's not the only antiques dealer I talked to. Won't be the last, either."

"And?"

"He didn't have it."

The detective sighed. "I figured as much." He tapped the brim of his hat. "Keep in touch, Mr. Chandler."

Alan watched him leave, then turned toward the hotel, pleased to see that Tom hadn't waited around. *Wouldn't have done anybody any good if Parks had seen the duffel bag.*

Tom was waiting at the elevator. On the way up, Alan filled the boy in about the latest police visit. Tom tried a theatrical wipe of his forehead, but with his hands full of bags, it was a lost cause. "I didn't even notice you weren't with me until I got into the lobby. Good thing I didn't go back."

"We got lucky. If he saw the duffel at all, he probably figured it was more laundry. Can't count on that happening again. We'll have to be more careful."

"He's making progress."

"Not much. It's a long sideways jump from Maggione to the Nowlins."

Once inside the room, they shoved the clean clothes into drawers, pulled archival gloves from Alan's suitcase, and turned to the music.

Tom scratched his head. "The table isn't going to be big enough. How do you want to do this so nothing hits the floor?"

"Hmm. Sort it into stacks on the bed. Four piles, I think. Printed sheet music, full manuscripts, individual manuscript sheets with no corrections, and everything else—all the scrap paper and drafts."

"Okay. What about the stuff that isn't by Joplin? We saw some when we were at Mickey's."

"Don't sweat it for now. We'll do that on a second pass."

They worked in silence for a few minutes before Tom laughed. "Got a copy of 'Alexander's Ragtime Band' here. If Mr. Joplin knew, he'd choke."

"Maybe it was his copy. He would have had to have one to decide if he should sue Berlin."

"Not this one. It's got a photo of some girl group. The Star Sisters? Who the heck are they?"

Alan laughed. "They were in the eighties—nineteen eighties, that is. Wonder how that got in the bag. Well, put it on the sheet music pile and we'll figure it out later."

● ● ● ● ●

"What have we got?"

"Four big piles of paper."

"Cute." Alan gently bopped the top of Tom's head. "You know, if even a quarter of this is new Joplin, it really *is* the biggest musical find of the century."

"And it's all yours."

"There are a few people who would argue otherwise." Alan pursed his lips. "Now that I see it spread out like this, it's starting to sink in just how big it is. Much bigger than it felt, leafing through a few sheets at a time at Mickey's. No wonder there are so many people chasing it. Amazing that the Nowlins sat on it for so long."

Tom nodded and stretched.

Alan caught the motions and realized his own back was protesting about the amount of time he had spent bent over the bed. "I better stretch out for a bit. Why don't you start sorting the printed music: Joplin, other rags, and everything else? Wake me up when you're done with that."

"Sure, Alan. Need any meds?"

"Nah. Just need to give my body and brain some downtime."

• • ● • •

Tom glanced at the clock.

Only fifteen minutes. Hardly enough of a rest. I'll give him another ten or fifteen. I'm pretty sure he's not going to care about any of the sheet music. The Joplin titles are well-known, and the rest are crap—hell, more than half of it has copyright dates after 1950. He set his piles on the table and started to sort the handwritten manuscripts.

• • ● • •

After Alan woke, he went right to the scraps while Tom continued through the complete manuscripts and single pages. A little over an hour later, Alan paused to look at the neat piles Tom had made of the manuscripts and clean single sheets, then at his own untidy, half-sorted piles of scraps, ideas, and heavily annotated pages.

"You're making much better time than I am."

Tom shrugged. "Some of these have names on 'em. Makes it easy to tell what's who's. And Joplin's handwriting is pretty recognizable. I can't match up most of the separate sheets—but I did find another page of the piece with that card theme. I think we've got the entire second half of it now."

Alan picked up the pile. "How much is in here?"

"Close to two dozen complete, including the piano concerto. And I only recognized maybe five or six of them. The single sheets, I think they come from maybe a dozen pieces. None of them are complete, but they're all new."

"More than *two dozen* new Joplins?" Alan's jaw was nearly resting on his knees. "Holy shit!"

Tom's grin threatened to wrap around the back of his head. "Even if I'm wrong about them all being new, it's one hell of a haul. Add in the bits and pieces you've got, and holy shit doesn't even begin to cover it."

Alan took a deep breath and carefully set down the pile of manuscripts. "And most of the bits and pieces look to be Joplin as well." He shook his head in amazement and his eye fell on the non-Joplin manuscripts. "Anything interesting in those?"

"Well, there're four or five manuscripts signed 'Wilbur Sweatman.' You said the duffel bag used to be his?"

"Possibly. If his music's in there, that makes it more likely. Ought to help establish the chain of ownership. What else?"

Tom squinted in thought. "A bunch of one-offs, mostly by people I've never heard of. You'll have to take a look. Oh, and a couple from 'A. No-land'." He pronounced it Betty-style.

"Who?" Alan said with a straight face. After a second, they both grinned conspiratorially before Alan's lip curled into an involuntary sneer. "*Two* by Angeline? God help us."

Tom flipped through the pile of manuscripts and shuffled pages out of the middle. "'Will's Way' and, uh, 'The Queen of Calico Rag'."

"'Queen of Calico'? Let me see that!" Alan grabbed the pages and studied them for a moment. He laughed and held them out to Tom. "You've seen this piece before, only with a different name."

"I have?" Tom studied the manuscript for a moment before a lightbulb came on over his head. He pulled out his phone and swiped through the photo roll. "It's exactly the same as 'Lowdown Rag'—that piece in Abigail's shrine!"

Alan rubbed the side of his nose. "Why would Joplin have kept a copy of Angeline's music all those years? His own drafts, sure. But this other stuff?"

Alan's gaze fell on the pile of non-ragtime music and he slapped his forehead. "Idiot! He didn't keep it—he never had it. God only knows where half this stuff came from. Sweatman, some of it, sure, but I bet we've got generations of additions here. Sweatman's daughter, maybe, or whoever had the bag before Charles Blackstone's father bought it. The Nowlins, for whatever stupid reasons they had. We're lucky there's anything of Joplin's left, let alone a bonanza like this! And maybe because it's such a mishmash is part of the reason why the Nowlins could never get together on it. They probably didn't know which pieces were Joplin's, and which weren't."

Alan waved "Will's Way" at Tom. "We've probably got Ms. Abigail Nowlin to thank for inflicting this on us." He eyed the title suspiciously. "Named for Angeline's son with Lathan, I suppose. I wonder if she wrote it before or after they split up."

Curiosity battled briefly with sense and emerged victorious; Alan played the song in his head. "It's not actually that bad. More of a unified piece than 'Queen of Calico,' and some decent musical ideas. Nothing to distinguish it from the herd, but it might have made her a few dollars if she had published it."

Alan waved at Tom's piles of music. "The ladies could be back any time and I'm getting too wrapped up in these bits and pieces. Better I should leave them for later, when it won't matter how much I get lost in the music. Let's start making lists of what you've found."

He pulled out his notebook and settled carefully against the headboard. "You call 'em off, I'll write 'em down. Then pack 'em up: each piece into an envelope, handful of envelopes in a folder, stack 'em in the duffel."

• • ● • •

Miriam moved quickly and quietly through the small house, sliding drawers open, pushing them shut. Nothing in the living room, or the dining room, or the TV-music den. In the bedroom, she made a point of looking carefully through the underwear drawer, but all she found there was underwear.

Best she could tell, there was no accessible attic or basement, so she was spared decades of cobwebs, but the amount of dust everywhere except the bedroom made her wish for a face mask. Jarvis' housekeeping was a little better in the improvised little office off his bedroom: the floor needed a good vacuuming, but the working surfaces weren't an immediate hazard to anyone's lungs.

The big find was in the top right drawer of the computer desk. Seven yellowed music manuscript sheets, filled with music. Miriam had picked up a smattering of musical terminology—it would have taken a determined effort not to learn something in the decades she had been exposed to Alan's influence—but reading a handwritten manuscript was far beyond her capabilities. These weren't even clean copies. They were filled with scratched out passages and ink blots, and the notation had the sloppy look of something intended as a memory aid for the writer. Given what Alan and Tom had been searching for, Miriam was confident she had just made a significant find. She tapped the sheets even, then slipped them into her clipboard, behind the few pages of note paper that had been there when JJ gave it to her.

A sepiatone photograph of two men, one white, one black, shaking hands, had been under the music. Miriam was already pushing the drawer closed when it hit her. Squinting, she read in faded blue ink, "To Scott Joplin, of whom I expect great accomplishments. Alfred Ernst."

She had no idea who Alfred Ernst was, but if Scott Joplin was in the photo, it was going to Alan. Miriam slid it under the music sheets.

The computer desk yielded no further treasures. Miriam looked around the room, decided she'd done as well as she was going to. She walked briskly back into the living room and through it toward the front hall...just in time to see a large black man push the outside door open and walk inside.

The two stood for a moment, staring at each other. Miriam took the initiative. "Mr. Nowlin?"

Jarvis held a half-empty bottle of Royal Emblem Scotch in his right hand. With his left hand, he scratched at his head. "Yeah, you got me there, Lady." A loud hiccup. "Now, who the hell are you…and what the hell you doin' inside my house, huh?"

"They didn't tell you I was coming out?" Miriam shook her head sadly. "They get worse and worse." She tucked the clipboard under her left arm, then extended her right hand to shake Jarvis' hand. "I'm Miriam Broaca, Domestic Violence Unit. I need to have a talk with you about what happened last night. Routine."

Thank goodness, she'd kept her maiden name for professional purposes. If he asked for I.D., she could wave a card past his face, too quickly for him to see it was from her investment business in Seattle.

But he only shook his head slowly back and forth, and wavered slightly in place. He clearly was exhausted, at least a little drunk, and just wanted to get this stuff done, whatever it was. "No, nobody tell me you was comin'. And they sure's hell didn't tell me you was gonna be *inside* a my house."

"Oh, I understand, and I'm very sorry. I expected you to be here. The door wasn't quite latched, but I rang the bell anyway. When you didn't answer, I thought you might have dozed off, so I pushed the door open and came inside to look for you. I suppose the police didn't lock up properly." She gestured at the bottle in his hand. "It looks like you'd have been here if you'd come straight from the courthouse, and hadn't made that stop."

Jarvis shrugged, then put the bottle down, not gently, onto a little side table. He sighed. "Okay, Lady, you say you gotta talk to me, let's talk. My head still hurt like hell from last night. I jus' wanna get this shit…'scuse me…over and done."

"That would be fine with me."

Miriam settled into a small padded chair; Jarvis plopped onto one end of the sofa opposite her. "Okay, shoot. What you want to know?"

Miriam pulled a mechanical pencil out of her purse, giving the bump key and knife a little shove to the very bottom. Then she picked up the clipboard. "Tell me what happened last night, and why."

"I already told the cops that, ten different times. Why I gotta do it again?"

"It's what I said, routine. I'm a social worker, not a cop, and it just might be I'll make sense out of something that sails right past their thick heads."

She didn't miss Jarvis' smile.

"Okay, Lady, here it is. That bitch, Abigail, she and me're sorta cousins. Her daddy and my granddaddy was brothers. But you could say we don't 'zactly see eye to eye. We've had troubles in our families, goin' all the way back to 1899, it's got to do with my great-great gramma and a composer named Scott Joplin. You ever hear of him?"

Miriam put on a thoughtful look. "Yes. 'The Sting,' right?"

"Yeah, right. Well, he wrote a bunch of music besides what was in that movie, and some of it, most people don't even know it exists. It's been in and outa our family for most all these years and we can't get together on what to do with it. It's worth a little fortune if we sell it, which is what makes a ton a sense to me and some of the others. But my cousin Abigail, she's just damn crazy. She thinks that Great-great got screwed on the music by Joplin, and she wants to publish the stuff and give Great-great the credit for writin' it. When she was a li'l girl, Great-great made her promise to do that one day. 'Course if that happens, there's no money in it for nobody. The whole family's been fighting about what to do since we found out about the music.

"So Cousin Abigail gets ahold of the music and one day she has herself a yard sale. Some scumbag antique dealer walk away with all the music. Shouldn't a never happened. He sells it to an old piano player in Sedalia, Mickey Potash, 'cause he thinks maybe Mickey'll help him make a fortune on it.

"When I find that out, I go and talk to Mickey. I tells him, 'Let's you and me work together, get the music copyrighted as Joplin's, we'll get the most for it that way.' He said that sounded pretty good. Meanwhile, this antique dealer, Maggione, he's like a leech on your skin, wanted to make sure he got a good cut, and if he didn't, he was gonna queer the whole deal by tellin' people the music was really not by Joplin. We'd have to get experts to say Maggione's fulla shit, and that'd take forever and cost a bunch of money, so I figured we should just stonewall him. We'd be fine, get the music out, copyrighted, then what could he do? And then he ends up dead in his shop."

Miriam squeezed her stiff fingers. "Do you have any idea about how that happened?"

Jarvis waved his hands before his face. "Nope, no idea at all. I ain't gonna tell you I was sorry to see we had one less problem, but I had nothin' to do with it. The cops asked me that too, and like I told them, I was clean as a whistle. When he got whacked, I was at a jazz concert downtown, ended up reviewing it. Hundreds of people saw me there."

"Good. I'm glad to hear it. But what happened then? What I really need to know is why you ended up crashing into your cousin's house and beating the hell out of her. Domestic violence…?"

"Well…Mickey told me he'd called in this friend of his, Alan Chandler, another piano player, and the biggest Joplin expert in the world." Jarvis pursed his lips, shook his head. "Two things about Chandler—one was that if he said the music was Joplin's, then it *was* Joplin's, period. And the other was Mickey figured Chandler would come across with some nice dough t' get his hands on th' music. And the more I thought about that, the more I started to get a little nervous. Seemed t' me, Mickey was tryin' t' cut me outa the deal. So I went into Sedalia the other night, I was gonna talk to Mickey and y'know, get him and me back on the right track."

Jarvis paused, rubbed fingers across his mouth. Miriam stiffened, and made a stern face. "Just tell me straight. The way it happened."

"Mickey, he was a guy liked his sauce, an' when I went into his house, I call his name, but he don't answer. So, good, I think, maybe he ain't home, an'…y'know, maybe I can put my hands on the music, skip out, and I'm back where I started, it's me got the music. And maybe *I* can make a deal with Chandler. So I go lookin', but no luck. I check almost the whole house, nothin'. He got music in cabinets, shelves, everythin', but no sign of *my* music. There's even this one closet got a lock on the door, but somebody'd bashed the lock off, it was layin' on the ground, an' the door was wide open. An' then I go in the bedroom, and yeah, there's Mickey in his bed, and he's drunker'n any skunk I ever laid eyes on.

"I try askin' him what happened, and he just giggles, and says the music, it's all gone, Fats Waller was Misbehavin', he busted in and ran off with all the music. I tried soberin' him up, tried to find out what really happened, but the more I tried, the more he giggled, and then he started cryin', and I told myself shit, this ain't gonna work. So I snagged this picture of Joplin and his Kraut buddy off the wall. Mickey was real fond of it, so I figgered I could come back th' next day, tell him I holdin' the picture hostage till I get what's comin' t' me, we go from there.

"But there I am, goin' on back home, and the more I think about it, the more I'm sure what the hell is happenin'. It could on'y be one other person, broke in there and copped the music. My crazy-ass sorta-cousin Abigail. The more I thought about it, the surer I was, and also the more pissed off. Then last night some asshole kid breaks inta my house, I figure Abigail sent him to give me what that Maggione jerk got. I goes over to Abigail's. Woke her up, she said, and she started callin' me names. Next thing I knew, there was blood all over, she was screamin' t' bust my ears, and here come the cops, and there I go. Dumb move, I gotta admit, but fuck!" Jarvis belched mightily and swayed in his seat. "She's still gotta have that bag fulla music someplace in her house, and I'm gonna get it off her somehow. But I promise, no more trouble. No rough stuff. That just don't work."

"Well." Miriam favored Jarvis with her patented tight-lipped smile, then drummed fingers on the clipboard papers. "That's quite a little story."

"Well, it's true. Every word. What happens now?"

Miriam rose slowly, stretched. "I go back to the office, get your story typed up, and file my report."

Jarvis squinted. "Am I gonna have to get some kinda counseling? Like anger management?"

Miriam edged past him toward the door; he stayed seated. She thought he looked like a penitent little boy. *Why the hell can't I have this kind of effect on Alan?* "I'm not supposed to comment to clients," she said. "But really. Don't you think a big man like you who beats up an old woman…for any reason…ought to try to do something about it? But on the good side, everything considered, I suspect if you do get counseling, you won't get any jail time."

On her way past the little side table, Miriam paused, picked up the whiskey bottle, and dropped it into the wastebasket. "Good luck, Mr. Nowlin. Use your head. Behave yourself. Maybe if your head isn't full of booze, you can make better decisions."

Once out the door, it took all Miriam's self-control to keep from breaking into a run, but she maintained social-worker demeanor all the way back to the car. Saramae gave her a sullen look as she returned to the passenger seat. "Get anything useful?"

Miriam slid behind the wheel, turned the key, and peeled away from the curb. "Bet on it. I think I may have discovered a new career. I'll fill you in on the way home, but the important thing is that Jarvis isn't the killer."

The young woman's expression brightened. "Then it's gotta be Abigail! We could zip over there and take her down!"

"No. Absolutely not. I'm not prepared to break the law more than twice in one day."

Saramae flopped back in her seat and folded her arms over her chest as Miriam headed for the freeway.

● ● ● ● ●

Hours later, Saramae was still sulking. She felt ridiculous pacing in the tiny hotel room, twisting around the corner of the bed every few steps, and that just added to her frustration. Still, pacing beat all hell out of sitting down and staring at the wall.

And griping to an audience of furniture was better than listening to lingering doubts about her father's innocence.

"Damn it!" she said for at least the fifteenth time. "Everyone agrees! If it wasn't Jarvis who killed Mickey, it *had* to be Abigail." She stomped across a pillow she had earlier thrown on the floor. "Argh! I coulda handled her all by myself—and we were right there in Kansas City. We shoulda gone to her place and made her spill her guts."

She stopped to glare at her reflection in the TV. "But no. Buncha crap!" Saramae didn't give her reflection a chance to respond. "We came all the way back here, and the guys are too excited about the music to do anything! Jeez!"

Saramae glanced guiltily at the manuscript of "Will's Way" on the table and dropped into the room's only chair. "Okay, I'll admit, that's kinda neat—I mean, a song my own triple-great grandma wrote for my double-great granddaddy? That she wrote with her own hands, not a printed copy? And Mr. Chandler let me keep it, just because I thought it was cool. He's an okay guy, and I know he's sick and hurtin', but damn it, he can't go to Kansas City to look for evidence at Abigail's place any more than he could go to Jarvis' house. So why are we all hangin' around here?"

She jumped to her feet and started pacing again. The pillow tried to trip her, and she snatched it up and hurled it onto the bed. "Triple-great Angeline didn't sit around waiting on some man to fix her problem. She was bat-shit crazy, yeah, but she got in there and started swinging, even against Mr. Scott Joplin. And Abigail's not some big-ass celebrity, she's just my auntie. Okay, so I haven't actually met her, but it's never too late to meet relatives, right? I can talk to her, find out what she knows about Mickey, and get a line on the real killer."

She stopped, again facing the TV. Hands on her hips, she studied her reflection. "One gal doing something by herself's worth a dozen guys sittin' around a hotel room workin' their jaws." A sharp nod. "Right. Daddy'll be at work for hours yet. He'll never know if I take the car for a little trip to K.C."

Saramae slid "Will's Way" back into its manila envelope, and scribbled a note on the notepad next to the phone. "Going to K.C. See you when I get back with the proof I need for my daddy." She propped the pad against the phone to make it obvious. "Miriam's got a spare key. They'll find that when I don't show for dinner."

Chapter Eighteen

Miriam looked at the clock. "I'd have thought Saramae would have cooled off and come back by now."

"I'll text her, Gramma!" Tom was already pulling out his phone.

"Thomas…" Miriam shook her head. "She's already feeling like she's being ordered around. How do you think she'll take it if she gets a message, 'Quit sulking and come upstairs'?"

"Jeez, Gramma, credit me with some sense. I woulda asked nicely."

"There's no such thing as a nice text." She tossed the spare key onto the bed in front of Tom. "Go down and ask her politely if there's anything she needs."

Tom caught the key on the first bounce and was on his way to the door while Miriam's hand was still in the air.

Alan grinned at his wife when the door clicked closed. "She's going to eat him alive. You know that."

Miriam smiled back. "It'll be good for him to get gnawed on a bit. Builds character. Look how much good I've done you."

Tom knocked on Saramae's door. After a moment, he knocked again, harder, and called the girl's name. Still no response. He unlocked the door and pushed it open, visions of catching her napping or showering flashing through his mind.

No Saramae. Nobody on the bed, no sound from the shower. "Saramae?" No answer. It took Tom less than thirty seconds to find the girl's note and grab his phone.

"Alan! Saramae's on her way to Kansas City! By herself!"

• ● **●** ● •

"Editorial, Charles Blackstone."

"It's Alan Chandler, Mr. Blackstone. If you had to get to K.C. right now, couldn't wait for the next train, how would you go?"

"What do you think I am, a travel agency? I'd drive, of course!" A wary note crept into Charles' voice. "Dare I ask what you've done with my daughter this time?"

"Absolutely nothing. She's done it herself—she decided to take charge of our case and took off for K.C. on her own." Alan hesitated, then quickly added, "We know who she's going after, and we're heading out now."

"Hang on." Charles' chair creaked and then there was a long silence. Alan was just about to call Charles' name when he heard another creak. "She took my car right out of the *Democrat's* lot." A sigh. "I'll be at the Bothwell in ten minutes. Don't you dare leave without me."

• ● **●** ● •

Before he even shut the car door, Charles demanded, "Have any of you tried to call Saramae?"

"Yes, Mr. Blackstone," Tom said. "Gramma and I both called. She didn't answer."

"She didn't pick up when I called, but I thought her co-conspirators might have had better luck."

"Hopefully it's because she was driving," said Miriam. "If she's on the road now, we might catch up while she's still looking for Ms. Nowlin's house."

"Maybe. But you've met my daughter. She's probably ignoring our calls just because she can."

• ● **●** ● •

Picking up JJ and squeezing him into the backseat between Miriam and Tom didn't add more than another ten minutes to the trip. They rode in silence for a quarter of an hour before JJ could no longer contain himself.

"Why'dja take th' bag, Boss? That music, it mean more to Mickey than anythin'. Only thing coulda made him happier woulda been t' meet Mr. Joplin hisself."

Charles twisted in his seat to look at his accuser. "I know, JJ. I could claim I was just taking back something that rightly belonged to me—it was stolen from my father, remember. But since it's you who's asking, I have to admit it was mostly about the money." He turned back the other way and stared vacantly out the passenger-side window. "Putting a kid through college— a really good one—isn't cheap. I worked my way into a good job, one I love. But I wanted to make life easier for Saramae, and that bag would have gone a long way to turning her into a successful lady." He shrugged. "Not going to happen now." He coughed. "Hard to believe my own daughter stole the bag from me—but better she should have it than those Nowlins. If she's smart enough to get some help without losing the music, it'll still do her good."

A long silence followed Charles' speech. Alan's mind wandered from the bag to Mickey's torture. He glanced at Charles' hands. No rings, as Saramae had said. Abigail wore a ring—Alan clearly remembered seeing it when he and Tom first went to her house—but how could she have held Mickey down and beaten him, let alone strangled him? Jarvis was probably right: she hired some muscle. But what kind of criminal for hire would be dumb enough to wear a large, heavy ring on a job?

His train of thought crashed when Charles spoke again. "Saramae didn't leave that duffel bag at the hotel, did she?"

Alan tucked his tongue firmly into his cheek and readied an accurate but misleading response, but Miriam beat him to the punch. "Not likely, Mr. Blackstone. Give the girl credit for her brains. She knows better than to trust anything valuable to a hotel lock."

Charles nodded. "Good to hear." He laughed briefly. "We'd likely be having a very different conversation right now if Mr. Potash had been as smart. The lock he used was a real piece of junk. Barely slowed me down."

"I tol' him that a whole buncha times," JJ added. "Tol' him it just call attention t' the closet, too. If he hadda keep it close, he shoulda jus' depend on nobody knowin' about th' hidey-hole. Hey! How'd *you* know 'bout that, anyways?"

"Mickey showed it to me," Charles said with a small chuckle. "Back when I was a reporter, I interviewed him for a local history piece on bootleggers. The story never ran, but I still had my notes." He gave JJ a sharp look. "Never throw away anything you write. No way to tell when it'll be useful. I figured Mickey would use that space for something as important as Joplin's music."

Alan shook his head. "That was Mickey, all right. Couldn't resist telling a good story. And he'd never have put the music anywhere that would've prevented him from gloating over it whenever he felt the urge."

"At least that's a mistake Saramae won't make," Tom said. "She's not a hoarder."

"No? You should have seen her with her first baby doll." Charles stretched his legs, making the seat creak. "She doesn't have too many choices. Car trunks aren't any more secure than Mr. Potash's safe room. You wouldn't believe how many car thefts we get every summer when the tourists come in for the Joplin Festival and the State Fair."

Was that a hint? Damn it, now I'm going to have to keep him away from this car's trunk. Alan spent the rest of the ride trying to figure out how to alert Tom and Miriam to stay between Charles and the car, all speculations about rings and stupid criminals forgotten.

• • ● • •

Saramae drove slowly up the street, looking carefully for the house. The only other time she'd seen it, she hadn't noticed the number. But it hadn't been hard to find online: Nowlin, A., 5708 Virginia. Saramae parked at the curb, picked up the manuscript of "Will's Way" from the passenger seat, and got out of the car.

She walked slowly up to the front door, feeling the hammer of every heartbeat. Yeah, she was scared a little…but why?

She needs a cane for Christ's sake. Try anything funny, I'll make hamburger outa her.

The girl set her chin, and pushed the doorbell.

A couple of minutes later, the door slowly swung open. Abigail Nowlin squinted at Saramae. "Who you be, and what you want?"

A faint sound of ragtime piano music came from back in the house. The girl swallowed the lump in her throat and waved the manuscript. "You're Ms. Nowlin, right? I was hopin' you could help me, I've got this music that was written by a lady with a name like yours, Angeline Noland, and it looks real old…"

A large man stepped up behind Abigail, and Saramae's voice trailed off. The girl blurted, "Oh fuck! You're the one that did it!" She turned to run. But Nelson Nowlin grabbed her by the arm, his heavy ring bruising her bicep, before she got off the porch. He yanked her into the house, slammed the door, and snatched "Will's Way" from her hand. Abigail grabbed the music and hobbled behind Nelson as he dragged Saramae into the living room.

The big man threw the girl into an ancient, overstuffed chair and stood over her. "Now, you tell me, who you be?" Nelson growled.

"And where it was you got this music," Abigail shrieked.

"Don't you try no funny stuff," said Nelson. "I ain't the most patient man in the world."

Saramae snuffled. "Hey, Mister, Lady, please don't hurt me. I'm doin' a project for my high school class, I found the music at the library, and I'm supposed to write a paper about it. So I went lookin' for somebody who can tell me somethin' about it, and I found Abigail Nowlin—that's kinda like Angeline Noland, y'know, so I figured maybe—"

Nelson raised a fist. "Girl, what be your name, huh? An' where you be livin'?"

Saramae shrank back in the chair. "Hey, Mister, come on, huh? I ain't done anything wrong. Please—"

The big man ripped Saramae's purse from her shoulder, and was fumbling at her wallet when a young girl ran in from the back room. "Hey, what's everybody shoutin' about…oh, *Sara-mae*. You come to hear my songs, like you said you would!" She ran over and threw her arms around her older friend.

Nelson peered into Saramae's face. "Well, goddamn! You the girl had dinner with Li'l Angeline th' other night, ain't you? An' now, here you is again." He shook the wallet open, held her driver's license up to Abigail. "Looky here, Mama. Her name's Saramae, all right—Saramae *Blackstone*. From Sedalia. Betcha my las' nickel her daddy be Charles Blackstone!" He leaned close. "Is I right, Girl?"

Abigail held up a hand. "Nelson, hush!" She turned a cold eye on Saramae. "Got the music from the liberry, huh? And how you know her name was Angeline?" The old woman shook the manuscript in Saramae's face. "Look, she sign her music with jus' her initial." Abigail put her hands on her hips, glared at Saramae. "Lyin' to an old lady. Oughta be ashamed. Nelson! We need to talk."

The big man straightened and patted the puzzled Angeline's head. "Sure, Honey, sure. Saramae come to hear your songs, all right. You take her in the music room and play 'em for her, okay?" He glared at Saramae. "Don't you be thinkin' 'bout trying to get away, neither. Only way out is past me." He tossed Saramae's license and wallet into her purse and stepped back, staying between her and the doorway to the front hall.

Saramae grabbed the purse and hugged it to her chest. Angeline took her by the hand. "Come on, Saramae. I gonna play every one of my songs for you."

The two girls had barely vanished when Abigail stage-whispered, "Those fucking Blackstones. They must have the duffel bag again."

Nelson answered in a rough whisper. "Mama, they're on to us. They know what we did. We gotta get rid a her."

"Jesus, boy! Don't be such a pussy. If they be on to us, you think Charles gonna send his daughter here to haul you off to the jail? Just keep your fool mouth shut and we be fine. But this girl come in with one of Angeline's manuscripts, one I put in the duffel bag myself. I gotta see what other music she got. An' why she really come here to talk to me about it. You get rid a her, we ain't never gonna find out where that duffel bag is."

"Damn it, Mama. You be lookin' fo' a few pieces a hundred-year-old music. But me? I went and killed two people fo' you, that ol' man in Sedalia an' that douchebag antique dealer. So I be lookin' at the rest of my life in stir. An' that just ain't gonna happen, hear?"

"Nelson, it's you be the douchebag if you says anything about that to her. Think! The Blackstones ain't gonna send no li'l girl to talk to you about no murders. She be here about the music."

The big man shook his head in disgust. "Mama, that girl jus' can't walk outa here alive."

He lumbered back into the piano room, and returned a moment later with Saramae in tow. Behind them, the piano music continued, much louder and with considerably more mistakes. Nelson practically threw Saramae back into the over-stuffed chair; he and Abigail hunched over her.

"Now!" the big man roared. "You tell us, Saramae Blackstone, tell us fast and tell us straight. What you be doin' here?"

Abigail waved the manuscript in the girl's face. "And what you be doin' with this music, and what other music you got?"

Tears—real ones—started down Saramae's cheeks. "Okay, okay! I came here because I know a little bit from my daddy about how the Nowlins and the Blackstones have been fightin' over this music for a zillion years. I found this music in Daddy's filin' cabinet, and figured it had somethin' to do with my double-great granddaddy Will and his mama, my triple-great grandmamma." She grabbed a tissue from the box on the table, blew her nose. "I've never met you, Ma'am, but I know you're descended from that same lady, Angeline No-land, and I wanted to find out what you could tell me about her and Will."

Nelson made a shut-off motion toward Abigail. "I wants to know what you was talkin' about when you said 'You did it.' I did what, huh?"

Before the girl could answer, Abigail whacked Nelson's shin with her cane. "*I* wants to know the truth. How'd you really get your hands on this music…and where be the rest of it?"

"I already told you, Ma'am," Saramae said, trying to make the story sound reasonable. "I found it in Daddy's stuff, and I had no idea at all there was any more."

"You ain't never seen no duffel bag with music inside?"

Saramae shook her head, sniffled. "No, Ma'am. Only this piece. And I just wanted to find out more about my ancestors, that's all."

"A Blackstone caring 'bout her ancestors?" Abigail said in a softer tone of voice. "Must be 'cause you the first girl I know born in that fam'ly since Angeline herself." She turned on Nelson. "See here, Boy? She be a close relative. Her daddy's your half-first cousin, 'r something like that. An' I am your mother! I tell you to show respect to fam'ly, you do what I tell you!" The old woman turned to take hold of Saramae's arm. "You wants to know about your great-great-great gramma? Well, I'll tell you. Up, young lady. Come with me."

She gave her son a look that warned him to behave or else, and led Saramae into the piano room. She pointed a finger at Angeline, squawked, "Don't go bangin' away like that, hear? Practice right." With a grand gesture, she threw open a door on the other side of the room and led Saramae inside. "Shut th' door, Child," she said, clearly expecting instant obedience.

Saramae recognized the room from JJ's pictures. A former walk-in closet, converted into a shrine through a rough white paint job and a blinding overhead lighting fixture. Table under the light holding a stack of music and several short pieces of corroded wire. Shelves on either side full of memorabilia: lipsticks, hair ornaments, and a few pieces of cheap jewelry; pens, pencils, and dried-up bottles of ink; faded photographs and badly executed pencil portraits. All rendered trivial by the large black-and-white photograph of an old woman on the rear wall. Her eyes projected an intense glare even more disturbing than in JJ's smartphone photo.

The old woman nodded at the picture, almost a bow. She picked up the top few sheets from the pile of music on the table and set "Will's Way" in their place. "There she be, your great-great-great gramma. *Angeline*. She also be my great-gramma…I coulda been named Angeline too, but my mama, she was bound and determined I was gonna be named for somebody in *her* family, her Gramma Abigail. She tol' my daddy, well, that was close enough to Angeline for her, 'cause my great-gramma was crazy. Can you imagine that?" A loud thump of her cane punctuated the question.

"Well, they never got over that argument, an' after Mama die, Great-gramma, she help bringin' me up. I stay with her for days at a time, an' I heard all about how she wrote some music for Scott Joplin, for his "Maple Leaf Rag." Abigail spoke louder and louder. "But when she tried to get him to give her credit for it, he jus' got real nasty. Then her…friend, Otis Saunders, tol' her he'd get it done, but know what he did? He tol' Joplin that *he* wrote that music." Another thump of the cane. "So Great-gramma went out and wrote up her work herself, called it "Lowdown Rag" to rub that bastard Joplin's face in it."

She waved the pages in her hand at Saramae. "Here it be, better'n anything ol' Scott Joplin ever wrote. And she wrote a lotta other pieces, great music, too. But she couldn't never get it published."

The more Abigail talked, the faster she went, a train with malfunctioning brakes on a downhill slope. "But Angeline was gonna make sure her music didn't just get lost. When I was a child, she spent all kinda time with me, taught me piano and how to play her work right, and makin' me promise I'd get her work published if she never did. An' I promised, over an' over, every day. She always tol' me my real name was Angeline, an' when she died, which she did when I was six, then I'd take over for her, and I should never tell my mama that I really *was* Angeline."

She raised the cane, waved it in tight circles just below the light fixture. "But I can tell *you* everything, Saramae, 'cause I *be* my great-gramma now, been her for full-on fifty-five years now. Fifty-five years, I been tryin' to get my music published, but the Blackstones and them other Nowlins just been stoppin' me at every turn. So I be doin' with Li'l Angeline now what Great-gramma done with me, an' if I die before I get this music published—" The cane jabbed at Saramae's face—"Li'l Angeline'll get it done. An' even better now, I got you to help. I bet you can find the rest of the music, an' then we'll get it all published, you an' me, and your great-great-great gramma will give you her undying blessing. And so'll I. 'Cause we be the same person, and so will you be. An' Li'l Angeline, too."

Saramae shivered. She felt more creeped out than she ever had in her life. She fought a terrible urge to make a run for safety—useless with Nelson standing guard—but just then the door flew open and Nelson blasted into the shrine. "Fuckin' doorbell just rang again—you expectin' more company, Mama?"

"No, you damn fool, who the hell would I be expectin'?"

Nelson growled an undecipherable message, then turned and left the room. Abigail gently set "Lowdown Rag" back on top of the pile of music, then followed him as fast as she could shift her cane.

Rather than try to find "Will's Way," Saramae shoved the entire pile of music into her oversized purse as she fled the shrine and its scary photograph of creepy Old Angeline. Little Angeline was still banging out error-filled ragtime in the piano room, and Saramae made a beeline for the comparative normality of a reluctant young piano student.

● ● ● ● ●

In a perfect fury, Nelson threw the front door open and found five people, all shouting at him. "Shut the fuck *up*," he roared at the top of his voice, hands raised, fists clenched. "Who the *fuck* are you, and what the *fuck* are you doing here?"

As the overhead light glittered off the ring on Nelson's right hand, time seemed to stop for Alan. A double image came before his eyes, Abigail's ring…and the matching ring he'd seen on Lathan's hand in 1899. And here was Lathan's ring, more than a hundred years later, on the right hand of the huge Nowlin man Alan had glimpsed at the restaurant.

Of course Abigail would give the second ring to her son! And the autopsy said a right-handed person gave Mickey those bruises. Abigail had to have had help, and who better than her son? He's got to be the one who killed Mickey!

In a unit, the gang shoved past Nelson, into the living room where Abigail, befuddled, leaned on her cane. Alan snapped, "Where's the young woman who came here just a little while ago?"

Charles Blackstone elbowed Alan aside. "Yeah," he barked. "Where is my daughter?"

Abigail shrugged. "Don't know who you be talkin' about."

Nelson shook his head in mock ignorance.

Saramae rushed into the room, trailed by young Angeline. "I heard you, Daddy." Nelson grabbed her roughly by the arm as she tried to run past him.

Which set all Niagara bustin' loose.

Charles lunged at Nelson, but years of political infighting in the City Room of the *Sedalia Democrat* hadn't prepared Charles for the physical fighting skills of his huge opponent. Nelson released the girl and grabbed an antique table lamp. He swung it, catching Charles across the face, shattering the glass shade and spraying fragments everywhere. As Charles staggered back, Nelson dropped the base of the lamp and caught Charles with a right cross that sent him to the floor.

Miriam took a step toward Charles, then stopped, yanked out her cell phone, dialed 911.

Tom and JJ exchanged a quick glance, then both rushed Nelson.

"Sorry, Daddy!" Saramae shouted over her shoulder as she snatched Angeline by the hand and took off toward the door.

In one smooth movement, Nelson shot a mean left fist into Tom's solar plexus and followed it with a right-handed punch to his jaw. Tom went down like a poleaxed steer, twitched a couple of times, then lay still.

JJ came in low, but the big man ignored the blow to his ribs. As Tom fell, Nelson spun and launched a vicious knee to the young man's crotch, followed by a descending double blow to the crown of his head. JJ rocked back and forth on the floor, clutching his lower abdomen.

"You have reached 911, Kansas City, Missouri," spoke the recorded voice on Miriam's phone. "Do not hang up."

Meanwhile, Abigail, spluttering incomprehensibly, began to slap at Miriam with her cane.

"Hang up? Are you insane?" Miriam shrieked as she dodged. "We have a homicidal maniac here at 5708 Virginia Avenue. Get us the police before we have a house full of dead people!"

Abigail took another shot at Miriam with the cane, the last straw. Miriam slapped her phone down on an end table, slammed Abigail into the overstuffed chair, yanked the cane away, and took a batting stance with it.

"Just one more move from you—*one goddamn twitch*—and your head goes rolling across the floor."

Nelson, eyes bulging, spit flying from both corners of his mouth, started toward Alan, the last man standing in the room.

Alan sighed. *I thought it might come to this.* He reached into his pocket, pulled out the pistol JJ had taken from Jarvis, and pointed the muzzle squarely at Nelson's abdomen.

"Yes, it's loaded and I do know how to use it," he said calmly. "And I will, if you take another step. You won't be the first man I've had to kill."

"Fucker!" Nelson roared, shaking from top to bottom.

"Turn around," Alan snapped. "Stand in that corner, hands up on the wall. Now!"

• • ● • •

Ten minutes later, Alan and Miriam heard the door slam open, then close behind them. "Kansas City police. Put the gun down, Mister. Now!"

The old couple exchanged a smile. "Gladly," Alan murmured.

Chapter Nineteen

"Just once more, Miriam."

"And then one more after that, and then another."

Alan shook his head. "This is probably my last chance. First thing in the morning, we're going home, and I'm as sure as I can be I won't be able to time-travel in Seattle."

Miriam lifted an eyebrow in what Alan had long recognized as her "You'll have to pile it higher to convince me" expression.

"It's an unusual situation. The music on the invitation is something that was important to Scott Joplin, something he spent a lot of time working over. We're here in Sedalia where the music was written, and that's got to be part of it too. If you could time-travel just anywhere and any time, people would be doing it constantly."

Miriam's eyebrow was still raised.

"Maybe if I find the right piece of paper in the duffel bag *and* go to St. Louis or New York, I *might* be able to time-travel there. But he never visited Seattle."

"Well…"

Alan knew he was close. "When we get home, we can both talk to Dr. Fisch. He can check me over any way you want." He held his breath.

Miriam knew when to stop pushing. She sighed and shook her head. "All right. I don't like it, but I can't stop you."

• ● ● ● •

Alan looked at the sign advertising Bast Storage, two blocks from the former location of the Maple Leaf Club. Twenty minutes later, he let himself into his freshly rented storage unit.

Cheap. If it works, I'd've been happy to have paid five times as much. Let's see... The street is that way.

He taped the envelope containing the invitational card to the south wall, locked the door, and counted his steps down the length of the building, then took the same number of steps up the sidewalk. As close to the card as he could estimate, he leaned against the building.

He pulled Miriam's phone, last year's top-of-the-line Samsung model, from his inside jacket pocket. His wife had stood between him and the hotel room door.

"If you go off again, you're going to settle the question of what's really happening when you think you're time-traveling. Take some pictures while you're there. We'll see what the camera shows. If you come back with a good shot of Scott Joplin, we won't bother Dr. Fisch."

Alan unlocked the phone, launched the camera app, and stared at the screen.

Yes, I'd love a picture of Mr. Joplin. Or better yet, a video of him playing. But if someone sees...?

His thumb brushed the screen as he shoved the phone back into his pocket without shutting it off.

He took a deep breath and pictured the card in its envelope on the wall, tried to make it as real as if it were on a table in front of him. Next, he imagined it in the lockbox under the bar at the Maple Leaf Club. He pictured Joplin and Lathan standing by the bar. Alan smiled—the sense of right and wrong he associated with time-travel was there, telling him his image was off. He seated the men at one of the tables. That felt a little better; he moved them to another table, one near the pool tables instead of the piano. Much better. He changed the light to late afternoon or early evening instead of mid-morning. Added a crowd of men around the room, drinking and talking. Someone at the piano.

That was right. A final tweak—a ginger—no, cream soda—on the table in front of Joplin, nothing for Lathan.

Alan stepped forward.

"Alan! What fortunate timing! Please…take a seat and explain to this person that I'm in no danger."

"First I'd prefer to hear what kind of danger he thinks you're in, Mr. Joplin." Alan pulled a chair away from the next table. "Hello, Lathan. Are you okay?"

"Tol'rable, Mr. Chandler. Jus' tol'rable."

"Sorry to hear it. More trouble with Angeline?"

Lathan nodded. His hands fidgeted on the table. "I throwed her out. I had to. She laugh at me after—" He stopped abruptly and glanced at Joplin before he went on. "When I get home, she were already packin' up her clothes. Musta started even befo' she an' Otis go to, uh, you know."

Alan's eye caught the small band of callus on Lathan's finger where his ring had been. He nodded.

"I tells her she gotta stop this messin' 'round. It be too big, too dangerous. I tells her that an' she laugh. She say nothin' gonna stop her from gettin' what she deserve. Then I knows I cain't do nothin' mo'. I gives her my ring and tells her she best not be there when I comes back. Been walkin' 'round town all day. Don' wanna go home."

Joplin stood. "Excuse me a moment." He walked toward the bar.

Lathan didn't seem to notice Joplin's departure.

"What about Will?" Alan asked. "Where's your son?"

"Huh? Will? He be fine. Lady next do' watch him when Angie an' I be at work. He with her since las' night." Lathan put his head in his hands. "Gotta make up for what Angie done," he mumbled.

Joplin set a shot of whiskey in front of Lathan and resumed his seat.

"I ain't a drinkin' man, Mr. Joplin." Lathan's gaze was slightly unfocused, and Alan realized belatedly Lathan had been awake and moving for at least a day and a half.

"It's not drinking when it's medicinal." Joplin's expression was an odd mix of exasperation and pity.

Lathan shrugged and downed the whiskey in a single gulp. After a moment, he said "Angie, she not gonna give up chasin' you, Mr. Joplin. Tha's why I be here. Gonna keep close, make sure she don' do nothin' she shouldn' oughta do."

"I told you already, Mr. Blackstone, I don't need a bodyguard." He looked at Alan. "Nor do I expect to remain in Sedalia much longer." He returned his attention to Lathan. "Even if your wife harbors plans to do more than bombard me with letters, she can hardly follow me about the country any more than you can."

A stubborn look spread across Lathan's face. "You keep close watch, then. Mebbe I cain't stay near t' you, but Angie, she *determined*. She gonna do whatever she think she gotta do." His head sank lower as he spoke. "An' when you comes back here t' Sedalia, I be here, an' I help you watch." Lathan's head slowly lowered to the table, and a moment later, he was snoring.

"Alan? Should I take this warning seriously?"

"I can't say for sure, Mr. Joplin. Nobody in my time knew anything about Angeline until recently. But all that means is she never succeeded in doing anything significantly harmful to you. It doesn't mean she didn't—or won't—try." He shrugged. "I'd say to be careful, but don't obsess about it."

Joplin sighed. "Very well." He stared into his soda for a moment, then looked back to Alan. "You're leaving, aren't you? Or is that the right way to put it?"

Alan nodded. "It's as good a way as any. Yes, I did come to say goodbye. I hope to see you again, here or in, uh, some other places, but I don't know if it'll be possible."

"Hmmm…yes, I see." Joplin stood and extended his hand. "It's been a pleasure meeting you, Mr. Chandler, and I hope we *will* meet again."

They shook, and Alan stood. "I wish I could stay longer, but I had to promise my wife I'd return quickly." He gently knocked twice on the sleeping Lathan's head with a knuckle. "Live your own life, Lathan. Angeline isn't your responsibility any more." Alan looked back at Joplin. "When he wakes up, tell him I said everything'll turn out fine if he brings Will up right."

"Is that true?"

Alan smiled. "I have reason to think so. And either way, wouldn't you rather have him concentrating on his son than on you?"

Joplin's mouth twitched, not quite a smile, but almost. "That I would. I'll tell him."

"Thank you, Mr. Joplin. For everything." Alan took a deep breath. "Until next time."

"Until then."

A few steps away from the table, Alan stopped and looked back. *Damn it, I've got to take one.* Joplin had returned to his seat and was looking across the table at Lathan with a rueful expression. *Yes! It would be worth ten times the risk. Can I get Lathan into the picture too? That'd tickle Saramae.*

He pulled Miriam's phone out of his pocket, quickly lifted it to get Joplin and Lathan in the center of the screen, and tapped the capture button.

At that moment, one of the men at the pool table raised his head, and shot a mean stare at Alan. *Don't know if he saw what I was doing, but no way do I want to field any questions about it.* He returned the camera to his pocket, and walked to the stairway, where he made certain to grip the wooden handrail as he rushed down the stairs and outside. *Last thing I need is to slip and break a leg.*

Alan strolled north on Ohio Avenue toward the J.A. Lamy Manufacturing Company building. Just past the railroad tracks, he stepped from a clear evening to an overcast afternoon. *Huh. Easiest return I've had. Wish I had thought of this sooner.* The outside of the building hadn't changed much, but the blue ADA sign next to the office door confirmed Alan's return to the twenty-first century. He retrieved the invitation from his storage unit and drove back to the Bothwell.

● ● ● ● ●

Miriam snatched her phone from Alan, tapped a couple of times, glared at the screen, then launched an ear-splitting "Jesus Christ! Alan, what is this supposed to be?"

"Well…it's a picture of Scott Joplin at the Maple Leaf Club… with another man who's been important to this story." There was a nervous edge to his voice.

"And I'm supposed to believe that?" Miriam held up the camera in front of Alan's face. "All I see is a fuzzy, near-black photo. Couldn't you have held still long enough for the auto-focus to work?"

Alan grimaced and shook his head. "I think one of the men playing pool, one of the guys at the right edge there, saw me taking the picture. It looked like he was about to come after me, so I got out in a hurry."

"But why is it so dark…? The auto-flash is turned off. Did you—"

Alan raised both hands, unconditional surrender. "I don't think I did anything but tap the take-the-picture button."

"And you always hit the screen too hard, make the phone shake like crazy." Miriam blew out a mouthful of exasperation. "I *knew* I should've gotten a new phone this year…the focus is faster and low-light performance is so much better…Jesus *Kuhryst!*" She waved the camera before Alan one more time. "So… where…is…Scott…Joplin?"

"He should be sitting there right in your hand," Alan murmured. "Maybe we should give it to Tom. Let him see if he can fix it up on his computer."

Miriam snorted. "And for an encore, he can make a million dollars before lunch. He's got a better chance of doing that than of salvaging this mess."

● ● ● ● ●

That evening, the gang gathered at the Bothwell. From the desk chair, Charles Blackstone regarded his companions with vague pain. None of the men were moving very easily and the jagged cuts on Blackstone's face from Abigail Nowlin's lampshade resembled a roadmap. He pulled a piece of paper from his pocket, unfolded it, cleared his throat. "See what you all think of this." Then he began to read from the paper.

"An amazing century-long story came to a striking conclusion Tuesday evening in Kansas City. For more than 100 years, members of the Nowlin family fought over possession of musical manuscripts by the great composer, Scott Joplin. The Nowlins, descendants of long-time Sedalia resident Angeline Noland, had been accumulating the manuscripts by various means, not all of them legal, since the 1970s. Some of the music had found its way to Mickey Potash, a local ragtime performer. Mr. Potash was murdered, and the music stolen from his house. Members of the *Democrat* staff and Sedalia resident Saramae Blackstone assisted ragtime pianists Alan and Thomas Chandler in tracing the culprits to Kansas City. The police were called in and Abigail Nowlin, 71, and her son, Nelson, 40, were arrested. Both made full confessions regarding the murder; however neither admitted to any knowledge of the current location of the music. See the sidebar for full details of the confessions and an analysis by *Democrat* psychiatric consultant, Dr. Elliot Funderburk.

"Mr. Chandler remarked, 'Mickey Potash was a good friend. I'm glad his killers have been caught. But Scott Joplin's music must be recovered, and I will devote whatever time and effort it takes to do that…though I'm sure Detective Parks of the Sedalia Police will succeed in turning it up.'"

A quiet chuckle made its way through the group as Blackstone set the page back onto the desk. Side-by-side on one bed, Tom and Saramae exchanged high fives; then the girl turned to give JJ a quick hug. On the other bed, Alan smiled at Miriam; she sent him a tight-lipped nod, then couldn't hold back a smile of her own.

"From there it goes into background on Joplin and ragtime. It'll run in Friday's paper." Blackstone waved toward Alan. "Sure that'll give you enough time to get out of town with the loot?"

Alan spoke through a grin. "We're hitting the road first thing in the morning. By the time Parks sees the story, we'll be safely back in Seattle." He turned to JJ. "You did a great job of talking around what really happened with the music."

JJ made the go-way motion. "Shit, man. How dumb you think I am?"

"Not dumb at all, not in any way," said Alan. "All considered, I'd say you're a pretty smart cookie."

"I suppose I'm not so dumb, myself," said Blackstone. "If I'd let JJ mention that music, or if I'd done it myself, I'd be up for theft right now. And Alan, you'd never get out of town with the loot. Our friend Parks is really pissed off at having been cut out of the case, and made to look like a fool."

Miriam sneered. "Handsome is as handsome does."

"Well, thank you for your silence," Alan said quietly.

Blackstone smiled and picked up the sheet of paper, scanned the story. "JJ really does have potential. But he needs to work on his punctuation, grammar, and spelling. As of this day, he is no longer on the night shift; he's a reporter, working under *me* in the City Room. And I'm a goddamn demanding boss. I spent more time making this story publishable than he spent writing it, and I'm not about to spend the next twenty years doing the same thing to all his stories. He's going back to finish school, or do a GED. One or the other."

Tom groaned. "Yeah. And I'm on my way back to school, too. Blech."

A quick look at Miriam's face set Alan to thinking, then speaking. "Yes, you need to at least graduate from high school," he said. "But I'm going to need a lot of help getting that music authenticated, copyrighted, and published, and you're it. Someday that music is going to be yours. You're going to be playing it at a lot of festivals and concerts. 'Tom Chandler, Joplin's…Apostle?'"

Tom smiled weakly. "Maybe something a little less religious?"

Alan patted the boy's shoulder. "We'll work on it. And Sara-mae, anything to do with Angeline's music, I'd say you have the most valid claim. It could bring you a little money, especially when the story gets out about the old woman. Also, it's an important part of musical history now. It needs to be preserved for scholars and musicians." He grimaced. "Too bad you lost 'Will's Way.' Musically, it was much more interesting than that 'Queen of Calico' piece."

Saramae smacked her palm to her forehead. "Completely slipped my mind in all the fuss. I did get it back, along with a bunch of other music. I wasn't gonna leave Triple-great's music with that smelly ol' bitch, so I snatched it all out of the shrine before I took off." She plopped the pile down on the bed between herself and Tom. "I don't think they got too badly mussed in my bag. Couldn't have been any worse for 'em than that duffel, anyway."

Alan's eyes widened. "Oh, my. The career output of a previously unknown composer—and a well-preserved family history of her career? You're going to have academics offering to have your baby to get their hands on that music."

"I'm not ready to have kids yet, thanks." Saramae stopped and reparsed Alan's statement, then grinned. "And when I *am* ready, I'll do it the old-fashioned way. No test tubes with some dusty lady music professor for me."

While Saramae and Alan were talking, Tom had been leafing through the stack. "Hey, Saramae, some of this ain't Angeline's. Looks like Abigail pulled some music out of the duffel bag, same as Jarvis did."

Saramae drew herself up and gave a queenly wave of her hand. "Since your granddaddy gave me Triple-great's music for myself, why don't you pull out anythin' that *ain't* hers and give it to him?"

"Sure thing, Your Royal High-and-Mightiness."

Alan grinned indulgently while Tom finished his survey, and pulled a baker's dozen sheets out of the pile. He sorted them quickly and handed all but two to Alan. "I think this is it—looks like random pages from some of the incomplete pieces in the duffel." He thought for a moment. "I wonder how many other Nowlins have pages squirreled away."

"Probably a bunch of them," Blackstone said. "From what my father said, almost everything in the bag was complete when he and *his* father got it. Those damn Nowlins have been fighting over it for decades. Probably every time someone new got their hands on the bag, they snagged a few sheets, just in case they lost it again."

"I doubt we'll ever know for sure what's been lost," Alan added. He leaned forward, squinted at the pages Tom was holding with the reverse, unmarked sides toward the room. "What are those?"

Tom shrugged elaborately. "Well…you were right about the invitation strain being for a cakewalk. With the pages we got from Mickey and the one Gramma swiped from Jarvis—"

"Watch your mouth, Thomas. I've never swiped anything in my life." She smiled faintly. "Certainly not from that Jarvis fool. I was just reclaiming something he never should have had."

"Yes, Gramma. As…I…was…*saying*," Tom continued in theatrically martyred tones, "with those sheets and these, we've got the whole composition. He grinned and handed the pages to Alan.

Alan quickly scanned the first page. When the words registered, he redirected his eyes back to the top of the sheet.

The Chandlers Cakewalk
Scott Joplin
New York, 1915

Is that an apostrophe before the "s" or an inkblot? Alan wiped his eyes, looked closer, wiped his eyes a second time.
Can't tell. Well, good enough. So be it.
"Are you okay, Alan?"
"Fine, Tom."
Alan held up the page to show the title to the rest of the group. "Ragtime composers *did* enjoy using cryptic titles."

Saramae grinned and, after a few seconds of thought, JJ did as well. Blackstone and Miriam looked puzzled.

Tom said "From the last couple of pages, Alan figured it's got an ABACA structure. Repeating the first theme that many times is pretty odd for a cakewalk, but there it is. Interesting, the way the piece keeps *going back* to its beginning like that."

After a moment, Miriam got it and she squeezed Alan's hand. "It's a nice thought, certainly."

"There's obviously something I'm missing here," Blackstone said. He waited a few seconds, and when nobody chose to enlighten him, he went on. "Be that as it may, I'm still not clear on what 'Mae's going to get out of having Angeline's music."

Tom nudged Saramae. "Penny for your thoughts."

She smiled weakly. "I don't give away thoughts for less than a buck."

The boy pulled a bill out of his pocket, and pressed it into her palm.

She snapped it open, folded it, opened it again, then kept folding the bill while she talked. "Okay, what I'm thinkin'. I don't know much about copyrighting and publishing, and nothin' about what I could do on my own with this music. So, y'know? I wanna go to Seattle with you guys. You've got schools; I can finish up high school there as easy as here—and I could work with you and Alan on the music. Somethin' else, too. I wanna learn how to play ragtime. I've been takin' piano lessons for—how many years, Daddy?—and I can play whatever you want by Chopin and Liszt and all those dead white German guys too." She gestured toward Alan. "But if you can teach me how to play ragtime, I'd love that. I could play at festivals too."

Saramae dropped the dollar bill, now an origami heart, into her purse and flashed Tom a look whose meaning held no ambiguity. "Be fun to play four hands with Tom."

The boy's cheeks flamed.

Blackstone stiffened and pulled forward in his chair, but ducked away from the palm Miriam held up before his face.

"Let's think about that a little," she said. "You're going to take on JJ and his career in a big way. Why *not* let Alan teach Saramae ragtime, and get her a start in performing? But in no manner, shape, or form would I release your daughter to my husband's social custody; I would personally take full responsibility for her well-being. Would that make you feel better?"

Blackstone guffawed. "Infinitely."

Saramae leaped across the room to throw herself into her father's arms. "Oh, Daddy, that's so cool...and y'know what? I'll even miss you. But I'll come back for visits—and to pick your brain for everythin' you can remember about Great-great Will and Triple-great Lathan."

"Scott Joplin Ragtime Festival, every June," said Alan. "I think you just might see a six-hand piano performance there next summer."

JJ took Alan's hand, and gave it a firm shake. "I done promise Gramma I wouldn't forget t' thank you." The young man picked up the *Democrat* article, pointed to a passage, and read, "'The investigation also revealed that the longstanding injuries suffered by "Big Jack" Jackson, which confined him to a state care facility for several years, were inflicted by a member of the Nowlin family in the course of their extra-legal ventures related to the Joplin music. Mr. Jackson recently returned to the home of his mother, Elvira Jackson, who expressed great happiness to have her son back.'"

Miriam's eyes filled. Alan put his arm around her. "Are you and your grandmother going to move into Mickey's house, JJ?"

"Not any time soon, we ain't. Lawyer say Mickey's estate be held in trust fo' me till I twenty-five. Say Mickey want me to become a respect'ble citizen like he weren't. Don't sound like much fun, but if it what Mickey want, I give it a shot." The young man glared at Alan. "An' speakin' of shootin', I can't believe you made me get rid a Jarvis' fire iron, but you keep his gun."

"Tell you what, JJ. When you get to be eighty years old and have Stage Four cancer, you have my permission to play with guns all you want."

"Like you be able to stop me then!"

Alan winked at the young man and gave his wife's shoulders a squeeze. "You know, Miriam, you seemed to be having a good time yourself—with JJ getting out of the business, there's an opening for a slick housebreaker."

"Oh, Alan. You damn wooden nickel. I think I'd better stick to what I've been doing. Somebody's got to support you penniless musicians. I'll tell you this, though: I sure as hell would've enjoyed giving that nasty, evil old bat a few good smacks across the chops with her own cane."

• • ● • •

The hum of the airplane engines was hypnotic, but Alan was wide awake, his mind filled with kaleidoscopic passages of Scott Joplin's music. In the seat next to him, Miriam snored softly. For the umpteenth time, he glanced at the overhead bin where the duffel bag was hidden, folded inside his carry-on suitcase.

From the seats behind him, he heard muffled conversation, punctuated by giggles.

Those kids…would I like to be sixteen again? No. I wouldn't have missed it for anything, but once was enough. I wouldn't even want to time-travel to 1951 and see myself then.

Again, his eyes strayed to the overhead bin. *Time-travel…I'll never believe I was hallucinating or dreaming. It was all too real, too consistent, too coherent, both while it was happening and afterward. Maybe I pulled it off because I have some kind of sense that most people don't have…Tom is so much like me at that age—might he have it too? If I help him develop it, then he could find me after I…What an adventure that would be!*

But wherever I was, wherever 1899 Sedalia is, Scott Joplin is there. Alive, talking, writing music—My God, writing music! Maybe death is just a change of location, outside of time.

Forget about personal annihilation, Mr. Chandler. Just keep on composing. Keep on researching.

Keep on playing.

Authors' Note

Some of the characters in *The RagTime Traveler* were real people; some were imaginary.

Scott Joplin, Arthur Marshall, Scott Hayden, Otis Saunders, Tom Ireland, and Walker Williams really did exist, and with the help of David Reffkin and various recorded histories of ragtime (most prominently Edward A. Berlin's definitive biography, *King of Ragtime, Scott Joplin and His Era*), we have done our best to present them faithfully to reality.

There are two Betty Singers associated with the book. The contributions of the real-life Betty are described in the Acknowledgments section. The fictional Betty, who helped Alan uncover historical information necessary for him to solve the murder and theft, is based directly upon her corporeal counterpart.

Brun Campbell is also both real and fictional. The actual Brun was—briefly—a student of Scott Joplin, and late in his life, a historian of the ragtime era. Larry's biography, *Brun Campbell: The Original Ragtime Kid*, is a highly praised account of both parts of Brun's life. The fictional Brun stars in *The Ragtime Kid* and *The Ragtime Fool*, two of Larry's ragtime-based historical mysteries.

As sixteen-year-olds, the fictional characters Alan and Miriam Chandler played central roles in *The Ragtime Fool*. Now, some sixty-five years later, they've returned in *The RagTime Traveler*, with their grandson, Tom.

Mickey Potash; Detective David Parks; Rudolph Korotkin and Sylvester Maggione; Jackson "JJ", Elvira, and "Big Jack" Jackson; Saramae and Charles Blackstone; Lathan and Will Blackstone; Angeline Noland Blackstone; and Abigail Nowlin and the rest of the present-day Kansas City Nowlins are imaginary. No resemblance or relationship to any person, living or dead, is intended or should be inferred.

Then there's the matter of time-travel. Do the authors believe that Alan did in fact travel back in time, or do they think he was hallucinating? We have our opinions, but will not exercise auctorial fiat on Alan's experience. That said, we believe Alan was wise to resist making changes to the past. Altering history is likely to be as addictive as eating potato chips.

Acknowledgments

The authors thank three friends who provided critical help with regard to history, geography, and the language of music.

David Reffkin, musician, arranger, historian, and founder/ director of the American Ragtime Ensemble, answered innumerable questions having to do with ragtime history and the intricacies of ragtime music, and read the final version of the manuscript to pick up on inconsistencies and errors.

Neither of the authors is familiar with Kansas City, and so they are indebted to the energetic and gracious Margot Sims, who did a thorough job of orienting them to the city, supplementing her verbal descriptions with excellent photographs.

Whenever questions arose in the minds of the authors regarding the history or the geography of Sedalia, Betty Singer (the real one, the inspiration for the fictional Betty) was Betty-on-the-Spot, always providing the necessary answers, usually by return email.

Without the kindness of these three friends, the authors would still be trying to write the book, and no matter how long they might have worked at it, it would never have been satisfactory.

In addition, the authors wish to thank Sharon Kingsford and Deborah Kelch for their fashion advice, especially regarding the awesomely horrific hats.

Sheriff Kevin Bond of Pettis County answered all of our questions about 911 service in Missouri.

Peg Kehret and Stef Maruch read the manuscript and offered helpful suggestions, most of which we accepted with gratitude.

Thanks to Myra and Maggie for their support and encouragement.

For any errors or inaccuracies, the authors take full responsibility.

To see more Poisoned Pen Press titles:

Visit our website: poisonedpenpress.com/
Request a digital catalog: info@poisonedpenpress.com

CPSIA information can be obtained
at www.ICGtesting.com
Printed in the USA
BVOW04s0727110517
483801BV00003B/6/P

9 781464 208140